Shadows Through Time

MADELINE BAKER

Cerridwen Press

A Cerridwen Press Publication

www.cerridwenpress.com

Shadows Through Time

ISBN 9781419960307
ALL RIGHTS RESERVED.
Shadows Through Time Copyright © 2009 Madeline Baker
Edited by Meghan Conrad.
Cover art by Dar Albert.

This book printed in the U.S.A. by Jasmine-Jade Enterprises, LLC.

Electronic book publication August 2009
Trade paperback publication February 2010

With the exception of quotes used in reviews, this book may not be reproduced or used in whole or in part by any means existing without written permission from the publisher, Ellora's Cave Publishing Inc., 1056 Home Avenue, Akron, OH 44310-3502.

Warning: The unauthorized reproduction or distribution of this copyrighted work is illegal. Criminal copyright infringement, including infringement without monetary gain, is investigated by the FBI and is punishable by up to 5 years in federal prison and a fine of $250,000.
(http://www.fbi.gov/ipr/)

This book is a work of fiction and any resemblance to persons, living or dead, or places, events or locales is purely coincidental. The characters are productions of the author's imagination and used fictitiously.

Cerridwen Press is an imprint of Ellora's Cave Publishing, Inc.®

Shadows Through Time

Dedication

೦೦

For all my readers who asked for another time travel story. This one's for you. I hope you enjoy the journey.

Trademarks Acknowledgement

೦೦

The author acknowledges the trademarked status and trademark owners of the following wordmarks mentioned in this work of fiction:

Donna Karan: Gabrielle Studio, Inc.

Godiva: Godiva Brands, Inc.

Gunsmoke: CBS Broadcasting Inc.

Hopalong Cassidy: U.S. Television Office, Inc.

iPod: Apple Inc.

Jacuzzi: Jacuzzi Inc.

Liz Claiborne: Liz Claiborne, Inc.

Manolo Blahnik: Blahnik, Manolo

Mustang: Ford Motor Company Corporation

Nikes: Nike, Inc.

NFL: National Football League

Nordstrom: NIHC, Inc.

Red Ryder: Red Ryder Enterprises, Inc.

Starbucks: Starbucks U.S. Brands, LLC

The Lone Ranger: Classic Media, Inc.

The Rifleman: Levy-Gardner-Laven Productions, Inc.

Wells Fargo: Wells Fargo & Company

Chapter One

༺༻

Kelsey St. James had always hated vacations. She hated the last-minute rush at work to get everything in order so she could take four weeks off, she hated trying to decide where to go, she hated packing, she hated coming home and unpacking and getting ready for work again.

But she didn't hate anything as much as she hated scraping old wallpaper off walls, which was how she was spending her vacation. After several years of indecision, her grandmother, Nana Mary, had decided to redecorate the old place with the idea of perhaps renting it out in the summer since no one in the family had used it much in the last few years. So, here she was, on a beautiful day in mid-April, doing what she hated the most.

With a sigh, Kelsey brushed a lock of hair from her forehead and regarded the wall in front of her. The first layer of paper, put up in the last couple of years, had come off with ease. The layer underneath, which was a faded red-and-gold stripe that must have been a knock-out in its day, had been hung sometime in the late 1800's and seemed determined to stay on the wall for another century or two.

Shaking her head, Kelsey reached for the spray bottle wondering, for perhaps the twentieth time that day, why she had ever agreed to do this. She could have hired someone to do it for her, but somehow that just didn't seem right, not when Nana Mary had asked Kelsey to do it. The sly old dear. Nana Mary knew full well that Kelsey would do anything she asked. Nana usually had an ulterior motive whenever she asked Kelsey for a favor, knowing that Kelsey would never refuse, but if her grandmother had some hidden agenda this time, Kelsey was at a loss to figure out what it might be.

"After all," Nana Mary had said cheerfully, "your father's right. If we don't fix it up, it's going to fall down before I can rent it out."

Kelsey had to agree with that. The old house was just a summer place located on an acre and a half of land just outside of Rapid City. She had to admit it was in pretty bad shape. Kelsey had spent her vacations here with her grandparents when she was a little girl. She remembered sitting in front of the fireplace, roasting marshmallows, while her grandfather told her stories about the Old West, exciting tales of Wild Bill Hickock and Calamity Jane, Doc Holliday and Big Nose Kate, Pat Garrett and Billy the Kid, Frank and Jesse James, the Dalton gang, George Armstrong Custer and his ill-fated battle against the Sioux and Cheyenne at the Little Big Horn.

Of course, Papa Joe had idolized all the old cowboy stars like Gene Autry and Roy Rogers, Lash LaRue and Red Ryder, Hopalong Cassidy and the Cisco Kid. His especial favorites had been The Lone Ranger and Tonto and The Rifleman. Papa Joe's favorite western movies had been the ones directed by John Ford and starring John Wayne and Ward Bond.

Papa Joe had been quite a history buff, too. He liked nothing better than to talk about the Old West. He often declared he had been born in the wrong time, that he should have been born back in the early 1800's, when men were men. He had loved telling stories about the old days. He described places like the Custer battlefield and Deadwood Gulch so vividly, it was almost as if he had actually lived there when the Indians roamed the land and Wild Bill Hickock played cards at Saloon No. 10. Wild Bill had been one of Papa Joe's favorite characters. Papa Joe had told Kelsey so much about Wild Bill she sometimes felt as if she had known Hickock personally. During his life, Hickock had been a Deputy Marshal at Fort Riley and a scout for Custer. He'd been a sheriff in Ellis County, Kansas, a marshal in Abilene and he'd spent a year with Buffalo Bill Cody's Wild West Show. But the thing most people remembered about Wild Bill was that he had been shot in the back of the head by Jack McCall while he was playing poker. Hickock had been holding an ace of spades, an ace of clubs, the eight of spades and the eight of clubs and the jack of diamonds, a hand that was known forever after as a dead man's hand.

Over the years, Papa Joe had collected stacks of books, both fiction and nonfiction, about lawmen and gunfighters and men like Wyatt Earp who had worked on both sides of the law. Papa Joe's intense fascination with Wyatt Earp and the gunfight at the O.K. Corral was the reason he had bought the old house in the first place. Somewhere along the way, Papa Joe had gotten hold of the notion that Wyatt had once lived in the house. Whether that was fact or fiction didn't matter. Papa Joe had bought the house for a song back in 1949, now the land alone was worth a small fortune. At the moment, Kelsey was sorry she hadn't suggested they level the house and sell the land!

Kelsey muttered a mild oath as she scraped her knuckles against the wall. She hated tedious work like this. She ripped off another strip of stubborn red and gold paper and tossed it into the large cardboard box sitting in the middle of the floor. The box was almost full. Next time she took a break, she would have to empty it or bring in another one.

She squirted more water on the wall, wondering, as she did so, what was going on at Russell, Russell and Raglan. She loved her job to the exclusion of pretty much everything else, which was a good thing, because it was her job that had kept her going when she filed for divorce five years ago. She shook her head. Had it been that long already?

For a moment, she let herself remember the past. She had married Nick right out of high school. Some girls were young and foolish, she had been young and stupid. Nick had encouraged her to go to work and once she was working steadily, he had conveniently lost his job. To her dismay, he seemed perfectly content to stay at home and watch TV. She couldn't remember when he started drinking. She had tried to get him to go to AA, had pleaded with him to stop drinking. She had nagged him and then she had ignored him and immersed herself in her work. She had started working at Russell, Russell and Raglan's as a lowly clerk typist. Five years later, she had a management position with a secretary of her own. Two years after that, she had been promoted to Vice President in Charge of Sales.

With a shake of her head, she banished her memories into the past where they belonged.

She pulled another strip of paper off the wall. It was a little depressing, tearing down a part of something that her grandfather had loved so much. She had never truly shared her grandfather's fascination with the Old West. It had been a rough, untamed time in the history of the United States. Had she lived back in those days, she would have stayed in the east, safe from Indian attacks and flash floods and the myriad other catastrophes that had assailed the pioneers who had been adventurous enough to go traipsing off across the plains. She couldn't imagine anything that would have dragged her from the security and comfort of life in the East for the wild, untamed frontier.

Not for her the rigors of moving westward, traveling by covered wagon, fighting the elements and the dust and the wild terrain, sleeping outside in all kinds of weather, praying that no one would get sick or break a leg or need a dentist, hoping that your food and water would last from one stop to the next. Not to mention the ever-present threat of attack from Indians and outlaws and other unscrupulous characters who had populated the Old West.

No doubt about it, she would have made a lousy pioneer. But she would have given anything to hear one of her grandfather's stories again. His disappearance was a mystery. Nana Mary declared she had no idea where he'd gone. One day he had been there, she had said with a shrug that seemed completely out of character considering the gravity of the situation and the next he had been gone. That had been over a year ago and no further explanation had been forthcoming. It was most peculiar. At his age, it was unlikely that he had run off with another woman, though anything was possible. Kelsey secretly feared he had been the victim of foul play, though she never voiced her opinion aloud because Nana Mary was convinced that Papa Joe would return.

Kelsey blew out a sigh as she yanked the last strip from one wall. She had moved all the furniture out of this room except for a tall, narrow bookcase. Taking hold of the bookcase, she rocked it back and forth until it was in the center of the room.

Turning back toward the wall, Kelsey frowned at the door that had been hidden behind the bookcase. Why would anyone put a piece of furniture in front of a door? And where did that door lead to? A room that held only sad memories, perhaps?

She thought of all the times she had stayed in this house, both as a child and as an adult. Nana Mary had ever mentioned a hidden room. What was through that door? A sudden shiver ran down Kelsey's spine as her imagination sprang to life. If she opened the door, what would she find? A long forgotten fortune? A room full of cast-off clothing and old furniture? A dead body? She shook off her morbid thoughts. Maybe it just led into a closet, though she couldn't imagine anyone blocking a closet. No one ever had enough closet space. Maybe it just led out into the side yard.

Curious now, Kelsey wiped her hands on her bright pink jeans and turned the old glass knob. She had expected some resistance from a door that hadn't been opened in who knew how long, but it opened without a hitch. None of the things she had imagined lay on the other side. Instead, she looked out on a narrow dirt road that separated two tall wooden buildings. But that was impossible. There were no other buildings this close to the house.

In the distance, she heard the mournful howling of a dog and what sounded like a car backfiring.

Feeling a little like Alice in Wonderland, Kelsey stepped through the doorway.

Chapter Two

T. K. Reese sat back in his chair, his hat pulled low while he regarded the cards in his hand. He had three queens and a pair of deuces—a full house. He tossed five dollars into the pot, then glanced around the saloon, thinking he had stayed in this one-horse town long enough. It was time to move on before someone recognized him, before a wanted poster wearing his name and description showed up on the bulletin board outside the sheriff's office.

Reese glanced at the two other men at the table. Ed Booth raised Reese's bet. Old man Neff folded and Reese raked in the pot.

"That's it for me, gents," Reese said. Pushing away from the table, he scooped up the greenbacks and shoved them in his pocket.

Going to the bar, he ordered a whiskey. He knocked it back in a single swallow, wiped his mouth with the back of his hand and left the saloon.

Outside, he glanced up and down the street. It was near dark, and quiet save for the notes of a tinny piano coming from a saloon across the street. He stood there a moment, enjoying the quiet, a quiet that was suddenly punctuated by a gunshot and the mournful howling of a dog somewhere in the distance. Reese shook his head. No doubt some of the cowboys from the neighboring ranches were letting off a little steam.

Shoving his hands in his pockets, Reese strolled down the street. Except for Saturday nights, Grant's Crossing was a peaceful town. No one knew him here, no one cared about where he came from or where he was going. The chances of being recognized were pretty slim. Maybe he would stick around for another couple of days.

He was headed for the hotel at the end of the street when he heard a woman scream, followed by a strangled cry for help.

Running toward the sound, Reese darted around the corner of the hotel and almost slammed into a man and a woman who were locked in a violent struggle. The woman screamed again, then scrambled backward as Reese grabbed the man by the arm, spun him around and drove his fist into his face. The man dropped like a poleaxed mule.

The woman stared up at him, her eyes wide and wary.

Reese lifted his hands in a gesture of surrender. "Hey, I don't mean you any harm. Do you know this *hombre*?"

The woman glanced at her attacker. "No."

Kelsey stared at the man who had come to her rescue. He was tall and broad-shouldered, muscular but not beefy. And good-looking, though that didn't begin to describe him. With his long black hair, dark brown eyes and dusky skin, he reminded her of the way Antonio Bandaras had looked in the movie *Desperado*. Tall, dark and dangerous, she thought. But it was his clothing more than his good looks that held her attention. He wore a long-sleeved gray shirt, black trousers and a black cowboy hat. There was a black kerchief knotted at his throat. And a big gun holstered on his right hip.

She shook her head. Men didn't walk around with guns strapped to their hips, not in the twenty-first century.

A noise at the mouth of the alley drew her attention. Looking past the man who had come to her rescue, she watched a heavyset man mounted on a dark horse trot by.

"You all right, miss?" Antonio's double asked.

Kelsey looked at him and slowly shook her head. "No," she murmured. "I don't think so."

Reese swore softly. Unless he missed his guess, the woman staring back at him was about to faint. The thought had no sooner crossed his mind when thought became fact. Darting forward, he scooped her into his arms before she hit the ground.

She was a pretty little thing, he mused, with her long dark hair and pretty green eyes. But what the hell was he going to do with her now?

* * * * *

Kelsey woke with a start. Feeling slightly disoriented, she sat up, her gaze darting around the room. Where was she? Not home, that was for certain! The room was small and square. The walls were white and bare. A white porcelain bowl and pitcher sat atop a scarred, mahogany chest of drawers. Limp white curtains hung at the room's single window.

The man who had come to her rescue sat in a chair by the window, regarding her through narrowed eyes.

"What am I doing here?" she asked.

"Lying in my bed at the moment," he replied.

She scrambled off the mattress as if it had suddenly caught fire.

"Whoa, girl, slow down. I don't want you fainting on me again."

She blinked at him. "I fainted?"

Reese nodded. "That guy you were wrestlin' with, was he a friend of yours?"

"No, I never saw him before in my life! And I hope I never see him again." She crossed her arms over her chest in an age-old gesture of self-protection. "I...thank you for...for what you did," she said, edging toward the door.

His gaze moved over her. He had seen women in trousers before, but never in trousers that fit like a second skin and never in such a bright shade of pink. He had never seen a shirt quite like the one she was wearing, either. It was white and it clung to her upper body, outlining her breasts. The words *I'm PMSing and I've got a gun, so look out buster, you'd better run* — whatever the hell that meant — were printed in blood-red letters across the front of the shirt. He didn't know what PMSing was, but there was no way she was hiding a gun, not in that outfit.

"You're not from around here, are you?" he remarked.

"No. Well, thanks again. I think I'll be going now."

"Suit yourself."

She hurried toward the door as if she was afraid he would stop her, muttered, "Thanks again," as she opened it and bolted out of the room.

Reese stared after her, then shook his head. Pretty or not, she was a strange one and he was well rid of her.

* * * * *

Kelsey stood on the boardwalk outside the hotel, her mind whirling as she tried to make sense of what she saw. The world as she knew it appeared to have vanished. There were no sidewalks, no paved streets, no electric lights, no mailboxes, no automobiles, no houses with neat green lawns and three car garages. Instead, the sidewalk was made of narrow wooden boards, the streets were hard-packed dirt and people apparently rode horses, judging by the number of four-legged creatures she saw tied to hitching posts along the street. The few men she saw were dressed in old-style Western clothing. They all wore hats of one kind or another, though cowboy hats prevailed, and they all wore gunbelts.

She was dreaming, she thought. That had to be it. There was no other logical explanation. She had been reminiscing about Papa Joe and his fascination for the Old West and she had fallen asleep. And now she was dreaming.

And she was ready to wake up. She pinched herself and it hurt. It never hurt in dreams. But what else could it be? Good

Lord, was she losing her mind? Hallucinating? Lying in a hospital bed, unconscious? In a coma? Maybe she had died. She glanced around again. No, heaven couldn't possibly look or smell this bad!

Closing her eyes, she willed herself to wake up. "Just a dream," she whispered, "it's just a dream. When I open my eyes, I'll be back where I belong." She nodded. "I'll count to three and open my eyes and I'll be home. One. Two. Three..."

She opened her eyes but nothing had changed. Two cowboys trotted past. One of them tipped his hat in her direction. A boy ran down the street, a puppy yipping at his heels.

Fighting a rising tide of panic, she spent the next two hours trying to find her way back to Nana Mary's house but to no avail. She went up and down every street twice but nothing was familiar. She saw houses, but none looked familiar. She found what she thought was the narrow street that she had seen when she opened the door, but it led to a dead end.

It was full dark and Kelsey was on the verge of tears when she made her way back to the hotel, only then realizing that she was starving and that she didn't have any money with which to pay for a meal or a place to spend the night. She glanced through the window of the hotel, wondering if the desk clerk would let her spend the night on the small sofa in the lobby.

Blinking back her tears, she went inside and approached the man behind the desk.

His gaze moved over her in blatant disapproval, but he pasted a smile on his face and said, "May I help you?"

"I don't have any place to spend the night."

"Well, you've come to the right place," he said, plucking a key from a board on the wall behind the desk. "Room Six is available."

"I'm afraid I don't have any money just now," she said.

The desk clerk replaced the key with a flourish. "Then I'm afraid Room Six just became unavailable."

"Would it be all right if I spent the night on your sofa?"

"I'm sorry, but no."

With a nod, Kelsey left the hotel. Outside, she sat down in one of the wooden rocking chairs. Fighting the urge to cry, she stared into the growing darkness. Where was she? And how was she going to get back home where she belonged?

She shivered as a chill wind blew down the street. Folding her arms over her breasts, she rubbed her hands up and down her arms, hoping this nightmare would end before she froze to death.

* * * * *

Reese sat at a back table in the corner saloon, one hand fisted around a glass of beer. He had spent the last hour trying not to think about the woman in the alley, but try as he might, he couldn't seem to get her out of his mind, couldn't stop worrying about her. He knew two things for certain—she wasn't like any woman he had ever met before and she didn't belong here. He told himself she was none of his concern. He had his own problems to worry about. He didn't need to take on any more. And that woman was trouble from head to foot, in spite of all the lush feminine curves in between.

Muttering an oath, he grabbed his hat from the rack and headed for the door. He would just make sure she was all right and then he would forget her.

Stepping out of the hotel onto the boardwalk, Reese saw the object of his unrest huddled in a rocker on the hotel boardwalk across the way.

With a shake of his head, he crossed the street. Her eyes were closed and she was shivering.

"Hey." He tapped her lightly on the shoulder.

Her head jerked up, her eyes wide and scared. "Oh," she murmured, pressing one hand over her heart. "It's you."

"Yea. What the devil are you doing out here at this time of night?"

She shrugged. "I don't have any money and...I don't have anywhere else to go."

Reese grunted softly. Trouble, he thought again. She was nothing but trouble. Sweeping her into his arms, he pushed the hotel door open and stepped inside.

"Are you crazy?" she exclaimed. "Put me down this instant!"

"Hush."

"Here now," the desk clerk said as Reese strode toward the staircase, "what do you think you're doing?"

"I'm taking this woman to my room."

"Now, see here," the clerk said indignantly. "This is a respectable hotel. We don't allow that sort of thing..."

"Don't be such an old fussbudget, Wexler. She's my sister."

The desk clerk stared at Reese dubiously. "Your sister, huh? Well, you'll have to pay double for the room."

Reaching into his pants' pocket, Reese pulled out a silver dollar and tossed it to the clerk, then continued toward the staircase.

"I can't stay here with you," Kelsey protested as he carried her up the stairs and down a narrow corridor.

"Well, you sure as hell can't stay outside," he retorted, awkwardly unlocking the door to his room with one hand while clutching her to his chest with the other. Stepping inside, he kicked the door shut with his boot heel, then set her on her feet. "There's a storm comin'."

"But I don't even know you. I don't even know where I am."

Removing his hat, he hung it on the hook beside the door. "You lost?"

"Yes," she said, "I think I am."

"Well, you're in Grant's Crossing."

"I never heard of it."

He shrugged. "I'm not surprised. It's not much of a town."

"What...what year is it?"

"Last time I looked, it was 1871."

Feeling suddenly lightheaded, Kelsey sat on the edge of the bed. "No, that's impossible."

"I think you must have taken a bump on the noggin during your scuffle with that *hombre*," Reese said.

That had to be it, Kelsey thought. She had fallen off the ladder at Nana Mary's and she was lying unconscious on the floor having a nightmare. Of course, what other explanation could there be?

"You're not real," she said, which was too bad, because he was easily the most gorgeous hunk of man she had seen in a long time. She glanced around. "None of this is real. I'll just lie down for a little while and when I wake up, I'll be home and you'll be gone." The thought saddened her. She hadn't been attracted to a man in months. Just her luck that the one man who sparked her interest was just a figment of her imagination.

Reese stared at her as she removed her funny looking shoes and socks, then stretched out on his bed. She looked normal enough, he thought, but she was at least one ace short of a full deck.

To his astonishment, she was asleep the minute she closed her eyes. Moving toward the bed, he picked one of her shoes up off the floor, thinking he had never seen anything quite like it before. Dropping her shoe, he picked up one of her socks and turned it over in his hand. It was fuzzy and white with little pink and red hearts sewn around the top edge. He dropped the sock on the floor, then looked at the woman again. Where the hell had she come from? She was sleeping on her side, her head pillowed on her hand. Her skin was smooth and unblemished, her eyelashes thick and dark against her cheeks.

For a moment, he considered doing the gentlemanly thing and sleeping in the chair, then grunted softly. What the hell! It was his room and his bed. Blowing out the lamp, he removed his gun belt and hung it over the bedpost, then sat on the edge of the bed and pulled off his boots and socks, removed his hat, kerchief and shirt and slipped under the covers.

He swore under his breath when the woman rolled over and snuggled up against him, warm and soft and curvy in all the right places.

Damn. It was going to be one hell of a long night.

* * * * *

Kelsey sighed and nestled closer to the source of the warmth at her back. A warmth that snored softly.

Suddenly wide awake, she rolled over, a gasp escaping her lips when she saw the man lying beside her. Apparently the dream or nightmare or whatever it was, wasn't over! She stared at him a moment, admiring the width of his shoulders, the thickness of his lashes against his cheeks, his fine straight nose. She was tempted to run the tip of her finger over his full bottom lip, to run her fingers through his thick black hair.

Before she lost the battle and gave in to temptation, she slipped out of bed and crossed the floor to the window. Drawing back one of the limp, white lace curtains, she gazed down at the scene below, unable to believe what she was seeing. As her rescuer had predicted, it had rained last night as evidenced by the puddles in the muddy road. But now the sky was blue and clear and the sun was shining.

Across the street, a woman wearing an apron over a long gingham dress was sweeping the boardwalk in front of her shop. A few doors down, two old men sat in the shade playing a game of checkers. A wagon loaded with hay rumbled down the muddy street. A big spotted dog sniffed at a pile of horse manure that was still steaming. Several horses were tied to hitching posts up and down the street. In the distance, a clock chimed the hour.

She glanced back at the bed as the stranger stirred. She didn't know a thing about him, not even his name. For all she knew, he could be an outlaw or a murderer, although that seemed out of character. After all, he had saved her from the clutches of that horrid man in the alley and offered her a place to spend the night. But the night was over now and like Dorothy, all she wanted to do was get out of Oz and go home. If only she had a pair of ruby slippers and a good witch to show her the way.

Tiptoeing across the floor, she was about to open the door when a sleep-roughened masculine voice said, "Going somewhere?"

Lifting her chin and squaring her shoulders, Kelsey turned to tell him she was leaving but the words died in her throat. He was sitting up in bed now, the covers pooled around his hips. His long black hair was sleep-tousled. The stubble of a beard shadowed his jaw. But it was his broad chest and six-pack abs that drew her gaze. That and the fine line of black hair that arrowed down his chest to disappear beneath the covers. She had seen numerous men without their shirts, both in real life and in movies, but never, ever, anything to compare with this man.

"You all right?" he asked, one brow arched quizzically.

"What? Who, me? Oh, yes, fine," she replied, then felt her cheeks grow hot when her stomach growled.

"Sounds like you need some grub." He threw back the covers and slid his legs over the edge of the bed. "Just let me get my shirt and my boots and I'll take you to breakfast."

"You don't have to do that."

"I do if you're gonna eat."

She couldn't argue with that, nor could she stop watching the play of corded muscles in his arms and back as he shrugged into his shirt and pulled on his socks and boots. She watched, speechless, as he slung his gunbelt around his lean waist, buckled it and settled it on his hips. He ran a hand through his hair, then plucked his hat off the bedpost and set it on his head.

"Ready?" he asked.

She stared at him. Ready? She couldn't go out to eat looking like this. She needed to shower and wash her hair and change her clothes. She needed deodorant and a toothbrush. And a toilet!

"Something wrong?" he asked.

"I need to... I need a..." She searched her mind, her cheeks burning as the word she was looking for popped into her head. "A privy."

"Under the bed."

She blinked at him, then nodded.

"I'll wait for you in the hallway."

Kelsey waited until he left the room, then peered under the bed. As she had feared, there was a white enamel pot there. To her horror, she saw that he had apparently used it sometime during the night.

It wasn't until she was almost finished that she wondered what people in the Old West had used for toilet paper.

* * * * *

Reese paced the hallway. She was a strange one, all right, with her funny clothes and odd footwear. Where had she gotten such fripperies? Not from around here, that was for damn sure.

He turned as the door to his room opened and she stepped into the hallway.

With a nod, he moved toward the stairs, glancing back to make sure she followed.

Downstairs, Reese led the way into the dining room. He chose a table in the far corner, away from the windows. Ever aware of the price on his head, he sat with his back to the wall. The woman sat across from him, her hands folded primly in her lap. Eyes wide, she stared around the room like she'd never seen a hotel before.

"You got a name?" he asked.

"Kelsey. Kelsey St. James."

"Strange name for a female, Kelsey."

She shrugged. "My dad was hoping for a boy. Are you going to tell me yours?"

"Reese. T. K. Reese."

"Pleased to meet you, Mr. Reese," she murmured.

He doubted that. "Just Reese," he said. "So, how'd you happen to wind up here in Grant's Crossing?"

"You wouldn't believe me if I told you." She chewed on the inside of her cheek. "I don't believe it myself."

"You're not married or anything, are you?" One thing he didn't need was an angry husband beating on his door.

A look he couldn't quite fathom flashed in her eyes and was gone. "No, I'm not married. Are you?"

"No, ma'am, and I don't intend to be."

The waitress came to take their order, her eyes widening when she saw Kelsey's attire. Reese couldn't blame her. He found himself staring, too.

Reese ordered steak, eggs and black coffee.

Kelsey started to ask for a blueberry bagel and a latte but swallowed the words and asked for bacon, eggs and coffee instead, since she was pretty sure bagels were as much a rarity in this place as hot running water and mint-flavored toothpaste.

The food, when it came, was plentiful and good. She hadn't eaten since lunch the day before and she ate quickly, then sat back in her chair and sipped her coffee, which was definitely not Starbucks.

Reese gestured at her empty plate. "You want some more?"

"No, thank you. Well, do you think they have any muffins?"

"Only one way to find out." Reese motioned the waitress to their table. "Hey, Caro, you got any muffins?"

"For you, Reese, I'll find one."

"That's a good girl. Bring us a couple, will ya? And some more coffee? So," he said when the waitress was gone, "what are your plans?"

Kelsey shook her head. "I don't have any. I guess I'll have to find a job." She breathed a sigh, thinking she was probably overqualified for any job she could find in a hick town like this.

The waitress, Caro, brought a plate with two muffins and set it on the table, along with some butter and a pot of honey. She refilled their coffee cups. Then, with a smile at Reese, she walked away, her hips swaying provocatively.

Kelsey spread a little honey on one of the muffins. It was surprisingly good and she ate it quickly, then licked the honey from her fingertips.

"Go on," Reese said, gesturing at the plate, "you might as well eat the other one, too."

"I...I think I'll take it with me for later," she said, thinking it would likely be the only thing she'd have to eat the rest of the day.

"You about finished then?"

"Yes. Thank you for breakfast. I'll pay you back when I can."

He waved her thanks away. "No need."

Kelsey followed him out of the dining room and onto the boardwalk, squinting against the sunlight. "Thank you again," she said, "for the room and everything."

He nodded. "Take care of yourself."

She forced a smile. She was used to taking care of herself back home. She only hoped she could do so here.

"Well, goodbye," Kelsey said, and, squaring her shoulders, she turned and walked down the boardwalk. Before she did anything else, she was going to have a try at finding the door to Nana Mary's house one more time.

* * * * *

Reese watched her go. Kelsey. It still struck him as a strange name to hang on a female. And she was all female. Being a red-blooded male, he couldn't help admiring the sway of her hips or noticing the way her trousers outlined her long legs and shapely behind. He had felt that shapely behind pressed against his backside last night. It had provoked a number of interesting fantasies, all of them involving the two of them getting to know each other better. Much better. Her scent had teased him all night long, her nearness had been both torment and temptation.

Glancing down the street, he noted that he wasn't the only man watching her progress. Several men along the boardwalk stopped whatever they were doing to admire her as she passed by. The thought that other men found her attractive rankled somehow. Admitting that it bothered him rankled still more.

Turning on his heel, he headed for the nearest saloon. A good game of poker and a glass of whiskey would soon put him to rights again.

Chapter Three

Kelsey walked slowly down the boardwalk. She had spent the last two and a half hours looking for the elusive door to Nana Mary's house but to no avail. She still couldn't believe she had stepped through a doorway in the twenty-first century and been zapped into the Old West, but there was no denying the proof of her own eyes. It was there, in the Wells Fargo stagecoach pulling up in front of the depot, in the mud that splattered from the wheels of the coach, in the distant ring of a blacksmith's hammer.

She wanted to believe she was still dreaming, but, like it or not, she seemed to have landed in the past, for who knew how long. And if that was the case, then she needed to find a job. She needed money, enough to pay for a place to stay, meals and a change of clothes. She glanced down at her pants and t-shirt. She definitely needed something else to wear. Everywhere she went, people stared at her. She wasn't sure if it was her outfit or the fact that she was the only woman in town wearing pants. Especially hot pink stretch pants.

For now, it was time to stop looking for a way home and find a job, however menial it might be. With that thought uppermost in her mind, she went into Irma's Millinery Shop and was politely turned away. She tried Houghton's Bootery, Osgood's General Store, Cosgrove's Mercantile and Aunt Sally's Boardinghouse. No one wanted to hire her. She didn't know if it was because of her attire or because she was a stranger in town, but no one was willing to give her a chance.

Standing in the shade of the newspaper office, she ate the muffin she had saved from breakfast. It took the edge off her hunger but did nothing to ease her thirst.

Looking around, she crossed the street and entered the Square Deal Saloon. As her eyes adjusted to the dim interior, she noted that there were less than a dozen men inside. Four stood at the long mahogany bar against the back wall. A brass rail stretched the length of the bar, brass spittoons were located in strategic places around the room.

Keeping her eyes straight ahead, she walked toward the bar. The back wall held several shelves of glasses in various sizes. The requisite painting of a nude reclining on a curved red settee hung above the shelf. She was a buxom beauty with long black hair that fell over her shoulders, barely covering her breasts. She looked a little the worse for wear. There were several small rips in the canvas, no doubts incurred during bar fights. A piano stood silent in one corner. Sawdust covered the raw plank floor. Several poker tables covered with green felt were scattered around the room. Only one was occupied. In addition to the poker tables, she recognized a faro table and a roulette wheel.

The bartender's shaggy brown brows rose when he saw her. "You want something?" he asked gruffly.

"I need a job."

"Is that right?" He was as wide as he was tall, with squinty blue eyes, brown hair and a deep cleft in his chin. "What can you do?"

"Serve drinks?"

He grunted. "Is that all?"

"What do you mean?"

"You willin' to entertain the customers?"

She frowned. "You mean like singing or dancing?"

He barked a laugh. "I mean like lifting your skirts in one of the rooms upstairs."

It took her a moment to realize what he meant. "Definitely not!"

His gaze moved over her. "You got anything else to wear?"

"No."

He grunted again. "I reckon that outfit might do, at that. Men might get a kick out of seein' a woman in pink breeches." He ran a hand over his jaw, then nodded. "You can start today. Four to midnight. You can take your supper whenever you've a mind to."

"Thank you, Mr...?"

"Call me Pete."

"Thank you, Pete. And you won't be sorry you hired me, I promise."

"We'll see."

She refused to let his lack of enthusiasm discourage her. "Do you think...could I please have a drink of water?"

"Water!" He shook his head as he filled a glass from a pitcher behind the bar. "Never had anyone ask for just plain water before."

She drank it quickly and knew why no one had ever asked for it. It tasted nothing like what she was used to. "I don't suppose you could pay me in advance?"

"Not hardly." He frowned. "You busted?"

"Yes."

He looked thoughtful. "You got a place to stay?"

"No."

"Tell Wexler over to the hotel that I said to put you up. I'll pay for your room and grub for a week 'til we see how you work out. If I decide to keep you on, you can pay me back out of your first week's pay."

"Thank you."

"Be back here at four o'clock sharp."

"Yes, I will. And thanks again."

"Hold on, gal. You got a name?"

"Kelsey," she said. "Kelsey St. James."

"St. James," he repeated, his brow furrowing. "Used to have a customer by that name. You any kin?"

"I don't know, but I doubt it."

Pete shrugged. "Haven't seen old Joe in a while. Reckon he must have moved on."

A sudden chill passed down Kelsey's spine. Her grandfather's name was Joe. But she was being foolish. Papa Joe couldn't be here. Besides, there were probably hundreds of men in the world named Joseph St. James.

"Thanks, again," she murmured.

Nodding, Pete moved down the bar.

Telling herself that it was all a coincidence, Kelsey left the saloon and turned down the boardwalk toward the hotel. The man at the desk listened to what she had to say, then asked her to sign the guest book.

"St. James," he said. "You any kin to Old Joe?"

That same shiver ran down Kelsey's spine. "I don't think so. When was the last time he was here?"

The clerk scratched his jaw thoughtfully. "Must be nigh on to, oh, I don't know, about nine months ago, I suspect. He was a strange old cuss, likeable though, always telling tall tales."

Was it possible? Kelsey wondered. Was it possible that her grandfather had found his way back here, to this time and place? Was that the reason the door had been hidden behind a bookcase? So that no one else stumbled through it and into the past? Oh, but surely if her grandfather had traveled into the past, Nana Mary would have known about it. There was no way her grandfather would ever have been able to keep a secret like that.

"Miss?"

She shook her head. "I'm sorry, did you say something?"

He dangled a key in front of her face. "Room number nine."

"Thank you. Is there someplace where I can get a bath?"

"The bathing room is at the end of the hall. I'll send a boy up with some hot water. He'll knock on your door when it's ready. Towels are in the cupboard."

"Thank you."

Going up to her room, Kelsey closed and locked the door. The room was small and square, with a double bed, a dresser that had seen better days and an equally scarred rocking chair. It was similar to the room she had shared with Reese the night before. And no wonder, she thought, only then realizing that this was same hotel. And that not only was her room on the same floor as his, it was right next door.

She wondered where he was, then told herself it didn't matter. With a sigh, she moved to the window. How long did it take to heat enough water to fill a bathtub? Moving the curtain aside, she gazed at the street below. It was a scene right out of Gunsmoke. Cowboys rode down the middle of the muddy street. Men and women hurried along the boardwalk, while others stood in the shade, talking. The women all wore long dresses and bonnets, some wore gloves and carried parasols. The men wore whipcord trousers, long-sleeved shirts, boots and hats, some wore leather vests. Most of them wore guns. A wagon rumbled past, digging deep furrows in the mud. She imagined those same wheels stirring up a cloud of dun-colored dust when the weather was warm. A couple of boys ran by, laughing and poking at each other. A little girl sat on the edge of the boardwalk across the way playing with a rag doll.

From her vantage point, Kelsey could see the sheriff's office, the blacksmith's shop, the stage coach depot and the Wells Fargo office. A number of small shops were sandwiched in-between, including the saloon where she was now employed. A bar girl, she thought ruefully. Fat lot of good a college education was doing her now!

She had to find her way back home! If she couldn't...she wouldn't think of that. The mere idea of being stuck in this time and place was beyond comprehension.

A knock at the door interrupted her thoughts.

"Bath's ready, miss," a young male voice called.

Opening the door, Kelsey thanked the young man, then made her way down the hall to bathe and wash her hair. She would have liked to wash her clothes, as well, but she didn't have anything else to wear while they dried. At least she could wash her underwear.

Oh, but this just gets better and better, she thought as she got her first look at the zinc bathtub.

"Lord, have mercy," she murmured, and locked the door.

* * * * *

Leaning back in his chair, Reese waited for old man Neff to decide whether to stay in or fold. Reese shook his head. If he had any sense, he would get out of the game himself. Instead of concentrating on his cards, his mind kept wandering toward that fool girl. Time and again he found himself wondering where she was and what she was doing. It was going on four o'clock and unless her circumstances had changed since this morning, she was most likely in need of vittles and a place to stay the night. He didn't know why he was so worried about her, but for some reason, he didn't like to think about her wandering around town alone, with nothing to eat and no place to stay the night. If she had no objections, he reckoned he could put her up in his room again.

He tossed a dollar into the pot. After this hand, he'd go and see if he could find her, he thought, and then chuckled inwardly. Shouldn't be too hard to spot those bright pink breeches.

He was about to gather his winnings and push away from the table when the object of his thoughts appeared beside him.

"Hi," she said with a bright smile that looked forced, "can I get you anything?"

"What the hell are you doing in here?"

"Trying to earn my keep. Can I get you a drink?" She glanced at his glass. "Another beer?"

"Sure, why not." Scowling, Reese watched her take orders from the other men at the table, then sashay back to the bar. Damn.

Kelsey and her breeches were the main topic of conversation at the table for the rest of the evening. He blamed her for the fact that he lost more than he won, but how the devil could he concentrate with her sashaying around the room and his companions commenting of her odd-looking duds and the way they fit. After a while, the men started speculating on what the word "*PMSing*" meant and how she managed to get the words printed on her shirt and after a few more drinks, they started taking bets on what the chances were of getting her upstairs and out of that shirt and those breeches.

For Reese, that was the last straw. Tossing his cards into the center of the table, he grabbed his hat and stalked out of the saloon.

He went to the hotel for dinner, determined to avoid the Square Deal for the rest of the night.

Forty minutes later, he was walking through the saloon's bat-wing doors. There was a new group of players at his usual table, but the main topic of conversation hadn't changed.

Muttering an oath, Reese dropped into a vacant chair. He couldn't seem to keep from watching Kelsey as she moved around the room, serving drinks, smiling at the customers, occasionally laughing at something one of the men said.

Behind the bar, Pete Muldoon was looking almighty pleased with himself and who could blame him? His customers polished off their drinks in a swallow or two just so they could get Kelsey back to their tables so they could order another round. At this rate, the whole saloon would be roostered before midnight.

When Kelsey left the saloon an hour later, Reese threw in his hand and followed her.

"Hey, Miss...!" What the devil was her name? "Miss St. James, slow down a minute."

She turned at the sound of his voice, stood waiting for him to catch up with her. "Is something wrong?"

He shook his head. "No, I just wanted to make sure you were doing all right."

"You really don't have to worry about me, you know. I can take care of myself."

"I noticed that in the alley the other night."

She didn't like being reminded of that. Thinking of it now made her wonder if she really could take care of herself in this place.

"So," he said, "you're doing all right?"

"I'm fine, except that my feet are killing me and my cheeks hurt from smiling so much."

He chuckled. "Guess you've never worked in a saloon before."

"No." Nor seen one, at least not one like the Square Deal.

"Ole Pete put up much of a fight before he hired you?"

"Not really," she said, puzzled by the question. "Why?"

"Kind of surprisin', seeing you in there. He's never had any help before." Reese slapped his thigh. "You've sure been good for business."

"Well, it's only temporary, until I can find...until I go home."

He shifted from one foot to the other. "You got a place to stay?"

"Yes, at the hotel. Pete's paying for my room and board out of my wages."

"So, where you headed now?" He hadn't meant to ask, told himself he didn't care, but he couldn't help feeling responsible for her.

"Just over to the hotel for a cup of coffee."

"You could have had a cup at the saloon."

She looked at him in horror. "Are you kidding? Have you tried that stuff Pete calls coffee?"

"Yea, once," he said with a wry grin. "Mind if I join you?"

She shrugged. "It's a free country."

Puzzling over her reply, he fell into step beside her.

It was near the end of the dinner hour and the dining room was almost empty. There was a new waitress on the floor. Like Caro, she smiled warmly at Reese. Kelsey doubted it was just because he was a big tipper.

"Evenin', Reese," the waitress purred.

He inclined his head in her direction. "Peggy Jo."

"Sukie made an apple pie this afternoon. I saved you a slice."

"No, thanks, just coffee."

"I'd like a slice of that pie," Kelsey said. "And coffee."

"Sure, honey," Peggy Jo said. With a last, lingering look at Reese, she left the table.

Reese leaned back in his chair, his gaze drawn toward the words on Kelsey's shirt again.

"What the hell is PMSing?"

"What?" She glanced down at her shirt and felt her cheeks grow hot. With everything else that had happened, she hadn't given any thought to the words on her tee shirt. She was pretty sure women in the old west had experienced PMS, too. They just hadn't called it that. "It's..." How on earth was she supposed to explain it to a man, especially a man who was a stranger? Men in the twenty-first century had pretty much grown up knowing what it meant. She had never had to explain it to anyone before and she didn't think she could do it now.

Peggy Jo's appearance at their table put an end to their conversation. Kelsey smiled at the waitress, grateful for the reprieve. She had never given much thought to the men and women who provided service in restaurants and hotels and the like. Now that she was one of them, she would be more appreciative in the future…the future, she thought, and wondered again if she would ever get back where she belonged and what she would do if she didn't.

Reese sipped his coffee, his curiosity growing. Whatever PMSing was, she obviously didn't want to talk about it.

"You said you were lost," Reese remarked. "Is anyone looking for you?"

"I don't think so." She took a bite of pie. Surprisingly, it was almost as good as the apple pie her mother made.

"No husband?" he asked. "No family?"

"No husband and no family around here." Of course, that might not be strictly true, she mused, thinking about her grandfather. For all she knew, Papa Joe might be the Old Joe that Pete had mentioned. Wouldn't it be something if Papa Joe were wandering around here, too, lost and unable to find his way back home?

She sighed wistfully, thinking about the family she had left behind in another century. Her parents, her sisters, Megan, Amy and Rose and her brothers, Keith and Ryan, not to mention Nana Mary, would all be worried sick when she didn't call. She took another bite of pie. Her brothers would probably go to Nana Mary's house looking for her. Her eyes widened at the thought. What if Keith or Ryan walked through that door and ended up here? Good grief, what if her whole family ended up here? She grinned inwardly. At least then she wouldn't be so alone, but what if her brothers didn't end up in exactly this time and place? She frowned, wondering again if Nana Mary knew about that damn door.

"Miss St. James?"

Drawn back to the present, she looked up. "Did you say something?"

"You about ready to go?"

"What? Oh, yes. And please, call me Kelsey."

"You sure everything's all right? You look a little...distracted."

Distracted, she thought. Who wouldn't be? "I'm fine."

With a shrug, he tossed a couple of greenbacks on the table, stood and grabbed his hat off the back of his chair.

Kelsey followed him out of the dining room. What if she couldn't find her way home? The thought of never seeing her family again filled her with despair. Her mother and her sisters were her best friends. Her brothers had teased and tormented her unmercifully when she was a little girl but they had redeemed themselves by looking out for her all through her teen years. Her father was a rock she could depend on, always there when she needed advice, or just a shoulder to cry on. And Nana Mary...those times when Kelsey couldn't talk to anyone else, she could always confide in Nana Mary.

"You don't have to walk me back to the saloon," Kelsey remarked.

"Who said I was walking you back?"

"Where are you going?"

"To the saloon," he said, grinning.

"Why?"

He shrugged. "I left a hot poker game."

"Oh."

"It's a good way to pass the time," he said. "And it pays the bills."

"You gamble for a living?"

"Among other things."

"What kinds of other things?"

He shrugged. On occasion, he hired out his gun, but it wasn't something he talked about. The fewer people who knew, the better, as far as he was concerned.

"Well," she said when they reached the Square Deal. "I hope you win."

"Obliged." Winning was never a problem. He had the devil's own luck where cards were concerned.

He held the door for her, then made his way to his usual table in the back. Dropping into a chair, he watched Kelsey move from table to table while he waited for the dealer to shuffle the cards. He didn't have to worry about Miss St. James anymore. She had a job and a place to stay. Too bad, he thought as he picked up his hand. Looking after her hadn't been that much trouble.

Chapter Four

Kelsey closed and locked the door to her hotel room, lit the lamp on the dresser, then fell back on the bed. Her feet were killing her. She was used to walking and jogging, but she wasn't used to being on her feet for eight hours a day. Right now, all she wanted to do was soak her feet in a tub of hot water. Only there wasn't any hot water available at this time of night. Which meant she couldn't soak her aching feet, she couldn't wash her clothes, or, more importantly, her underwear and her socks and she couldn't wash her face before she went to bed. She ran her tongue over her teeth and grimaced. What did people in the Old West do about brushing their teeth? And flossing?

Maybe she should invent the toothbrush, if it hadn't already been invented. And if it had been invented, maybe she could encourage her customers to use one. Most of the teeth she had seen tonight would benefit immensely from a good brushing. For some of the men, it was too late, they had no teeth left to brush.

With a groan, she sat up. After removing her shoes, she peeled off her grimy socks and wiggled her toes. Say what you would about the so-called romance of the Old West, she wanted to go home, back to hot running water, flush toilets and washing machines. She was hungry and there was no upscale café on the corner where she could get a latte and a slice of chocolate cheesecake. Walking to the hotel earlier, the only places that had still been open were the two saloons. She didn't know if the Red Queen served food, but the Square Deal didn't offer anything in the way of food except for hard-boiled eggs.

Rising, she took off her tee shirt and jeans and laid them over the back of the chair, hoping a little airing out would make them less offensive when she had to put them on again in the morning. She had a feeling she was going to be awfully tired of those clothes before she could afford to buy new ones. Tomorrow, before she went to work, she would search for the door to Nana Mary's house again.

Pausing on her way to the bed, she glanced out the window. A man stood on the boardwalk across the street. He lit a cigarette and in the brief faint glow of the match, she recognized T. K. Reese. She wondered what T. K. stood for and why he was against marriage. Maybe he'd had a bad one, too, she thought, and then shrugged. It didn't matter what he thought about marriage or if he had ever been married. She had no intention of ever getting married again. Once was enough, thank you very much!

Kelsey watched Reese cross the street toward the hotel. He moved with a lithe grace uncommon in most men of his size. There was a hard edge about him that should have frightened her. Instead, she found it oddly comforting, even a little sexy.

As though sensing her gaze, he glanced up toward her window. She jerked backward, hoping he hadn't seen her staring at him.

Moments later, she heard the faint sound of his footsteps in the hall, a creak as he opened the door to his room.

Feeling suddenly flushed, she put out the light and went to bed. Pulling the covers up to her chin, she stared into the darkness. Had he seen her at the window? She took a deep breath, willing her heart to stop pounding. She hadn't done anything wrong, for crying out loud. There was no law against looking out the window.

With a sigh, she closed her eyes. His image came swiftly to mind and followed her to sleep.

* * * * *

She woke to the *clang, clang, clang* of a blacksmith's hammer and the rumble of a wagon rolling down the street. For a moment, she lay there with her eyes closed, hoping she was dreaming, hoping she would wake up in her own bed, in her own room, in her own time.

After several moments, she sat up. Dream or not, she was hungry and she wanted food and a bath, not necessarily in that order.

Dressing, she went downstairs. There was a different man behind the desk.

"May I help you, miss?" he asked, trying not to stare at her outfit.

"Yes, I'd like some hot water for a bath, please."

"Right away. Anything else?"

"No, thank you."

Knowing it would take a while before her bath was ready, Kelsey went into the dining room for breakfast. She ordered ham and scrambled eggs and coffee, then sat back in her chair and perused her surroundings. A subdued blue print paper covered the walls. Blue and white curtains hung at the windows, matching cloths covered the tables. The chairs were oak with blue padded seats. A fireplace occupied one corner, there was a hat and coat rack near the front door. All things considered, she thought the room was rather cozy.

She glanced furtively at the other customers, wondering what they would think if they knew she had come here from the future. A rather rotund man in a striped suit occupied the next table. A large suitcase sat on the floor beside him. A traveling salesman, perhaps? A middle-aged couple sat at a table near the window. He read a newspaper. She sipped a cup of coffee. Kelsey decided they had probably been married a long time, since they seemed to have nothing to say to each other. A man and a woman and a young girl sat at another table, their conversation lively.

Kelsey ate quickly, then hurried upstairs to the bathroom. After locking the door, she undressed, then washed out her bra, panties, socks and tee shirt. She didn't dare wash her jeans for fear they wouldn't get dry in time for her to go to work.

She spread her clothing out to dry, then stepped into the tub. Was there anything as relaxing as a hot bath? She wished fleetingly for some scented bubbles, her strawberry shampoo, her body lotion. And her toothbrush, of course.

She lingered in the tub until the water turned cool, then, with the towel wrapped tightly around her, she gathered her clothes and ran down the corridor to her room. She spread her still wet garments in front of the open window, then climbed back into bed and took a nap.

When she woke again, her tee shirt, underwear and socks were dry. After dressing, she left the hotel and went for a walk through the town to pass the time until she had to go to work. Pausing in front of Cosgrove's Mercantile, she looked at the items in the window and then opened the door and entered the building.

She wandered up and down the aisles, amused at how inexpensive items like soap and sugar and flour were in this day and age. There were shelves stacked with bolts of cloth and toweling, a pile of shoes in assorted sizes, a jumbled display of men's shirts and trousers, a rack of ladies' ready-to-wear dresses. One of them, a green and white gingham with a square neck, short, puffy sleeves and a full skirt, caught her attention. Pulling it off the hanger, she held it up in front of her. It reminded her of a dress her mother used to wear when she went square dancing. The price tag said four dollars. Kelsey blew out a sigh. Might as well be four hundred, she thought irritably.

She was putting the dress back on the hanger when a deep voice from behind her said,

"You should buy it."

Kelsey's heart fluttered strangely at the sound of his voice. Turning, she came face to face with Reese. "What are you doing here?" she asked.

He shrugged. "I needed some papers."

"Papers?"

"Cigarette papers."

"Oh, of course." She had never known anyone who rolled their own cigarettes. Well, except for Serge in college, but he had smoked pot. She hung the dress back on the rack.

"You really should buy it," Reese said.

"I can't afford it," she said bluntly.

"I was headin' over to the hotel for a cup of coffee. Wanna come along?"

Kelsey nodded. With the current state of her finances, she couldn't afford to turn down a free cup of coffee. Or anything else, for that matter.

The waitress, Caro, hurried over to their table when she saw Reese. A blind man could have seen that the woman had the hots for the man, not that Kelsey could blame her. He was a twenty-four-carat hunk, after all. He ordered steak and potatoes, then looked at her.

"I thought you just came for coffee?"

He shrugged. "Changed my mind. What'll you have?"

Kelsey ordered a steak, too, medium rare, with biscuits and gravy and a slice of apple pie.

Reese grinned at her when the waitress moved away from the table.

"What's so funny?" Kelsey asked.

"You eat like a hard-rock miner."

"Thanks a lot."

"I can make you a loan, if you like."

It was tempting, but she shook her head. "No, thank you." With any luck at all, she wouldn't be here long enough to pay him back.

"Suit yourself," he said, "but the offer stands."

She wondered suddenly if he was really hungry or if it was just his way of buying her lunch without making it seem like charity. "Do you really earn a living gambling?"

"Yep."

"Is it hard to learn?"

"You thinkin' of givin' up servin' drinks for playing cards?"

"It probably pays more."

Reese laughed. "I'm sure even the losers make more than whatever old Pete is payin' you."

"Could you teach me?"

"To play poker?"

She nodded.

"Sure, but I can't think of too many men in town who'd be willing to sit at a table with a woman. Hell, I doubt Pete would let you through the door if you weren't workin' for him."

"Why not?"

"Why not? Decent women don't frequent saloons." A slow smile spread over his face. "Or wear breeches in town."

Kelsey blew out a sigh of exasperation. She had forgotten, for the moment, that she was back in the nineteenth century. Equal rights were unheard of in this time period. Except in large cities, women rarely worked outside the home. They were expected to dress and act like ladies, to please their husbands and raise their children and if they had any strong opinions, they were supposed to keep them to themselves. Of course, there had been exceptions, like Susan B. Anthony and other women like her who had spoken their minds and went against the mores of the day—strong, forceful women who had paved the way for their less outspoken sisters.

"Well," Kelsey said, "I'd like to learn anyway." How hard could it be? Even though she had never played poker, she knew how to play pinochle and canasta and rummy.

Reese shrugged. "Okay by me."

Their meal arrived then. Reese thanked Caro with a smile and a wink. He knew the waitress was hoping he would come courting, but it wasn't going to happen. She was a decent sort and she deserved a man who stayed in one place, a man who didn't have a price on his head.

Kelsey was a nice girl, too. He watched her eat in wry amusement. For a little bit of a thing, she sure packed away the grub. He felt a sudden rush of desire when she licked a bit of gravy from her lower lip.

Kelsey sat back in her chair, thinking she had never been so full in her whole life. When she had ordered a steak, she hadn't expected it to be almost as big as her plate. Back home, a steak at a restaurant was usually measured in ounces, not pounds. Along with the steak, there had been enough mashed potatoes to feed a small army, along with a heap of green beans and the best biscuits and gravy she had ever tasted.

Her eyes widened when the waitress delivered the pie. Kelsey looked at Reese and shook her head. "There's no way I can eat that, too. Do you want it?"

"Don't tell me you're full?" he exclaimed.

She stuck that delightfully pink tongue out at him.

Laughing, he pulled the pie plate toward him and took a bite. "It's mighty good."

"Don't tempt me."

"You tempt me," he muttered.

Kelsey stared at him, wondering if she had heard him right. "What did you say?"

"Nothin'," he said. "Forget it."

"Did you say what I thought you said?"

"I don't know," he hedged. "Depends on what you think I said."

"Never mind." It would be too embarrassing to repeat it, especially if he hadn't said what she thought she'd heard.

Reese finished the pie and drank the last of his coffee. "You about ready there?"

"Yes."

"Were you serious about learning to play poker?"

"Yes."

"All right, let's go."

She followed him up the stairs to his room, stood by the door while he shrugged out of his coat, then pulled a deck of cards from the top drawer of the dresser.

"Sit down," he said, gesturing toward the bed.

She sat on one side and he sat on the other.

"All right," he said, "we're playing five-card-draw poker. The highest hand you can get is a royal flush, which is the ace, king, queen, jack and ten of any suit. Hearts, for instance. Next is a straight flush, which is any five cards of the same suit in sequence— three, four, five, six, seven. Next is four of a kind— four aces, four kings. A full house is three of a kind and a pair. A flush is five cards of the same suit in no particular order. A straight is any five cards in sequence. Then comes three of a kind, then two pair, then a pair. If no one at the table has anything, then whoever has the highest card wins the pot. You got that?"

"I think so."

"Don't worry about remembering it all. It'll come to you as we play. Aces can be high or low. First thing we do is ante up." Reaching into his pants pocket, he pulled out a wad of greenbacks and handed her half.

"I guess gambling really is profitable," she exclaimed softly.

He tossed a dollar bill into the middle of the bed and she did the same.

She watched him pick up the deck and shuffle the cards, noting the ease with which his long fingers manipulated the deck.

He dealt a hand, then picked up his cards. "Now, you look at your cards and decide if you want to open. If you don't want to open, you can pass, which leaves the decision to open to the next player, or you can fold."

Kelsey looked at her cards. They were different from any she had ever seen in that they had no numbers on them, just spots. She studied her hand. She had a pair of threes, a six, a four and the queen of hearts. It didn't seem like a particularly good hand, but since she wasn't playing with her own money, she tossed another dollar into the pot.

Reese looked at his cards. "Raise you a dollar," he said, and threw two dollars into the pot. "If you want to stay, you have to match my bid."

She placed another dollar in the pot.

"All right now," he said, "you can discard any cards you don't want."

She tossed the six and the four into the middle of the bed, face down. Reese dealt her two new cards. She picked them up one at a time. A ten and the queen of spades.

"Dealer takes three," he said. "Now you bet again."

She added five dollars to the pot.

Reese whistled softly. "You must have a good hand."

"It'll cost you five dollars to find out," she said with a sassy grin.

"I'll see your five and raise you five more."

"So I have to put another five in?"

He nodded.

Kelsey stared at him, wondering if he was bluffing.

He stared back at her, his expression giving nothing away.

"All right." She added another five dollars to the pot. "What do you have?"

He spread his cards out, face up. "Three jacks."

"I don't remember. Does that beat two pair?"

"Yes, ma'am, it surely does," he said, and raked in the pot. "You game to try again?"

She tossed a dollar into the pot. "You bet."

Chapter Five

Kelsey crowed out loud when she finally won a hand — her four tens beating Reese's full house.

Reese smiled as she raked in the pot. With her cheeks flushed with victory and her eyes shining, she was prettier than a newborn filly.

The chiming of the town clock drifted through the open window.

"Three-thirty!" Kelsey exclaimed. "Where did the time go? I've got to go get ready for work." She pushed the pile of greenbacks in front of her toward Reese, then stood up.

Rising, Reese stretched his back and shoulders. She was a quick study. Another few lessons and she'd be a hell of a player — if she could just keep from grinning every time she had a good hand. Of course, the way her eyes sparkled with delight was a dead giveaway.

"Will you be at the saloon later?" she asked.

"I reckon so." Earlier, she had removed her shoes. Now, she reached down to pick them up, giving him a nice view of her backside.

"Well, I'll see you then," she said, tying first one shoe and then the other. "Thank you for the lesson."

He nodded. "My pleasure."

After she left, he ran a comb through his hair, scooped the cash off the bed, then grabbed his hat and coat and left the hotel. He had a present to buy before he headed for his usual game at the Square Deal.

* * * * *

Kelsey found herself glancing toward the table in the back corner of the saloon time and again. She told herself it didn't matter whether Reese showed up or not, but she couldn't stop looking for him, nor could she stifle the rush of excitement she felt when, at last, he entered the saloon. In his striped trousers, white shirt, black hat and long black coat, he looked like he had just stepped off a Missouri riverboat. Catching her attention, he smiled at her, then took his customary seat with his back against the wall.

The very air in the saloon felt different now that he was here, Kelsey thought, though she didn't know why that should be. The same miners, outlaws, cowboys and soldiers filled the saloon. The piano player was pounding out the same off-key ballads on the battered upright piano, the notes mingling with the tinkling of shot glasses, the rattle of dice and the soft whisper of cards being shuffled. And over all, the low drone of conversation. Sometimes the men's voices rose, either in a joyful hoot when someone raked in an exceptionally large pot, or in a flood of obscenities that turned the air blue when one of the men lost a pot he had been sure of winning. A thick haze of gray smoke hung heavy near the ceiling. She tried not to imagine her lungs turning black from all that second-hand smoke.

The next few hours passed quickly as more and more men sauntered into the saloon. There was no room at the bar, every table was filled. She was surprised to see such a crowd on a week night. Was it a holiday or something? It wasn't until she overheard two men talking that she realized it was her presence that had drawn the crowd.

"Told ya, didn't I?" the first man said smugly. "She's wearing pink breeches."

"Wouldn't have believed it if I hadn't a seen it with my own two eyes," the second man said. "A gal, in a saloon, in breeches!"

"Breeches that look like they was painted on," a third man chimed in.

Kelsey shook her head, wondering whether to be flattered or angry and then she grinned. If she was the big draw around here, maybe it was time to ask for a raise.

At eight o'clock, she left the saloon for a much-needed break.

As he had the night before, Reese followed her outside.

"Nice night," he remarked, coming up behind her as she walked along.

"Yes." It was more than nice, it was beautiful. And quiet save for the soft strumming of a guitar coming from somewhere in the distance. Millions of stars twinkled in the dark skies. Even the full moon couldn't dim their brightness. "Have you decided to be my bodyguard?"

In the moonlight, she saw him lift one shoulder in a negligent shrug. "Pretty girl like yourself shouldn't go wanderin' alone in the dark."

Pretty? He thought she was pretty? The thought made her smile inwardly. And then her stomach growled.

"When's the last time you ate?" he asked.

"I had a glass of milk and a muffin before I came to work." Even though Pete was paying for her meals, she usually skipped lunch. She needed cash for clothes and the more she spent on food, the less cash she would have coming when Pete paid her. Tonight, she had skimped on dinner, too.

"I reckon you're hungry."

"I reckon so," she replied, and then she laughed. She sounded just like Clint Eastwood.

"Come on, I haven't had supper yet."

"I already ate," she said. And then her stomach growled again.

"Sounds to me like you're still hungry," he drawled.

"Well, I am, but you can't keep buying me supper." It was only a token protest. Every meal he bought her meant money in her pocket.

"Sure I can. Come on."

Without waiting to see if she followed, he stepped off the boardwalk and crossed the street.

After a moment, she followed him. One day she would pay him back, she vowed. No matter how long it took, she would repay him for every cent he had spent on her. He wasn't her husband and he wasn't her boyfriend and she hated feeling like she was living on his charity, even though she was.

The dining room was virtually empty when they arrived. Reese took a table in the back. As usual, he sat with his back against a wall. Curious, she asked why.

"Let's just say I've got a few enemies who'd just as soon plug me in the back as the front."

"What kind of enemies?"

He snorted softly. "There's only one kind."

"You're not an outlaw, are you?" she exclaimed. She had wondered about that before and then dismissed it. Of course, he could easily pass for the bad guy, what with that long black hair, the gun that looked so at home on his hip and that aura of danger that surrounded him. Still, it was hard to think of a man who had saved your life as being one of the bad guys.

"I'm not wanted by the law, if that's what you mean." He chuckled. "At least not in Grant's Crossing."

"In other places?"

He shrugged. "One or two."

She stared at him, speechless. What kinds of crimes had he committed? And what was she doing, sitting here eating dinner with a criminal? Good Lord, he could be a bank robber or a murderer...or worse.

Reese swore softly. Her thoughts were as easy to read as the menu on the table.

"Take it easy, sweetheart," he muttered. "Even if I were a killer, I wouldn't gun you down before supper."

"Very funny! Is that supposed to make me feel better?"

"You've known me for what, three days? Have I done anything to make you think your life's in danger?"

"Well, no..."

"Have I hurt you in any way?"

Feeling suddenly foolish for what she had been thinking, she shook her head. "No."

The waitress sashayed up to their table. "So, Reese," she asked with a wink, "what'll it be tonight?"

"Roast beef, Peggy Jo, and whatever goes with it."

Peggy Jo wrote it down on her pad, then looked at Kelsey.

"I'll have the same," Kelsey said. She waited until they were alone, then summoned her courage and asked, "Why are you wanted by the law?"

"Are we back to that again?"

"I can't help being curious. I never met an outlaw before."

He grunted softly. "Maybe someday I'll tell you."

One look at his face and she knew she would have to be content with that.

Silence fell between them. Kelsey stared out the window into the darkness. It was still hard to believe all this was real, that she was stuck here, in the middle of the Old West. Harder still to believe that Papa Joe might be here, too. Tomorrow morning she would search for the door to Nana Mary's house one more time, even though her hope of finding it had dwindled considerably. If it was possible to find the way back to the future, wouldn't her grandfather be at home now?

*****

Kelsey blew out a sigh of exasperation. She had risen early this morning, gulped down a cup of coffee and left the hotel. She had been searching for over three hours now and all she had to show for it were a bunch of scratches from crawling about in the underbrush. She had tried every door she could manage without arousing suspicion. She had prowled through the outskirts of town, twisted her ankle when she stepped in a gopher hole, snagged the hem of her shirt on a nail. The door had to be here somewhere! But where? It was as if Nana Mary's house had vanished off the face of the planet, but how could that be? The door had to be some kind of time portal to the past, but how could the door open into the past if the house itself didn't exist yet?

It was all so confusing. She was tired and thirsty and hopelessly discouraged. Why had this happened to her? How was she ever going to find her way back home?

She stood in the scant shade offered by a stunted tree. There had to be an answer. Maybe something to do with timing…maybe the portal only opened at a certain time of the day, she thought, frowning. It had been on a Monday around five o'clock when she stepped through the doorway. Maybe the portal only opened on one particular day and time each week. Or each month. Or, oh Lord, each year.

Hunger propelled her back toward town. She had been so anxious to look for Nana Mary's house, she had skipped breakfast. Now, discouragement weighed heavily on her shoulders. What if she had to wait a whole year before she could find the doorway again? And what about her job? They must be missing her at work and at home, too.

Dark clouds were gathering overhead as she made her way back toward town.

Wrapping her arms around her middle, she walked faster. She couldn't afford to get caught in the rain. If her clothes got wet, she didn't have anything else to wear.

She reached the hotel one step ahead of the storm. She waved to the clerk on duty, then ran up the stairs to her room, intending to wash her hands and face and finger comb her hair before she went down to get something to eat.

Opening the door to her room, she stepped inside, only to come to a halt when she saw several packages wrapped in brown paper and string scattered on the bed. Frowning, she picked up the largest one. She turned it over, but there was no card, nothing to indicate who it was from.

Curious, she tore off the string and peeled back the paper, gasped in surprise when she saw the green gingham dress she had admired in Cosgrove's Mercantile.

"Reese." She murmured his name. It had to be from him. He was the only one who had seen her looking at the dress.

She opened the other packages. One held a pair of white cotton stockings and garters, a pair of drawers and a chemise. Another held a ruffled petticoat, another held a comb, a brush and a package of hairpins and the next one contained a long white nightgown. The last package held a white shirtwaist and a long brown skirt.

Kelsey blinked back her tears as she stared at the bounty before her. God bless T. K. Reese, she thought, sniffling. Even if she could afford to repay him for what he had spent, she could never repay him for his thoughtfulness.

Stepping out of her muddy shoes, she peeled off her grimy jeans, tee shirt and underwear then, using the cold water in the pitcher on the dresser, she quickly washed her hands, face and arms. After drying off, she pulled on the peculiar underwear and the petticoat, then slipped the gingham dress over her head. Except for being a little too long, it fit as if it had been made for her.

Standing in front of the mirror, Kelsey smiled at her reflection. The color of the dress complemented her hair and eyes, the square neckline was flattering. She couldn't remember the last time she had worn a long dress. At work, she wore slacks and silk blouses or skirts and jackets. On dates, she dressed casually. On special occasions, she wore cocktail dresses that were short and slinky.

She brushed her hair until it shone, then sat on the edge of the bed and pulled on her new stockings, thinking that the only thing Reese had neglected to purchase was a pair of shoes.

She cleaned off her Nikes as best she could and put them on. They didn't show at all beneath her long skirts.

Feeling remarkably feminine except for her clunky running shoes, she went downstairs.

* * * * *

Reese looked up as Kelsey entered the dining room. Damn, he thought, if she hadn't been wearing the garb he had bought, he might not have recognized her. The dress emphasized her lush curves, the color made her green eyes glow. She smiled when she saw him. The look went straight to his heart and then arrowed downward where his baser instincts resided.

"Reese," she said as she hurried toward him, "I don't know how to thank you for this."

She smoothed her hands over the front of her skirt. "I'll pay you back, I promise, just as soon as I can."

"No need."

"But I want to."

"Forget it, honey. Seeing you in that dress is payment enough. Sit down and have some breakfast. Or would you rather have dinner?"

"How do you know I haven't eaten?"

"I asked Caro. She said you hadn't been in yet. Where'd you rush off to so early this morning?"

"How do you know I went anywhere?"

"I knocked on your door around ten-thirty."

"Checking up on me again?" she asked petulantly.

He shrugged. "So, where did you go?'

"I was looking for…" She bit down on her lower lip. She couldn't tell him the truth. He'd think she was crazy. "I was just out looking around."

"Uh huh."

"You don't believe me?"

"Honey, if you don't wanna tell me where you've been, that's up to you, but if you wanna make any money playing poker, you're gonna need to learn how to bluff." He looked up as Caro approached. "Steak and eggs for me," he said.

"I'll have the same," Kelsey said, her voice subdued.

"So, you up for another lesson this mornin'?"

"I don't think so."

He grunted softly. "Got somethin' better to do?"

Kelsey shrugged. "I thought I'd go shopping." She wasn't really going shopping, but she needed to check the doors inside the shops on the off-chance that one of them would take her back home.

"Shoppin', huh?"

"Oh!" she exclaimed. "It's very annoying that you don't believe a word I say."

"Then don't lie to me."

Too late, she realized her mistake. She couldn't afford to go shopping and Reese knew it. She didn't have any money and she didn't have any credit. Not only that, but she had always been a terrible liar. Why did she have the feeling that Reese was good at it?

Breakfast was a silent meal. Tension hummed between them. For the first time, she was uncomfortable in his presence. As soon as she finished eating, she murmured a quick thank-you for the meal and fled the hotel.

As soon as she stepped outside, she knew it was a mistake. A steady downpour had turned the streets to mud and sent everyone inside. She felt a rush of pity for the horses standing out in the rain.

Hugging herself for warmth, she hurried down the boardwalk to the general store and ducked inside. A bell over the door announced her presence.

Heat emanated from a big pot-bellied stove beside the front counter. She stood there a moment, basking in the warmth.

A few moments later, a big, barrel-chested man emerged from a door in the back of the store. He came forward, smiling.

"A good day to you, miss," he said, his big voice booming. "Nasty day to be out and about."

"Yes, indeed."

"I'm Nate Osgood," he said jovially. "Can I help you find something?"

"No, I just came in to get out of the rain. I hope you don't mind."

"Not at all. Stay as long as you like." He studied her a moment. "You're new in town, aren't you?"

"Yes."

"Well, it's a nice place."

Kelsey nodded.

"Look around, if you like. Got some new dress patterns over on that table yonder. Got some new fabric, too, fresh from New York City. We even have a few ready-made dresses on a rack at the end of the last aisle." His gaze moved over her in a quick assessment. "I think we might even have one or two in your size."

"Thank you."

Kelsey was about to do a little looking around when two men pushed their way into the building, admitting a blast of cold air and a sprinkling of raindrops.

"Afternoon, gents," Mr. Osgood said.

One of the men grunted a reply. The other moved toward the shelves, picking up items as he went.

Kelsey glanced surreptitiously at the man standing near the door. He was tall and lean, with a sweeping mustache and cold brown eyes.

The second man returned to the counter several minutes later, his arms filled with canned goods. He dumped them on the counter. "I'll take some of that there jerky, too. And a couple of them cigars."

"Yes, sir," Mr. Osgood said. He added the jerky and the cigars to the pile on the counter, then picked up a piece of paper and a pencil and began adding up the man's purchases.

"That won't be necessary," the man with the mustache said.

Mr. Osgood looked up, frowning at the man near the door. "Excuse me..." he began, then blanched when he saw the pistol in the man's hand.

"Shut up, old man. Garrett, get the money."

The other man, Garrett, went behind the counter and opened the cash drawer.

Kelsey's gaze darted between the two men, one hand pressed to her chest. Her heart was pounding so hard, she thought she might faint.

Garrett scooped up the cash and thrust it into his coat pocket. "Hardly worth taking," he muttered sourly.

"Maybe you want to put it back," the first man said with a snarl. "Let's get out of here."

Grunting softly, the man called Garrett pulled his pistol and struck Mr. Osgood across the back of the head. Osgood dropped to the floor without a sound.

Emerging from behind the counter, Garrett headed for the door.

The man with the mustache regarded Kelsey through narrowed eyes, then grabbed her by the arm.

"Colville, what the hell are you doing?" Garrett asked.

"Taking her with us," Colville said. "Let's go."

"Are you crazy?" Garrett asked. "We don't need a woman slowing us down."

"Can't leave her," Colville said. "She knows who we are. She'll alert the whole town as soon as we're gone." A nasty smile spread over his face. "Besides, she'll keep me warm later."

Kelsey shook her head. "I won't tell anyone." She tugged against the man's hold on her arm. "Let me go! I won't tell anyone, I promise!"

With a snort, Colville dragged her out of the store and down the boardwalk to where three horses stood huddled in the rain.

A third man armed with a rifle materialized from the side of the building. "'Bout time," he muttered, and then, seeing Kelsey, his eyes narrowed. "What the hell are you doing with her?"

"Mount up!" Colville said. "We're wasting time."

Kelsey screamed in protest when he thrust her onto the back of one of the horses, but her voice was blown away by the wind.

Colville swung up behind her, one arm snaking around her waist.

The next thing she knew, they were riding out of town at a gallop.

* * * * *

Reese stood on the boardwalk, his hat pulled low against the rain. He had paid for their meal, then followed Kelsey out of the hotel, determined to find out what she was hiding. He was headed for the Square Deal, figuring she might go there, when the sound of a woman's scream drew his gaze. Glancing over his shoulder, he saw a man swing onto the back of a horse and light out as if his tail was on fire. But it wasn't the man who had drawn his gaze, it was the flash of a green gingham dress. Reese's gut clenched. Had it been Kelsey? He stared after the riders, but they were soon swallowed up by the rain.

Reese was debating whether to ride after them when Nate Osgood stumbled out of the general store, one hand pressed to the back of his head.

"Help!" Osgood shouted, his voice ragged with pain. "Help! I've been robbed!"

Reese swore. "Was there a woman in there? Dark brown hair, about this tall, wearing a green dress?"

Nate Osgood nodded. "Is she all right?"

"I don't know." Reese helped the man back inside, out of the rain. "Here, now," he said, guiding the injured man to one of the chairs near the pot-bellied stove. "Sit down before you fall down."

Once the storekeeper was settled, Reese hightailed it down the street toward the Square Deal. He elbowed open the door and told Pete that Osgood needed a doctor right quick. He didn't wait for a reply. Taking up the reins of the nearest horse, Reese swung into the saddle. He didn't hold with horse stealing as a rule, but it was a hell of a lot quicker than hot-footing it down to the livery and saddling his own mount. He didn't have time to waste, not now, when the rain would quickly wash out the tracks of the men who had kidnapped Kelsey.

He head someone holler, "Hey, that's my horse!" as he lashed the animal into a gallop.

* * * * *

Kelsey wrapped her arms around her middle in a vain effort to stop shivering. She didn't know if she was shaking because she was soaked to the skin or because she was scared out of her mind. Fear coiled like a snake in her belly, making it hard to think coherently. In the movies, there was always a hero waiting in the wings, ready to ride out and save the heroine at the drop of a hat. Only she didn't have a hero waiting in the wings. Pete Muldoon wouldn't miss her until later this afternoon. Reese would probably notice her absence when he went to the saloon later that evening. But she could be dead by then...

Revulsion twisted in her stomach when the man behind her pulled her up against his chest. His arm was like an iron band around her waist, making it difficult to breathe. His hand brushed the underside of her breast, filling her with revulsion. The words, *She'll keep me warm later*, replayed endlessly in her mind. She had no doubt as to just what it was he had in mind, nor did she doubt that his two friends would be involved... Oh, Lord, this couldn't be happening.

She watched the countryside fly by. The storm raged on, making the landscape look eerie and foreboding behind a thick curtain of rain. Lightning sizzled across the lowering skies. Thunder shook the earth. And still they rode on.

Tears welled in Kelsey's eyes as the town fell farther and farther behind and with it any hope of rescue.

She was going to die here, she thought, here, in this godforsaken place, and no one in this time or her own time would ever know what had happened to her.

After what seemed like an eternity, the three men pulled up in front of a dilapidated structure that could only be called a shack.

Colville dismounted. "Hatch, you look after the horses. Garrett, see if you can find any wood fit to burn."

Without waiting to see if his orders were obeyed, Colville yanked Kelsey off the back of the horse and half-pulled, half-dragged her into the shack. "Don't move," he said tersely.

Kelsey huddled in the dark. She could hear Colville moving around. A few moments later, the smell of sulfur filled the air, along with a faint yellow light.

Colville placed the lantern on a battered table.

Kelsey swallowed hard as she looked around. Shack was too kind a word. The wooden floor was warped. A board covered the single narrow window. Two bunks were built into one wall. There was no furniture save for the battered table and two equally battered chairs. A small fireplace took up most of one wall. A couple of empty wooden crates were stacked in a corner. A narrow shelf held a couple of tin plates, two blue speckled cups and some dented pots. A faded picture of a nearly nude woman, obviously torn from a magazine, was tacked to one wall.

She cringed when the other two men entered the cabin. Fear was a solid lump in the pit of her stomach. She couldn't stop shivering, she was cold and wet and more scared than she had ever been in her life.

Hatch dropped three pairs of saddlebags and three canteens on the floor beside the fireplace.

"No dry wood anywhere," Garrett announced. He tossed their bedrolls on the top bunk

Hatch muttered an oath.

"Shut up," Colville snapped. "We've made cold camps before."

Hatch glared at Colville. "This whole idea was a bust from the beginning. We should have taken the bank."

"It was closed and this idiot..." Colville glared at Garrett, "forgot the dynamite."

"Then we should have waited until it opened," Hatch said irritably.

"Quit yer bellyachin'," Colville snapped. "Let's eat."

With a grunt, Hatch began rummaging through one of the saddlebags.

* * * * *

Outside the line shack, Reese stood behind a tree that dripped rain down the back of his shirt. With the window boarded up, he couldn't see a thing. Earlier, he had made his way around the place, looking for another entrance, but there was none. So now he waited and considered his options. He could rush the place, but if the door was barred from the inside, it would accomplish nothing other than to alert those inside to his presence, which might put Kelsey's life in danger. If he'd had any matches, he might have tried setting the place on fire, though the rain would likely put out the flames before the fire got hot enough to drive the occupants outside. His best bet seemed to be to wait until morning and hope he could pick the men off one by one when they came out. That option held little appeal. It was a long time until morning and Kelsey was inside with three hard cases. He didn't like to think about what they might do to her—what they would surely do to her. Why else would they have brought her here?

Dammit! He hated waiting, hated feeling helpless. But at the moment, waiting seemed like the only sensible thing to do.

* * * * *

Kelsey remained still and silent, her heart pounding, as Hatch dumped supplies on the table while Garrett carried their saddles inside and dropped them on the floor in the corner.

Hatch used his knife to open several tin cans and the men gathered around the table to eat. Using spoons that they had pulled from their saddlebags, they ate directly out of the cans.

Colville glanced over his shoulder at Kelsey. "You want some of this grub?"

"No, thank you."

With a shrug, he resumed eating.

When they were all pigging out again, Kelsey inched slowly toward the door.

"Dammit, Hatch, stop hogging the peaches!"

"Back off, Garrett," Hatch retorted.

"Dammit!" Colville said irritably, "you two squabble more than a couple of old hens!"

It was now or never, Kelsey thought. Bolting for the door, she yanked it open and darted outside. It was still raining and she couldn't see a thing in the dark, but she ran blindly, more afraid of what she had left behind than of anything that might be waiting ahead. She heard shouts behind her, the sharp report of gunshots followed by a harsh cry of pain and then the world went suddenly silent.

She ran until she couldn't run any more. Wrapping her arms around her middle, she stood there in the darkness, waiting for her breathing to return to normal, for her heart to stop pounding. Listening, she heard nothing but the steady drip-drip-drip of water off the trees as the rain slowed and stopped.

She wondered who had cried out. Had one of the outlaws taken a shot at her and hit one of his companions instead? Or had their verbal arguing turned more deadly? Maybe they had killed each other...and maybe they were prowling through the dark looking for her, even now.

She stood where she was, wondering what to do. Should she keep running and hope she could find a safe place to hide? Or hope that, by some miracle, she could find her way to a town, any town? One thing she knew for certain, she was ill-equipped to survive out here in the wilderness on her own.

Pressing one hand to her heart, she debated the wisdom of sneaking back to the shack. Maybe while the men were looking for her, she could steal one of their horses and find her way back to Grant's Crossing. She'd have a much better chance on horseback than she would on foot...what on earth was she thinking? Going back to the cabin would be the height of foolishness. If they caught her again, there was no telling what they'd do.

She stood there for a long time, every muscle tense, her eyes and ears straining for some indication that she had been followed. She shivered as drops of rain splashed down on her head and neck, trickled between her breasts.

She was breathing a sigh of relief when she heard the unmistakable sound of a horse picking its way through the tangled underbrush.

Adrenaline shot through her. With a cry, she turned and ran, only to trip over a fallen branch. She landed hard, the air whooshing out of her lungs. Stunned, she lay there for a moment, then scrambled to her feet.

Too late. A horse whinnied behind her.

Trapped, her right knee bleeding from where she had scraped it on the branch, she glanced behind her, afraid of what she'd see.

"Reese!" Her shoulders slumped in relief.

"Are you all right?" he asked, his voice tight.

"Yes," she said, brushing wet leaves off her skirt. "I am now..." She stared up at him. Something was wrong. His face looked pinched. His voice sounded funny, too, now that she thought about it. "Are you all right?"

He grunted softly and then he sagged forward and tumbled out of the saddle.

Chapter Six

Kelsey stared at Reese, the pain in her knee forgotten as her initial relief at seeing him riding toward her turned to horror. Good Lord, was he dead? Had he been killed trying to save her?

Running forward, she knelt beside him. "Reese?"

She placed her hand over his heart, breathed a sigh of relief when she felt it beating sure and strong beneath her hand. Had he fainted? The mere idea of such a strong man fainting seemed ludicrous. And then she saw the blood staining his shirt sleeve, just above his left elbow. She stared at it a moment, numb with the realization that he had been shot. And then she noticed another ugly red stain spreading slowly across his shirtfront, just above his waist. Pushing his coat aside, she felt her stomach churn. So much blood! She stared at it in horror.

"Reese?" She shook his shoulder gently. "Reese, wake up."

He groaned softly.

"Reese, please wake up."

His eyelids fluttered open and he stared up at her, his gaze slightly unfocused. "You all right?"

"Yes." She glanced past him. "Those men...?"

"Dead."

"All of them?"

He nodded.

The lump in her stomach grew larger, colder. "You're bleeding."

"Yea. I know."

She had never seen so much blood. "We've got to stop it."

He grunted softly.

She pulled his shirt out of his trousers, more concerned about the wound in his side than the one in his arm. Blood leaked from an ugly hole just above the waistband of his trousers. She needed something to stop the bleeding, but what? Her petticoat, of course. That's what they always used in the movies.

Bending over, she lifted her skirt, took hold of the ruffle on her petticoat and gave a yank, wondering as she did so if this was the reason ruffles had been invented in the first place.

Tearing the material in thirds, she folded the first piece into a pad and placed it over the wound, then wrapped the second strip about his middle and tied the ends off tightly. She wrapped the third piece around his arm.

"Now what?" she asked.

"Help me up."

"Is that a good idea?"

"Better than…lying here…in the mud."

She glanced at his blood-stained shirt, wondering how much blood he had lost. Taking a deep breath, she slipped her arm under his shoulders. His face went white as she helped him sit up.

He sat there a moment, breathing heavily, his lips compressed, his eyes closed.

She stood, waiting. Several minutes passed before he reached for her hand. He was a big man, solid and well-muscled. Trying to lift him was like trying to move a mountain, but she finally managed to get him to his feet.

"My horse." He ground the words out through clenched teeth.

With a nod, Kelsey walked over to his mount. Taking up the reins, she led the animal to where Reese waited.

"Get on," he said.

She didn't argue. Putting one foot in the stirrup, she pulled herself into the saddle. She stared down at Reese, her gaze drawn to the strip of cloth around his middle, which was even now turning red.

Reese closed his eyes a moment, then he put one foot in the stirrup, took a deep breath and heaved himself onto the horse's back, sitting behind the saddle. Gritting his teeth, he reached around her for the reins and clucked to the horse.

Kelsey bit down on her lower lip. She could feel the heat of Reese's body against her back as they rode. Was he heading back to town? When she asked, he grunted, "Shack," and then fell silent. She prayed he would remain conscious until they arrived, afraid that if he fell off the horse again, she wouldn't be able to get him back on his feet.

She breathed a sigh of relief when the cabin came into view, felt her stomach knot with revulsion when she saw the three rain-soaked bodies sprawled in the mud. Even without being told, she would have known they were dead.

Reese drew rein in front of the shack.

Kelsey lifted her leg over the pommel and slid to the ground, then looked up at him.

He stared back at her, his face a mask of pain, his jaw rigid. Dropping the reins, he grabbed hold of the saddle horn and eased out of the saddle, then sagged against Kelsey.

She reeled under his weight. Slipping her arm around his waist, she guided him into the shack toward the bunks. They staggered across the floor like a couple of drunks. With a groan, Reese fell heavily across the bottom bunk.

Kelsey blew out a breath. What now, she wondered.

As though reading her mind, Reese said, "Build a fire."

With what? She glanced around the shack. The only things that would burn were the two chairs, the table and the wooden crates.

She carried the large, rough-hewn chairs outside, one at a time. She had seen an axe lodged in a tree stump alongside a pile of wet wood. It took all her strength to pull the axe from the stump. Hoping she didn't slice off her own foot, she chopped the chairs to pieces, then carried the wood back inside. She piled half of the pieces in the fireplace and dumped the rest on the floor. She broke up the wooden crates, as well and added the pieces to the pile on the floor. Going outside again, she toppled the neatly stacked wood pile, pleased to find several large, mostly dry pieces near the bottom. It took several trips to carry the wood inside where she spread them out in front of the hearth.

She located a box of matches on the mantel. Crumbling a couple of old newspapers she found on the floor, she shoved them under the wood in the hearth, struck one of the matches and touched it to the paper. The wood from the chairs was old and dry and caught fire immediately.

When the fire was burning brightly, she returned to Reese's side. "Now what?"

"Take my knife..."

"Why?"

"You need to...dig the bullet...out of my side."

She stared at him as if he was speaking a foreign language. Dig a bullet out of his side? Who did he think she was, Florence Nightingale? She was an executive, not a doctor.

He looked up at her, his eyes dark with pain. "Can you do it?"

"I don't know..." How could she refuse to help him? He had come after her, risked his life to save hers and been badly hurt in the process. "I've never..."

"Heat the knife in the fire." He paused to take several shallow breaths. "Then bring it to me."

"What are you going to do?"

"Take the bullet out."

"Are you kidding me?"

He shook his head. "I've done it before."

"Never mind," she said. "I'll do it."

Though she had little training in first aid, she had watched enough movies to have a pretty good idea of what had to be done. Doing it was something else.

She dragged the rickety table closer to the bunk.

She found a small enamel pot, filled it with water from one of the canteens and set it on the edge of the hearth to heat.

She found a sliver of soap near a rusty dishpan and carried both to the table.

Bandages, what could she use for bandages? Her petticoat was wet and dirty. Her gaze fell on the saddlebags piled in the corner. Maybe she could find something inside. Rummaging through the first one, she found a couple of shirts, none of which looked too clean, three boxes of ammunition, a box of matches, a sack of tobacco, a package of cigarette papers, a couple of bottles of whiskey and a length of clean linen wrapped in brown paper. She frowned, wondering if the outlaws carried the cloth for just such an emergency as this.

Picking up the paper and the linen, she placed them on the table, then went to check and see if the water was hot. It was. Using her skirt for a pot holder, she carried the pan to the table.

"Reese?"

He opened his eyes.

"Can you raise up a little?"

Teeth clenched, he did as she asked.

Being as careful as she could, she removed the bandages from around his arm and his middle and tossed the bloody bandages. She helped him out of his coat and laid it on the foot of the bed, noting that the shallow gash in his arm had already stopped bleeding. His gunbelt came next. Unbuckling it, she dragged it out from under him. She was about to drop it on the floor when he stayed her hand.

She frowned when he pulled the gun from the holster and slipped it under the pillow.

When she started to unbutton his blood-stained shirt, he waved her off.

"I can do it," he said through gritted teeth.

"Let me help you."

"No."

Puzzled by his behavior, she waited while he removed his shirt. Careful to keep his back toward the wall, he tossed his bloody shirt on the floor and then lay back on the bed.

"Where's your knife?" she asked, dreading the thought of what she was about to do.

"Inside my right boot."

A strange place to keep a knife, she thought as she withdrew the weapon from a sheath inside his boot. She held the blade over the flames in the fireplace, her mind shying away from what she was doing and why.

She removed the blade when it turned red, stared at it while waiting for it to cool. Nausea roiled in her stomach at the thought of guiding the blade into Reese's flesh. In an effort to buoy up her flagging spirits, she told herself that if he could stand to have it done, then she could stand to do it. Nevertheless, she felt the need for a little fortification. Rummaging through the saddlebags again, she pulled out a bottle of whiskey. Ordinarily, she wasn't much of a drinker, but right now a good stiff shot was just what she needed. With a hand that trembled, she pulled the cork, wiped off the mouth of the bottle and took a drink. And then she took another. It burned all the way down.

"I'll take some of that," Reese said.

Going to the bunk, she lifted his head, held the bottle to his lips while he took a drink. And then another. And another. When she set the bottle on the table, it was nearly empty.

She wet the soap with water from one of the canteens and then, trying not to think of what she was doing, she washed the blood from his stomach. Under other circumstances, she would have taken time to admire his physique, but not now. Now, she took pleasure in noting that the bleeding had dwindled to a mere trickle.

"I don't think it's too deep," he said, his words slightly slurred. "Just dig the damn thing out. If it bleeds a lot, heat my knife and slap it on the wound. If it doesn't, pour what's left of the whiskey over the hole, then bandage it up."

Kelsey nodded. The whiskey she had consumed gave her a warm, detached feeling as she picked up the knife. She could do this.

As though watching someone else, she probed the wound with the point of the blade. Found the bullet. Slid the knife under it and popped it out. Bright red blood flowed freely in the wake of the blade. She watched it, hoping it would stop, but it didn't.

She looked at Reese. His eyes were closed, his jaw rigid with pain. He had told her what to do. It couldn't be any worse than what she had already done.

She added more wood to the dwindling fire. Heated the knife. Mopped up the blood oozing from Reese's side with a piece of linen.

Placed the hot blade over the raw wound.

Pain hissed through Reese's clenched teeth.

The stink of burnt flesh filled her nostrils.

She wrapped the last of the linen around his middle, tied it tightly with fingers that trembled.

And then she fainted.

Chapter Seven

Kelsey woke reluctantly. Her head ached. Her back ached. There was a bad taste in her mouth.

Opening her eyes, she was surprised to find herself lying on the floor. Why was she lying on the floor? And then she remembered.

Lurching to her feet, she stumbled toward the bunk where Reese lay. His eyes were closed, his body sheened with perspiration. A touch of her hand to his forehead confirmed that he had a fever.

She drew a blanket over him, then went to the hearth and started a fire. Her stomach growled loudly, reminding her that she hadn't eaten since the day before. Pulling a piece of jerky from one of the saddlebags, she gnawed on it while she warned herself by the fire.

She wondered how soon Reese could travel and what she would do if his fever worsened and how she would find her way back to Grant's Crossing if, God forbid, he should die.

She didn't want him to die. Moving toward the bunk, she gazed down at him. He had broad shoulders, a flat belly that looked as hard as a rock and long, muscular arms. There was a puckered scar on his left forearm, another one on his shoulder and yet another wicked-looking scar across his belly. Apparently gambling for a living was more dangerous than one would expect.

Gathering up his bloody shirt and her sash, she carried them outside. She was glad to see that the sky was clear and the sun was shining. Raindrops sparkled like diamonds on the leaves of the trees. It looked like a beautiful day, until she saw the bodies.

How could she have forgotten about the dead men, or the fact that Reese had killed them to save her?

The bodies looked oddly pathetic, sprawled face down in the mud. She felt her gorge rise when she realized that scavengers had already been at work. What was she going to do with the bodies? It went against everything she believed in to leave them lying there in the open, but she didn't have any way to bury them. Frowning thoughtfully, she went back into the cabin. Picking up the saddle blankets laying atop the saddles, she carried them outside and draped them over the heads of the dead men, wrinkling her nose against the stink of death. Lowering her head, she closed her eyes and murmured a brief prayer for the welfare of their souls, then, feeling as though she had done all she could do for them, she walked away.

The outlaws' horses whinnied at her from the corral. Reese's horse stood nearby, reins dragging on the ground. She supposed the animals were hungry but there was nothing she could do about that now. Taking up the reins to Reese's horse, she opened the gate and led it into the pen. After securing the gate, she relieved herself behind the shack, then went back inside.

Reese was awake. He had managed to pull on his jacket while she was outside.

She hurried toward him. "How are you feeling?"

It was a stupid question. He was pale and shivering uncontrollably, his dark eyes were filled with pain. She pulled one of the bedrolls from the top bunk, unrolled the blanket and spread it over him, tucking it in as best she could.

"Water." The word rasped through his lips.

Grabbing a canteen, she held it to his lips. He drank greedily, then closed his eyes.

"Reese?"

He must have heard the fear in her voice. His eyelids fluttered open again. "I'll be all right...the fever...it'll pass in a day or two."

She nodded. But what if it didn't?

"Don't worry." He managed a weak smile. "I won't die...and leave you here...alone."

He closed his eyes again. Moments later, he was asleep.

Kelsey moved about the cabin. She emptied the contents of all the saddlebags onto the table and sorted through them, separating the items into piles—clothing here, food there. For men on the run, they hadn't carried much in the way of food and they had eaten most of it last night. She put the bottles of whiskey and the boxes of ammunition on the floor beside the saddles, placed the matches on the mantel, the coffee pot on the hearth. She found a sack of coffee beans, but had no idea how to make coffee that didn't come already ground and flavored with vanilla.

Filled with nervous energy, she found an old broom and swept the floor. She heated a pot of water and washed the dishes, the cups and the cook pots. There were no dishtowels so she put the dishes on the table to air dry, then wiped her hands on her dress.

She looked over at Reese. He needed something to eat, something to keep his strength up, but what? She looked at the foodstuffs on the table—beef jerky, tinned peaches, some stale biscuits. She eyed the beef jerky, then shrugged. It might work. She heated water in the coffee pot and added a couple strips of the jerky. Flavored water, she thought, but it would be easy for him to swallow and serve to warm him up besides.

When it was ready, she poured some into a cup and carried it to the bed. "Reese, wake up."

With a low groan, he opened his eyes.

"Here," she said, slipping one arm under his shoulders, "drink this."

"What is it?"

"Poison. Just drink it, you'll feel better."

A grin twitched his lips before he took a swallow. Grimacing, he looked up at her. "Poison is right...what the hell...is that?"

"Beef broth, sort of."

He drank it all.

Easing him back down on the bunk, she asked, "Is there anything I can do?"

"No. How about...you? You doing...all right?"

"Oh, don't worry about me," she said brightly. "I'm fine."

"Yea," he muttered. "I can see that."

"Get some rest."

He didn't argue.

She stood there, looking down at him, pleased that he seemed to be shivering less. His color looked a little better. She frowned. His skin was a lovely shade of reddish-brown. At first she had simply thought he had a nice tan. She realized now that he was the same color all over. Was he an Indian? She shook her head. He couldn't be. He didn't sound like one, she thought, and then laughed. She had no idea what Indians sounded like except for the ones she had heard in movies and somehow she doubted that real Indians had ever talked like that.

Moving away from the bed, she looked for a place to sit but of course, there wasn't any. She had burned all the chairs and the crates.

Grabbing one of the bedrolls from the top bunk, she opened it and spread it on the floor. She looked at it a moment, wondering which man had slept on it. Hoping it wasn't full of fleas or worse, she sat down, her knees drawn up to her chest, her head resting on her folded arms.

At this rate, she would never find her way back home.

* * * * *

Kelsey was on the brink of sleep when she heard Reese cry out. Scrambling to her feet, she hurried to his side. He was tossing restlessly. Sweat ran down his face and dotted his chest. He clutched one corner of the blanket so tightly that his knuckles were white. Fresh blood spotted the bandage wrapped around his middle.

His body arched, then convulsed. A curse hissed through his teeth. He muttered something she didn't understand and then his body convulsed again.

A strangled sob rose in his throat, a sound that was filled with such pain and anguish it brought quick tears to her eyes.

"No!" Sobs racked his body. "Dammit, leave her alone! Chumani, no, no. No!"

She couldn't stand to hear any more. Putting her hand on his shoulder, Kelsey shook him gently. "Reese? Reese, wake up."

He came awake with a start. Jackknifing into a sitting position, he glanced around, his eyes wild.

"Shh, it's all right," she said, "you're safe now."

He blinked up at her, but there was no recognition in his eyes. She had the feeling he was looking at her, but seeing someone else.

"Reese, it's me, Kelsey."

The breath left his body in a long, shuddering sigh that seemed to come from the very depths of his soul. He lifted a hand to his face, swore when he felt the tears on his cheeks. And then he fell back on the bed. Closing his eyes, he released his death grip on the blankets.

Kelsey stared down at him, her mind filling with questions. Who was Chumani and why did mentioning that strange name cause him such pain? The answers would have to wait until another time, she thought. Right now she had to re-bandage his wound.

* * * * *

His fever wasn't much better the next day. Kelsey was terribly afraid he was going to die and there was nothing she could do about it. She washed the wound in his side, appalled to see that it was swollen and hot to the touch. The lesser wound in his arm had already scabbed over.

She stayed close to his side, plagued by the irrational thought that he would die if she left him alone. She mashed the peaches and managed to get him to take a few bites. She forced him to drink as much water and broth as he could hold, helped him to relieve himself when necessary. He didn't seem to feel any embarrassment and she was too worried about him to give it any thought.

She didn't leave the shack except for those brief moments when she had to go outside to relieve herself or to bring in more wood. She dragged the bodies of the dead men as far away from the shack as she could, not only because of the awful smell, but because she could see that scavengers had been preying on them.

Standing in the open doorway, Kelsey decided it was time to leave, the sooner, the better. She would get Reese on a horse somehow. He could tell her how to get back to town.

As soon as the thought crossed her mind, she put it into action.

She gathered up the remaining foodstuffs and the matches and jammed them into one of the saddlebags. She stuffed a couple of the spare shirts into another saddlebag, figuring Reese might want to put one on later.

She didn't know how to saddle a horse but she dragged one of the saddles outside and into the corral. Picking out the smallest horse, a gray with a black mane and tail, she pulled the saddle toward it and heaved it onto the animal's back. It took her ten minutes to figure out how to cinch the saddle and another ten minutes to get the bit into the horse's mouth and the bridle over its head. When that was done, she led Reese's horse and the gray out of the corral and tied them to one of the rails, then left the gate open so the other two horses could get out.

Returning to the shack, she picked up the saddlebags, the canteens and two of the bedrolls and carried them outside. She looped the canteens over the saddle horns, then tied the bedrolls behind the saddles. Lastly, she shook out the smallest of the dead men's jackets, wrinkling her nose at the overpowering scent of sweat and tobacco smoke as she pulled it on.

She was out of breath when she finished.

Now all she had to do was get Reese outside and into the saddle.

"Reese, wake up," she called softly. "We're leaving." She slipped her arm under his shoulders and helped him to sit up. She had removed his boots earlier, now she helped him put them on. She debated trying to get him into one of the shirts, but decided against it. He should be warm enough in his jacket.

"Where are we going?" he asked.

"Back to town. You need a doctor."

He grunted softly as she helped him to his feet. "Wait."

"What?"

"Get my gunbelt."

She plucked it off the top bunk where she had thrown it and buckled it around his waist.

With a nod, he reached under the pillow for his pistol and dropped it in the holster.

"Can we go now?" she asked.

"I'm game to try," he muttered.

She put her arm around his waist and they staggered out of the cabin toward the horses.

Reese rested his forehead against his horse's neck for a moment; then, taking a deep breath, he put his foot into the stirrup and hauled himself into the saddle.

"Are you all right?" Kelsey asked, looking up at him. "Can you ride?"

He snorted softly. "I can ride in my sleep."

"That's great, but try to stay awake, okay?"

She handed him the reins, then stepped into the stirrup and pulled herself onto the back of the gray. She looked over at Reese, who sat very still. She had a feeling he was gathering his strength for the ride ahead. After a few moments, he lifted the reins. His horse moved out at a brisk walk and Kelsey's followed behind.

Kelsey stared at Reese's back. If she ever got back home, no one would ever believe her story. She wasn't sure she believed it herself. How could she be here, riding a horse in the middle of nowhere, following a man who had been shot by outlaws?

They rode for several hours. Reese swayed in the saddle from time to time, making her fear he was going to pass out but he rode steadily onward, refusing to stop when she suggested he should rest.

After a time, she began to suspect they were heading the wrong way. Even allowing for the time difference in riding a horse that was walking as opposed to one that was running, it seemed that they should have reached Grant's Crossing by now.

She was about to ask Reese what was going on when a dozen Indians suddenly appeared before them. Kelsey shook her head in disbelief. Where had they come from? One minute the prairie was empty and the next there were a dozen mounted warriors in front of her. Feathers fluttered in their long black hair. Streaks of paint adorned their faces and cut across their chests. Some carried feathered lances. Others held rifles. Several of the warriors lead pack horses.

Reese reined his mount to a halt.

Kelsey glanced around, looking for a place to hide, but of course, there was none. And then it was too late, because the Indians were practically on top of them. Had she been rescued from her kidnappers only to die a worse death at the hands of savage Indians?

One of the Indians rode forward and then, to her amazement, began speaking to Reese, who answered in the same harsh guttural tongue. Reese gestured once in her direction. He spoke to the warrior for a few more minutes and then urged his horse forward. The warriors fell in around Reese. They paid her no attention at all.

She stared after Reese and the Indians. Then, resigned to her fate, she urged her horse after his.

Out of the frying pan and into the fire, she thought hopelessly. But it was better than staying out there alone.

*****

She lost track of time as they rode across the prairie. She kept waiting for the Indians to stop and take a break but they rode steadily onward. It gave her a lot of time to study the Indians, a lot of time to think. After a while, she decided that the Indians must be Reese's friends. They hadn't tried to kill him. They hadn't tied him up. It occurred to her that maybe the reason they weren't stopping was because they were as worried about him as she was. She only hoped they could help, though she didn't know what they could do out here, where there were no doctors and no medical help and the wonders of modern medicine were far in the future.

It was near dusk when she saw the village. It lay in a shallow green valley, looking for all the world like a scene straight out of *Dances With Wolves*. She wouldn't have been surprised to see Kevin Costner stride into view with Mary McDonnell at his side. Conical lodges, blackened at the tops, were spread beside the slow moving river. Dogs and children ran along the shoreline. A large herd of horses grazed on the lush grass. A haze of blue-gray smoke drifted in the breeze. A woman clad in a buckskin dress shooed a dog away from a high wooden rack laden with strips of meat. Across the way, two women knelt on either side of what looked like a bear skin, painstakingly scraping the inside of the hide. Men moved through the village or sat in the shade, talking and smoking. Several tall young warriors strolled through the camp, pretending not to notice the young women who watched them.

Filled with trepidation, Kelsey followed Reese and the warriors into the heart of the village. Their arrival brought all other activity to a halt. Warriors clustered around the returning men. Women came forward to take the horses. Children ran back and forth, their black eyes wide with curiosity as they stared at the newcomers.

Kelsey stayed on her horse, trying to be as inconspicuous as possible.

A short time later, an old woman with long gray braids emerged from the nearest tipi. She spoke to one of the warriors, then turned and went back into her lodge.

The warrior who had conversed with the old woman helped Reese from the back of his horse and the two of them went into the tipi, with Reese leaning heavily on the other man.

Kelsey sat there for a minute, wondering what she should do and then, not wanting to be separated from Reese, she slid off the back of her horse and ducked inside the tipi.

It was gloomy inside. Reese was reclining on a fur robe, his eyes closed. Riding such a long distance hadn't done him any good, she thought. Someone had removed his jacket and his gunbelt. Perspiration dotted his forehead and his chest. He looked pale, his face drawn and haggard.

The warrior that had helped Reese into the tipi nodded at Kelsey, then stepped outside, leaving her alone with the old woman and Reese.

The old woman stirred something in a small clay pot. Kelsey studied her a moment. The woman's face was lined with the passage of many years. She wore a shapeless tunic and a pair of moccasins that were beaded in black and yellow. Tiny silver bells were sewn along the hem of her skirt. They made a pleasant tinkling sound when she moved.

"How are you called?" the old woman asked, looking up at Kelsey.

"You speak English!" Kelsey exclaimed.

The old woman nodded. "I am Hantaywee."

"I'm Kelsey."

"*Hohahe*, Kel-sey."

"Are you a doctor?"

"I am a medicine woman. Is Tashunka Kangi your man?"

"Who's Tashunka Kangi?"

The old woman pointed at Reese. "Are you his woman?"

"No, we're just...friends."

"He is bad hurt," the old woman remarked.

"Yes, I know." Kelsey looked at the concoction in the clay bowl, wondering what it was. Though she had little faith in the primitive medicine practiced by the Indians, she reminded herself that they had survived out here for hundreds of years. She just hoped the medicine woman knew what she was doing.

The old woman placed a few sticks of wood on the fire, sprinkled a handful of what looked like dried grass into the flames and then picked up a long white feather. She murmured something in her own language as she passed the feather through the smoke, drawing it over Reese.

She did that four times, murmuring what sounded to Kelsey like a prayer, and then she drew the feather through the fire four more times.

White smoke drifted over Reese. As Kelsey watched, the smoke took on the shape of a wolf. Kelsey closed her eyes and opened them again, certain she was seeing things. But the wolf remained. Fascinated, she stared at the hazy figure. It had to be some kind of hallucination, she thought, and wondered what the old woman had added to the fire.

Twice more, the medicine woman murmured softly and drew the feather through the smoke. Then, setting the feather aside, she picked up a narrow, wicked looking knife, which she passed through the flames four times.

The smoky wolf hovering over Reese threw back its head and howled. The sound sent a shiver down Kelsey's spine.

Chanting softly, Hantaywee passed the knife through the flames again.

Kelsey was afraid she knew what was coming. She looked down at Reese. His eyes were open now and he was looking up at her.

"Whatever happens," he said, his voice raw with pain, "don't be afraid. My people won't hurt you."

"I think *she's* about to hurt you," Kelsey said, jerking her chin toward the knife in the old woman's fist.

"Yea. The wound's infected. She's gonna drain it."

"Oh." Her voice was no more than a squeak. Feeling a sudden need to console him in some small way, Kelsey knelt beside him and reached for his hand. She meant to comfort him, but she had a feeling she was more afraid than he was.

Reese squeezed her hand. "If I don't make it…"

"Don't say that!" She couldn't help it, she had always been superstitious when it came to talking about death.

"If anything happens to me, Wehinahpay will take you back to Grant's Crossing."

"All right, just hush."

Kelsey kept her gaze on Reese's face. Nevertheless, she knew the exact moment when the woman began to drain the wound. Reese's fingers tightened around her hand, tighter, tighter, until it was all she could do not to cry out. She told herself she was nothing but a coward. If he could endure what he was going through without so much as a whimper, she should be able to endure a little discomfort.

Eyes closed, his breath coming in harsh gasps, he clung to her hand. She wondered if he was even aware of what he was doing.

Kelsey risked a glance at the old woman, felt her stomach churn when she saw the dark red blood oozing from the wound, dripping down Reese's side, pooling on the cloth Hantaywee had spread beneath him. Hantaywee let the wound bleed until the blood was bright red and then she smeared a thick yellow paste over the wound.

An oath escaped Reese's lips. His hand squeezed Kelsey's so tightly, she was certain he was going to break a few bones.

And then, with a sigh, his body went limp and his hand fell away from hers.

Kelsey looked up at the wolf. Even as she watched, it grew fainter, smaller, until it was gone.

Kelsey looked at Hantaywee. "Is he all right?"

Hantaywee nodded. "Do not worry about your man. He is strong. Tomorrow, he will be better."

"He's not my…"

The medicine woman's hand sliced through the air, cutting her off. "You may not have accepted it here," she said, pointing at Kelsey's heart, "but he is your man and you will be his woman."

Startled by the conviction in the old woman's voice, Kelsey didn't argue and as she thought about it, she discovered that she rather liked the idea of being Reese's woman, but it was impossible. She didn't belong here, in this time, would never belong here, nor did she want to stay in this wild, untamed land. She just wanted to go home.

Hantaywee examined the wound in Reese's arm then, apparently deciding there was nothing more to be done, she bandaged it with a strip of clean cloth.

"You will sleep here tonight," Hantaywee said. "Tomorrow, you will see. He will be better."

Kelsey nodded, grateful that she would be allowed to stay there, with Reese. Grateful that she would have a place to spend the night.

Later, Hantaywee offered Kelsey a bowl of what appeared to be some kind of soup. Kelsey took a small taste, surprised to find that it was quite good, or maybe she was just really hungry. In either case, she ate it all and accepted more.

Shortly after that, Hantaywee spread a furry robe along the back wall of the tipi. "Sleep now, Kel-sey," she said, handing her a blanket. "Tomorrow will be better."

"Thank you." Removing her shoes, Kelsey stretched out on the robe and pulled the blanket over her. She glanced at Reese, reassured by his presence.

Closing her eyes, she tried to sleep, but to no avail. Strange odors assaulted her nostrils. From outside, she heard the murmur of voices speaking in a strange tongue. The robe beneath her, while soft, did little to cushion the hard ground. The dying fire cast dancing shadows on the hide walls of the tipi.

The old woman sat near Reese, chanting softly as she rocked back and forth. Oddly, Kelsey found the sound comforting, almost like a lullaby.

Opening her eyes, she glanced at Reese one more time and then she followed the lullaby to sleep.

Chapter Eight

ഔ

Reese woke slowly. For a moment he lay there with his eyes closed, unmoving as he waited for the pain of the night before to make itself known, but there was none to speak of, only a mild ache in his arm and along his side.

Opening his eyes, he saw that he was alone in the tipi. Hantaywee's lodge looked just as he remembered it. Two willow backrests sat on either side of the firepit. Parfleches and soft leather storage bags that held food, utensils, clothing and other goods were stacked along the side walls, firewood was stacked near the door. As in all Lakota lodges, the fire pit was located under the smoke hole, a small altar was located behind the pit. The floor was carpeted with buffalo robes with the hair side up, making the floor soft to walk on.

Overhead, a bit of clear blue sky was visible through the smoke hole. It had been years since he had been inside a Lakota lodge, yet the furs beneath him felt familiar, the scent of the sweet grass Hantaywee had burned in the fire the night before lingered in the air.

He had known Hantaywee could heal him but he was still surprised that he felt so much better and that so little pain remained. She really did work miracles.

Where was she? And where the devil was Kelsey?

Moving like an old, old man, he sat up, one hand pressed to his side. A strip of soft cloth was wrapped around his middle. A blanket covered his nakedness from the waist down.

His stomach growled.

He was thinking of getting up and going in search of food when the tipi's door flap opened and Hantaywee stepped inside, followed by Kelsey. At least he thought it was Kelsey.

Her green dress had been replaced by an ankle-length doeskin tunic with a beaded yoke and ties at the shoulders, she wore a pair of moccasins instead of her strange-looking shoes. Her hair fell down her back in rippling waves save for two skinny braids that framed her face. Both the dress and the moccasins looked like they had been made for her and perhaps they had. He had no doubt that Hantaywee had forseen his arrival in a vision; perhaps she had seen Kelsey, as well.

Kelsey smiled shyly at him. "You're looking much better!"

"I'm feeling much better."

"You are hungry," Hantaywee said.

Reese grinned. "You got that right."

Hantaywee motioned for Kelsey to sit down.

She sat beside Reese, all too aware of the fact that he was very nearly naked. Her gaze moved over him. "Are you really all right?"

"Yea."

It was amazing, Kelsey thought. Last night, he had seemed to be at death's door. This morning, his eyes were clear and his color was back to normal. She looked at Hantaywee with new respect.

The old woman handed them each a bowl of soup that was heavily flavored with sage and spoons that looked like they had been made from the horn of an animal.

Reese ate quickly and asked for more. Kelsey ate more slowly, hoping she might be able to identify just what it was she was eating.

After his third helping, Reese put his bowl aside. "Hantaywee, where are my clothes?"

"Drying outside with Kel-sey's."

"I need something to wear."

Hantaywee grunted softly. Reaching into a nearby parfleche that was hanging from one of the lodge poles, she pulled out a buckskin clout and a sleeveless vest and handed them to him.

Reese wasn't the least bit surprised that the old woman had something for him to wear. Hantaywee might call herself a medicine woman, but Reese thought she was a witch, a very old witch. As near as he could figure, she had to be at least a hundred years old.

Reese murmured his thanks. It had been years since he had spent any time with his mother's people. He wasn't sure why he had let Yahto bring him here. He must not have been thinking clearly, that was the only explanation. He had avoided this place for years; under normal circumstances, he would never have come here. It had been home once, now it held only memories he had spent the last nine years trying to forget. Memories of Chumani...

He would not think of her. She had loved him and she had died because of it. With a shake of his head, he put her out of his mind.

"Reese, are you okay?"

He glanced at Kelsey, wondering what she would think when she saw him wearing nothing but a buckskin clout and vest.

"I'm gonna get dressed now," he said, holding the blanket around his waist. "You're welcome to stay and watch if you've a mind to."

Kelsey was sorely tempted to do just that until she got a glimpse of the knowing look on Hantaywee's face.

"Maybe another time," Kelsey muttered, and ducked out of the lodge as fast as her feet would carry her.

As soon as she stepped out of the tipi, she came to an abrupt halt. For a moment, she had forgotten where she was.

She stared at the scene before her, a scene totally alien to everything with which she was familiar. There were hide tipis instead of houses. The people wore animal skins instead of spun cloth. The children were virtually naked. The boys played with small bows and arrows instead of Hot Wheels and Game Boys, the girls played with homemade dolls, but in no way did they resemble the dolls Kelsey had played with as a little girl. The women, clad in tunics much like the one Kelsey wore, cooked outside over open fires. Dogs of all sizes ran underfoot, barking and chasing each other and generally getting in the way. The horse herd grazed in the distance, a shifting mass of color. The men, most of them wearing little more than a strip of cloth for modesty's sake, strolled through the village, talking and laughing, while the women cooked. That, at least, was familiar.

It was unbelievable that she should be here, in this time and place. Totally unbelievable. She wondered again if she was dreaming, but no dream had ever been this realistic. Once again she wondered if she was lying in a hospital bed somewhere while her family hovered around her, waiting for her to regain consciousness. Or maybe she was just out of her mind. Any of those options seemed far more likely than believing she had traveled backward through time.

She glanced over her shoulder as Reese stepped out of the tipi, her eyes widening at what she saw. She was no stranger to scantily clad men. In her world, naked and nearly naked men could be seen on magazine covers, in movies, on television, in advertisements for practically anything and everything. But she had never seen anything the equal of T. K. Reese. He was tall and lean, with broad shoulders, a washboard stomach and well-muscled arms and legs. The white bandages wrapped around his middle and his left arm looked incredibly white against his copper-hued skin. His hair fell past his shoulders, thick and inky black. Odd that she hadn't realized sooner that he was an Indian when it was so obvious now and not just because of what he was wearing.

Her heart skipped a beat. He was a man to make a woman think of warm nights and cool satin sheets and she had a sudden image of herself wrapped in his arms, his dusky skin sheened with sweat.

She couldn't stop staring at him. Couldn't believe it when he actually blushed.

"Quit that," he muttered.

"Quit what?"

"Staring at me like I'm the last cookie in the jar."

Now she was blushing. Murmuring, "sorry," she tore her gaze away, grateful that he didn't know what she had been thinking. She smiled inwardly, thinking that his image had been forever imprinted on her mind.

With a shake of his head, he turned and walked away from the tipi.

Kelsey hurried after him. "Reese, wait! Where are you going?"

"I just had three bowls of soup and I haven't been out of bed since yesterday," he called over his shoulder. "Where do you think I'm going?"

"Oh." She skidded to a halt, her cheeks flaming, but she couldn't help noticing how good he looked walking away.

Reese swore under his breath. He could feel Kelsey's gaze on his back as he walked into the woods behind the lodge. He hadn't missed the look in her eyes when she had first seen him emerge from Hantaywee's tipi. He'd had women stare at him before, but never quite like that. He swore softly. He couldn't remember a time when a woman had made him blush, but that hungry look in Kelsey's pretty green eyes had done the trick.

He took his time walking back to the village. He had come here for Hantaywee's help, had planned to leave as soon as he felt up to it, but now... He took a deep breath, inhaling the scent of sage and earth and wood smoke. Timbered mountains loomed in the distance. A red-tailed hawk soared effortlessly overhead.

Home, he thought. No matter where else he went, no matter how long he stayed away, no matter that being here stirred a host of bittersweet memories, this would always be home.

He found Kelsey waiting for him where had left her.

She was a beautiful woman, warm and desirable and he was tired of fighting his longing for her. He didn't know which of them was more surprised when he pulled her into his arms and kissed her.

For a moment, she stood rigid in embrace and then, with a funny little sigh, her arms slid around his waist and she leaned into him. Reese drew her body close to his, one hand sliding up and down her side, skimming the edge of her breast, the indentation at her waist, the softly rounded curve of her hip. Lord, but she was sweet. One kiss and his whole body came alive. He knew the moment she became aware of his desire. A little gasp escaped her lips, it could have been desire, it could have been dismay. He thought it was the former, since she didn't pull away from him.

She was breathless when they parted.

"I've been wanting to do that since the first day I saw you," he said without apology.

A faint smile curved her lips. "And I've been wanting you to."

He lifted one brow. "Is that right?"

She nodded. "What took you so long?"

"I didn't want to rush you."

Kelsey looked up at him, thinking how different he was from every other man she had ever known. Not rush her? She had met men who expected her to sleep with them simply because they had bought her a drink!

Kelsey licked her lips as heat flowed between them. He was still holding her loosely in his embrace. Needing to touch him, she slid her hand under his vest. His skin was warm. Beneath her palm, she could feel the steady beat of his heart. Would he kiss her again? She moved a little closer, hoping he would interpret it as the invitation it was.

He didn't move, simply continued to look down at her. His eyes were dark, turbulent with an emotion she didn't understand. It wasn't desire. It was more like…fear.

"We'd better get back," he said.

"What?" She stared at him, wondering if she had missed something.

He took a step away from her, then reached for her hand. "Come on."

She told herself it was just as well. The last thing she needed was to get involved with T. K. Reese. Sooner or later, she would find the door that led back home where she belonged and when she did, she didn't want to leave her heart here, in the past.

* * * * *

Reese stood in the shadows staring out into the darkness. Hantaywee and Kelsey had gone to bed hours ago, but he couldn't sleep. Every time he closed his eyes, he saw the hurt and confusion on Kelsey's face. He never should have kissed her, never should have brought her here.

Chumani's image rose in his mind, as vivid as if she were standing beside him, her blue eyes shining, her long black hair tumbling over her shoulders. Both half-breeds, he supposed it was only natural that they had become friends. They had grown up together, played together as children. He had endured the teasing of the other boys because he preferred Chumani's company to theirs, but he hadn't cared. She understood him as no one else did. He figured it had been inevitable that as they had grown older, their friendship had deepened, just as it had been inevitable that once she became a young woman, the unmarried warriors began to take notice, especially Wahchinksapa. Wahchinksapa, who had once been his best friend. Over time, the amiable rivalry between them had grown stronger and more antagonistic until there was no longer anything friendly about it.

When Chumani turned seventeen, Reese had offered her father six horses in exchange for her hand in marriage.

Not to be outdone, Wahchinksapa had sent ten horses to Chumani's father.

Chumani had pleaded with her father to accept Reese's horses, but her father had refused to let her marry a half-breed, even though Chumani herself was a half-breed.

Reese had refused to accept her father's decision.

"Come away with me," he had pleaded. "It's the only way we can be together."

Chumani looked up at him, her blue eyes wide. "Run away?"

He nodded. "Others have done it." It wasn't uncommon for lovers to elope in the face of parental disapproval. "Once it is done, they will have to accept it," he said with a smile. "Remember the games we played as children? The packing game? The first love game?" They were games played by the very young wherein they pretended to be make-believe lovers and parents.

Chumani nodded, but still looked doubtful. "What if my parents refuse to accept us once we are married?"

"Then we will find somewhere else to live!" Filled with the audacity and impatience of youth, certain that her parents would approve once the deed was done, he would not be swayed. "Come with me, Chumani! Now, tonight."

And when she still looked uncertain, he drew her into his arms and kissed her. Though she was still a maiden, they had often snuck away together. Hidden from her mother's eyes, they had given in to their natural curiosity and explored each other's bodies. Though he had yearned to possess her, he had kept a tight rein on his passion, refusing to yield to temptation until she was truly his.

That night, he kissed her until she agreed to run away with him.

"You will not find any answers out here."

Hantaywee's voice chased the memories from his mind. She was the closest thing he'd had to a mother since his own parents were killed by the Crow when he was thirteen. She knew him better than any other living soul. Better, perhaps, that he knew himself. He loved her for that. Sometimes, he hated her for that.

Taking a deep breath, he turned to face her. "I'm not looking for answers."

"What are you looking for?" she asked.

"You know damn well what I'm looking for," he said bitterly.

"If she were here, she would forgive you."

"It doesn't matter."

"You must accept the past and then forget it."

"Forget it?" Hands clenched, he fought down the anger rising within him. "How can I forget it?"

"You cannot change the past, *chaska*. Surely you have learned this by now."

"What are you doing out here, old woman?"

"Offering comfort to one who needs it." She canted her head to the side. Though he could not clearly see her face in the darkness, he knew her eyes were filled with compassion. And love. He had never known anyone like Hantaywee. She was *wakan*—holy. But for her, he would have died long ago. Sometimes, like tonight, when the past refused to be ignored, he wished she had not succeeded in saving him. Sometimes, like tonight, he was certain the only forgetfulness he would ever find would be in the grave.

"Is Wahchinksapa still here?" It galled him to speak the man's name aloud.

"Yes. He is a Shirt Wearer now."

Reese grunted softly. To be a Shirt Wearer was a great honor and carried great responsibility. Shirt Wearers were given special shirts to wear, either red on top and blue on the bottom, or blue on top and yellow on the bottom—blue represented the sky, yellow represented the rock, red stood for the sun, green for Mother Earth. The shirts were fringed with locks of hair, which represented all the people of the tribe. The welfare of the People rested on the shoulders of the Shirt Wearers.

Moving closer, Hantaywee placed her hand on Reese's back.

He flinched at her touch.

"The woman with you. Who is she?"

He shrugged. "Just a woman I met in town. She needed someone to look after her."

"She is a stranger here."

Reese turned to look at her. Of course Kelsey was a stranger here. She was a white woman in a Lakota camp.

Hantaywee shook her head. "She is a stranger from another time."

"Another time? What the hell are you talking about?"

"She has come here from a time far in the future."

"You're talking nonsense, old woman," Reese muttered. But it explained so many things, like Kelsey's peculiar clothing and her funny shoes and socks. He remembered asking her if she was lost and her reply—*yes, I think I am*. He shook his head. What Hantaywee suggested was impossible. And yet, there were tribal medicine men who claimed to have traveled from this world to the next. But not physically.

Reese swore softly as he tried to wrap his mind around it, but it was beyond his comprehension. Hell, even Hantaywee couldn't travel through time. Yet how could he doubt her? In all the years he had known her, none of her visions had been wrong. If she said Kelsey had come from the future, it was probably true, whether he wanted to believe it or not.

"She may be just what you need, *chaska*."

"No," he said bitterly. "I don't need anyone."

* * * * *

Kelsey slid a glance at Reese. They had taken a walk earlier that morning and now they were sitting on the banks of the river that ran behind the village. It was a pretty setting, with the river running in front of them and the mountains looming in the distance. A few scattered clouds, looking like fluffy powder puffs, drifted across the sky. Birds twittered in the branches overhead, squirrels darted from tree to tree.

Reese had been unusually silent ever since last night. She wondered if he was sorry he had kissed her, then shook her head. Sorry or not, that was no reason for his behavior. There was a haunted look in his eyes, as if some demon plagued him. And maybe it did. She knew so little about him.

"Reese?"

He looked over at her, his expression closed. She would have given a month's pay to know what he was thinking.

"Are we going back to Grant's Crossing soon?" If he wouldn't take her, she would have to find the way on her own. She would never find her way back home from here.

"In a few days."

She nodded. Though she was anxious to get back to Grant's Crossing, she couldn't very well insist they leave right away. He had been badly wounded only days ago and even though he seemed to be feeling much better, his wounds were still healing.

"So tell me," he said after a while. "Just where are you from?"

"New York City," she replied.

"City girl, huh?" he said, grinning.

"You got a problem with that?"

"When were you born?"

"Why?" She plucked a long blade of grass and twirled it between her fingertips.

"Is it a secret?"

"Are you trying to find out how old I am?"

"I'm trying to find out when you were born."

"I'm twenty-eight," she said. "You do the math."

"Math?"

"Arithmetic."

"What year were you born?"

"You're very persistent, aren't you? Why are you asking me all these questions, anyway?" She might have told him the truth, except she was sure he would think she was crazy.

"I just want to know what year you were born."

She did some quick math of her own. "1843."

"You wouldn't lie to me, would you?"

He knows, she thought. Somehow, he knew she didn't belong here, that she was from the future. But how could he know that? And why would anyone believe it? She hardly believed it herself.

Kelsey took a deep breath. "Just what are you trying to find out?"

"Hantaywee told me you were from another time, somewhere in the future."

Kelsey stared at him, stunned. How could the old Indian woman know such a thing? She forced a smile. "Don't tell me you believed her?"

He was watching her, his expression serious. "She knows things, sees things that others don't."

"Well, it's true," Kelsey said, suddenly eager to have everything out in the open. "I was born in 1981."

He shook his head. "How is it possible?"

"Beats the hell out of me." She tossed the blade of grass into the river and watched it float away. "All I know is, one day it was 2009 and in the blink of an eye, it was 1871."

2009? Reese swore under his breath. It wasn't possible. No matter what Hantaywee had said, it just wasn't possible for a body to travel backward through time.

"That shirt you were wearing the first night I saw you," he said, "is that what women wear in the future?"

"Well, not all of them. But clothes have changed, like everything else. Where I come from, women don't just stay home and have a baby every year. They wear pants, they run companies, they're doctors and lawyers and architects and senators."

"Women in Congress?" He shook his head in disbelief.

Kelsey nodded. "Yes, women can own property now. Not only that, but we have the right to vote and not just in New Jersey but in every other state in the Union."

"When did that happen?"

"In 1920, as I recall."

"No wonder women are wearing pants in your time," he muttered.

Kelsey laughed. "It's a world you wouldn't recognize, believe me. There have been so many inventions, things that weren't even thought of in this day and age." She glanced around, thinking that, in some ways, life was better in his time. It was less hurried, less hectic, less confusing. The land was beautiful, the air was clean, the sky so bright and blue it almost hurt her eyes to look at it. As far as she knew, parents didn't have to worry about their children smoking anything stronger than tobacco. Kids didn't get shot walking down the street or sitting in a classroom or ordering a hamburger at McDonald's. Sure, there was crime in the Old West. Banks got robbed, stagecoaches got held up, crooks cheated honest people out of their land or their hard-earned money, but at least you didn't have to worry about some terrorist hijacking a plane and using it as a weapon.

"So, you don't know how you got here?" he asked.

"Not exactly. I was in my grandmother's house, removing some old wallpaper. I found a door behind a bookcase and when I stepped through the door, I was here, in the past."

"That was the night I found you in the alley?"

"Yeah. I tried to find the door again, but..." She shrugged. "It's like it disappeared."

"That's why you're so anxious to go back to Grant's Crossing."

She nodded.

"And if you can't find the door, what then?"

"Then I guess I'm stuck here." She glanced around, thinking again how incredible it was that she was here, in this place, in this time. Across the way, a young mother sat in the shade of her lodge, an infant cradled in her arms. In front of another tipi, two little girls were playing with dolls made out of scraps of buckskin. Further on, she saw a man sharpening an arrowhead. "I don't belong here," she murmured.

Reese grunted softly. They were both in places where they didn't belong.

Kelsey rubbed her hands over her arms. "The funny thing is, I think my grandfather came through that same door."

"Why do you think that?"

"My grandfather's name is Joseph St. James. Pete says a man by that name used to frequent the Square Deal. Mr. Wexler from the hotel remembers him, too. Said he was a strange old man who liked to tell stories and that he hadn't seen him in the last year or so. My grandfather disappeared just over a year ago. I think he's stuck back here somewhere."

"Sounds like some kind of tall tale to me," Reese muttered. "People walking through doors into the past." He shook his head. "It isn't possible." And yet, as farfetched as it seemed, he had to admit that Kelsey wasn't like any other woman he had ever met.

"Maybe it isn't possible," Kelsey said, "but here I am." She sighed, her shoulders slumping in despair. Reese was right, it sounded like a tall tale, only it was real. Either that, or this was the longest, most vivid dream she'd ever had.

At the sound of laughter, Reese glanced upriver. Several women had brought their children down to the river. In minutes, the little ones were splashing in the water while their mothers looked on.

"Looks like fun," Kelsey remarked, following his gaze.

Reese nodded, remembering the carefree days of his own childhood when he had splashed in the water with Chumani and Wahchinksapa. He wondered if Wahchinksapa had married and had children. Once, Reese had hoped to see Chumani's belly grow big with his child. Nothing had turned out as he had planned...

He persuaded Chumani to run away with him and they had left that night. Once they were married, all her doubts had faded away. A week later, more in love than ever, they had decided to return home.

That night, they camped near a shallow stream. They had made love and then gone to the stream to bathe. Reese had seen the riders first. Too late, he had realized that his weapons were out of reach.

"Well, now, looky here," one of the white men had said. "Ain't' she the purtiest little thang I ever did see."

Reese had stepped in front of Chumani, blocking her nakedness from the three white men.

"Right purty," the second man agreed.

The third man swung out of the saddle. "Come on outta there, honey. We ain't gonna hurt you none."

"Leave her alone," Reese had said. "She is my wife."

The first man drew his gun and leveled it at Reese. "She's gonna be a widow if you don't get out of the way."

Reese glanced at the shore where his knife and his rifle lay. He was wondering what his chances were of reaching his rifle when a rope settled around his upper body, pinning his arms to his sides. The man gave a sharp jerk on the rope, yanking Reese off his feet. Before he could react, the other two men dragged him to a tree, shoved him against it face first and looped the rope around him from neck to heels.

With a cry, Chumani ran out of the water and threw herself at one of the men. Uttering a vile oath, the man spun around and backhanded her across the face. She reeled backward, gathered herself and lunged at him again. He hit her harder this time and she crumpled to the ground and lay still.

"What'll we do with him?" one of the men asked, gesturing at Reese.

"Kill him."

With a grunt, the second man pulled his gun.

"Hold on," the third man said. "No use wasting a bullet." He lifted a whip from his saddlebags. "I always wondered how many lashes it would take to kill a man. What do you think? A hundred?"

The first man shrugged. "Beats the hell out of me."

"I'd say less than that," the second man said.

The man with the whip smiled maliciously. "Only one way to find out, I reckon."

"Well, you can waste time with him if you've a mind to," the first man said, "but she's more to my liking."

And so saying, the first man picked Chumani up and carried her into the shadows beyond the trees.

"I'm next," the second man called.

Reese struggled against the rope that bound him. He had to get free before it was too late, before the three *wasichu* defiled Chumani. Ignoring the rough bark that scraped his chest, arms and legs, he turned and twisted, trying to loosen the rope, but to no avail. He'd been so intent on trying to escape, he had forgotten the man with the whip. Until it came whistling down across his shoulders. He choked back a cry of pain, his body going rigid as the whip fell again and yet again, driving everything else from his mind. His skin split beneath the onslaught. Blood flowed down his back, hot against the chill of fear.

As from far away, he heard Chumani struggling against the men who held her.

The whip fell again, driving the breath from his body. Just when he was certain he couldn't stand it any longer, one of the men hollered, "Look out! She's got a knife!"

The man wielding the whip tossed it aside. With a whoop, he went to join in the fun of helping the other men disarm Chumani.

Weak with the loss of blood, knowing it was useless, Reese renewed his struggles to get free. He had to save Chumani before it was too late, before the *wasichu* violated her.

Ignoring the pain that engulfed him, he fought against the rope, felt it begin to give. His blood made the hemp slick. Gritting his teeth, he twisted his body back and forth, loosening the rope still more until he was able to slide it down over his shoulders.

Breathing heavily, he stepped away from the tree. The men had Chumani cornered now. No one paid him any mind as he moved as stealthily as possible toward his weapons. There was a sharp cry from one of the men as Chumani's blade found flesh.

Another man shouted, "Look out, he's loose!"

All three men glanced in Reese's direction. One of the outlaws pulled his gun and leveled it at Reese as Reese dove for his rifle.

There was a moment when he knew he was a dead man.

And then Chumani threw herself in front of the man with the gun.

Reese screamed, "No!" as time slowed to a crawl. He saw the dark stain that blossomed over Chumani's left breast, the look of pain and surprise in her eyes as she took a step forward, one hand reaching out to him. A thin ribbon of blood trickled from a corner of her mouth as she stumbled forward, then fell at his feet.

With a wild cry, he raised his rifle.

There was a flurry of gunfire. When it was over, the three men were dead.

Reese dropped to his knees beside Chumani. Oblivious to the blood oozing from a gunshot wound in his shoulder, he gathered her into his arms.

She stared up at him. "Husband..."

"Shh," he said. "Don't try to talk. You'll be all right..."

"Do not be sad...do not..." She lifted one hand, only to have it fall limply to her side.

He shook his head as the light went out of her eyes.

"Chumani, no!" He clutched her body to his, willing his strength, his life, into her, but to no avail. "No! No!" He sobbed the words over and over again, not wanting to believe she was gone.

He held her until his strength gave out, until the pain and the amount of blood he had lost took its toll and he pitched headlong into unconsciousness.

When he woke, it was morning. Chumani lay stiff and cold beside him. He wrapped her in a blanket and laid her body over the back of her horse. Teeth clenched against the throbbing agony in his back and shoulder, he mounted his own horse and started for home.

He left the white men where they had fallen.

Hantaywee met him before he reached the village. Later, he learned that she had seen the whole thing in vision.

It had been Hantaywee who treated his wounds, who cared for him while he wandered in and out of consciousness. Hantaywee who spoke to him in the quiet of the night when he couldn't sleep, Hantaywee who soothed him when he woke in a cold sweat, tormented by nightmares.

When his back was healed, he left the land of his mother's people, certain he would never return...

"Reese? Hey, earth to Reese."

He looked at Kelsey blankly.

"Where were you just now?"

He frowned at her, then shook his head ruefully. "I guess you're not the only one living in the past."

Chapter Nine

Kelsey studied Reese. His face was drawn and pale, his eyes tormented. What had he meant about both of them living in the past?

"It's obvious that something's bothering you," she remarked after a moment. "Do you want to talk about it?"

"No."

"It might help." She remembered the dark days after Nick had died. If she hadn't been able to talk about it with her mother and Nana Mary, she never would have gotten through it. Sometimes they had just listened. Wise women, both of them, they had known she needed to get it all out, the anger she felt because her marriage had ended so abruptly with nothing solved between them, the regret she had felt because Nick had been on his way to meet her when he died, the relief she had felt that it was over, the guilt she had suffered because Nick's death had solved the problem of whether she should end their marriage or keep trying to make it work.

"Nothing helps," Reese said. He had tried pickling himself in alcohol, hoping to find forgetfulness. He had turned to soiled doves, seeking comfort in their arms, only to find that his body refused to cooperate. He had tried running away from his memories. He had tried facing them head-on. Nothing had eased the guilt that tormented him. She was dead and it was his fault. If he hadn't wanted to get the best of Wahchinksapa, if he hadn't been so certain he knew what was best for Chumani, if he hadn't talked her into running away with him, she would still be alive. She might be married to Wahchinksapa, but she would still be alive...

Kelsey bit down on her lower lip. She couldn't bear to see the pain in his eyes. She didn't know what had caused it, but she knew that look. She had seen it reflected in her own eyes often enough after Nick died.

Taking a deep breath, she laid her hand on his arm.

Slowly, Reese turned to look at her.

She waited, certain he was going to brush her hand aside and tell her to mind her own business. Instead, he rested his head on her shoulder.

That simple gesture of defeat tore at her heart. She didn't know what tragedy lay in his past, but whatever it was, she knew he hadn't yet come to grips with it.

Murmuring, "It'll be all right," she patted his back lightly.

He went rigid at her touch and then, with an effort that was almost visible, he relaxed again. They sat that way for some time, until a couple of boys came running down river, yelling and splashing in the water.

Reese sat up and put a little space between himself and Kelsey. "Do you want to go for a swim?"

"Here?" She looked upriver to where the mothers and children were frolicking in the water. "I don't think so."

"We can go down river a ways," he said, "if you want some privacy."

It was tempting. The sun was warm on her back, the water looked cool and inviting.

But she shook her head. "I don't have a suit."

He frowned. "A suit? For swimming?"

Kelsey laughed. It was obvious that he thought she meant a business suit, like men wore to work. "A bathing suit," she explained. "It's something people wear to swim in."

"Doesn't it just get wet?"

"Well, yeah."

He shrugged. "So, why bother?"

"For modesty's sake," she said, her mind filling with vivid images of Reese swimming in the buff.

Rising, he held out his hand to help her up.

She might have rejected such an old-fashioned gesture in her own time but here, in this time, it seemed charming and chivalrous. Putting her hand in his, she let Reese pull her to her feet.

They walked a while in silence. Kelsey was a little nervous about skinny-dipping with Reese, although it had little to do with being naked in front of him and everything to do with her growing affection. Maybe she would just wear her bra and panties. They covered a lot more than some of the bathing suits she had seen lately.

Rounding a bend in the river, they came to a sunny spot where the river widened. Grass lined the banks, trees provided shade, a large flat rock offered them a place to sit.

"This is nice," Kelsey remarked, sitting on the rock.

He nodded. "I'll be just down there a ways."

"Oh."

"Something wrong?"

"No, I just thought… You can swim here, if you want."

"I thought you wanted privacy?"

"Oh, sure, whatever," she said, but she couldn't help feeling a little twinge of disappointment that she wouldn't get to see Reese in the buff, after all. Of course, his clout and vest didn't cover all that much anyway.

She watched him walk away, thinking it was odd that he was even more modest than she was. Stepping out of her buckskin dress, moccasins and underwear, she slid into the water. It was cool but not cold, deep enough in the middle to cover her up to her shoulders. She swam for a few minutes, then sat in the shallows, enjoying the eddy and flow of the water around her. She had never been skinny-dipping in a river, though she had gone swimming in the nude in a girlfriend's pool late one night during one summer vacation. She had been fourteen at the time and remembered feeling very daring and naughty.

It was pleasant, sitting in the shallows with the sun warming her head and shoulders. Birds chirped in the treetops. A squirrel scolded her from a branch overhead. A lizard sunned itself on a rock.

But it was thoughts of Reese that crowded her mind. Had he shed his clout and vest and gone swimming in the river's other fork? She imagined all that bronze skin sleek and wet, his long black hair glinting blue-black in the sunlight... Just thinking about it did funny things in the pit of her stomach. She wasn't looking for anything permanent. She wasn't looking for a new husband, especially here, in the Old West, but...she felt a rush of heat climb into her cheeks. She had never had an affair, never indulged in casual sex like so many of her friends. She had been a virgin when she married Nick. But she wasn't a virgin anymore...

What on earth was she thinking? She didn't know how long she was going to be in this time, this place. Even as she tried to tell herself it would be a mistake to get involved with Reese, a little voice in the back of her mind said this might be the perfect time and place for an affair. No one knew her here. She could do whatever she wanted, within reason, because sooner or later, she was bound to find her way home and whatever she did here, in the past, would stay here, in the past...unless she got pregnant!

With a shake of her head, Kelsey waded out of the river and stood in the sun to dry herself. She didn't know where this line of thinking had come from but, as Don Knotts used to say on the old Andy Griffith show, it was time to nip it! Nip it in the bud! Besides, she didn't think she could give her body to a man without giving him her heart, as well.

Said heart skipped a beat when she heard Reese's voice calling her name.

With a start, she grabbed her tunic and yanked it over her head, then rolled her underwear into a ball to put on later. She was sitting on the rock, pulling on her moccasins, when he appeared.

"You about ready to go back?" he asked.

She nodded. His wet hair proclaimed that he had also gone swimming.

The village was humming with activity when they returned. Kelsey saw women cooking over open fires, sewing, nursing their children, hanging meat to dry on long wooden racks, laughing together as they watched a baby take a few wobbly steps. The Indian women glanced up as she passed by, their dark eyes filled with quiet curiosity. She saw a few of the younger women looking at Reese speculatively, saw recognition in the eyes of some of the older ones.

A few of the warriors nodded at Reese. One older man glared at him, his eyes filled with hatred. Reese saw it, too. He paused briefly, his body tensing, and then he continued on, his gaze focused straight ahead.

Kelsey hurried after him, her own curiosity mounting.

Hantaywee was waiting for them when they reached her tipi. She handed them each two bowls, one filled with soup, one filled with strips of roasted meat. Kelsey looked at the meat, wondering what it was.

"It's venison," Reese said, noting her wary expression.

"Oh." Relieved, Kelsey sat down in the shade of Hantaywee's tipi. She knew that some Indians ate their dogs and even their horses when they were starving.

Reese sat beside her, apparently intent on what he was eating.

"How long has it been since you've been back here?" she asked.

"A long time."

"I thought so."

He looked over at her. "What makes you say that?"

She shrugged. "Just the way people look at you."

He grunted softly. "I'm not welcome here."

"Why not?"

"It's a long story."

"I'd like to hear it."

"Maybe someday I'll tell you."

"If you're not welcome," Kelsey asked, frowning, "why did we come here?"

"Because Hantaywee is here and I needed her help."

"Is she related to you?"

"No." He blew out a sigh. "But she raised me after my parents were killed."

At his words, a number of questions rose in Kelsey's mind. She swallowed a spoonful of soup, wondering if she dared ask any of them. One thing she was sure of, he didn't want to talk about his past.

With a sigh, she reined in her curiosity and drank her soup.

* * * * *

Reese stood at the outskirts of the village, grateful to be alone. He had been aware of the looks cast his way earlier in the day. There were those in the village who didn't know who he was or what he had done, but most of them were familiar with the story. He had ignored those who had regarded him with ill-disguised interest, but he couldn't ignore Chumani's father. A cold and bitter hatred had burned in the older man's eyes. Reese had looked away, stricken by the pain and loathing in Iron Wolf's expression, by the sharp stab of guilt that had pierced his own heart.

He had been near death when he arrived back at the village all those years ago. As soon as he was able, he had gone to Chumani's mother and father to tell them how sorry he was about what had happened, but they had refused to listen. Hantaywee had advised him to give them time to grieve, time to heal, but he had taken the coward's way out. He had left the village, left the blatant accusation, real or imagined, that he saw on every face, the sorrow and condemnation on the faces of Wahchinksapa and Chumani's parents.

Now, standing there in the moonlight, he wondered again why he had come here. Better to have died out on the prairie than to return home and reopen old wounds that had never fully healed.

But his death on the prairie would have meant Kelsey's death as well. She was a stranger in this place, ill equipped to survive in the wilderness alone.

Kelsey... He wished fleetingly that he was a whole man, one whose heart didn't lie cold and dead under a bier of bitter grief and regret.

* * * * *

Kelsey stood in the shadows, watching Reese. In the moonlight, his face looked like something carved from stone. She wondered what it was that tormented him so. If she went to him now, would her presence comfort him? Or would he be angry because she had followed him?

As she watched, he bowed his head. At first, she thought he was praying, but then she realized he was crying. Harsh sobs racked his body.

The sound tore at her heart. She was tempted to go to him, to wrap her arms around him, to cuddle him as if he were a little boy in need of comfort. But he was a man grown, not a child. And she didn't know him well enough to know if he would welcome her touch or turn away from it.

Another sob was her undoing. Unable to watch any longer, she went to him, overcome by the need to take him in her arms, to whisper words of solace and assure him that everything would be all right.

"Reese." She whispered his name.

He looked up, startled, so lost in his own misery that he had been unaware of her presence.

Wordlessly, she drew him into her arms and held him while he cried, wondering, as she did so, if he would hate her now that she had seen this vulnerable side of him.

Not knowing what to say, she remained silent, one hand stroking his hair, his hard body pressed against hers.

Gradually, his sobs subsided and he stood quiet in her arms, his forehead resting lightly against hers.

Gradually, the atmosphere between them changed until she wasn't just a woman holding a man in a comforting embrace, but a woman keenly aware of the man in her arms — the heat of his skin, the thick texture of his hair beneath her hand, the sudden increase in his breathing, the sexual tension that blossomed between them.

He lifted his head and gazed into her eyes. Desire flared between them, hot and unmistakable. The urge to console him was still there, but now Kelsey wanted to pull him down onto the ground, to comfort him with the warmth of her body, to make him forget, if only for a little while, whatever it was that caused him such distress.

She wanted to give him solace.

She wanted to ease his heartache.

She wanted him.

Taking a deep breath, she lowered her arms to her sides and took a step backward. In spite of her earlier thoughts, this really wasn't the time or the place for an affair. She had to concentrate on what was important and that was finding her way back home. She didn't belong here, in the past and she never would. Letting herself care for Reese was a mistake she couldn't afford to make. Getting physically and emotionally involved with him was just asking for heartache and she'd had enough of that to last a lifetime. Or so she told herself.

There was a moment when she thought he wouldn't let her go, a moment when she hoped he would pull her into his arms and to heck with the consequences. But the moment passed.

The fact that he let her go so easily convinced her that he was thinking along the same lines she was. They were literally from two different worlds, it would be foolish for the two of them to become romantically involved.

But as she turned to walk back to Hantaywee's lodge, she couldn't shake the feeling that they were fighting a battle that was already lost.

Chapter Ten
୨୦

When Kelsey woke in the morning, Reese had already left the lodge.

"Gone hunting," Hantaywee told her.

Kelsey nodded, wondering if he had actually gone hunting or if, after last night, it was just an excuse to put some distance between them.

So, he would be gone for the day. Now was the perfect time to find out what Hantaywee knew about Reese. If anyone would know what was troubling him, she was sure it was the old woman.

Kelsey waited until after they had eaten breakfast; then, taking her courage in hand, she asked the question uppermost in her mind.

"What's troubling Reese? Why is he so sad?"

Hantaywee canted her head to one side, regarding Kelsey through all-knowing eyes. Then, as if making up her mind about whether to answer or not, she sat down and motioned for Kelsey to do the same.

"It happened a long time ago," Hantaywee began. "Tashunka Kangi was young and very much in love with Chumani. They had grown up together and everyone expected them to marry. But there was another young man, Wahchinksapa, who also had warm eyes for Chumani. Wahchinksapa and Tashunka Kangi had grown up together, like brothers. Their rivalry for Chumani changed that. Friends became enemies. Everyone in the village knew that Chumani's parents favored Wahchinksapa. When Tashunka Kangi offered six fine horses to Chumani's father, Wahchinksapa offered ten.

Chumani wept when her father promised her to Wahchinksapa. On the night before she was to marry, Tashunka Kangi convinced her to run away with him. It had been done before. It has been done since. Chumani agreed to run away with Tashunka Kangi and they left the village."

Hantaywee paused a moment and then went on. "Chumani and Tashunka Kangi were returning to the village when they were set upon by three white men. Tashunka Kangi was captured and badly beaten. His back still wears the scars."

Was he ashamed of those scars, Kelsey wondered. Was that why he was so careful to make sure she never saw his back, why he hadn't wanted to swim with her?

"Chumani was killed trying to save his life. He cannot forget that, nor forgive himself for it. He killed the three white men and brought Chumani's body home. When his wounds healed, he left the village."

It was a tragic story. She could see it all in her mind, feel Reese's pain, his guilt at being unable to save Chumani. He carried the scars to this day and not just the ones on his back. Her death had scarred his soul, as well. Blinking back her tears, Kelsey thanked Hantaywee for sharing it with her and then left the lodge.

She spent the day sitting in the sun, watching the people in the village as they went about their daily routine. She had never really known any Indians, though she had met one or two during the summers she had stayed at the cabin with her grandparents. The Lakota seemed like a warm and friendly people, nothing at all like the Indians portrayed in old Westerns. Her grandfather had scorned the old movies and their stereotypes of stone-faced Indians who spoke broken English and never laughed or smiled.

She wondered what Reese had been like as a child. As soon as the thought crossed her mind, she knew she was in trouble. Once a woman started wondering what a man had been like when he was a little boy, it was a sure sign that she was beginning to care! But she couldn't help it.

She watched a handful of young boys at play. Had Reese been one of the bold ones, like that little fellow over there, or one of the quiet ones? Smiling, she watched two of the boys wrestling on the ground, growling like young puppies while the others looked on. Later, she watched them shoot at targets with small bows and arrows. And still later, filled with energy and the exuberance of youth, she watched as they raced each other from one end of the village to the other and back again. Ah, to be young again and have that kind of unbridled energy. She wondered what the boys' reaction would be if she had joined in the race.

Her gaze drifted to a little girl who sat beside her mother. Had Chumani looked like that, all big dark eyes and long black hair? She felt an unexpected twinge of jealousy as she imagined Reese courting Chumani, begging her to run away with him. No wonder he was so torn with guilt. He had defied her father's wishes and taken Chumani away from her home and she had died because of it. And yet, it wasn't really his fault. He wasn't responsible for the actions of the men who had killed her. It had just been bad luck that those men had found them. Still, putting herself in his place, she knew that, under the circumstances, she would probably feel the same way he did.

She looked up when Hantaywee emerged from the lodge. What was it Reese had said? *She knows things.* Maybe Hantaywee could tell her how to get home again.

With that thought in mind, Kelsey followed the old woman into the woods.

"Hantaywee?"

The old woman turned at the sound of Kelsey's voice.

"Do you mind if I walk with you?"

Hantaywee shook her head. "I came here to gather wood."

Kelsey glanced around, only then noticing the fallen branches and sticks that littered the ground beneath the trees. "Oh, let me help."

"Pilamaya."

Not certain how to broach the subject she wished to discuss, Kelsey concentrated on gathering wood and then she recalled that Reese said Hantaywee had told him that she, Kelsey, was from the future, so maybe the subject wouldn't come as a shock after all.

"You wish to ask me something," Hantaywee said.

"Yes." Kelsey stopped walking, the wood she had gathered cradled in her arms. "Do you know how I can get home?"

Hantaywee turned, her arms also filled with wood. "Do you wish to go home?"

"Yes, of course."

"Perhaps you should think on it before you answer so quickly."

Kelsey frowned. What was there to think about? Of course she wanted to go home...didn't she?

Reese won't be there.

Did Hantaywee say the words aloud, Kelsey wondered, or had she only heard them in her mind?

"Sometimes the path we follow is not the one we meant to take," Hantaywee said quietly. "But in the end, we find that it is the path that leads us to where we want to go."

"Are you saying that my coming here was meant to be?"

"Perhaps."

"Well, that's an interesting theory, but I don't think it's true in my case. I don't fit in here."

Hantaywee shrugged. "Only time will tell."

And with that, the old woman went back to collecting firewood. When her arms were full, she walked back to her lodge.

Kelsey trailed after the old woman, her mind replaying their conversation. Surely it wasn't her fate to spend the rest of her life here in the nineteenth century! Reese or no Reese, she didn't want to stay here. She wanted to go home, back to electric lights and computers and television, back to pizza delivered to your door and online shopping and dark chocolate ice cream. She wanted to see Gerard Butler's upcoming movie and read her favorite author's next book and spend Christmas at the cabin with her family and...

Her thoughts scattered like dandelion fluff in the wind when she looked up and saw Reese striding toward them from the direction of the village. Her heart did a happy little joy-joy dance while butterflies fluttered in the pit of her stomach. How was it possible that this man, who was little more than a stranger, could make her feel as if she had just won the lottery?

He smiled at her, a slow, sexy smile, and then he took the wood from Hantaywee's arms and carried it the rest of the way to the village.

Kelsey followed him, her gaze moving over his broad shoulders, his tight butt, his long, long legs. His hair glistened blue-black in the late afternoon sunlight, the smooth copper color of his skin tempted her touch. She didn't want to stay here indefinitely but, for now, there was no place on earth she would rather be.

Inside the lodge, she piled the wood she had gathered next to the door, then ducked back outside.

Reese emerged from the lodge on her heels.

"I thought you went hunting," Kelsey said.

He jerked a thumb over his shoulder to where Hantaywee was already busy at work skinning a deer.

Grimacing, Kelsey looked away. She knew cows and chickens were killed so that she could eat, but when your meat came in neat little cellophane-wrapped packages, it was easy to forget how it got there.

"I don't suppose you've ever butchered a deer," Reese remarked.

"No."

"City girl," he scoffed but his eyes were kind.

She nodded. "Shouldn't you be helping Hantaywee?"

He looked aghast. "Skinning and butchering are woman's work."

"Why is that?"

"It just is."

"Well, we have a saying where I come from. If you catch it, you clean it."

He chuckled. "Our way is better. Tell me more about what it's like where you come from."

He started walking away from the village and she fell in beside him.

"Well, it's very different from what it is here. Better in some ways, worse in others. There have been many wars, some of them involving other countries. There are some people who have more than they need while others don't have enough. Life is more hectic. Divorce is common and no longer frowned upon..." She looked up at Reese. "Do Indians ever get divorced?"

"Sometimes."

"Is it complicated?"

"No, it's a simple thing with us. When a man wants to divorce his wife, he waits until his society has a dance. Sometime during the night, he asks for a drumstick and then he beats the drum once and announces that he no longer wants his wife."

"What if the wife wants a divorce?"

"Then she leaves him and goes back home."

"Who gets the children?"

"The woman, usually. Tell me more of your time."

"Gosh, there's so much. We have cars now...carriages with engines that can go much faster than a horse."

"You don't have horses?"

Kelsey grinned. For a Lakota not to have a horse would be beyond comprehension. The acquisition of the horse had given the Lakota a freedom they had never known before. "Of course we still have horses, but now they're ridden for pleasure."

He grunted softly. "Go on."

"I don't know how to explain things to you," Kelsey said. "There have been so many innovations in the last hundred years. Airplanes and computers, iPods and cell phones, moving pictures. We have machines that wash your clothes for you and others that dry them and machines that wash dishes and vacuum the carpets and..."

"Enough," he said.

She grinned at him. "Like I said, a lot of changes."

"The words on your shirt, you never told me what they mean."

"Oh, that," she said. "PMS means pre-menstrual syndrome."

"What the hell does that mean?"

"It's a term to describe the cranky, out-of-sorts feeling a lot of women get before they start their..." What on earth did women in the Old West call it when they had their period? "You know, their monthly..."

"Ah," he said, "I think I understand."

She smiled up at him, pleased to see that the dark, haunted look was gone from his eyes. Maybe going out and killing something had been good for him.

* * * * *

Reese had said they would leave the village in a few days, but a week went by and then two. Living with the Indians was different from anything Kelsey had ever known. The Lakota had no clocks, kept no time. They ate when they were hungry and slept when they were tired. The men hunted when they needed meat. When they weren't hunting, they strolled through the village, repaired old weapons, or fashioned new ones. The women were always busy cooking or cleaning or just looking after their children. All in all, it seemed a pleasant way to live, not at all like life in the twenty-first century, where everyone was always in a hurry and there was never enough time to just sit and relax.

Her thoughts scattered as Hantaywee emerged from her lodge. A few minutes later, a dozen children were gathered in front of the old woman's tipi.

She was wondering what was going on when Reese came up beside her.

"It's story time," he explained.

"Like at the library?" Kelsey wondered aloud, and then realized he probably had no idea what story time at the library was all about.

"She's telling them about the pipestone quarry," Reese said. "It's located to the northeast. The People go there to cut pipestone, which is a soft red rock the men use to make pipes. Legend has it that the stone was formed from the flesh of our ancestors who were destroyed in a great flood. The Lakota ran to the quarry to escape, but they were all drowned except for one maiden. She was caught by an eagle and carried to safety. We come from her descendents."

"Interesting," Kelsey remarked. She remembered reading somewhere that almost every race of people had a story about a great flood that had covered the earth. "She must have been pregnant when she was saved."

Reese laughed. "Maybe so. Another legend says that *Wakan Tanka* called all the Indian nations to the quarry at a time when all the tribes were at war. *Wakan Tanka* made a great pipe from the red rock. He smoked it and commanded the people to be at peace. Still another legend says the quarry is where mankind was created."

"What's she telling them now?" Kelsey asked as a hush fell over the children.

Reese listened a moment, then smiled. "She's telling them about *Wakinyan*, the Thunder Beings."

"Thunder Beings?"

"They are creatures of power, like the thunder birds. The *Wakinyan* bring rain and hail, thunder and lightning. They bring new life to the earth after the winter. Long ago, the *Wakinyan* used their powers to fight the *Unktehila*. The *Unktehila* were evil water monsters with scaly skin and horns."

"Like lizards?"

"Yes, but bigger and more deadly. And they weren't particular about what they killed, or what they ate. So *Wakan Tanka* sent the Thunder Beings to kill the *Unktehila*. The *Wakinyan* struck the water with their lightning and made it boil, so that the rivers and lakes dried up and the *Unktehila* died."

"Kind of a scary story for kids, don't you think?" But even as Kelsey posed the question, she saw that the Lakota children were enthralled by the tale. When Hantaywee started another story, Reese took Kelsey aside.

"I was about to go for a walk," he said. "Do you want to come along?"

"Are we going anyplace in particular?" she asked.

"No. I just need to stretch my legs."

"Sure, I'll tag along."

They had almost reached the edge of the camp circle when a tall warrior emerged from one of the lodges.

Reese came to an abrupt halt as the tall warrior stepped into his path. He hadn't seen Wahchinksapa since Chumani's death but the years had not diminished the tension between them.

A woman stepped out of the lodge behind Wahchinksapa, a baby in her arms, a toddler at her heels. Reese recognized Takchawee. When they were growing up, it had been no secret that Takchawee was in love with Wahchinksapa, just as it had been no secret that Wahchinksapa had been in love with Chumani.

Reese clenched his hands at his sides. It was hard to see Takchawee and her children, to know Wahchinksapa and Takchawee had gone on with their lives. But for him, Chumani would be alive today, perhaps with children of her own.

Wahchinksapa folded his arms across his chest. He was a few inches shorter than Reese, a little meatier around the middle. "Why have you come back here?" he asked in curt Lakota.

"This is my home."

"You are not wanted here."

Reese gestured at Wahchinksapa's shirt. "You are an important man here now. Are you going to run me off?"

Wahchinksapa's gaze slid toward Hantaywee's lodge.

Reese grinned inwardly. He might not be welcome here, but not even a Shirt Wearer had the guts to throw him out, not when he was staying here with Hantaywee's blessing.

Wahchinksapa looked past Reese to where Kelsey was standing quietly. "A white woman," he said, his voice thick with scorn. "But then, no Lakota woman would have you now."

It was the wrong thing to say. Rage boiled up inside Reese. His first instinct was to plant his fist in Wahchinksapa's face, but for once in his life, he took a deep breath and kept a tight rein on his temper. Brawling with Wahchinksapa would only shame Hantaywee.

Head high and back straight, Reese walked past Wahchinksapa with as much dignity as he could muster.

Kelsey hurried to catch up with him. "What was that all about? Who was he? What did he say that made you so angry?"

"I don't want to talk about it," Reese retorted. He walked briskly for a few minutes, then slowed. "His name is Wahchinksapa."

Kelsey's eyes widened. Wahchinksapa was the other man in the Chumani triangle.

Kelsey looked up at Reese, thinking how difficult it must be for him to be here, to be constantly reminded of the woman he had loved and lost.

Reese stopped at the river's edge. Stooping, he picked up a handful of rocks and tossed them, one by one, into the water.

Kelsey watched the ripples spread as each rock hit the water. Life was like that, she thought. A man loved a woman and that simple act spread in ever-widening circles, touching other lives for better or worse.

She stood beside Reese, listening to the plop-plop-plop of rocks hitting the water, ready to listen if he wanted to talk.

"She was so young," he murmured after a time, his voice so low she didn't know if he was talking to her or to himself. "I loved her my whole life. But I wasn't really thinking about that when I convinced her to run away with me." He shook his head. His voice was bitter when he said, "I was thinking about me, about what I wanted, about proving to Wahchinksapa that I was the better man." He shook his head again, his gaze fixed on something only he could see. "I defied her parents because I thought I knew what was best for her. I was stubborn and proud." He swallowed hard, his voice thick with unshed tears. "I might as well have put that bullet into her myself."

"Reese, that's not true! You were both young and in love. No one could have known things would turn out the way they did."

"Hantaywee knew."

"What do you mean?"

"She warned me to wait, but I didn't listen."

Kelsey didn't know what to say. Hantaywee hadn't mentioned that part to her when she related the story.

"Maybe if she had told me what was going to happen instead of just telling me it would be better to wait until spring…hell, maybe she didn't know how it would turn out. I probably wouldn't have listened to her anyway. I was young and invincible…"

He stopped as if suddenly realizing that Kelsey was there. "Sorry," he muttered. "Can you find your way back?"

"Aren't you coming?"

"No."

She didn't want to leave him there alone, but she didn't know how to convince him to let her stay. "Well, I guess I'll see you later, then," she said.

But he didn't answer.

Hantaywee was sitting outside when Kelsey returned to the village. The medicine woman looked up, her wise old eyes sad.

"Did you warn Reese not to run away with Chumani?" Kelsey asked, dropping down beside Hantaywee.

"He told you that?"

Kelsey nodded. "Would it have made any difference if he had waited?"

"It is difficult to say. The future is not always as easy to read as the past. Only the Great Spirit knows all. Perhaps waiting would have changed nothing. Perhaps Chumani would have died some other way. Perhaps she would have lived and Tashunka Kangi would have died," she said with a sigh. "Perhaps they would have grown old together. Who can say?"

"I hate to see him blaming himself," Kelsey said. "It really wasn't his fault." She knew why he felt guilty, but he wasn't to blame for the actions of those men. Like Hantaywee had said, waiting might not have changed anything. Maybe it had been Chumani's fate to die young. Maybe, if she hadn't been killed by those men, she would have been killed some other way, as Hantaywee had mentioned. Kelsey had always believed that when it was your time to go, you'd go. How else did you explain it when a plane crashed and killed everyone on board except for one person? Didn't people always say it just wasn't their time to go?

Time, she thought. That was the only answer to the pain and guilt that tormented Reese. She just wished she could speed it up a little.

* * * * *

Reese seemed to be in better spirits in the morning. After breakfast, Hantaywee sent them out to look for pine nuts.

Kelsey strolled along the river, ever aware of Reese beside her. They walked in silence until the village was far behind, but it was a comfortable silence. Kelsey couldn't seem to stop looking at Reese. Talk about a babe magnet, she thought. He couldn't be more perfect if she had called Cupid and ordered a man to fit her own specifications.

The thought made her smile. Still, with his tawny skin and long black hair and killer smile, she doubted any woman who had reached the age of puberty would be able to resist him.

She had dreamed of him last night, a dream that had lingered in her mind when she woke. And made her blush whenever she thought of it.

They walked through a grassy meadow until they came to a small pool shaded by tall pines.

It looked like a storybook place, Kelsey thought as she sat down on the grass, the kind of place where the handsome prince rendezvoused with the beautiful princess.

Her handsome prince stretched out beside her, his hands folded underneath his head as he gazed up at the sky. In her mind's eye, she pictured him on a white charger riding to her rescue. The thought made her smile inwardly.

Plucking a long blade of grass, she twirled it between her thumb and forefinger, hoping he wouldn't notice that she couldn't stop staring at him. He was simply beautiful, from the top of his black-thatched head to the soles of his moccasins. She wished her skin was as dark as his. It really wasn't fair, she thought. She spent a ton of money every year trying to get her skin to be that same smooth shade of brown that his was naturally. She yearned to feel his mouth on hers, the heat of his skin beneath her hands.

Feeling her gaze, he looked over at her. Was he thinking what she was thinking, wanting what she was wanting? When he didn't move, didn't speak, she thought maybe she was imagining the tension that hummed between them. But then his hand closed over hers, pulling her down until her upper body lay across his.

He stroked her cheek with the back of his hand. "Don't make more out of this than it is."

"No," she murmured. "I won't."

He pulled her closer, crushing her breasts against his chest. His eyes grew darker, more intense, as he cupped the back of her head in his hand, drew her head closer and kissed her.

His lips were warm and firm, filled with magic as they played over hers. She ran her tongue across his lower lip, felt his body tighten as his lips parted under her gentle assault.

Her tongue dueled with his, sending fingers of fire streaking down to her belly and beyond.

With a groan, he rolled over, tucking her beneath him as he deepened the kiss.

Clutching at his shoulders, she thought she might go up in smoke. Never had a man's touch inflamed her so quickly, never had a man's kisses aroused her so thoroughly.

Needing to touch him, she slid one hand under his vest, her fingertips kneading his back, reveling in the powerful muscles that quivered at her touch. Hardly aware of what she was doing, she let her fingers trace the line of ridged flesh that started at the point of one shoulder and ran diagonally across his back.

With a sharp intake of breath, Reese rolled away from her and sat up.

Startled and bereft, she looked up at him, wondering what had just happened. And then she knew. His back, the scars. She had been tracing one of them with her fingertips. "Reese?"

He stood abruptly, his body tense, his hands tightly clenched at his sides.

"I'm sorry." She sat up, her arms folded under her breasts. "Reese?"

"It's time to go."

She wanted to argue with him, to force him to tell her more of what had happened the day Chumani died, to make him see that it wasn't his fault, but one look at his face, at the pained expression in his eyes, put the idea right out of her mind.

"All right." Taking a deep breath, she stood and brushed a stray leaf from the hem of her tunic.

Not meeting her gaze, he started back toward the village.

Kelsey followed a few moments later, wishing that she had kept her hands to herself.

He was silent and withdrawn when they returned to Hantaywee's lodge. The old woman was sitting in the shade, a bit of sewing in her hands, when they returned. She took one look at Reese's face and wisely held her tongue, at least until Reese went inside and closed the door flap, the Lakota way of saying, keep out.

Hantaywee looked up at Kelsey. "It is not your fault."

Kelsey looked at the old woman, wondering how she knew what had happened in the meadow.

Hantaywee put her sewing aside, the lines around her mouth and eyes deepening. "I saw that look in his eyes many times when I was caring for him," she said quietly, "that look of shame and guilt and despair. His body has healed. In time, his heart and soul will heal as well."

Kelsey nodded, hoping the medicine woman was right.

Later that night, after dinner, Kelsey heard drumming. When she asked Reese what it was, he told her, in a voice devoid of emotion, that the Kit Fox Society was having a dance.

"What's the Kit Fox Society?" she asked.

"It's a warrior society. There are several. The Kit Foxes, the Tokalas, the Badgers, the Crow Owners, the Brave Hearts."

"Sort of like social clubs for men?"

Reese nodded. He had once belonged to the Kit Foxes. If he went to the dance, would they welcome him? Or would they turn their backs on him while the drum fell silent?

"Reese?" She tugged on his arm, refusing to let him shut her out.

"Tomorrow we'll head back to Grant's Crossing," he said.

"Is that what you want?"

"It's for the best." He couldn't stay here any longer, an outcast among his own people. "You should get some sleep," he said. "We'll be leaving at first light."

* * * * *

Kelsey lay curled up in her blankets, unable to sleep. She stared at the sprinkling of stars visible through the smoke hole of the tipi and listened to the sounds of the night—the whisper of the wind against the sides of the lodgeskins, the chirrup of a cricket, the stamp of a horse's hoof. Quiet sounds, peaceful sounds, so different from the sounds of home.

Home. She was anxious to get back to Grant's Crossing and continue searching for the door to Nana Mary's house and yet she would be sorry to leave this place. Her grandfather had loved the Old West and now she was here, a part of it. And, if Pete was to be believed, Papa Joe was a part of it, too. It explained how he had known so much of life in the Old West. She wondered where her grandfather was and if he was still alive. The wild west really was wild. Her grandfather could have died or been killed and she would never know.

With a sigh, she rolled onto her side and closed her eyes. She had to get some sleep. Reese had said he wanted to leave at dawn. She didn't know what time it was now, but it felt late and first light came mighty early.

It seemed she had just fallen asleep when a harsh cry rent the stillness of the night. Bolting upright, Kelsey glanced over at Reese, wondering if he was having a nightmare, but Reese was also sitting up, his head canted to the side, listening.

She was about to ask what was wrong when he grabbed his rifle and padded toward the door of the lodge.

Hantaywee had also gained her feet. Kelsey's eyes widened when she saw the long-bladed skinning knife clutched in the old woman's hand.

Scrambling to her feet, Kelsey pressed her hand over her rapidly beating heart. Something was definitely wrong.

From outside, a dog began yapping furiously and soon all the camp dogs were howling.

"What is it?" Kelsey whispered. "What's happening?"

Reese glanced over his shoulder. "I don't know. Stay here."

Silent as a shadow, he slipped out of the lodge.

Kelsey tiptoed to the doorway and lifted the hide flap so that she could see outside. The sky was just brightening in the east. At first, she didn't see anything out of the ordinary and then she saw three warriors skulking around the lodge next to Hantaywee's.

She stared at the warriors. They were tall and bronze, bare chested, with roached scalp locks and painted faces. But it was the feathered tomahawks in their hands that sent a chill racing down her spine.

As she watched, she realized they hadn't come to take lives but to steal the horses tethered in the front of the lodge across the way. Hantaywee had told her that Lakota men tied their favorite war ponies close to their lodges at night and that it was considered a great coup for an enemy warrior to sneak into camp and steal such horses, horses that one of the warriors was even now leading away while the other two warriors threw chunks of meat to the nearest camp dogs in an effort to keep them quiet.

Where was Reese?

The thought had no sooner crossed her mind than he appeared in her line of vision, along with four other Lakota warriors.

The Indian leading the horses dropped their tethers. A spine-tingling war cry rose from his throat as he sprang forward, his tomahawk raised. His companions also took up the cry.

Warriors brandishing weapons erupted from nearby lodges. Dogs who had fallen silent began barking again.

Kelsey stood there, mouth agape, as dozens of armed Lakota warriors surrounded the three intruders.

Women were emerging from their lodges now, some of them armed with knives or clubs, adding their ululating cries to the angry voices of their men.

Justice came swiftly. There was no trial. The Lakota warriors were judge and jury. They found the intruders guilty and extracted their vengeance quickly and with finality.

Kelsey turned away as the horse thieves were beaten to death without mercy.

She knew, by the exultant cries that rang out a short time later, that the intruders were dead.

Stunned by the sudden outburst of violence, Kelsey crept back to her bed and slipped under the covers, one hand pressed over her heart. She had seen violence in movies and tv, she had never seen it happen right in front of her eyes. It was brutal and all too real.

She was drifting, not quite asleep, when a slight noise drew her attention. Through heavy-lidded eyes she saw Hantaywee add a few sticks to the hot coals, followed by what looked like a handful of dried grass.

A shiver slid down Kelsey's spine when a small blue flame rose in the center of the firepit, followed by a soft whooshing sound. A cloud of blue-gray smoke gathered in the air over the firepit and in the smoke she saw two wolves, one red and one white.

Hantaywee glanced over at Kelsey, then turned back to the fire, chanting softly as she added another handful of sweet grass to the fire. She had prayed to the Great Spirit for a woman to ease Tashunka Kangi's pain and the white woman, Kel-sey, had appeared. Now Hantaywee watched the two spirit wolves as they circled each other, curious to see what the outcome of their meeting would be.

Twice more Hantaywee added sweet grass to the fire, chanting all the while. She smiled to herself when Kelsey fell asleep, lulled by the soothing notes of her chant.

The two wolves stopped circling each other. Whining softly, the white one rolled onto her back while the red one licked her head. Then, with a joyful bark, the white wolf gained her feet and bounded away. The she-wolf paused a moment to glance over her shoulder, grinned a wolfish grin when, with a low growl, the red wolf gave chase.

Hantaywee smiled as the two wolves ran off together. And then she went back to bed.

Chapter Eleven

It was early afternoon when Kelsey left the tipi. She looked around, wondering where Reese had gone. Was he upset because they hadn't been able to leave as planned? Or, merciful heavens, had he left without her?

Fighting down a sudden panicky feeling, she went in search of Hantaywee.

She found the old woman behind her lodge, hanging long strips of meat on a wooden rack. Several dogs and puppies paced back and forth a few feet away, no doubt waiting for her to drop a piece.

"Hantaywee, have you seen Reese?"

"He has gone hunting."

"Again?"

The old woman smiled. "He said he wanted to make sure I had enough meat for winter before he leaves."

"Oh." Funny he hadn't thought of that before, Kelsey mused, and then shrugged. Maybe he had other things on his mind. Maybe he just wasn't ready to leave.

"There is something else that troubles you," Hantaywee remarked.

How did the woman always know? Kelsey was dying to ask about the strange vision she had seen before she fell asleep the night before except she wasn't sure if she had actually seen something, or merely dreamed it. Thinking of it now, she decided she must have imagined the whole thing.

"Do you know when Reese will be back?" Kelsey asked, changing the subject.

Hantaywee looked past Kelsey and smiled. "Here he comes now."

Kelsey turned, uncertain of her feelings. The violence she had seen earlier that morning had completely unnerved her. Had it really been necessary to kill the intruders just for trying to steal a couple of horses?

Reese dismounted with fluid ease. A deer and two rabbits were slung across his horse's withers, evidence that he'd had another successful hunt.

Hantaywee smiled broadly. "*Hecheto welo!*" she exclaimed. Well done.

Reese nodded as he handed his horse's reins to Hantaywee. When he looked at Kelsey, his expression was guarded. He took a step toward her. "You all right? You look a little pale."

She closed her eyes and took a deep breath. "I'm fine."

He regarded her a moment, his brow furrowed. "You're upset about what happened this morning."

"Why did they kill those men? Why didn't they just let them go?"

"They were trying to steal Wehinahpay's war ponies."

"And that was reason enough?" As soon as the words left her mouth, she wanted to recall them, but it was too late.

He reached for her, then drew back, as if afraid of being rejected. "It's like a game, Kelsey, a serious and deadly game. Had the Crow caught one of us stealing their horses, the results would have been the same."

"Did you...?"

"I didn't get any licks in, if that's what's bothering you." Was it her imagination, or did he sound disappointed?

She was glad he hadn't had a hand in the killing, though she didn't say so. "I guess I'm just not used to seeing people killed right in front of me."

"The Crow and the Lakota have been enemies as long as anyone can remember."

"It's none of my business, really. I shouldn't have said anything."

"Would it make you feel better if you knew they killed two of our sentries?"

"Yes. No. I don't know." She glanced hesitantly at the place where, hours earlier, three men had been killed. The ground had been swept clean. There was nothing to show that violence had erupted there only a few hours ago. "I'm just not used to seeing anything like that, at least not firsthand." She frowned, wondering why she was making such a fuss. At home, she had seen far worse things on TV every night of the week. Drive-by shootings, car bombs in foreign lands that killed dozens of innocent people, snipers that took pot shots at people on the freeway, wars in far-off places that were brought into her living room on the nightly news. But this...it had happened less than ten feet away, right in front of her eyes. She had seen the knives and war clubs descending, heard the meaty sound of those clubs striking living flesh, smelled the blood.

Reese was capable of killing, too, she thought, remembering the story Hantaywee had told her. He had killed the men who had raped Chumani, but Kelsey couldn't fault him for that. Surely those men had deserved to die for what they had done. She blew out a sigh. Perhaps all men were capable of killing, given the right provocation.

"Well, cheer up," he said, "we'll be leaving tomorrow."

"That's what you said yesterday," she reminded him, and oh, how she wished they had left as planned, before she saw a side of the Lakota that she hadn't wanted to see.

"Yea, well," he muttered dryly, "things happen."

* * * * *

Reese was ready to leave at first light the next morning.

Kelsey dressed quickly, then put on her socks and shoes. Even though she had only worn the garb of an Indian woman for a short time, it seemed odd to be wearing her own dress and petticoat again but then, she could hardly return to civilization wearing a doeskin tunic and beaded moccasins. Her dress, made of one hundred percent cotton, was badly wrinkled after being washed in the river. One thing about buckskin, she thought as she folded her tunic, it didn't have to be ironed.

Going outside, she saw that their horses were saddled and waiting. Reese had already tied their bedrolls and saddlebags in place behind their saddles. He had told her that Hantaywee had packed them enough food to last them a couple of days.

Kelsey glanced over at Reese, who was fiddling with one of the saddle cinches. His long black hair gleamed in the early morning sun. She rather missed seeing him in his clout and vest. Not that he didn't look good enough to eat in his shirt and trousers, but there was no denying the effect he'd had on her senses when he had worn only enough for modesty's sake.

Chiding herself for her wayward thoughts, Kelsey went to bid farewell to Hantaywee. In the short time they had been in the village, she had grown quite fond of the old woman.

"I will see you again," Hantaywee said, giving Kelsey's hand an affectionate squeeze.

"I hope so," Kelsey replied, though it seemed doubtful that she would be returning to the Lakota village any time soon.

Hantaywee embraced Reese. "Listen to your heart," she murmured for his ears alone. "Look inside and you will find the forgiveness you seek."

He hugged her in return. "Thanks for taking care of me."

"I will see you again."

"I don't think so."

Hantaywee smiled. "I know so, *chaska*."

With a wry grin, Reese lifted Kelsey onto the back of a chestnut gelding, then swung onto the back of his own horse. He waved at Hantaywee, then rode out of the village.

Kelsey looked back when they reached the outside of the camp circle. Hantaywee was standing where they had left her. Lifting a gnarled hand, she waved at Kelsey, then turned and went inside her tipi.

"I'm going to miss her," Kelsey remarked, urging her horse up alongside Reese's.

"Yea, me, too."

"Are you sure you want to leave?"

He grunted softly. "No reason to stay."

"No reason to go."

He glanced over at her, one brow arched. "I thought you were in a hurry to find your way back to wherever it is you came from."

"I am, but..." She shrugged. "It's a woman's prerogative to change her mind."

He grunted softly, but didn't turn back.

Knowing there was no point in arguing with him, Kelsey relaxed in the saddle and enjoyed the scenery. An eagle soared effortlessly overhead. In the distance, she thought she saw a deer but it was gone before she could be certain. The prairie seemed to go on forever, an endless sea of gently waving tall green grass beneath a bold, blue sky. The air was warm but not hot, the motion of the horse beneath her almost like a rocking chair. She found that the more she rode, the more she liked it.

At dusk, Reese reined his horse to a halt. "Why don't you make camp? I don't know about you, but I'd like some fresh meat for dinner."

Kelsey glanced around. Fresh meat? There was nothing to see for miles but prairie grass, an occasional stand of timber and the endless vault of the sky.

"I'm gonna see if I can hunt up a couple of rabbits." Removing the saddlebags from behind his cantle, he dropped them on the ground. "I won't be gone long. Think you could gather some wood?"

"Sure." Dismounting, she watched him ride away until he was out of sight. "He'll be right back," she told her horse, and then laughed self-consciously.

She tied her horse's reins to a low-hanging branch, then walked under the trees, picking up sticks and branches. When she had an armful, she carried them back to their camp site and dropped them on the ground. She looked at her horse for a minute; then, squaring her shoulders, she reached for the cinch. Unsaddling the horse wasn't as difficult as she had expected, certainly not as difficult as saddling one had been. She staggered backward under the weight of the saddle before regaining her balance. She dropped the saddle and blanket on the ground, spread her bedroll on a relatively flat spot and then glanced in the direction Reese had taken. There was no sign of him. Of course, he had only been gone a few minutes. Still, night was fast approaching and while she wasn't afraid of the dark, she was afraid of being alone in the wilderness. Heaven only knew what wild creatures lurked out there in the shadows.

She wrapped her arms around her body and told herself there was nothing to be afraid of and all the while bits and pieces of stories her grandfather had told her flitted through her mind—stories of women and children carried off by Comancheros and sold into slavery, tales of men set upon by wild animals. She recalled a story about a man who had been attacked by a bear. Badly wounded, the man had managed to crawl some unbelievable distance to the nearest town where he had gotten medical help and then, after he recovered, he had gone back and killed the bear.

She glanced around. Surely there were no bears around here!

Fire, she thought. That's what she needed. She piled a bunch of sticks and small branches together, dug the matches out of one of the saddlebags and after five tries, had a small fire going. It brightened the night, as well as her spirits.

Sitting cross-legged in front of the cheery little blaze, she chewed on a piece of jerky. There was something almost mesmerizing about watching a fire, the way the flames changed color as they writhed in the hot coals, the innate knowledge that the same fire that looked so inviting could, in an instant, turn deadly.

She guessed an hour had passed before Reese returned with two fat rabbits slung over his horse's withers.

Dismounting, he carried the carcasses toward the fire. "You ever skin a rabbit?"

She shook her head, her gaze fixed on the limp furry creatures in his hand.

"I didn't think so."

"I can unsaddle your horse," she offered.

"All right."

She took her own sweet time doing it so she wouldn't have to watch him cut into the rabbits. She'd had a fluffy white bunny for a pet when she was a little girl. She wasn't sure she could eat one of Mr. Cottontail's wild cousins.

Before long, the scent of roasting meat tickled her nostrils. All sentimental thoughts of Mr. Cottontail fled when Reese offered her a portion of the meat. She washed it down with water from one of the canteens.

He put the fire out as soon as the rabbit was cooked.

Kelsey looked at him askance.

"Fires can be seen a long ways off out here," he explained. "We don't want any unexpected company."

Thoughts of what had happened to Chumani flashed through Kelsey's mind.

"You'd best turn in," Reese said. "We'll be leaving first thing in the morning."

She didn't argue, was, in fact, almost asleep before he finished talking.

* * * * *

Kelsey groaned softly. They had been on the trail since early morning and her back and shoulders were beginning to ache. She didn't want to complain; after all, he had been injured not long ago and riding didn't seem to bother him. Still, he was used to spending long hours in the saddle and she wasn't.

She was about to ask Reese if they could stop and rest for a little while when she saw a thin plume of blue-gray smoke rising in the distance.

"What's that?" she asked, pointing.

"Dunno. You stay here. I'll go have a look."

Without waiting for an answer, Reese urged his horse to the top of the next ridge and disappeared down the other side.

Kelsey sat there a moment, then followed Reese up the hill. When she reached the summit, she drew back on the reins. A stagecoach lay on its side at the foot of the hill, one of its wheels slowly spinning. A man lay sprawled face down the dirt. Half a dozen arrows protruded from his back. A second man was tied head down to one of the wheels on the stagecoach. The wheel had been set on fire. It was still smoldering and so was the man. An errant breeze wafted her way, carrying the scent of burning hair and charred flesh.

Another body lay a few feet away. Several arrows protruded from its back. There was a raw red patch where his hair should have been.

Kelsey looked away, afraid she was going to be sick to her stomach. Indians had done this. Indians like Reese and Hantaywee.

Turning her horse around, she rode back the way she had come. Swinging one leg over her horse's back, she slid to the ground and dropped to her knees.

She was still vomiting when Reese rode up beside her.

He didn't ask what was wrong. Dismounting, he removed his kerchief and handed it to her, along with his canteen.

She rinsed her mouth, then wet a corner of his kerchief with water from the canteen and wiped her face.

"I thought I told you to stay here," he said.

Keeping her back toward him, she nodded.

He blew out a sigh. "I'm sorry you had to see that."

She nodded again. She was sorry, too. Oh, she had known that in the old days Indians had scalped and tortured whites and that whites had tortured and killed Indians. Hadn't her grandfather told her one grisly tale after another? She had seen massacres in movies and on TV and read about them in history books, but to actually see such torture firsthand was just too horrible. On top of what she had seen the Lakota do to the would-be horse thieves, it was just too much.

Rising, she handed Reese his kerchief and canteen.

His eyes were cold when he looked at her. "Would you be looking at me like that if you'd seen me shoot those three men who kidnapped you?"

She stared at him, her conscience pricking her. She hadn't given those men another thought, nor experienced a moment's sorrow for their deaths, only relief that Reese had come along when he did, that those men would never be a threat to anyone else. How quickly one's perspective changed, she thought, when it was one's own life that was in danger.

Ashamed, she turned away.

He came up behind her, his breath warm against the side of her neck.

She leaned back against him, reveling in his touch, in the warmth of his hands on her shoulders. His breath stirred the tendrils of hair along her cheek.

"I'm sorry," she said, "I was wrong to judge your people so harshly."

"I guess I can't blame you. You've had a rough couple of days."

Rough was putting it mildly, she thought. But surely the worst was behind them now.

His next words shattered that illusion. "There was a woman on the stage," he said. "I'm going after her."

"A woman! How do you know?"

"I saw her belongings scattered on the other side of the coach. There's no sign of her body, so I reckon the warriors took her with them."

"How many Indians are there?"

"Not more than three or four. The trail's fresh. We can't be more than half an hour behind them. One of the dead men was a whiskey salesman."

"How do you know that?"

"The warriors emptied a couple of bottles before they took off. I figure by nightfall they'll all be passed out dead drunk."

"And the woman?"

"I reckon they'll be too liquored up to bother her much."

Kelsey nodded. Though the idea of chasing after a bunch of drunken Indians was not her idea of a good time, it was something that had to be done. Squaring her shoulders, she put her foot in the stirrup and pulled herself into the saddle.

"Let's go," she said with forced bravado. "We're burning daylight."

Grinning at her, Reese swung onto the back of his horse. Taking up the reins, he followed the tracks of the Indians.

* * * * *

It was two hours after sundown when they caught up with the Indians. As Reese had predicted, the warriors were all drunk as skunks. Hiding behind a tree a safe distance away, Kelsey watched as the four liquored-up warriors whooped and hollered around a blazing campfire. Several empty whiskey bottles littered the ground.

The woman sat with her back against a large boulder. She wore a long black traveling cloak. The hood hid her face. Her hands were tied behind her back. A rope secured her ankles.

Kelsey looked over at Reese, who was standing beside her. "Now what?"

"We wait until they pass out, then I'll go get the woman."

"Just like that?"

"If I'm lucky," he said with a wink. "You might as well sit down and make yourself comfortable. This might take a while."

Nodding, Kelsey sank down on the ground, her back braced against the trunk of the tree, her arms folded over her bent knees. If she ever made it back home, she was going to have one heck of a story to tell, she thought, and then wondered who would ever believe it. Sometimes she didn't believe it herself.

"What's he saying?" she asked when one of the warriors started singing.

"He's bragging about what a brave warrior he is," Reese answered, and she heard the grin in his voice. "He's telling his *compadres* that he killed a Crow warrior with his bare hands when he went on his first raid and that he's counted coup against a dozen bluecoats."

"Do you think it's true?"

Reese shrugged. "Probably, since the others aren't denying it."

"What's he saying now?"

"He's saying that the woman will be singing praises to his manhood come morning."

Kelsey bolted upright. "I thought you said..."

"Don't worry, I won't let them touch her."

"Are these warriors...are they Lakota?"

"No. Hunkpapas."

The thought that the Indians weren't from Reese's village made her feel a little better about the whole thing.

She was half-asleep, her head resting against the trunk of the tree, when Reese shook her shoulder.

"Mount up and be ready to ride," he whispered, thrusting his horse's reins into her hand. "I'm going after the woman."

Reese dropped down on his belly and snaked his way toward the now quiet camp. It had been years since he had been on any kind of raid against an enemy but the things he had been taught in his youth quickly came to the fore. As he drew closer, he gained his feet and padded quietly toward the camp, his feet carefully testing each bit of ground before he took his next step.

The fire had burned down to a bed of smoldering coals. The warriors were sprawled on their blankets in that odd, boneless way of drunken men everywhere. The woman looked to be sleeping.

Reese hesitated at the outskirts of the camp, his gaze sweeping back and forth. One of the horses snuffled softly. Reese waited, eyes and ears alert, but none of the warriors stirred. Moving slowly, he picked his way around the sleeping men.

When he reached the woman, he bent down and placed one hand over her mouth.

She came awake with a start, her eyes wide and scared.

Reese shook his head, then placed one finger over his lips, cautioning her to be quiet.

When she nodded, he untied her hands and feet, then helped her to stand.

He froze when one of the warriors stirred, mumbled something unintelligible in his sleep and then rolled onto his stomach.

When all was quiet again, Reese swung the woman into his arms and carried her out of the camp.

When he reached the place where Kelsey waited, he lifted the woman onto the back of his horse. He glanced from the woman to Kelsey. "Stay here and stay quiet," he said curtly.

Without waiting for a reply, he made his way back toward the sleeping Indians.

Huddling deeper into her cloak, the woman looked at Kelsey and whispered, "What's he doing?"

"I don't know," Kelsey replied. She watched, her heart in her throat, as Reese padded quietly to where the Indians had tethered their horses. Stopping along the way, he picked up a couple of blankets before continuing on toward the horses. Untying the lead ropes, he swung onto the back of a gray gelding, dropped the blankets over the gelding's withers and then led the rest of the horses to where Kelsey and the woman waited.

"Mount up," he told Kelsey, "and let's get out of here."

Wordlessly, Kelsey and the woman followed Reese away from the camp. Once they were well away, he put his horse into a gallop.

Kelsey found herself grinning as she rode after him. Even though she hadn't done anything, she felt an unexpected sense of exhilaration. *We came, we saw, we conquered*, she thought, and felt like shouting it to the night.

They rode for what seemed like forever. The sky behind them was growing light when Reese reined his horse to a halt near a shallow stream. Dismounting, he turned the extra horses loose, then led his mount to the stream.

Kelsey slid off the back of her horse, grateful for a chance to stretch her legs. The other woman also dismounted. She stood there a moment and then threw back the hood of her cloak.

Kelsey stared at the woman, who wasn't a woman at all, but a very pretty teenage girl, with big blue eyes, pale skin and waist-length hair the color of cornsilk.

A girl who took one look at Reese, then threw her arms around his neck and kissed him full on the mouth, making Kelsey suddenly sorry that they hadn't left her with the Indians.

Reese put his hands on the girl's shoulders and held her away from him. "Whoa, now."

The girl batted her eyelashes at him. "I'm sorry," she murmured, widening her eyes. "I just wanted to show my gratitude."

"Yea, well, a 'thank you' will do well enough."

"Oh, not nearly," she said.

"Hold on now," Reese said. "Who are you?"

"Angelina Ridgeway, but you can call me Angel."

"You got kin hereabouts, Angelina?"

She shook her head, her eyes growing misty. "No. No one."

"So, where were you headed?"

"Grant's Crossing." She batted her thick blonde eye lashes at Reese again. "Do you think you could take me there?"

"As it happens, that's where we're headed."

Angelina smiled at Reese. "I guess this is my lucky day."

"Lucky!" Kelsey exclaimed, thinking of the three dead men the Indians had killed. "I'd hardly call it that."

"What else would you call it when you meet a gent as handsome as..." She smiled up at Reese. "What did you say your name was?"

"Reese."

Angelina looked at Reese as if she was a cat and he was a bowl of fresh cream. "He's quite handsome," she purred, glancing at Kelsey, "don't you agree?"

Reese cleared his throat. "That's enough, you two. Kelsey, dig some jerky out of my saddlebags. We'll camp here for the night and get an early start in the morning."

Dropping his hands from the girl's shoulders, Reese went to look after the horses.

Angelina stared after him a moment, then turned to look at Kelsey, her expression thoughtful. "You're not married to him or anything, are you?" she asked.

Kelsey shook her head. "No."

"I think he might be just what I've been looking for."

"Really?" Kelsey retorted. "Well, stop looking."

"But you said..."

Kelsey thrust a chunk of jerky into the girl's hands. "He's old enough to be your father."

"I don't mind."

A wave of jealousy rose up in Kelsey's breast, so hot and so unexpected, all she could do was stare at the girl in front of her, speechless.

Removing her cloak, Angelina spread it on the ground and sat down, her gaze fixed on Reese, who was hobbling the horses a short distance away.

"Were your parents on the stagecoach?" Kelsey asked, thinking that no mother in her right mind would let her daughter travel in the outfit Angelina was wearing. Or almost wearing. Her white off-the-shoulder blouse was shockingly low-cut for this day and age, her skirt, while ankle length, had a slit up one side that revealed a length of long creamy leg almost to the thigh.

"What?" Angelina glanced over her shoulder. "Oh, no. I don't know where they are."

"Aren't you rather young to be traveling by yourself?"

"I'm almost seventeen."

Kelsey didn't say anything, but she would have bet her new baby blue Mustang that Miss Angelina Ridgeway wasn't a day over sixteen, if that.

The girl bit off a piece of jerky, chewed and made a face. "Is this breakfast?"

"I'm afraid so."

With a shrug, Angelina went back to watching Reese.

Kelsey couldn't blame her. He drew her gaze, as well. There was a latent sensuality in the way he moved. As he stroked the neck of one of the horses, she imagined that big, long-fingered hand stroking her back, her thigh, her...

With a start, she dragged her thoughts from a road best left untraveled.

Angelina smiled up at Reese when he drew near. "I'm cold," she said, "can't we have a fire?"

"You got any wood in that cloak?"

"No," she said, pouting prettily, "but you could keep me warm."

"Turn in and get some sleep," he said brusquely. "We'll be lighting out again in a few hours."

Turning his back to the girl, Reese grabbed a piece of jerky and then sat down.

"She's something, isn't she?" Kelsey remarked, sitting down beside him.

He grunted softly. "She's trouble, is what she is."

Kelsey nodded. She had no doubt of that. No doubt at all.

* * * * *

Angelina complained all that day. She didn't like horseback riding, it made her back hurt. She didn't like the heat. She didn't like the dust. She didn't like having nothing but jerky to eat. She wouldn't touch the pemmican that Hantaywee had provided.

Kelsey was sorely tempted to smack the girl, but then she reminded herself that Angelina was young and had been through a terrible ordeal. Looking at the expression on Reese's face, she was sure he was having some of the same thoughts she was, though from time to time he looked like he wanted to put Angelina over his knee and give her the back of his hand.

They stopped at a waterhole at midday. Angelina slid off her horse with a loud groan.

Dismounting, Reese gathered the reins and led the horses to the waterhole.

Angelina followed, mincing along behind as him as though she were wearing a pair of Manolo Blahniks instead of a pair of well-worn half-boots.

Angelina put her hand on Reese's arm to get his attention. "How much longer until we get to Grant's Crossing?"

"We should get there some time tomorrow night. You got kin waiting for you?"

She shook her head. "No, no one," she said in a small voice. "I'm all alone in the world."

"Uh huh."

She gazed up at him, her eyes shining with unshed tears. "Will you take care of me, Reese?"

"I don't cotton much to kids."

"I'm not a kid!" Angelina fisted her hands on her hips, her left leg thrust out so that the slit in her skirt parted, revealing her leg from ankle to mid-thigh. "I'm a woman."

Reese muttered an oath, then jerked his thumb over his shoulder. "If you need to take a..." He cleared his throat. "If you need privacy, go over there, behind that bush. We're leaving as soon as the horses are watered."

With a small humph of pique, Angelina turned and flounced away.

Shaking his head in exasperation, Reese filled their canteens, then led the horses over to where Kelsey waited in the shade.

"Angelina seems quite taken with you," Kelsey remarked. And why wouldn't she be? Reese was, to say the least, a hunk and a half. In his own time or hers, women would be drawn to his good looks, his sense of chivalry, that air of self-assurance that made a woman feel that he could take care of her, no matter what.

Reese made a sound of disgust low in his throat. "Don't be ridiculous."

"Ridiculous? She's practically panting after you." And it was driving Kelsey crazy. She told herself it was none of her business, that she had no reason to be jealous of Angelina. But she was.

Reese grinned at her. "Does it bother you, her 'panting after me' as you put it?"

"Of course not!" Kelsey replied hotly. "Why should it?" She had no claim on Reese and didn't want one. But every time Kelsey saw Angelina flirting with Reese, she wanted to scratch the girl's eyes out. Kelsey's reaction shocked and surprised her. She had never succumbed to the green-eyed monster before.

"Too bad," Reese drawled, a teasing glint in his eyes. "I was hoping maybe you were a little jealous."

Kelsey snorted softly. "Now *you're* being ridiculous."

"Not even a little jealous?" he asked.

He sounded disappointed. Well, that was just too bad. She refused to stroke his male ego by admitting he was right. She had her pride, after all. Gathering her dignity, she opened her mouth to tell him she wasn't the least bit jealous, then blew out a sigh. She had never been any good at lying.

"All right," she confessed, refusing to meet his gaze, "maybe I am a little bit jealous. Are you happy now?"

He grinned, looking extraordinarily pleased with himself. "You don't have anything to be jealous of, Kelsey," he murmured, drawing her into his arms.

"No? She's lovely and young and thin and…"

"I don't want a skinny little girl, sweetheart, I want a woman." He looked at her, his dark eyes smoldering. "I want you."

The heated look in his eyes, the husky tone of his voice, went straight to Kelsey's heart and then arrowed downward. Had they been alone, she might have surrendered to the desire she saw in his eyes, to the restless wanting that plagued her.

But they weren't alone.

"Well, well," Angelina said, smiling archly, "I hope I'm not intruding."

Kelsey bit back a sharp retort. She would have pulled away from Reese, but his arm remained firm around her waist. Then, as if Angelina wasn't standing there watching them avidly, Reese lowered his head and kissed her, not some little peck, but a kiss that made Kelsey's toes curl with pleasure, made her forget, for the moment, that there was anyone else on the planet.

She was breathless when Reese lifted his head. "Are you ready to go?" he asked.

Kelsey stared at him blankly for a moment. Go? And then she remembered where they were. "Yes, of course."

He winked at her, then lifted her onto the back of her horse and handed her the reins.

Reese lifted Angelina onto the back of her horse, dropped the reins into her lap and then swung into the saddle.

Angelina immediately rode up beside him, but Kelsey hung back a little, her fingertips sliding back and forth over her lips. She felt as if she had been branded by his kiss. It was a good feeling.

And then she frowned. Had he kissed her because he wanted to, or had he kissed her hoping that Angelina would take the hint and leave him alone?

Chapter Twelve

Reese gazed up at the sky, his arms folded behind his head. How the hell had his life gotten so complicated? He had gone from being a loner to being saddled with two females. He grunted softly. Saddled probably wasn't the right word, at least where Kelsey was concerned.

He hadn't wanted to care for her but he couldn't help it. Somehow, in spite of his resolve to the contrary, she had managed to work her way into his heart. The fact that she had admitted she was jealous of Angelina made him smile. And then he frowned. What in hell was he going to do about Angelina?

The thought had no sooner crossed his mind than she was there, sliding into his bedroll.

"What the hell do you think you're doing?" Mindful of Kelsey sleeping nearby, he kept his voice low.

"I was cold. I thought you'd keep me warm."

She didn't feel cold. Her lithe body snuggled against his, her young, firm breasts pressing against his side, her long legs twining all too intimately with his.

He jackknifed into a sitting position. "Dammit, girl, you can't sleep here!"

"Why not?"

Reese swore. "You know very well why not."

She wriggled against him, then laughed softly. "You don't really want me to go, do you?"

He moved away from her, cursing his body's automatic reaction to being in such close proximity to a desirable female, even if that female was little more than a child.

Rising, he jerked Angelina to her feet, then thrust his blankets into her arms. "Here, you'll be warm enough now."

"But what about you?"

"Go. Back. To. Bed." He spit the words through gritted teeth.

"Oh! Are you always this stubborn and pig-headed?"

"Pretty much."

"Keep your old blankets!" she said, throwing them in his face. "I don't want anything of yours."

"Good. Let's keep it that way."

Glaring at him, Angelina turned and stomped back toward her own bedroll, her cheeks burning.

Oh, but he was the most aggravating man! She smoothed her blankets, then slid underneath the top cover and pulled it over her head. Maybe he didn't like girls! No other man had ever pushed her away. Old or young, they always leered at her as if they knew what she looked like in her chemise. Not that she had ever let any of them actually touch her. Oh, no, if there was one thing she had learned early, it was that a man quickly lost interest and respect for a woman he could talk into his bed. Her mama had taught her that, if nothing else!

With a sigh, Angelina flounced over on her stomach, wondering if her mother had missed her yet. Sometimes, if Mama was really busy, she didn't pay any attention to Angelina for days at a time. The bigger question was, would Mama come looking for her? Or, worse, would she send Mr. Wellington after her? The thought made Angelina shudder with dread. Mama had promised Mr. Wellington that Angelina would spend the night with him if he would pay off Mama's loan at the bank. Mr. Wellington had readily agreed.

Five days ago, Mama had informed Angelina that Mr. Wellington would be coming to collect her on the night of her sixteenth birthday and that after Mr. Wellington had had his way with her, Angelina would be serving drinks in the saloon instead of just cleaning up at closing time. Angelina had also learned that after she had entertained Mr. Wellington, she would be expected to "pleasure" certain other customers who were willing to pay the right price.

Angelina had smiled and nodded and pretended everything was fine, but that night, after Mama was asleep, Angelina had stolen all the cash money Mama kept hidden in the bottom drawer of her dresser and hightailed it out of town like a thief in the night.

Angelina flopped over onto her back and stared up at the stars. So many stars. She blew out a sigh, wondering how she could convince Mr. Reese to take her to bed and still keep his respect. He seemed like a gentleman. If she could seduce him, he would surely do the right thing and marry her and then she would never have to worry about Mama or old Mr. Wellington ever again. She blinked back the tears that welled in her eyes. She had to find someone to marry her. It was the only way to be free of Mama. Running away from home had seemed like the best solution at the time, but what was she going to do now?

She chewed on her thumbnail, her brow furrowed in thought. Maybe she could just tell Mr. Reese the truth. But, no, when had the truth ever done her any good? Besides, if he knew she was only fifteen, he might send her back home and she would rather go off with the Indians than go back home.

Turning onto her stomach again, she closed her eyes. She was safe now, at least until they reached Grant's Crossing.

* * * * *

Kelsey rolled onto her side and tried to relax, but every time she closed her eyes, she saw the way Angelina had looked at Reese and the way Reese had looked at Angelina. Not that she could blame him. Angelina was a beautiful girl. A man would have to be blind in both eyes and dead six months not to notice her!

Kelsey told herself she was behaving like a love-struck teenager, jealous of her first crush and that no matter how she felt about T. K. Reese, it didn't matter. She wasn't in this time period to stay. She was, as it were, just passing through. As soon as she found the door back to her own time, she was outta here! Letting herself fall in love with Reese, or any other man, would be sheer stupidity. The only thing was, she was afraid that no matter how hard she tried to deny her feelings for Reese, it was already too late. She loved the way he looked after her, the way he cared about what happened to her. She loved the sound of his voice and the touch of his hand. She even loved it that he had gone after Angelina when he could just as easily have turned his back on the girl and let the Indians have her. But, even more than that, she wanted to comfort him, to wipe away the pain that lingered in his eyes, to banish the demons that haunted him.

Mostly, she just plain wanted him.

Unable to sleep, she crept out from under her blankets and walked a little ways away from their campsite. Sitting on a large rock, she propped her elbows on her knees, cupped her chin in her hands and stared into the distance, listening to the quiet.

Overhead, the stars followed their set patterns, winking down at her as if they knew the answers to all of life's questions. Large billowy white clouds drifted across the face of the moon. A gentle breeze sang a soft serenade, accompanied by the whisper of the leaves in the trees.

Nana Mary would be missing her by now. No doubt Nana had called Kelsey's parents to see if Kelsey was there. Kelsey didn't know if time in the past moved at the same rate as time in the future, but if it did, she had been gone longer than twenty-four hours. Her parents had probably notified the police.

She frowned, thinking of the pictures of young women she had seen on the nightly news from time to time, women who just disappeared without a trace. Maybe they weren't victims of violent crimes, after all. Maybe they hadn't run away or been abducted, maybe they had just stumbled into the past and couldn't find their way back home. After all, if it could happen to her and her grandfather, it could happen to anyone!

Home. She clicked her heels together three times, murmuring, "There's no place like home, there's no place like home." And then she laughed. Of course it wouldn't work, not without the ruby slippers.

"You shouldn't be out here alone." His voice poured over her like molasses warmed by the sun, deep and dark and rich.

"I couldn't sleep."

Grunting softly, he sat beside her. "Something botherin' you?"

There was a loaded question if she'd ever heard one. She was debating between the truth and a lie when he said, "I couldn't sleep either."

"Something bothering you?" she asked, a smile in her voice.

"Someone."

"Oh." She didn't have to ask if that someone had long blonde hair and sky blue eyes.

"Kelsey, I..."

She turned so she could see his face. "What?"

He didn't say anything, just slipped his arm around her shoulders and drew her up against him. "What am I gonna do about you?"

"Me?" she said, her voice little more than a surprised squeak. "What do you mean?"

"I can't stop thinking about you." His knuckles brushed her cheek. "I can't stop wanting you."

While she was trying to think of an answer, he leaned forward and kissed her. The touch of his mouth on hers drove every coherent thought right out of her mind. She wrapped her arms around his waist, needing something solid to hold onto while her emotions soared and her body seemed suddenly lighter than air. He wanted her. And she wanted him. What difference did it make if she wasn't here to stay? She was here now, in his arms, with his mouth warm on hers, his tongue playing havoc with her senses. What if she woke up back home tomorrow? Would she be glad she hadn't surrendered to the desire pulsing through her, or would she forever regret letting this incredible moment pass by?

His hand caressed her back, her thigh, skimmed the area just under her breasts and each touch aroused her still further. What could it hurt to give in? It wasn't like she had to save herself for marriage. She had been married once and she wasn't likely to get married again. What harm could one indiscretion committed in the nineteenth century do?

His tongue teased her lips as his hand continued to move over her body, never trespassing where it shouldn't, yet arousing her just the same.

She moaned softly as pleasure engulfed her. Just one night, what could it hurt? One night of unprotected lovemaking...who would ever know?

She drew back. In high school, how often had she heard one of her girlfriends say, *I can't be pregnant. We only did it once.* Once was all it took. She couldn't risk getting pregnant, not here, not now.

"I'm sorry," she stammered, "I can't."

He released her with good grace. "Can't blame a fella for tryin'."

"It's not that I don't want to," she blurted, then pressed her hand to her mouth.

"No?"

"It's just that, well, the time's not right...I mean..." But that pretty much said it all, she thought. Not only was the timing wrong. She was in the wrong time.

He seemed to know exactly what she meant. "I guess you're still hopin' to find your way back home."

"I don't belong here." She lifted one shoulder and let it fall. "Look at it from my point of view. How would you feel if you suddenly found yourself over a hundred years in the past where you didn't know anyone and you weren't sure how to behave?"

He nodded. "I reckon I wouldn't like it."

She smiled. "I reckon not."

Drawing her into his arms again, he gave her a squeeze, then stood and offered her his hand. "I reckon we'd best get some sleep."

With a nod, she let him help her to her feet and then they walked hand-in-hand back to camp.

But later, lying in her blankets, half-asleep, Kelsey couldn't help wishing that, just once, she had followed her heart instead of her head.

Chapter Thirteen

Kelsey was relieved when they reached Grant's Crossing late the following night. If she'd had to spend one more day watching Angelina shamelessly flirting with Reese, she didn't know what she would have done. No matter how many times she told herself that she had no claim on Reese and that they were literally worlds apart, it just didn't seem to sink in. She was jealous and there was no two ways about it.

When they reached the hotel, Reese secured a room for Angelina.

"Another sister?" Wexler asked with a leer.

There was no mistaking the look in the clerk's eye. He thought Angelina was a hooker. Kelsey's eyes widened with the sudden realization that Wexler probably thought the same thing about her! The mere idea made Kelsey want to sock him in the jaw. And then she grinned inwardly. What did she care what the clerk thought of her? She had other, far more important things to worry about, like finding her way back to where she belonged.

"Just give her a room on the same floor as mine," Reese said curtly. "And how about sending up some hot water? I don't know about the ladies, but I could use a bath."

"It's gonna cost you extra, this time of night," the clerk said.

"Just do it."

Wexler slid two keys across the counter. Apparently Reese rented the room he had shared with Kelsey on a long-term basis, because it was still there, waiting for him. He didn't say anything about a separate room for Kelsey.

There was a moment of awkwardness when she wondered if Reese expected her to arrange for her own room, but then he took her by the hand and led the way up the narrow, winding staircase.

Looking none too happy with the sleeping arrangements, Angelina followed Reese and Kelsey up the stairs and down the corridor.

Reese stopped in front of Angelina's room and handed her the key. "If you need anything, tell the clerk to put it on my bill."

"That's very generous of you," Angelina said sweetly.

"Yea, that's me," Reese muttered, "generous to a fault. Water for the tub should be up soon. We'll meet you downstairs for breakfast in the morning."

Angelina's eyes narrowed as she glanced at Kelsey, then looked back at Reese. "I thought she'd be sharing a room with me."

"Yea? Well, you thought wrong."

"Oh!" Angelina exclaimed. "I didn't know she was your..."

"Careful what you say," Reese warned, an ominous glint in his dark eyes.

Kelsey took a step forward. "I can fight my own battles, thank you very much." She lifted her chin belligerently. "Go on, Angelina, say it."

With a shake of his head, Reese stepped between the two of them. "It's been a long day, ladies. I'm about done in." He opened Angelina's door and gave her a little push inside. "Wait about half an hour before you go down for your bath. Kelsey can go first. I'll go last."

"All right, Reese," Angelina purred. "Whatever you say." Smiling a blatant come-hither smile, she blew him a kiss, then closed the door.

Muttering an oath, Reese turned on his heel and stalked down the corridor to his own room.

Kelsey followed, trying not to feel smug about the fact that she was the one sharing his room. Once inside, she reproached herself for her childish behavior. She was a grown woman. She had to stop behaving like a teenager with her first crush.

She looked at Reese, who sat on the room's only chair, pulling off his boots. Amazing, she thought, that he looked sexy as all get-out no matter what he was doing. The light from the lamp cast gold highlights in his hair. The shadow of a beard made him look dark and dangerous.

"Maybe I should get a room of my own," Kelsey suggested, thinking it would be for the best. And not because she cared what that little chit or the desk clerk or anyone else thought, but because being in the same room with Reese was like putting a woman in room filled with her favorite brand of chocolate and then telling her she couldn't have any.

"I'd rather you didn't." Rising, he gathered her into his arms. "I like having you nearby."

"Do you?" she asked, her heart beating a rapid tattoo in her breast.

He drew her up against him until they were only a kiss apart. "Can't you tell?"

"Reese..."

"I just want to hold you, that's all."

She would have argued, but it was what she wanted, too. So much had happened in such a short time. He had been wounded while rescuing her from those dreadful men. She had tended his wounds as best as she could, hovered over him, listened to the tragic tale of his love for Chumani. Though she had known him only a few weeks, it seemed as if they had spent a lifetime together. More and more, she found herself thinking about what it would be like to stay here, with Reese. Oh, but she couldn't. Her life, her parents and her job were all waiting for her. Did she really want to give up everything she knew, everything she loved, to stay here, in a time she had always thought she would hate? Did she want to give up civilization and all its wonders for life in the Old West? Funny, but being here didn't seem as bad as she had always imagined it would be.

She rested her cheek against Reese's chest. Would she still feel that way if he wasn't here? What if something happened to him and she couldn't find her way back home? Would she still think this wasn't such a bad place?

He stroked her back, his hand warm, comforting, as it moved lazily up and down her spine. Her skin tingled at his touch.

He held her close for a long moment, then brushed a kiss across the top of her head. "Your bath should be ready by now."

The words, *you could share it with me*, hovered, unspoken, in the back of her mind. With a sigh, she kissed his cheek. "I won't be long."

She walked down the hall to the room that held the tub. It was filled to the brim with steaming water.

After undressing, she stepped into the tub, wishing she had some of her favorite bubble bath to add to the water. She washed quickly, glad that Reese had said she could be the first one in the tub. She knew that, in the old days, it was common for everyone in a family to use the same bath water, starting with the oldest and working their way down to the youngest. By the time the last family member had bathed, the water was usually so dirty, you couldn't see the bottom of the tub. She had read somewhere that that was where the expression *don't throw the baby out with the bath water* had originated.

She closed her eyes, thinking she would just enjoy the warm water for another few minutes. Submerged to her shoulders, she let her thoughts drift. As usual, they drifted toward Reese. She wondered what the initials T. K. stood for, wondered what he was doing now. Was he pacing the floor, or relaxing in the overstuffed chair by the window, his long legs stretched out in front of him, while he smoked a cigarette?

Or, horrible thought, had he gone down the hall to keep Angelina company?

* * * * *

Reese experienced a rush of adrenaline when he heard a knock at the door. Hoping it might be Kelsey coming to tell him she had changed her mind, he struck a match and lit the lamp beside the bed. Then, always cautious, he grabbed his gun, holding it against his thigh while he opened the door.

Before he could say a word, Angelina slipped past him and hopped into his bed wearing nothing more than her chemise and a smile.

Damn, he thought as he shut the door, she was a persistent little thing! Dropping his gun back into the holster hanging from the bedpost, he crossed his arms over his chest and regarded her through narrowed eyes.

She looked up at him as if she had every right to be in his room and in his bed.

"Girl," he said impatiently, "what the hell are you doing here?"

"I know you want me." She was on her hands and knees on the mattress now, her chest thrust forward, giving him a clear view of her ample cleavage.

Reese shook his head. *Trouble*, he thought again. *Nothing but trouble.* "Stop wasting my time," he said, taking her by arm, "and go back to your own room."

"No!" She twisted out of his grasp, then sat back on her heels. "What's wrong with you?"

"Me?" he practically shouted. "What the hell is wrong with you?"

She frowned up at him. "Why don't you want me?"

"Why? Well, for one thing, you're about ten years too young! Now get out of my bed before I throw you out."

"I don't understand you." The sultry expression disappeared to be replaced by one of genuine confusion. "Men have been trying to get me into bed since I turned thirteen. Don't you like girls?"

"No." He crossed his arms over his chest. "I like women."

"I'm a wom..."

"Don't start in on that 'I'm a woman' crap," he muttered irritably, and then he frowned. "What men have been trying to get you into bed?"

"All the ones that visit the Magnolia."

"What's the Magnolia?" he asked, though he had a pretty good idea.

"My mama's house."

"Lot of men go there, do they?"

"Well, of course. It's a brothel."

"Your mama runs a brothel?"

She nodded. "In Golden."

Reese grunted softly. So, her mother owned a whorehouse in Colorado. Well, that explained a lot. "Does she know where you are?"

Angelina shook her head. "I ran away."

He couldn't say as he blamed her.

"How old are you?"

"Almost sixteen."

Reese swore under his breath. Not even sixteen and her own mother had her working in a house of ill repute! "So, why have you been coming on to me, what did you hope to gain by it?" he asked, though he was pretty sure he knew the answer.

"I need to get married."

"Married!" That was the last thing he had expected her to say. His gaze moved over her, settling on her flat stomach. "Are you...?"

"No! I've never taken a customer, at least not yet. But Mama promised one of her regulars that I'd spend the night with him when I turned sixteen if he would pay off the loan on the house." She crossed her arms over her breasts as if she was suddenly cold. "I won't sleep with him! He's a pig. So I stole all the money I could find and I ran away. I can't let her find me! She said after Mr. Wellington had me that I was going to have to pleasure some of her other customers."

Jumping off the bed, Angelina threw her arms around him. "If I was married, Mama couldn't do anything to me. Please, Mr. Reese, I'd make you a good wife, honest I would. I'd do anything you asked, anything at all..."

"Dammit, girl!" He grabbed her hands in his and held them tight. "Listen to me, we'll work something out, I promise."

"You'll help me?"

"I'll do what I can."

"You won't let Mama take me back, will you? Promise me you won't."

"I won't make you go if you don't want to."

"You promise?"

"I promise."

Two huge tears welled in her eyes. "Thank you, Mr. Reese."

"Go on back to your room now, hear? Kelsey should be about done with her bath."

Sniffling, Angelina rose on her tiptoes and kissed him on the cheek, then hurried out of the room.

Reese stared after her. What kind of mother sold her daughter's favors? Thinking he'd better check to make sure Angelina made it back to her room, he went to the door and looked down the corridor in time to see Angelina pass Kelsey on her way back to her room.

Reese swore softly. Of all the rotten luck. One look at her Kelsey's face and he knew she was thinking that he had taken Angelina to bed the minute her back was turned. Damn. He was going to have to do some fancy talking to smooth this over.

Kelsey forced herself to remain calm. Putting on her best corporate face, the one that said, kick butt and take names, she walked past Angelina with her head high. She walked past Reese without looking at him and went straight to the window, staring outside until she heard the door close.

After taking several deep breaths, she turned to face him. "I'll get my things and change rooms with Angelina."

"The hell you will."

"I'm sure that will be much more convenient for the two of you than having to wait for me to leave the room."

Reese shook his head. Women! Why did they always jump to the wrong conclusions? "You don't seriously think I'm interested in that... that...that child?"

"She doesn't look like a child," Kelsey retorted. "And she's certainly interested in you."

Fighting the urge to drive his fist into the wall, Reese took a deep, calming breath.

"She ran away from her mother's brothel. Seems her old lady promised her to some old fart and she's afraid to go back. She was coming on to me because she's looking for someone to protect her."

"She told you that?"

He nodded. "I guess she thought she'd be better off with me than some old fart."

"You think?" Kelsey said, laughing.

His gaze moved over her, hot and hungry. It sent a thrill of desire racing down her spine.

"You still want a room of your own?" he asked, his voice husky.

"What do you think?"

Closing the distance between them, he drew her into his arms. "This is what I think," he said, and lowering his head, he covered her mouth with his, chasing all rational thought right out of her mind.

Her arms went around him of their own volition as he deepened the kiss. Excitement fluttered in the pit of her stomach. Was there anything to equal the blush of first love, the wonder of those first kisses, the very newness of it that made you feel as if you were the only one in all the world who had ever experienced the joy and the wonder of it all? Love. Was there anything else like it?

She whimpered a soft protest when he took his mouth from hers, sighed with delight when his lips settled on hers again. Slowly, he walked her backward toward the bed. He eased her back onto the mattress and followed her down, turning so that his body aligned itself with hers, so that they lay facing each other, their bodies pressed intimately together from shoulder to heel.

His hands were rough from hard work and years in the sun, yet ever so gentle as they played lightly over her body, never demanding as they skimmed the surface, his fingertips barely brushing the curve of her breast, sliding down over her hip and up again to stroke her cheek. Each touch and caress built upon the last until she was trembling with desire, aching with need. She wanted to slip her hands under his shirt, to feel his skin beneath her palms but, mindful of the way he had reacted the last time she had caressed his back, she managed to stifle that particular urge, contenting herself with tracing the corded muscles in his arms.

She wanted him. Right or wrong, whether their time together was for this hour only or for years, she wanted him.

She drew him closer, closer, might have begged him to take her, then and there, if Angelina hadn't chosen that moment to knock on the door.

"Reese?" she called, opening the door to peer inside. "I'm through with my bath, so if you...oh!"

Kelsey felt a rush of heat flood her cheeks at the shocked look on Angelina's face even as she found herself wondering how a girl who had been raised in a whorehouse could look so stunned by something as ordinary as a kiss between two fully clothed adults.

Sitting up, Reese muttered, "I should have locked that damn door."

With a sigh, Kelsey slid her legs over the edge of the bed and stood up, straightening her skirt. Perhaps it was a good thing Angelina had burst in when she did, she thought, reminding herself again that it would be foolish to get any more involved with Reese than she already was.

Cheeks red with embarrassment, Angelina stammered, "I...I'm sorry, I didn't know...I didn't mean to...You said you weren't..." With a choked cry, she backed up and slammed the door.

Shaking his head, Reese turned to look at Kelsey. No one blushed prettier, he thought, quietly cursing Angelina's interruption. But maybe it was for the best. He hadn't been with a woman he cared for since Chumani, had vowed he would never put himself in a position like that again, never expose himself to the kind of hurt her death had caused him.

Clearing his throat, he said, "Maybe it would be best if we got you a room of your own."

Kelsey nodded, hoping her disappointment didn't show on her face. She knew it was the right thing to do, the smart thing, but she wasn't at all happy about it.

"I'll take care of it in the morning," he said. "Why don't you go to bed. I reckon I'll go take that bath now."

She nodded again, afraid to speak for fear her voice might betray her feelings.

When he left the room, she took off her shoes and stockings and her dress, then climbed into bed. Pulling the covers up to her chin, she turned on her side and closed her eyes, hoping she would be asleep before Reese returned.

* * * * *

For Kelsey, eating breakfast with Reese and Angelina the following morning was more than a little uncomfortable, to say the least. She glanced at Reese from time to time, wondering what he was thinking. She didn't have to wonder what Angelina was thinking. The girl had every reason to think Kelsey was doing more than just sleeping in Reese's bed. Kelsey thought about setting the record straight and then decided against it. What difference did it make what the girl thought? Besides, true to his word, Reese had gotten Kelsey a room of her own. He had given her the key that morning before they came down for breakfast. Was it by accident or design that her new room adjoined his?

Her gaze moved over him. He had changed into a clean gray shirt and black trousers. She heartily wished she had a change of clothes, as well. Her gingham dress looked like she had slept it in and of course, she had. After breakfast, she was going to walk down to the Chinese laundry at the other end of the street and ask if they could wash and press her dress while she waited.

"So," Angelina said brightly, "what are you two going to do today?"

Kelsey shrugged. "I don't know." Other than seeing about having her dress cleaned, she didn't have any plans.

Reese rubbed his hand over his jaw. "I'm thinkin' of gettin' a shave and playin' a little poker." Reaching into his pocket, he withdrew a handful of bills. He counted out twenty-five dollars and handed it to Kelsey, then counted a like amount and gave it to Angelina. "Why don't you ladies go buy yourselves whatever you need."

"Oh, Reese," Angelina squealed, clutching the greenbacks to her chest, "you're just the sweetest man I've ever met!"

He nodded. "That's me," he said dryly.

"Thank you," Kelsey said. "I'll pay you back somehow."

"No need." Rising, he dropped a couple of bills on the table, plucked his hat from the back of his chair and settled it on his head. "I'll see you ladies at suppertime."

Tucking the greenbacks into her skirt pocket, Kelsey pushed her chair back and stood up. "Well, see ya later, Angelina."

Angelina quickly wiped her mouth on her napkin and rose as well. "Can I go with you? I don't want to be alone…" She smiled uncertainly. "I don't know anyone here and…"

Kelsey's first instinct was to say no, but then she remembered what Reese had told her. How would she feel if she was young and on her own, afraid to go back home. To a brothel, of all places. Looking at it like that, she couldn't blame the girl for doing whatever she thought necessary to survive. All that flirting with Reese had probably just been the desperate act of a young girl with no one to care for her and no place to go.

Feeling ashamed for the way she had behaved, Kelsey smiled back at Angelina and said, "Come on, let's go."

Leaving the hotel, Kelsey headed for the general store. Since she had money for a new dress, she would take the one she was wearing to the laundry later.

Angelina trailed along beside her, looking in store windows, her eyes wide with wonder, like a child at Christmas.

"Haven't you ever been shopping before?" Kelsey asked.

"Oh, sure," Angelina said, grinning, "but I've never had money of my own before. And Mama always picked my clothes for me."

Kelsey glanced at the girl's outfit, amazed that any mother would dress her teen-age daughter in such a way, then shook her head. Angelina's mother wasn't like most mothers. She was a hooker and she dressed her daughter accordingly. And effectively, judging by the looks Angelina received from every boy over twelve and every man they passed.

Kelsey hesitated when she reached the general store. Things had gone horribly wrong the last time she had been there. Reminding herself that lightning didn't strike twice in the same place, she hoped, she opened the door and stepped inside, with Angelina at her heels.

Nate Osgood stood behind the counter. He looked up as Kelsey entered the building.

He looked at her a moment and then smiled in recognition. "You're looking well," he said.

"So are you."

He rubbed the back of his head. "That was a day I'd just as soon forget."

"Me, too," Kelsey agreed. "I thought we were both goners for sure that day."

He nodded. "And who's this with you?"

"This is Angelina Ridgeway. Angelina, this is Mr. Osgood. He owns the store."

"Pleased to make your acquaintance, Miss Ridgeway," Nate said.

"Likewise, I'm sure," Angelina replied, not quite meeting his eyes.

"Anything I can help you ladies with?"

"Not right now," Kelsey said, "we're just browsing."

"Well, let me know if you need anything," he said, and went back to whatever it was he had been doing.

Kelsey and Angelina went their separate ways inside the store. Kelsey moved along the first aisle, stopping now and then to look at whatever caught her eye. She was in no hurry. She had all day and nothing else to do.

She picked up a package of hairpins, a couple of ribbons so she could tie back her hair, several pairs of cotton stockings. She smiled her thanks when Mr. Osgood brought her a hand basket to carry her purchases.

Moving on, she dropped several bars of lavender soap into her basket. She grinned as she looked at some of the prices. Hard to believe that you could actually buy a dozen eggs for ten cents, or that butter was only twenty-three cents a pound, or that a pound of coffee was only thirteen cents. Of course, it wasn't Starbucks! As for eggs, the last time she had bought a dozen, they were over three dollars.

Wandering through the store, she was amazed that Mr. Osgood ever sold anything. There seemed to be no rhyme or reason for the way things were laid out. Bottles of whiskey were mixed in with bottles of quinine and something called Aunt Ru's Prickly Ash Bitters. One shelf held bottles of "cures" for a number of ailments, like Lou's Consumption Cure and Fletcher's Castoria and Dr. Dee's Obesity Powders, guaranteed to make you lose weight.

Kelsey had to laugh at that. Apparently the obsession to be thin wasn't limited to the women of the future!

She moved to another aisle. Haphazardly stacked in a pile on a long table were chamber pots and cuspidors, dish pans and coffee grinders, washboards and tea kettles, flour sifters and bread pans and a few items that left her wondering what they were.

She passed a glass case filled with an assortment of knives, another that displayed handguns, large and small.

The one thing she didn't see was ladies' underwear, which meant she would just have to keep washing her bra and panties out by hand every night.

When she reached the back of the store, she paused to pet a large black and white cat that was curled up on the window ledge.

Moving to the next aisle, she found a rack of ready-to-wear dresses. There were only a dozen or so. She held up two of them, thinking they looked like they might fit. The first was a green and brown stripe with long sleeves, a nipped-in waist and a ruffled skirt. The second was dark blue with a fitted bodice, a square neck and short puffy sleeves. They weren't Liz Claiborne or Donna Karan, she lamented, draping them over her arm, but they would have to do.

She found a pair of black kid half-boots and added them to her basket and she was ready to go.

Angelina was standing at the front counter, chatting with Mr. Osgood while he added up her purchases. Kelsey was happy to see that, among other things, the girl had chosen a couple of skirts and shirtwaists in subdued colors.

A short time later, her purchases wrapped in brown paper and tied with string, Kelsey left the store with Angelina again trailing at her heels.

"That was fun," Angelina said, hurrying up beside her. "And I have money left over!" Delving into a small sack, she pulled out two peppermint sticks. "I bought one for you," she said, offering the sweet to Kelsey. "I bought some divinity, too. And some licorice for Reese. Do you think he likes licorice?"

"I don't know, but thank you for the candy."

"You're welcome. Are you and Reese going to get married?"

"Married! Heavens, no, why would you think such a thing?"

"Well, you don't act like a whore and he doesn't treat you like one," the girl said candidly, "but I saw you two kissing, so I thought..." She licked her peppermint stick, then shrugged. "You know, I just thought you were engaged or something."

"No, we're not engaged or anything. We were just kissing."

"My mom never kisses the johns. She says it's too intimate."

Kelsey thought she might choke on her peppermint stick. Paid sex with a stranger was okay, but kissing was too intimate?

"Come on, Angie," she said, "let's go get some lunch. Or supper, or dinner, or whatever they call it here."

Reese took a deep breath as he stepped into the Square Deal Saloon. It was like coming home. He passed the roulette wheel, the faro table and the blackjack table, skirted a handful of cowhands playing three card monte. A couple of Chinese men were playing fan tan over in the corner.

Reese nodded at the bartender as he made his way to his favorite table in the back.

Old man Neff was already there, along with Ed Booth and a couple of other men Reese recognized though their names escaped him.

He nodded to the other men as he sat down.

"Hey," old man Neff said, shuffling the deck. "Where the hell have you been?"

Reese shrugged. "Can't spend all my time sitting here taking your money."

"Well, now," Neff said, chuckling. "I purely do appreciate that, yessir."

"I was hoping you'd left town for good," Booth remarked.

"Is that right?" Reese picked up the cards he'd been dealt.

"Yea," Booth said, fanning his cards in his hand. "I figure that's the only way I'll ever get ahead."

"You could quit playing," Reese suggested. "Spend your nights at home with the missus."

Neff laughed as he dealt the last card. "Why do you think he plays poker?"

"I heard you ran into some trouble over at Osgood's the other day," Booth said.

"Trouble's right," Reese muttered, thinking it had come in twos. Looking up, he saw one of them pass through the saloon's bat-wing doors. She was wearing a new dress that managed to be modest and enticing at the same time. Watching the sway of her hips, he decided it probably wasn't the dress at all. It was the woman.

How had he forgotten that Kelsey worked here?

Reese watched her go over to the bar and talk to Pete, probably asking him if she still had a job. He hoped the answer was no. She was far too tempting for his peace of mind. Seeing her in here every day was a torment he didn't need, especially now, when he knew how intoxicating her kisses were, when he knew the taste of her lips, the way the contours of her body molded against his. Damn! Sleeping beside her last night had been torture of the worst kind. He had no sooner fallen asleep than he woke with her shapely little fanny pressed up against his groin. Every in-drawn breath had carried the scent of her sleep-warmed skin to his nostrils, her silky hair had tickled his cheek. His reaction had been predictable and immediate. He'd gotten her a room of her own first thing that morning.

"Reese, you in?"

"Yea." He tossed two dollars into the pot, his gaze still on Kelsey and Pete. He could only hope that Pete was telling her that he had changed his mind and didn't want her working in the saloon anymore.

With a nod, Kelsey turned away from the bar. He knew, from the expression on her face, that Pete hadn't said no.

* * * * *

Kelsey hurried back to her room at the hotel. It was three o'clock. She was supposed to be at work in an hour.

Her room looked pretty much like Reese's—small and square, with a single window, a double bed and a four-drawer dresser with an attached mirror. A flowered bowl and pitcher stood on a tray atop the mahogany dresser. An easy chair covered in a faded print occupied the corner near the window.

She had left her purchases in her room before going to the saloon to talk to Pete. Now she unwrapped the packages and put her things away, then changed out of her dress and into her jeans and tee shirt, as Pete had directed. It seemed the men in the saloon liked her in pants. One thing was for certain, she was going to have them laundered in the morning.

She brushed out her hair and let it fall around her shoulders, then put on her tennis shoes. If she was going to be on her feet for eight hours, she was going to be comfortable!

With a last look at herself in the mirror, she left her room and walked down to Angelina's and knocked on the door.

Angelina opened it a moment later, her mouth forming an O when she got a look at Kelsey's attire.

"Where did you get that shirt?" the girl exclaimed, then frowned as she began reading the words aloud, "I'm P-M-S-ing and I have a gun...what does P-M-S-ing mean? A gun?" she exclaimed, her eyes widening. "Are you kidding?"

Kelsey sighed. "It's a joke back where I come from and I don't have time to explain it to you now, I've got to go to work."

"Work? You work? Where?"

"At the Square Deal Saloon across the street."

Angelina's eyes widened. "So you are a..."

"No, I'm not. I serve drinks and that's all, end of discussion, period."

"Oh, sure."

"I'm mean it, Angie, that's all I do. Will you be all right here, by yourself?"

Angie made a face at her.

"All right, stupid question. But listen, I don't think you should go wandering around town by yourself after dark."

"You're not my mother," Angie replied sullenly. "I don't have to listen to you."

"That's right, you don't. Do whatever you want. I have to go."

"Kelsey, wait!" Angelina grabbed Kelsey's arm. "I'm sorry."

"It's okay. Do you want to meet me downstairs for dinner at six?"

"All right."

"Okay, see you then."

Leaving the hotel, Kelsey admitted that sometimes she wanted to smack Angie up side the head and sometimes she just felt sorry for the girl. No doubt Angie had had a rough life, growing up in a brothel with a mother who saw her as nothing more than a potential whore.

Being careful to look both ways, Kelsey crossed the street and headed for the Square Deal. She wasn't looking forward to spending eight hours in a stinky saloon with men who didn't smell much better but it was the only job in town. And she needed a job, not only to pay for her room and board, but to pay Reese back for the money he had loaned her.

Taking a deep breath, she pushed her way through the bat-wing doors. The smell of alcohol and cigar smoke and perspiration was just as bad as she remembered. A rotund man in a plaid shirt, brown trousers and a black derby hat sat at the piano playing what sounded like *The Blue Tail Fly*, though it was hard to be sure, since the piano was so out of tune.

Whistles and cat calls followed her progress toward the bar where she checked in with Pete. Then, squaring her shoulders, she forced a smile and went to work.

Kelsey was delivering drinks to a table near the back when she saw Reese. He was sitting with his back to the wall, his gaze not on the cards in his hand, but on her.

She felt her cheeks grow hot under his warm regard as she handed out the drinks on her tray.

As the night wore on, she did her best to ignore him as she made her way back and forth between the tables and the bar, but time and again she caught him watching her, a speculative gleam in his dark eyes.

She was glad when dinnertime came.

Leaving the saloon, she paused on the boardwalk and took a couple of deep breaths to clear her nostrils of the smell of cigar smoke, then she crossed the street and went into the hotel dining room.

Angelina was already there, waiting for her. Clad in one of her new outfits, with her hair pulled away from her face by a pink ribbon, Angie looked young and vulnerable.

"So," Kelsey asked, "what have you been doing?"

"Doing?" Angie replied sullenly. "What's there to do in my room?"

"You should probably be in school during the day," Kelsey said, thinking that having homework would give Angie something to do in the evening.

"School!" Angie looked at her as if she had suggested she join a convent.

"You haven't graduated already, have you?"

Angie picked up her napkin and began pleating the edge. "Mama made me quit when I was thirteen, said she needed my help in the house."

"Doing what?" Kelsey asked, afraid of what the answer might be.

"Just changing the sheets and making the beds," Angie said with a sigh. "And dusting and sweeping and washing the windows and mopping the floors and emptying the spittoons, all the chores Mama didn't want to do."

And didn't want to pay someone else to do, Kelsey thought. The more she learned about Angie's mother, the more she disliked the woman. She reminded Kelsey of Cinderella's wicked stepmother, taking a lovely young woman and turning her into a drudge. But she didn't want to bad mouth the woman to Angelina, so she went back to her original topic.

"Going to school would give you something to do during the day," Kelsey said, "and you could do your homework at night, which would help keep you from being bored."

"I don't want to go," Angie said. "The kids my age will make fun of me because I won't know as much as they do."

"Well, I can't make you go," Kelsey said, wondering if kids in this day and time had been required to go to school until a certain age. "What are you having for dinner?"

"I don't care."

Kelsey ordered chicken and dumplings and Angelina decided to have the same.

"Do you like working in the saloon?" Angie asked when the waitress left to turn in their order.

"Not really, but it's the only job I could find. That's why you need an education. You don't want to end up working in some smelly saloon, or worse."

"Didn't you go to school?"

Kelsey laughed. "Yes, I went to school. I had a good job where I used to live, a beautiful condo...er, house, lots of clothes and nice things." And how she missed them! But more than her condo, she missed her family. Her brothers and their wives all lived reasonably close and the whole clan got together for birthdays and holidays and for barbecues and picnics in the summer. They were probably worried sick about her.

"Why did you leave home?" Angelina asked.

"It wasn't my idea, believe me."

"Are you going back?"

"I don't know," Kelsey said with a sigh. "I hope so."

Angie propped her chin in her hand. "Why aren't you married? Most women your age are married by now."

"I was married."

"Did he leave you?" Angie leaned forward, her eyes wide.

"No, he was...he passed away a few years ago."

"Oh, I'm sorry." Angie leaned back in her chair. "Do you have any children?"

"No."

Angie dropped her napkin in her lap. "Maybe I will go to school," she remarked. "I sure don't want to end up like my mother. Besides, what do I care what a bunch of kids I don't even know think about me?"

"Good for you."

Kelsey was back at work forty minutes later. She glanced automatically toward the back of the room, felt a keen sense of disappointment when she didn't see Reese sitting in his usual place.

With a shrug, she smiled at one of the other customers. It was Saturday night and the saloon was busy. And smoky. And noisy with conversation and deep laughter punctuated by an occasional raucous shout when someone raked in an exceptionally high jackpot.

Along about ten o'clock, four cowboys swaggered into the saloon. One look and Kelsey knew they were already drunk and loaded for bear. They pushed their way to the bar, elbowed the other customers aside and ordered whiskey.

To her surprise, Pete refused to serve them.

"You and your friends go on home and sleep it off, Meeks," the bartender said. "I don't want any trouble in here."

"You sayin' we're drunk?" Meeks demanded. "That *I'm* drunk?" He pounded his fist on the bar, a fist the size of a large ham. He was tall, probably six foot four, and built like an NFL linebacker.

"That's exactly what I'm sayin'," Pete replied.

"Four whiskeys, now!" Meeks said, his voice cutting through the noisy saloon like a hot knife through butter. "And leave the bottle."

Silence dropped over the saloon.

Reaching beneath the bar, Pete pulled out a sawed-off shotgun and eared back the hammer. It made an ominous *snick* in the silence. "And I said go home."

Meeks took a couple of steps backward, his hands raised shoulder high. "Hold on, now, no need for that." He glanced around the saloon, pointed his finger at Kelsey and smiled. "Instead of a drink, what say I just have me a dance with that pretty little gal?" He looked over at the piano player. "Tickle them ivories for me."

Wide-eyed, Kelsey watched Meeks saunter toward her. It was like watching a mountain move.

"Howdy, sweetheart," he said.

Kelsey looked up at him, wondering what to do. Should she just dance with him in hopes that he would go away? If she refused, would he leave quietly, or tear the place apart?

Meeks grabbed her hand when the piano player burst into a rousing rendition of *Buffalo Gals* and Kelsey found herself jerked up against Meeks.

She was trying to extricate herself from his hold when the piano fell silent again.

Meeks stopped in mid-step and stomped on Kelsey's toes. She gasped with pain, pain that was soon forgotten when she saw Reese striding toward her.

"Let the lady go, Meeks," Reese said. "She doesn't want to dance with you."

"Says who?" Meeks asked belligerently.

"Says me. Let her go."

Meeks smiled crookedly, but his eyes were cold. "Wait your turn, half-breed. This is my dance."

"I said let her go."

Kelsey stared at Reese. Was he out of his mind?

"Kelsey, do you want to dance with this *hombre*?" Reese asked quietly.

"I...I just don't want any trouble."

"Yes or no, Kelsey?"

Kelsey stared helplessly at Reese, not knowing what to say. She wrinkled her nose when Meeks tucked her under his arm, holding her so close she could smell the stink of him. He reeked of stale sweat and horse and something she couldn't identify and for which she was glad to remain happily ignorant.

A muscle twitched in Reese's jaw. "Turn her loose, Meeks."

"Well, 'breed," Meeks drawled. "If I can't drink and I can't dance, then I guess I'll just have to teach you to respect your betters."

Reese lifted one hand and motioned Meeks toward him. "Come and try."

Meeks pushed Kelsey aside and then, with a growl that shook the building, he lowered his head and charged.

Kelsey's hand flew to her mouth in horror, certain that Reese was going to be flattened to a pulp right in front of her eyes.

And then Reese moved. He drew back his arm and his fist lashed out and struck Meeks square in the jaw. And Meeks dropped to the floor as if he'd been poleaxed.

Reese turned to look at Meeks' companions, who were still standing at the bar. "Anybody else?"

The other three cowboys shook their heads.

Reese jerked his thumb over his shoulder. "Get him out of here."

Shuffling forward, the three men picked up their fallen comrade and left the saloon.

The piano player broke into *Old Dan Tucker*. Pete put his shotgun away. The whisper of cards and the rattle of dice once again vied with the hum of excited conversation.

"Did you see that? Decked him with one punch!"

"Dropped him like a bad habit!"

"Never thought I'd see the day anybody would get the best of old Meeks…"

Kelsey looked up at Reese, who was absently massaging his knuckles. "Are you all right?" she asked.

"You're a lot of trouble, Kelsey St. James, did you know that?"

"I didn't ask you to butt in," she retorted defensively.

He canted his head to the side. "Think you could have handled Meeks all by yourself, do you?"

She didn't, but she didn't want to admit it. With a shrug, she said, "He just wanted to dance."

Reese's hooded gaze moved over her, slow and insolent. "Is that what you think he wanted?"

Kelsey bit down on the inside corner of her mouth. "I didn't want to cause any trouble. I thought…"

"You thought if you danced with him, he'd just tip his hat and leave?"

Feeling suddenly naïve, she nodded.

"Girl, you've got a lot to learn."

Aware that they were being watched by most of the customers in the saloon, Kelsey turned on her heel and walked toward the bar.

Pete was waiting for her, one elbow propped on the edge of the bar. "You okay, girl?"

"I'm fine," she said, forcing a note of brightness she didn't feel into her voice.

He regarded her through narrowed eyes for a moment and she knew he was debating whether or not he should fire her.

Without looking, she knew Reese was standing behind her. His breath fanned her cheek when he spoke. "How about bringing a whiskey and a beer over to my table?"

Pete glanced past her. She couldn't read his expression but she had the distinct impression that something was going on between the two men, some sort of male communication that concerned her.

Pete splashed whiskey into a shot glass, filled a mug with beer and slid both across the bar top. "You heard the man."

Blowing out a sigh, Kelsey picked up the glasses and followed Reese back to his table. His impassive gaze met hers as she delivered the drinks. She would have given a week's pay to know what he was thinking.

Chapter Fourteen

༄

Curious to see what schoolhouses had been like in the Old West, Kelsey had gone with Angelina to meet the teacher. The schoolhouse was one large room built of logs. The teacher, Miss Naismith, informed Kelsey that she taught grades one through eight and had seventeen students.

"I work with them in groups," Miss Naismith explained. "Naturally, the older classes get more attention, since their lessons are harder and more complicated. Sometimes I ask the older students to work with the younger ones.

"School begins at nine and we finish at four. I give the children a fifteen minute recess in the morning. They get an hour for lunch and then another fifteen minute break in the afternoon. Our curriculum is mainly focused on reading, arithmetic and writing, with an emphasis on penmanship." Miss Naismith smiled. "I'm also expected to tutor them in deportment and morals, something few of the boys have any interest in."

Kelsey nodded, thinking it was too bad that schools in the future were forbidden to teach anything about morality. It was all right to discuss intercourse and safe sex, but not morality. Heck, she'd even heard that one high school had handed out goody bags on prom night and included condoms. She recalled hearing someone say that if the school was providing condoms, they should also pay for a hotel room.

While Miss Naismith took Angelina aside to ascertain what class she would be most comfortable in, Kelsey glanced around the room. The blackboard was just a wide wooden board painted black. Miss Naismith's desk stood in the front of the room, a small table beside her desk held a small world globe. A pot-bellied stove occupied one corner. There was also a bucket of water and a dipper, whether for putting out the fire or for drinking, Kelsey had no idea.

* * * * *

Kelsey's days soon fell into a regular routine. She rose at seven-thirty to have breakfast with Angelina before the girl left for school.

Sometimes Reese joined them, depending on how late he had stayed at the saloon the night before. Kelsey spent a part of every morning searching for the elusive door to Nana Mary's house. She didn't have any luck in finding it, but she spent so much time wandering through the town, she was certain she could navigate every street and alley blindfolded.

The afternoons were long and boring unless Reese came by to keep her company, which he did from time to time. Otherwise, there wasn't much to do. She was accustomed to spending her days immersed in meetings and paperwork, to taking long lunches with interesting people at expensive restaurants. Here, there was little for her to do until four, when she went to work at the saloon. After all, it didn't take much time to make the bed, or tidy her small room. She wished she could go to a movie or watch TV. She missed reading in the bathtub. She missed reading, period. There weren't many books or magazines to be had in town—a few penny dreadfuls, Miss Godey's Lady's Book, Peterson's Ladies' National Magazine, which was fashioned after Godey's, the Home Journal. There was a small lending library in the schoolhouse but the only books available were classics, like *The House of the Seven Gables, Moby Dick, Uncle Tom's Cabin, Madame Bovary, A Tale of Two Cities, Jane Eyre* and *Two Years Before the Mast.* Not exactly light reading. Except for *Jane Eyre*, which was out on loan, she didn't find any of them particularly appealing.

As the days went by, Kelsey found herself growing increasingly fond of Angelina. She was pleased that the girl seemed to be doing well in school and that she had made a few friends. She hated leaving Angie alone at the hotel at night, but what other choice did she have? One of them had to pay the bills.

Kelsey sighed, her thoughts turning to Reese. She didn't know what she would do without him, didn't know if he was as bored as she was, or if he just liked her company, but as time passed, they seemed to be spending more and more time together. Sometimes they sat in front of the hotel, talking. Sometimes they went to his room and played poker until it was time for her to get ready for work. She usually ate dinner with Angelina around six or seven and got off work at midnight. Reese often joined her and Angelina at the hotel for dinner.

Ah, Reese. He was constantly in her thoughts, whether they were together or not. Mostly, she wondered about their relationship. She knew he cared for her. Knew he was attracted to her, just as she was attracted to him. They had shared some sizzling kisses, had come close to making love. But since their return to Grant's Crossing, it was like nothing had ever happened between them. She knew he had issues and that he felt guilty for Chumani's death. She frowned. Did he feel guilty for wanting to make love to another woman? Was that the reason why he always backed off?

She reminded herself of all the reasons why it was for the best that nothing happened between them. She didn't belong here. She wasn't the kind of woman who slept around. Her first and only lover had been Nick. Reese was obviously afraid of making a commitment and even if he wasn't, it would be foolish for her to fall for him when she had no intention of staying here, assuming she could ever find her way back home...

Frowning, she went to the window and gazed down into the street. It was midmorning. Women clad in long dresses and colorful bonnets strolled along the boardwalk, moving in and out of the stores as they did their weekly shopping.

Several men were gathered together in front of the barber shop, others near the blacksmith's. A wagon rumbled down the street, leaving a cloud of dust in its wake. A couple of cowboys rode by, tipping their hats to the ladies they passed.

With a sigh, Kelsey turned away from the window. Maybe she was never going to find her way home. Maybe she was stuck here in the past, permanently. Maybe it was time to stop looking for the way back home and start making a life for herself here. She wasn't thrilled by the idea of spending the rest of her life in the 1800's but if that happened, she would just have to make the best of it. And if she was stuck here, then she needed to find some other way to support herself. Serving drinks was okay as a temporary line of work but she certainly didn't want to make a career out of it.

Sitting on the edge of the bed, she drummed her fingers on the mattress. So, what could she do? She wasn't much at sewing, so being a seamstress was out of the question. She was a pretty good cook, though she wasn't sure she could turn out a gourmet meal with what was available in town. She made a great cup of coffee…maybe she could start her own version of Starbucks. The idea held a certain appeal. She could sell flavored coffee and cookies. She made terrific chocolate chip cookies, if she did say so herself, and a fairly decent cheesecake. There was no place in town where a body could go to relax and enjoy a good cup of coffee and dessert. The hotel dining room served meals three times a day but the rest of the time, it was closed. Of course, she was used to making coffee in an automatic coffee maker, but she could learn to make it the old-fashioned way. She could get Angelina to help out after school…

Suddenly too excited to sit still, Kelsey began to pace the floor. She needed a building with a kitchen, tables, chairs, an oven, a large coffee pot, flavorings for the coffee. She wouldn't be able to find any chocolate chips for the cookies, but she could break up pieces of chocolate by hand. Of course, she didn't know if a coffee house would go over in a town like Grant's Crossing, but what the heck, it was worth a try.

Leaving the hotel, she strolled down the boardwalk, glancing at every building she passed. None of them were for sale or for rent. Besides the shops she had noted before, there was a small law office, a doctor's office, a dentist and the newspaper office.

When she reached the end of town, she kept walking. There were a few houses situated nearby. And one of them had a For Sale sign tacked to one of the porch uprights. Of course, a house would be perfect! It would give her a place to work and a place to live.

Picking up her skirts to keep them from snagging on the weeds that were almost as tall as she was, she climbed the porch stairs and peeked in the window beside the front door. The window was so dirty, she couldn't make out much more than the fireplace on the far wall. She walked all around the house, peering in the windows. There was a wood-burning stove in the kitchen, along with an old pie safe that looked to be in pretty good condition. There was a pump, too, which meant she wouldn't have to haul water from outside, assuming the pump worked and she could figure out how to use it! There were two small bedrooms and a fair-sized dining room. She looked around the backyard. It held a small corral, a shed and an outhouse.

Returning to the front of the building, she took another look around. Even though the house was in need of a ton of work and a coat of paint inside and out, it was perfect for her needs. She was certain she and Angelina could fix it up in no time at all.

Humming softly, she walked back to town only to come to an abrupt stop. She had forgotten one little thing. She didn't have any money. Maybe she could get a loan from the bank. And maybe not, since she didn't have anything to put up as collateral. But maybe the bank would be willing to take a chance on a new business. After all, a new business would be good for the townsfolk and good for the town.

Hopefully, the bank president would think so, too. Well, Kelsey thought, smoothing the front of her skirt, she'd never know if she didn't try and there was no time like the present!

Filled with purpose, she marched down the street to the bank, took a deep breath and stepped inside.

It looked just like a bank in the Old West should look. There were two tellers behind wooden cages. A bank guard stood to one side, idly thumbing through the morning newspaper.

A middle-aged man with a pencil thin moustache and a shock of white hair sat at a large desk located behind a wooden rail. He wore a natty pinstripe suit, matching vest and a black cravat. A gold chain spanned his ample belly.

He looked up when she entered the building. When she didn't go to either of the tellers, he rose and walked toward her. "Good afternoon. I'm Linus Piedmont, president of the bank. May I help you?"

Kelsey put on her best smile. "I hope so. My name is Kelsey St. James and I'd like to take out a loan."

"I see." He opened the small wooden gate in the rail. "Come in, won't you? Please, be seated."

Kelsey sat in the hard, ladder-back chair in front of the desk, her hands folded primly in her lap.

"I don't believe I've seen you in town before," Mr. Piedmont said, resuming his seat behind the desk.

"No, I've only been here a short time."

"I see. Do you have family in Grant's Crossing?" he asked. "A husband?"

"No." She wondered if mentioning Pete Muldoon's name would be a plus or a minus.

"It isn't company policy to loan money to single women. How much did you wish to borrow?"

"I'm not sure. I think about seven hundred dollars."

He lifted one brow. "And what do you have for collateral?"

"Well, nothing, but you'd have a note on the property. I intend to start a new business."

The banker put his elbows on the desk top and steepled his fingers. "What property? What kind of business?"

Kelsey frowned. Was he leering at her? Good Lord, did he think she meant to open a bawdy house? "A coffee shop," she said, holding onto her temper. "I want to buy the house at the end of town."

"The old Williams place?"

"Yes, that's the one."

"And you want to turn it into a coffee shop? You mean, a place that just sells coffee?"

"And cookies and cheesecake. A place where the town's ladies can gather," she said, her excitement growing as she expanded her idea. "The men congregate at the saloon and the barber shop and the blacksmith, but the ladies in town really don't have anyplace where they can get together to sit and talk, well, except the mercantile, but that's hardly a place conducive to conversation."

Mr. Piedmont leaned back, his brow furrowed. "You want me to lend you seven hundred dollars so the ladies in town will have a place to sit and gossip?" He shook his head. "I doubt if their husbands would approve."

Kelsey stared at him in disbelief. *Their husbands wouldn't approve? Give me a break!*

"I'm sure it will be a good risk," she said, again holding her temper in check. "I know quite a bit about selling and marketing."

"Indeed?" he replied, looking skeptical. "And where did you acquire this knowledge?"

"Time and experience, Mr. Piedmont."

"Well, Miss St. James, unfortunately, time and experience count for very little when one is applying for a loan of that size. I'd like to help you out, really I would, but you're new in town, you have no husband, no references and no collateral."

Inwardly seething, Kelsey clenched her hands in her lap to keep from screaming. She was a successful businesswoman. Back home, she handled accounts worth millions of dollars and this...this idiot refused to lend her a paltry seven hundred dollars.

Piedmont rose, indicating the interview was over.

Kelsey took a deep breath. "Won't you please reconsider?"

"I'm sorry, no. Good day to you, Miss St. James."

Biting back the urge to call him a spineless chauvinistic toad, she gained her feet and left the bank.

Standing on the boardwalk, Kelsey glanced up and down the street, hoping, somehow, that she would wake up and find herself at home. A foolish hope, at best. Muttering, "Now what?" she turned down the boardwalk toward the hotel.

She was about to open the door when Reese stepped out. As always, the sight of him did funny things in the pit of her stomach. Today, he wore black boots, black trousers and a black leather vest over a white shirt.

"Hey, girl," he said, smiling. "I was just about to come looking for you."

"Oh, why?"

He pushed his hat back on his head. "Do I need a reason?"

"I guess not."

Canting his head to one side, he regarded her through narrowed eyes. "Somethin' troublin' you?" he asked. "You look a mite upset."

"You've got that right!"

"Hey, don't bite my head off."

"Oh, I'm sorry, it's not you, it's just..." She waved her hand in a broad sweeping gesture that encompassed the whole town. "I don't belong here and I can't get home and I don't want to spend the rest of my life working in that smelly saloon and..."

"Whoa, girl! Come on," he said, taking her by the arm and leading her back into the hotel. "Let's get a cup of coffee and talk this over."

The hotel was closed, but a word and a smile from Reese and the waitress who had been sweeping the floor let them in. Even though the room was deserted, Reese sat with his back to the wall. He ordered coffee and a slice of apple pie and after a moment, Kelsey ordered the same.

"Why do you always sit like that?" she asked, dropping into the chair across from him.

"Like what?"

"Like you expect someone to come up behind you and shoot you in the back."

"It could happen."

"Is someone after you?"

"Several someones," he muttered.

"Really? Why?"

Settling back in his chair, he crossed his arms over his chest. "I was playing cards in Amarillo a couple of years back. I caught a fella dealin' from the bottom of the deck and I called him on it. He pulled a gun on me and I killed him."

"Oh, my."

"Yea. I went to jail. There was a trial. Judge said it was self-defense but the man I shot had brothers and they didn't see it that way." He shrugged. "There were three of them. Now there's only one."

She didn't have to ask what had happened to the other two. Their fate was clearly written in Reese's eyes. "Is the other one still looking for you?"

He nodded curtly.

"You said you were wanted by the law, too."

"They've probably forgotten about me by now. It was a long time ago."

"What did you do?"

He shrugged. "Robbed a bank in Kansas City and another one over in Hays."

Kelsey blinked at him and then she laughed.

"What's so funny?" he asked.

"Nothing," she said, wiping tears from her eyes. "It's just that when we were having dinner one night soon after we met, you told me you were wanted by the law in a couple of other places and I remember thinking you might be a bank robber. Turns out I was right!"

"Think that's funny, do you?"

"Well, sort of. Why did you rob a bank?"

He looked at her as if she wasn't too bright. "Why does anyone rob a bank? I needed a stake. Didn't amount to much more than a few hundred dollars either time. But enough about me. What's got you looking so down in the mouth?"

"Oh, that." She blew out a sigh. "I went to the bank to get a loan."

"Why do you need a loan?"

"I want to buy a house. The Williams house. Do you know it?"

"That old place out at the end of town?"

"Yes."

"Whatever for? Hell, the hotel's in better shape."

"I want to start a business."

He stared at her in much the same way Piedmont had. "What kind of business?"

"A coffee shop."

He grunted softly. "Why?"

"I don't like working in the saloon and I thought a coffee shop would be a nice addition to the town, a place where the women can go and just...well, you know, sit and chat."

He frowned. "Why do women need a place to sit and chat?"

"Oh! You sound just like that idiot, Piedmont!"

"I don't mean to interrupt," the waitress said as she delivered their order. "But I think it's a wonderful idea. A place just for ladies."

Kelsey looked up at her and smiled. "Thank you."

The waitress smiled back. "You let me know when it's open, you hear?"

"I'll do that."

Beaming, the waitress hurried toward the kitchen, no doubt to spread the latest bit of gossip.

"So, how much money do you need?" Reese asked.

"I'm not sure. I was hoping to borrow seven hundred dollars."

Reese leaned forward, his fingertips drumming on the tabletop. "I can let you have it."

"You can? You will?"

He shrugged. "Sure."

"Oh, Reese, that's wonderful! And I'll pay you back. What would you consider a good rate of interest?"

"Fifty percent?"

"Fifty percent!" she exclaimed, then, seeing his grin, she shook her head.

"I won't charge you any interest," he said. "Just consider me a partner."

"Really?"

"Why not? I've got the money, you've got the know-how, we'll split the profits."

"So you think a coffee shop will make money?"

"I don't know, but you seem to think so and that's good enough for me."

"To us," she said, lifting her coffee cup in a toast.

"To us," he repeated.

* * * * *

Leaving the hotel, Kelsey and Reese went to find the owner of the Williams place. They found Esau Williams at the barbershop, deep in a discussion with half a dozen other men about the price of beef.

Reese took Esau aside and told him they were interested in buying his house. Forty minutes later, the paperwork was done and Kelsey had the deed and the key to the house in her hand. She was a homeowner at last!

"Let's go look at it," she said.

"Now?"

"Yes, now."

Kelsey looked at the place through new eyes as they waded through the weeds up to the front porch. She would paint the house white, with yellow trim, plant flowers along the walkway, maybe put a couple of tables on the porch so the ladies could sit outside when the weather was nice. New curtains at the windows, maybe yellow to match the trim...

"You look like you're about to pop," Reese remarked as she slid the key into the lock.

"I've always wanted to be in business for myself," she admitted, opening the door.

Reese shook his head. "Women in business," he muttered. "It ain't natural."

"Excuse me?"

Laughing, he held up in hands in a gesture of surrender. "Hey, I was just joshin' ya."

Kelsey went from room to room. The curtains were faded, the floors covered with dust, but the building seemed solid enough. There was a dry sink and pump in the airy kitchen, along with the pie safe and several large cupboards. The two bedrooms were fairly small, but adequate for her needs. The living room was large and square, as was the dining room adjacent to the kitchen. She figured five or six small round tables would fit comfortably in the living room. She would need a sideboard and maybe a love seat. She had no idea where she would get the furniture she needed. Did people send back east when the things they needed weren't available in town?

She was standing in the kitchen, imagining how it would look once it was painted and furnished, when she heard the sound of footsteps. They were too light to belong to Reese. Glancing over her shoulder, she saw Angelina standing in the doorway.

"Hi," Kelsey said. "Welcome home."

"Home?" Angelina frowned. "What do you mean?"

"I just bought this place," Kelsey said.

"You did?" Angelina glanced around. "Why?"

"I woke up with a great idea."

Angelina grimaced. "You think buying this dusty old place was a great idea?"

Kelsey smiled at Reese, who had followed Angelina into the kitchen. "We're going into business," he said.

"We are?" Angelina asked, frowning.

"Yep. You and me and Kelsey."

"What kind of business?" Angelina asked suspiciously.

"We're going to open a coffee house," Kelsey said.

Angelina frowned. "What's a coffee house?"

"A place that sells coffee and cookies and cheesecakes. It'll be great, you'll see."

"What's Reese going to do?"

"He put up the money."

Angelina looked at him and shook her head. "You're as crazy as she is."

He shrugged. "A body has to do something crazy every now and then."

"So," Kelsey said, "first thing tomorrow, I'll start cleaning the place up. Then we'll see about some furniture...new curtains...dishes..." She did a slow turn around the room. "I'll need to find some coffee pots and experiment with flavors and things." She looked at the old wood stove and grimaced. "I'll have to learn how to bake in that monster."

"I'll help you clean after school," Angelina said.

"Thanks, Angie," Kelsey said with a grin. "This'll be fun."

Angelina and Reese exchanged dubious looks.

"Fun," Angelina said dolefully.

"Right," Reese said.

"You'll see," Kelsey said.

The chiming of the courthouse clock reminded Kelsey that she had to be at the Square Deal in less than an hour.

Reese and Angie followed Kelsey out of the house, waited while she locked the door.

"The Crossing House Cafe," Kelsey murmured. "That's what we'll call it."

Chapter Fifteen

Kelsey got several orders wrong that night, but maybe that was to be expected, since she was preoccupied with redecorating the Williams house instead of concentrating on what Pete was saying. Her house now, she amended with a smile. She had changed her mind about the color scheme. She had originally thought to do the house in shades of yellow and green but had decided to go with blue, lavender and pink instead, thinking the colors would be light and cheerful and feminine.

Reese grinned at her every time she glanced his way. And every time it made her heart skip a beat.

Kelsey was more than ready for a break when six-thirty rolled around.

She met Angelina at the hotel a few minutes later.

"How was school today?" Kelsey asked after they had ordered their dinner.

Angie shrugged. "Same as always. My teacher says I'm doing real good."

"That's great!"

Angie nodded. "I met a boy today…"

"At school?"

"No, he's out of school."

"Then where did you meet him?"

"I was at Osgood's, looking at some dress material, and he was there with his father." Her cheeks grew pink. "He smiled at me. It was such a nice smile," she said dreamily. "His name is Danny Hamilton and he lives out on West Road."

"He told you all this today?"

Angie nodded. "While his father was talking to Mr. Osgood. Danny asked if he could take me to the church social Saturday night."

"And what did you say?"

"I said yes!"

"Angie, I haven't even met him."

"What difference does that make?"

"Well...I'm responsible for you."

"I don't need anyone to be responsible for me," Angie said heatedly. "I'm almost sixteen!"

"Let's not go through that again."

"Hey, squirt," Reese said, tugging on a lock of Angelina's hair. "Is Kelsey giving you a bad time again?"

Kelsey glared at him as he pulled out an empty chair and sat down. "I'm not giving her a bad time. She met a boy and she wants to go to some church dance with him."

"What's wrong with that?" Reese asked. "She's a big girl."

"Nothing's wrong with it," Kelsey said, "except that I haven't met him."

"Ah. Well, I've got a good idea," Reese said. "You go to the dance with me and we'll both keep an eye on her."

"I have to work," Kelsey said.

"Just take the night off," Reese suggested. "You'll be quitting soon, anyway."

"I guess I could," Kelsey remarked thoughtfully.

"It's settled then." Reese grinned, looking incredibly pleased with himself.

Angie groaned. And then she looked at Kelsey. "I'll need a new dress."

"We both will," Kelsey said.

"Well, hell," Reese said, glancing from one female to the other, "maybe I'll pick me up some new duds, too."

* * * * *

Kelsey woke bright and early the following day. Putting on her jeans, tee shirt and tennis shoes, she grabbed a quick cup of coffee and a muffin in the dining room and then went to Osgood's, where she bought a broom, a mop, a bucket and soap and wished for a pair of rubber gloves. After charging everything on her new account, she hurried toward the Williams house. Her house, she amended.

Unlocking the door, she stepped inside. For a moment, she just stood there. It was the first piece of property she had ever owned. She and Nick had never bought a house, they had rented one with the idea of having one built some day in the future. When he passed away, she had rented a small condo. Now, she owned a house.

Taking up the broom, she began sweeping the living room floor. A good coat of wax would really make the floors shine, she thought, pleased.

When she had swept the whole house clean and mopped the floors, she began to wash the windows. She had never been crazy about washing windows but she soon found herself humming as she worked.

She bent down to wet her rag, reeled backward, one hand at her throat when she looked up again and saw a face peering at her through the window.

"Reese! Good lord, you scared me half to death!"

Grinning, he walked around to the front door and stepped inside. "You've been busy," he remarked, looking around. "What can I do to help?"

"You want to help?"

"Gotta protect my investment," he said with a wink.

"How'd you like to finish washing the windows?"

"Sure. What are you going to do?"

"Get to work on scrubbing the kitchen."

With a nod, Reese rolled up his shirtsleeves. Taking the cloth from her hand, he took up where she had left off.

Smiling, Kelsey went into the kitchen. She scrubbed and polished for a good hour before her back demanded a rest.

She went into the living room looking for Reese, but he wasn't there. She found him in one of the bedrooms, drying one of the windows.

She stood there a minute, one shoulder resting against the door frame, content to watch the play of muscles under his shirt. Sunshine painted gold highlights in his hair. Her gaze moved down his back, over his tight butt, down his long legs. She loved the way he moved, the sense of controlled power that emanated from him. It was a good thing there wasn't a bed in the room, she mused, or she might have turned her lusty thoughts into action.

As though sensing her gaze, he glanced over his shoulder.

"Ready for a break?" she asked, annoyed by the husky note in her voice.

"Sure." He dropped the cloth on the floor.

"Come on, I'll buy you lunch, I mean dinner."

"Maybe you'd better wait until you're turning a profit."

"All right, then, you buy me dinner," she said, grinning.

"I've got a better way to spend an hour or two." He moved toward her like a cat stalking its prey, his dark eyes smoldering.

"Do you?" she asked. Her voice, no longer husky, emerged as little more than a squeak.

He nodded. Closing the distance between them, he took her in his arms. "I can't fight it anymore." His hand slid up and down her back, slow and sensual.

"You can't?"

"No."

Lowering his head, he claimed her lips with his in a long searing kiss that burned away every thought, every objection, every doubt. Maybe she was here for a short time, maybe she was here forever, it no longer mattered. What mattered was now, this moment, this man. Maybe it was fate that had brought her here, maybe it was luck, but whatever it was, she was here now, in his arms and there was no place she'd rather be. She moaned softly when his tongue found hers, tasting, exploring, dueling in a dance as old as time. His hand slid down to cup her buttocks, drawing her body tighter to his, letting her feel the heat of his arousal, the depths of his need.

And she wanted him. Right or wrong, for this day or forever, she wanted him.

Taking him by the hand, she led him out of the house and down the street to the hotel.

Once they were in his room, with the door closed and the bed at her back, some of her courage deserted her. She had never been the kind to indulge in one-night stands, had never made love to any man but her husband.

Reese shoved his hands in his pockets. "Change your mind?"

"I've never done this before."

"Never had a man?"

"Just my husband…"

"Husband?" Reese exclaimed, rearing back. "Didn't you tell me you weren't married?"

"I'm not, not anymore."

"You a divorced woman?"

"No, he was killed in a car accident."

"Car?"

"An automobile. Oh, it doesn't matter how it happened, does it?"

"I reckon not. How long has it been?"

"Three years."

Reese tossed his hat on the bedpost, ran a hand through his hair. "I'm sorry. I guess you miss him." Crossing the room, he poured himself a shot of whiskey from a bottle on the dresser. "Want a drink?"

"No."

He leaned back against the dresser, glass in hand. "Were you happy together?"

"Not really. We got married too young and for all the wrong reasons. He was jealous of my career and he started drinking too much...I was thinking of asking for a divorce when he was killed." She crossed her arms over her breasts, saddened by the memory, surprised that it still had the power to bring her to tears.

Reese tossed off his drink and turned to pour another, then changed his mind. Setting the glass on the dresser, he ran his hand over his jaw, torn between the need to take Kelsey into his arms and comfort her and the need to bury himself in her sweetness.

Chivalry won out in the end.

Gathering Kelsey into his arms, he held her close and stroked her back. "It's all right now, girl. Go ahead and cry."

With a sob, she buried her face against his chest. She'd thought she had cried her last tears for Nick years ago but now, cradled in Reese's arms, she wept for the failure of her marriage, for the death of all her teenage dreams. She wept because she was far from home and didn't know if she would ever find her way back. She wept because going home again would mean leaving Reese. Lastly, she wept because as much as she wanted to make love to him right now, she knew it was wrong and would only complicate an already complicated situation.

Reese must have sensed what she was feeling, or maybe he had come to the same conclusion. Using his kerchief, he dried her eyes.

"Come on," he said with a faint grin, "let's go get something to eat."

"Reese..."

Using his thumb, he caught a stray tear trickling down her cheek. "It's all right, Kelsey."

"I love you." She hadn't intended to say the words out loud, but they whispered past her lips of their own volition.

Reese blinked at her. "Kelsey..."

She put her fingertips over his mouth. "You don't have to say anything. I shouldn't have said anything. I don't know what I was..."

Removing her hand from his mouth, Reese said, "Hush, girl," and kissed her before she could say anything else.

It was a gentle kiss, more promise than passion, more sweet than sensual, and yet she felt it clear down to her toes.

His eyes were filled with warmth when he looked at her again. "I don't know how you got here," he said quietly. "Maybe it was fate, maybe it was just my good luck, but whatever it was, I'm glad you're here." He stroked her cheek. "All I know is, I don't want you to leave, not now, not ever. Hantaywee said you would be good for me."

"She said that?"

"Yea. And she was right."

With a sigh, Kelsey rested her cheek on his chest, struck yet again by how right it felt to be in his arms.

He brushed a kiss across the top of her head. "I love you, too, you know."

She looked up at him, her heart swelling. "You do?"

"I tried to fight it," he said. "I've felt guilty because I lived and Chumani died." He blew out a sigh. "Being in love with you just made it worse. But all the guilt in the world can't change the past, or the fact that I love you."

"Oh, Reese!" She hugged him close, more torn than she had ever been in her life. She loved him so much, but did she love him enough to stay here, in the past, to never see her family again, to give up everything that was dear and familiar?

There was no point in worrying about it, she thought. For all she knew, the choice of whether to stay or go might never be hers. And if she was here to stay, well, now that she knew Reese loved her, the thought of spending the rest of her life in the past wasn't nearly as daunting as it had been.

* * * * *

They went to lunch—Kelsey didn't think she'd ever get accustomed to calling lunch dinner and dinner supper—at the hotel. Reese loved her! She smiled every time she thought about it. She felt like a teenager again in love for the first time, all bubbly and dreamy-eyed. She found herself just sitting there, staring at him, several times.

Now was one of those times. She couldn't stop looking at him, or thinking that he was surely the most handsome man she had ever seen. His face was strong and rugged. He had straight black brows and deep dark eyes and a nose that was slightly crooked, making her wonder if it had been broken. His cheekbones were high and prominent, his jaw square with a hint of stubbornness. His white shirt was the perfect foil for his dark good looks.

"Quit that," Reese muttered when he caught her staring.

"I'm sorry, I can't help it."

He grinned at her, so devastatingly handsome it took her breath away. He loved her!

Kelsey grinned back. "Are you going over to the saloon after lunch?"

He shrugged. "I reckon, unless you need my help at the house."

"Well, if you wouldn't mind, you could clean out the shed in the back."

"Consider it done. How much longer are you going to work for Pete?"

"I don't know. For a while, I guess. I need to have some money coming in regularly until the coffee shop is up and running."

Reese nodded. "You about ready to go?"

Kelsey pushed her plate away, took a last sip of her coffee. "Yes."

"All right, then, let's get to work."

* * * * *

Kelsey had the inside of the house spic and span by the time Angie arrived.

Angelina stood in the middle of the living room, her hands on her hips. "Looks like you don't need my help," she said, glancing around.

"Oh, there will be plenty for you to do before we're done, don't worry," Kelsey replied. "We need to make curtains for all the windows and tablecloths and napkins..."

"I don't know how to sew," Angie said.

"That's all right, I do. My grandmother taught me and I'll teach you. And once we're open, I'll need you to help serve and wash dishes."

"You seem awfully happy today," Angie remarked.

"I am happy."

Angelina regarded her a moment, her eyes narrowed, and then she looked around the house again. "You've got that look in your eyes," she remarked. "Reese must be around here somewhere."

"He's in the back, cleaning out the shed."

"Anything I can do?"

"I don't think so. I was just about to lock up and get ready for work. Why don't you go to the hotel and get started on your homework? I'll be there in a little while."

"All right."

After Angie left, Kelsey locked the front door, then went around to the backyard to see how Reese was making out.

Rounding the corner, she heard him cuss. A moment later, he stepped out of the shed, one hand rubbing the back of his head.

"Are you okay?" she asked.

"Fine," he muttered sourly.

"What were you cussing about?"

"Nothing. I was poking around in the corner and a crate fell off the shelf and hit me on the head."

"Let me take a look."

He started to argue, but when he saw the determined look on her face, he obligingly turned around.

She ran her fingers through his hair, checking his scalp. He winced when her fingertips slid across a bump the size of a golf ball. "At least it's not bleeding," she said. "Did you find anything interesting in there?"

"Just a bunch of junk. You ought to burn it and the shed, too."

Kelsey grinned at him. "One man's junk is another man's treasure."

He snorted softly. "If you find a treasure in there, it's all yours."

"Well, I don't have time to look for it today. I've got to get to work."

"Me, too," he said with a wry grin.

"I'd hardly call playing poker all night work," she muttered.

"Call it what you want," he said, "but it puts food on the table and pays the rent."

"And buys houses," Kelsey added with a smile. "Don't forget that. Come on," she said, taking him by the hand, "I've got to hurry."

Chapter Sixteen

Kelsey stood at the bar, joking with Pete while he filled a drink order, when she heard a familiar voice behind her. Unable to believe her ears, she slowly turned around.

"Papa Joe!"

"Kelsey? Kelsey!" His arms went around her in a bear hug. "What are you doing here? How did you get here? How's Mary?"

Kelsey's happiness at seeing her grandfather erupted in laughter and tears. Dashing the tears from her eyes, she said, "I'm so glad to see you!"

"Come and sit down," her grandfather said, drawing her toward a vacant table, "and tell me everything."

In short order, Kelsey explained how she had found the door and stepped through it and then discovered she couldn't find it again no matter how hard or how often she searched.

"The portal is only open a couple of days at a time in mid-April and mid-October," Papa Joe said ruefully.

"So, you've been back and forth before?"

"Several times over the years."

"Does it always open to the same time and place?"

"Not always."

"So you can't pick and choose where you want to go?"

"No, it seems random. But it's brought me here before." He shrugged. "I'm not sure what determines the time and place."

"Does Nana Mary know about the portal?"

"Of course, but I made her promise she wouldn't try to follow me if something delayed my return."

Kelsey nodded. That made sense, since there was no guarantee that her grandmother would have ended up in the same time and place. "You've been gone for over a year! We all thought you were dead or something. Why didn't Nana Mary tell us where you were?"

"I always wanted to tell you, but she was afraid you'd think the two of us were, you know, losing it. She's always been afraid of being sent to an old folks' home for wackos."

"As if we'd do that to either of you! So, what happened? Why didn't you come back? You've never been away this long before."

"Well, I missed the opening last April because I...well, I was in jail."

"Jail!" She stared at him in disbelief. "What on earth for?"

A faint red flush crept up his neck into his cheeks. "Being drunk and disorderly."

"You're not serious!" Kelsey stared at her grandfather in dismay.

He shrugged.

"You should be ashamed of yourself."

"Oh, I am," he said, but he didn't look ashamed. "Promise me you won't tell Mary."

"I promise." Kelsey could hardly believe what she was hearing. Her grandfather was sixty-eight years old. The idea of his being drunk and disorderly was ludicrous, yet in spite of his obvious embarrassment, he seemed almost proud of it. Men. She would never understand them.

Papa Joe cleared his throat. "Then, in October, I missed my window of opportunity because my horse went lame and I didn't get back to town in time. This April..." He shook his head. "I was laid up with a bad case of the gout and just couldn't make it."

"So the door won't be open again until October?" Kelsey asked.

"As far as I know. So, how's my old girl getting along?"

"She was fine when I saw her last. She's renovating the old house..." Kelsey frowned, Had Nana Mary known Kelsey would walk through the portal once she found it? Had she set the whole thing up, hoping Kelsey would somehow find Papa Joe? No, it was too farfetched, she thought. "Oh! Will renovating the house change anything?"

"I don't think so. We should be able to get back home in October."

It was the first of June, Kelsey thought. A lot could happen in the next four months, but at the moment, she had no intention of going back in October or April or anytime unless Reese went with her. Why hadn't she thought of that before? Of course, she didn't have to stay here, in the past. He could go with her to the future. It would be such fun, showing him all the wonders of the twenty-first century. Just thinking about it made her smile. And then she frowned. Maybe it wasn't possible to go from the past to the present...

"Something wrong?" Papa Joe asked.

"No. I was just wondering, is it possible for someone from this time to travel to our time?"

Papa Joe scratched his neck, his expression thoughtful. "I don't know. You got anyone in mind?"

"Maybe. I still can't believe you never told anyone about your little jaunts to the Old West. How on earth did you find the portal the first time?"

"It was just an accident. I only stayed a few hours the first time."

"What did Nana Mary say?"

"She didn't believe me, so I brought back proof the next time I went."

"What kind of proof?"

"A newspaper from Deadwood. A picture of me with Wyatt Earp. Stuff like that."

"You had your picture taken with Wyatt Earp?"

"I brought my camera with me on one trip. Mary couldn't doubt me when I took the photo myself."

"I can't believe you never told me! You always knew a lot about the Old West. Now I know why. You've been seeing it firsthand!"

"Enough about me," her grandfather said. His gaze moved over her. "So, how are you making out, Kels? And what the hell are you doing in a saloon?"

"Working."

His brows shot up. "Doing what, exactly?"

"Not what you're thinking, you dirty old man," she said with a grin. "I just serve drinks, but I'm going to open a coffee shop soon."

"A coffee shop? Where?"

"I bought the Williams place. We've already started renovating it."

"We?"

As quickly as possible, she told him about Reese and Angelina and how Reese had loaned her the money to buy the Williams house.

"So, when do I get to meet this guy?" Papa Joe asked.

"Here he comes now," Kelsey said, smiling as Reese approached their table.

"Mind if I join you?" he asked.

"Not at all. Reese, this is my grandfather, Joseph St. James. Papa Joe, this is T. K. Reese."

The two men shook hands, then Reese took the chair next to Kelsey's.

"So," Papa Joe said, leaning back in his chair, "you're the man who saved my granddaughter's life."

"Yes, sir, but she saved mine, too, so I reckon we're even." Reese shook his head. It was unbelievable that Kelsey and her grandfather had both come here from the future. Did the old man know how to get back to his own time? If so, Kelsey would undoubtedly go back with him. The mere idea filled Reese with a sense of loss, as if Kelsey was already out of his reach.

"So, Papa Joe," Kelsey said brightly, "where are you staying?"

"Over at the hotel. You?"

"I have a room there, too, but as soon as the house is fixed up, Angie and I will stay there. Reaching across the table, she squeezed his hand. "I'm so glad you're here!"

"It's good to see you, too, honey."

"We'll talk more later," Kelsey said. "Right now I'd better get back to work."

It wasn't until that night, lying in bed on the brink of sleep, that she wondered how her grandfather had managed to earn a living while he was here.

* * * * *

The next three days passed swiftly. Kelsey spent every free minute working on the house. With Papa Joe, Angelina and Reese pitching in to help, the work went quickly and by Friday afternoon, they had accomplished practically everything that had to be done. All that was left was painting the bedrooms and the kitchen, which she planned to do next week. Mr. Osgood had helped her order wallpaper from Boston for the tea room. She had thought she would have to order furniture from back east, but Reese had told her she could probably find what she was looking for in Bitter Ridge, which was a large town about twenty miles east of Grant's Crossing. Being the sweetheart that he was, he had offered to hire a wagon and drive her to Bitter Ridge whenever she was ready to go. Papa Joe had promised to keep an eye on

Angelina while they were gone, although Angie declared emphatically that she wasn't a baby and didn't need watching. Knowing it was just for show, Kelsey ignored the girl's outburst. Angie and Papa Joe got along just fine.

Kelsey decided to make the trip to Bitter Ridge on Monday, since the dance Angelina was so excited about was tomorrow night; the next day was Sunday and the stores would be closed.

The Square Deal was hopping on Friday night. It seemed to Kelsey that every man over the age of eighteen had decided to stop in to have a drink or two or to test his luck at one of the card tables. By eight o'clock, the place was packed. The air was pungent with the smell of tobacco smoke and booze and too many unwashed bodies squeezed under one roof. The piano player was in rare good form, pounding out one tune after another.

Reese and Papa Joe sat at Reese's usual table in the back corner. Kelsey passed by there every chance she got, surprised to see that Papa Joe had almost as much money stacked in front of him as did Reese. It seemed her grandfather was full of surprises, she mused as she picked up a drink order.

By midnight, she was more than ready for her shift to end. She bid good night to Pete, then stopped at Reese's table to see if he was ready to leave. It had become his habit to walk her to the hotel.

He looked up at her and winked, then tossed a dollar into the pot.

"Looks like you're on a hot streak," Kelsey remarked.

"Reckon so."

"Well, I'm going home," she said. "I'll see you tomorrow."

Reese frowned. "Hang on a minute and I'll go with you."

"No, that's okay."

Papa Joe scooped up his winnings. "I'll walk her home," he told Reese. "I was gonna call it a night anyway."

Reese nodded. Catching Kelsey's hand, he drew her down and kissed her. "Sweet dreams," he murmured.

She smiled at him. "Same to you."

Papa Joe held the door for her and they stepped out onto the boardwalk. The town was quiet as they walked toward the hotel.

"I've been wondering," Kelsey said.

"Wondering what?"

"How you managed to earn a living while you've been here."

"Oh, that." He cleared his throat. "Doing odd jobs, mostly," he said with a shrug. "It doesn't cost much to live here, you know. I moved around a lot, got to see a lot of the country."

"What kind of odd jobs?"

"Oh, mostly menial stuff, sweeping out saloons, currying horses and the like." He cleared his throat again. "My last job was doing some work for a widow woman."

"Here, in Grant's Crossing?"

"No, over in Greer."

Kelsey studied Papa Joe's profile as they crossed the street and entered the hotel lobby. Was it her imagination, or did she detect a note of guilt in his voice?

"Let's sit here a minute," she said, taking a seat on one of the sofas in the lobby.

Papa Joe sat beside her, his hands resting on his knees. He didn't meet her gaze.

"So, who was this widow woman?" Kelsey asked. "How did you meet?"

Papa Joe blew out a breath. "I met her in town. She'd come in to shop. I was working in the mercantile, sweeping up, and offered to help her load her wagon. And then, well, I drove her home. She'd been a widow about a year and her place needed some fixing up. She said she couldn't pay much, but that I could sleep in the barn and she'd do my laundry and fix my meals..."

Kelsey nodded, wondering if she wanted to hear the rest.

"I stayed there about three months, I guess." He dragged a hand across his jaw. "One night she came out to the barn after I'd gone to bed and..." He slid a glance at Kelsey. "She let me know, without saying a word, that if I wanted to sleep up at the house, it would be okay with her."

Kelsey stared at her grandfather. "Did you...?" She couldn't say the words. Good grief, Papa Joe was over sixty and a married man. Surely any relationship he had with a woman would have been purely platonic.

A deep red flush crept up his neck. "No, I didn't. I'll admit I was tempted. She was a fine-looking woman and I'd been away from Mary for a long time, but..." He shook his head. "Even though I knew I might never get back home again, I couldn't betray my wedding vows."

Kelsey breathed a sigh of relief. She had always respected and admired her grandfather.

"Anyway, I left her place the next morning and headed back here." Smiling, he met her gaze. "And a good thing I did, too."

Kelsey returned his smile. "Well, you'll be working for me now," she said. "That should keep you out of trouble."

* * * * *

Angelina was a mass of nerves as they got ready for the dance Saturday night. She stood in front of the mirror, fussing with her hair, putting it up, then down, then up again.

"Relax," Kelsey admonished with a smile. "It's just a dance."

"But it's the first time I've gone out with Danny," Angie said, "and I want everything to be perfect."

"Well, you look beautiful."

And indeed she did. Angie's dress was a light blue print with a narrow white sash, fine white lace edged the square neckline and the puffed sleeves. The color went perfectly with her blonde hair and blue eyes.

"So do you," Angelina said graciously.

Looking over Angelina's shoulder, Kelsey glanced at herself in the mirror. Would Reese think she was beautiful? Her dress was dark green, with a round neck and a full skirt that was gathered up on one side, revealing rows of white ruffles. She had opted to leave her hair down.

"Oh!" Angelina exclaimed. "I can't decide what to do with my hair!"

"Here," Kelsey said, taking the brush from the girl's hand, "let me fix it." Kelsey ran the brush though Angie's hair, then pulled the sides back into a pony tail with a white ribbon, leaving the rest of the girl's hair to fall down her back in soft golden waves. "How's that?"

Angie looked at her reflection in the mirror and smiled. "Thank you!"

Dropping the brush on the dresser, Kelsey picked up the small handbag she had bought at Irma's Millinery. "Let's go!"

They met Papa Joe and Reese in the lobby. Her grandfather looked rather dignified in a dark brown suit and cravat. His brown hat sat atop his head at a cocky angle, giving him a roguish look.

Reese looked ruggedly handsome in a pair of black whipcord breeches, white shirt and a buckskin jacket. "Evenin', ladies," he drawled. "You're both lookin' mighty fine this evenin'."

"Thank you, kind sir," Kelsey replied.

Reese put his arm around Kelsey's waist, Papa Joe took Angie's hand and they left the hotel.

The dance was being held at the Grange Hall at the end of town. Even before they reached it, they could hear the lively sound of a fiddle.

Kelsey glanced around as they stepped inside. Colorful paper streams and bunting decorated the hall. Long tables held baked goods and mulled apple cider. It looked to Kelsey like the whole town was there.

They had no sooner entered the hall than Danny Hamilton appeared. He was a handsome young man, tall and slim, with dark brown hair and guileless brown eyes. It was evident from the smile on Angie's face and the flush in her cheeks that she was fond of young Hamilton. And equally obvious that he cared for her. Introductions were quickly made, then Danny took Angie by the hand and led her onto the dance floor.

"They make a cute couple, don't they?" Kelsey remarked.

Papa Joe snorted softly. "He'd better treat her right, or he'll have me to answer to!"

Grinning, Reese took Kelsey by the hand. "Come on, let's dance."

"I never figured you for a dancing man," Kelsey teased as he swept her around the floor.

"I'm not, but it gives me a chance to hold you in my arms and maybe steal a kiss when nobody's lookin'."

"You don't have to steal it," Kelsey said. "Take as many as you want."

"Don't ask me twice," he replied, and drawing her closer, he kissed her long and hard.

The touch of his lips on hers blotted everything else from her mind. When she came up for air, she noticed several couples were staring at them, but she didn't care. Let them talk, she thought, a kiss like that was worth a little gossip.

The music slowed as the fiddler played a waltz. Kelsey settled into Reese's arms, amazed that they moved in such harmony even though they had never danced together before. He moved smoothly around the floor, carrying her with him, his gaze resting on her face, his eyes delivering a silent message that made her stomach curl with pleasure. It was a message that was old, yet ever new, the need of one man for one special woman. She wondered how much longer she could hold out against his need and her own desire. Would it be so wrong to give in to what they both wanted? Would she regret it if they made love? Would she regret it if they didn't?

"Kelsey?"

His voice drew her from her internal battle. "What?"

"You look troubled. Is anything wrong?"

"No, nothing," she lied.

He didn't look convinced. He twirled her around the floor until they came to a side door, then led her out into the night, away from the lights and the music. "What's wrong?"

"Nothing, honest."

"Why don't I believe you?"

"I don't know," she said with forced lightness. "Why don't you?"

He drew her into his arms. "You can tell me," he said quietly. "Maybe I can help."

"I doubt it." That would be like a hen asking a hungry fox for help, she thought, grinning inwardly.

"Have I done somethin' to upset you?" he asked.

"No, it's nothing like that."

"Dammit, woman, how can I help if you won't tell me what's wrong?"

"I love you."

Her soft reply squashed his rising exasperation. "I know. I love you, too."

"That's the problem," she said. "I love you."

He knew exactly what she meant. She wanted him but she was afraid of the complications involved, afraid that the day would come when she would go back to her own time. He had contemplated the same thing any number of times, wondering how he would let her go when the time came, knowing that, if they made love and she left him, it would haunt him the rest of his life. He had thought about ending their relationship entirely, leaving town, but he couldn't go. He wanted to be with her every minute that he could, for as long as he could, even though he knew making love to her would only complicate matters more, make their eventual parting that much more painful. Being a man, it was a risk he was willing to take, but he couldn't let Kelsey take that risk, because the consequences weren't the same. For Kelsey, making love carried the additional risk of pregnancy and that was a risk he wasn't willing to take. If she went back to her own time, it would break his heart, losing both her and a baby would shatter his soul.

She rested her cheek against his chest and he felt the damp heat of her tears soak his shirt.

"Don't cry, sweetheart," he murmured.

"I don't know what to do."

He drew her closer, his hand stroking her back, her hair, his thoughts tumbling through his mind like dice in a cup. He loved her. He wanted her, for now or forever, he wanted her.

He brushed his lips across her cheeks and when he spoke, his words were little more than a whisper. "We could get married."

"Married!" she exclaimed. "Do you mean it?"

He nodded. "Will you marry me, Kelsey?"

"But..."

"I know, it's a crazy idea, but it's the only one that makes sense."

"But, Reese, I don't belong here."

"But you're here now."

"But I can't stay…"

"It doesn't matter. I love you. You love me. Let's not waste whatever time we have together."

She stared up at him. Maybe he was right. There were no guarantees in life. She might never make it back to her own time. He could be killed in an accident. But they were together now.

"Will you marry me, Kelsey?"

"Yes, oh, yes!" She knew it was the right decision the moment she spoke the words, knew it in every fiber of her being.

"How about tomorrow?" he asked. "We can get married here in the morning and spend our honeymoon in Bitter Ridge, just the two of us."

"Tomorrow?"

He nodded.

"Yes," she said, blinking back tears of happiness. "Tomorrow."

Kelsey broke the news to Papa Joe and Angelina that night on their way back to the hotel.

"Doesn't surprise me," Angelina said with a knowing grin.

Papa Joe shook his head. "Have the two of you thought this through?" He looked at Reese. "What will you do when Kelsey goes home?" he asked. "And you," he said, turning his gaze toward his granddaughter, "have you thought about it? Really thought about it? What if there's a child?"

Kelsey held tight to Reese's hand. "Of course I've thought about it. But I love him, Papa."

"I think it's a mistake you'll regret," Papa Joe said.

"But you'll be there to give me away, won't you?" Kelsey asked.

"Are you kidding?" Papa Joe said. He kissed Kelsey on the cheek, then shook Reese's hand. "I wouldn't miss it."

Chapter Seventeen

୫୬

Kelsey was amazed by how quickly their wedding arrangements were made. At noon on Sunday, she and Reese stood in front of a preacher and exchanged their wedding vows. She wore the same dress she had worn to the dance, as did Angelina. Reese wore black trousers and a black leather jacket. Her grandfather wore his brown suit and cravat.

It wasn't the lavish kind of wedding most girls dreamed of, but as Kelsey looked into Reese's eyes and repeated the words that made her his wife, it didn't matter that her parents and her brothers and Nana Mary weren't there, or that she wasn't wearing a designer gown and veil or going to Hawaii on her honeymoon. The only thing that mattered was that she was marrying Reese.

Warmth spread through her as the preacher pronounced them man and wife and then Reese, her brand new husband, drew her into his arms and kissed her. She leaned into him, wanting to imprint this moment forever on her mind.

She was breathless, her legs like wet spaghetti, when he took his mouth from hers.

A rush of heat flooded her cheeks when his gaze met hers, his eyes hot, his smile filled with a promise of more and better things to come when they were alone.

Reese paid the preacher, then took Kelsey's hand and they left the church.

Outside, Papa Joe hugged Kelsey tight. "Be happy, sweetheart."

"I am happy."

Papa Joe slapped Reese on the back. "You take good care of my girl," he warned, "or I'll know the reason why!"

"Yes, sir."

Kelsey hugged Angelina. "Behave yourself while we're gone."

"Don't worry about us," Papa Joe said, draping his arm over Angelina's shoulders. "We'll be fine."

"Make sure she does her homework," Kelsey admonished. "And don't let her stay up 'til all hours."

Papa Joe made a shooing motion with his hands. "Get along with you," he said. "I raised eight kids, I think I can handle this little bitty one."

Grinning, Kelsey gave her grandfather another hug, waved to Angelina and climbed into the wagon Reese had rented for their journey to Bitter Ridge.

"How long will it take us to get there?" Kelsey asked as Reese picked up the reins and clucked to the team.

"About five hours."

Five hours, she thought as she settled on the hard plank seat. They could have been there in far more comfort and far less time in her Mustang. Still, there was something rather pleasant about sitting next to Reese, watching the countryside go by. In her Mustang, they would have been going sixty miles an hour, too fast to have noticed the small herd of deer grazing in the trees not far from the dirt road. She probably wouldn't have paid any attention to the tiny pink and white flowers nodding in the sun, or had time to watch the eagle that dipped and soared effortlessly overhead. Yes, there was a lot to be said for a slower lifestyle.

They had been traveling for about two hours when Reese pulled off the road.

"Why are we stopping?" Kelsey asked.

"I don't know about you, but I'm hungry."

She glanced around. There was nothing to see but prairie and blue sky for miles in every direction.

Reese hopped down off the wagon seat, came around and helped her to the ground, then reached under the seat and withdrew a covered basket and a blanket.

"A picnic?" she mused aloud.

He nodded. "Come on."

She followed him to a shady spot under a tree where they spread the blanket, then sat down. Reese uncovered the basket and set out a veritable feast—fried chicken, slices of cold ham and cheese, cornbread and potato salad, along with a couple bottles of sarsaparilla.

Everything tasted wonderful. She didn't know if it was because she was suddenly famished, or if it was because she was sharing her first meal with her new husband. She decided it was mostly the latter.

She was acutely aware of his presence, of the way his gaze continually moved over her, of the way butterflies danced in her stomach each time he looked at her. By the time she finished eating, she was quivering with desire and he hadn't even touched her! How would she wait until they reached Bitter Ridge?

It quickly grew evident that Reese didn't intend to wait. With his gaze hot upon her face, he quickly tossed their dishes and utensils back into the basket and put it aside and then he was reaching for her, drawing her down on the blanket beside him.

"What are you doing?" she asked breathlessly.

"What do you think?"

"But..."

"You're not gonna refuse me, are you? Not on our wedding day."

She glanced around, feeling horribly exposed. "What if someone comes by?"

"No one can see us from the road."

She supposed he was right. They were pretty far off the road and the wagon would block their presence from anyone passing by. She hoped. Still, she might have protested further but it was difficult to argue when he was trailing kisses across her cheeks, when his hands were slowly exploring the contours of her body.

She moaned softly as his hand slid under her skirt to caress her thigh. And then his mouth covered hers in a long, lusty kiss that drove all rational thought from her mind. She had wanted him for weeks and now, at last, he was hers. Excitement and anticipation fluttered in her stomach like drunken fireflies as she began an exploration of her own. His skin was hot beneath her fingertips, his body taut with desire. Impatient now, she quickly relieved him of his jacket and shirt, let her hands slide over his chest, down his belly.

"Turnabout is fair play," he drawled and in moments, she lay in his arms, the blanket soft beneath her bare skin, his heated body draped over hers.

She knew a moment of regret that he hadn't been her first lover, that she couldn't come to him pure and untouched, but before she had time to dwell on it, Reese was whispering in her ear, telling her that he loved her, proving it with long slow kisses that branded her as his even as it burned away the memory of another man's possession. It was as if no one else had ever kissed her or touched her, as if she were a new creature who had been born for this man, this moment. She knew only the taste of his mouth on hers, the pleasure of his hands stroking her, arousing her, worshipping her. Loving her. With Reese, each touch and caress was a new sensation. She gave him everything she had to give, her heart, soul and body, joining with his. It was the sweetest, most tender moment in her whole life as his body merged with hers, healing old wounds. Making her feel as if it was, indeed, the first time.

She cried his name as waves of pure sensual pleasure pulsed through her, clung to him as his body convulsed, carrying her to completion.

Later, with the blanket covering them, she rested in his arms, more content than she had ever been in her life.

Reese brushed a kiss across her cheek. "What are you smiling about?"

"I think from now on you'll be in charge of lunch."

Laughter rumbled in his chest. "You think so, huh?"

"Definitely."

He nibbled on her earlobe. "Okay by me, as long as you're dessert."

His hands drifted over her, lightly caressing.

"Give you an hour to stop that," she murmured.

"Only an hour?" He was teasing but she heard the husky yearning in his voice. He kissed her cheek, the back of her neck, rolled her over so he could possess her mouth with his. And then, reluctantly, he sat up. "We'd better get moving, unless you want to spend the night out here."

"Can we?"

"If you want, but you're gonna be mighty cold and mighty hungry come morning."

He was right, darn it.

Rising, they gathered up their clothes, kissing and caressing while they dressed.

"Next time in a bed," he said, "with a soft mattress and a feather pillow."

"All right," she agreed, "as long as you're there."

Reese picked up the basket and stowed it back under the wagon seat while Kelsey folded the blanket. Instead of throwing it in the back, she spread it across the wooden seat to cushion it.

A short time later, they were on the road again. Kelsey couldn't stop looking at Reese, couldn't stop touching him. She ran her hand along his hard-muscled thigh, over his shoulder, along his arm. She kissed his cheek and the line of his jaw, thrilled beyond words that he was hers now, that she could touch him wherever and whenever she wished.

"You keep that up," he warned, "and we'll never get to town."

"Promises, promises," she muttered with a saucy grin.

He slowed the team, a wicked look in his eyes. "We can do it right here, right now," he said, "if you don't mind a little company."

Her eyes widened. "Company?"

He jerked his chin at the road ahead. Two men on horseback were riding toward them.

"If you can restrain yourself for another half an hour or so," he said, "we can do it on clean sheets."

* * * * *

Angelina sat on a chair on the boardwalk, idly drumming her fingertips on the arm. It was Sunday evening and she was bored. Papa Joe dozed in the rocker beside her. She glanced down the street. She could hear music and singing coming from the church. She knew Danny was there, with his parents. She wondered what it was like to have a mother and a father, to go to church as a family. To be respectable. She was almost sixteen and she had never been to church. She didn't know who her father was. She had never been respectable. Growing up, she hadn't understood why the townspeople treated her the way they did. Mothers wouldn't let their children talk to her. Women crossed the street when they saw her mother coming. The men were friendlier, or so she'd thought. When she grew older, she knew that look in their eyes had nothing to do with friendship.

Angelina glanced down the street again, wishing for things that could never be. Even though she had never taken a man upstairs, she was tainted with her mother's blood, stained with her mother's reputation. No decent man would ever want to marry her.

She sniffed back a tear. It wasn't fair. But maybe she was worrying for nothing. Except for Reese and Kelsey, no one in Grant's Crossing knew who her mother was or what Charlotte did for a living. Sitting up straighter, she brushed the tears from her eyes. She'd never done anything wrong, well, except to steal money from Charlotte, but she'd had to do that. She was just as good as anybody else in this town!

Rising, she hurried down the street toward the church, drawn by the music and the singing and an overwhelming curiosity about what people did in church besides get married.

* * * * *

Papa Joe woke with a start. Must be getting old, he thought, falling asleep like that. He looked over to where Angelina was supposed to be, his eyes widening when he saw her empty chair. Damn, where had the girl gone off to and how long had she been gone?

Rising, he peeked into the hotel lobby, but there was no sign of her. Thinking she might have gone upstairs, he went up to check her room, swore when he saw it was empty.

Down on the boardwalk again, he glanced up and down the street. It was Sunday evening. Most of the stores were closed. Surely she hadn't gone into one of the saloons?

The sound of singing drew his attention. With a prayer in his heart, he headed toward the church.

He found Angelina sitting on the back row, her hands in her lap, her cheeks wet with tears. Scooting in beside her, he put his arm around her shoulders, wondering why she was crying. And then, as the preacher's words reached his ears, he knew. The preacher was decrying the sins of the flesh, admonishing the young women to protect and preserve their chastity, urging the men, young and old, to avoid harlots and shun the sins of adultery and fornication.

As soon as the service was over, Joe took Angelina by the hand and led her outside.

Once they were out of sight of the church, he drew the girl into his arms.

"There now," he said, patting her back, "there now."

"My mama's going to hell, isn't she?" Angelina asked, sniffing back her tears.

"Well, now, that's not for me to say, or for that preacher, either."

"He sounded so sure...he said harlots burn in hellfire forever." She looked up at him, her eyes red, her lower lip quivering. "I hate her," she said, "but I don't want her to burn."

Joe pulled his handkerchief from his coat pocket and dried her tears. "Only the good Lord is fit to judge your mama," he said. "She's in His hands, just like everybody else."

"Do you think she'll go to hell?"

"Now, how would I know that?" he asked with an affectionate smile. "I don't even know your mama."

"You're lucky," Angelina said. And wiping the last of the tears from her eyes, she made her way back to the hotel, more determined than ever never to return to her mother's house.

Chapter Eighteen

Kelsey's gaze darted from one side of the street to the other. Bitter Ridge was a good-sized town, far larger than Grant's Crossing. Though she had never been to the east in this time period, she had a feeling it would look a lot like this, with wide streets, lots of shops and houses that were well-cared for.

They left the wagon at the livery stable. With Reese carrying their bags, they walked down the boardwalk to the hotel. The Hopkins was larger and more luxurious than the hotel at Grant's Crossing and boasted a wide, double staircase and expensive carpets. Tiffany lamps adorned the marble-topped tables. Dainty settees covered in damask were placed around the spacious lobby.

Reese secured a room and they went upstairs to wash up. There was a tub in their room, partially hidden behind a folding screen. By the time they had settled in, the hot water had arrived.

Gentleman that he was, Reese graciously allowed her to bathe first. Knowing him as she did, she wasn't surprised when he appeared at the side of the bathtub and took the soap from her hand. Her heart skipped a beat as he proceeded to wash her, carefully and thoroughly, from head to foot. Having Reese bathe her was an erotic experience that had Kelsey blushing with pleasure as his large soapy hands moved over her.

Being a modern woman, she naturally turned the tables on him, unable to decide which was the most rewarding, being washed, or doing the washing.

The water was turning cool when Reese stepped out of the tub. In spite of the cold water, it was apparent that he was as aroused as she. Naked and dripping wet, he gathered Kelsey into his arms. The towel wrapped around her middle slipped unnoticed to the floor.

"Reese, what are you doing?" she exclaimed as he carried her to the bed. "You're soaking wet! The sheets..."

"We'll get dry ones later," he said, his voice a low growl. "I can't wait any longer."

Laughing, she locked her arms around his neck, pulling him down on top of her. Her hands slid up and down his back, thrilling to the play of muscles beneath her fingertips, reveling in the heat of his body, the taste of his kisses, the hungry look in his eyes as his gaze swept over her. She didn't think anything could have been better than the first time. Finding out otherwise proved to be a most pleasant surprise.

Later, after they each took another quick dip in the tub, they dressed and went out to dinner at the town's best restaurant.

After they ordered, Kelsey glanced around the room, noting the fine linen cloths on the tables, the delicate crystal vases filled with fresh flowers, the chandelier.

"Why don't you live here, in Bitter Ridge?" she asked, wondering why anyone would choose Grant's Crossing over this place.

Reese shook his head. "This town's too civilized for me. Might as well live in Boston."

"What's wrong with Boston?"

"Too civilized," he said with a grin. "I like a town that's still a little rough around the edges."

"I can't imagine why."

He shrugged. "Easier to go unnoticed in a town like Grant's Crossing."

"Oh, right." She had forgotten that he was wanted by the law. But then, how many people outside of Kansas City or Hays would be aware of that? Life in the Old West wasn't like it was today, when news spread across the globe at the blink of an eye, when pictures of wanted men could be seen on every TV screen and computer in America.

"Does it bother you?" he asked. "Me being wanted by the law?"

"Not really. Actually, I'd forgotten all about it. What will happen, if they catch you?" Nightmare images of Reese being led to the gallows and hanged flashed through her mind.

"I reckon I'd go to jail for a long time." He leaned forward, his dark eyes intense. "Would you wait for me, Kelsey?"

"Of course I would," she said, and then blinked at him as his words sank in. How could she make a promise like that when she didn't know how long she would be here?

He knew what she was thinking, she could see it in his eyes. "Don't worry about it," he said with a wink. "I'm not gonna get caught."

Famous last words, she thought, but didn't say them aloud.

After dinner, they walked hand-in-hand through the town, pausing now and then to look in shop front windows.

"Look." She pointed at a brown bowler hat in the window. "I've got to buy that for Papa Joe."

"We'll come back tomorrow," Reese said.

They walked a little farther down the street before she stopped again. "Oh! Angelina would look wonderful in that dress!"

"Which one?"

"The lavender one, there, in the corner."

"I thought we came to buy furniture?"

Kelsey looked up at him and smiled. "I think you should know that I love shopping, especially for other people. Now," she said, continuing down the boardwalk, "what shall we buy for you?"

"I don't need anything."

She stopped in front of a men's clothing store. "How about that vest?"

"That one?" He looked at her in mock horror. "The green and orange plaid one?"

Pursing her lips to keep from laughing, Kelsey nodded. It was ugly beyond words, from its puce-colored silk lining to its brass buttons.

Crossing the street, they started up the other side. "Wait," Reese said, stopping in front of *The Bon Ton for Ladies Shoppe*. "Since we're buying presents for everyone, I want to buy something for you."

"What?" she asked.

"That." She followed his gaze to the most hideous dress she had ever seen. It was brown and gold and pink, with a high collar, long sleeves and a bell-shaped skirt. "All right," she said, laughing, "you win."

* * * * *

In the morning, Reese got the wagon from the livery and they drove to Brown's Furniture and Carpentry Shop where Kelsey picked out two settees covered in a blue print, as well as five small round tables and one large square table, with matching chairs for each. She bought a long table for the kitchen, as well as a couple of chairs and a small glass-fronted cupboard.

The mercantile provided dishes, silverware and glassware, pots and pans, as well as material for curtains, tablecloths and napkins.

"You buy one more thing and we're gonna need a bigger rig," Reese said as they loaded her purchases into the back of the wagon.

"Oh, I think one hat and one dress will fit. I can't go home empty-handed."

Reese glanced at the overloaded wagon. "Empty-handed?"

"You know what I mean. When I was a little girl, every time Papa Joe went to town, he came back with presents for me and Nana Mary."

"All right, but make it quick," Reese said, patting her hand. "I'd like to make it home before dark."

Home. Warmth spread through Kelsey. Never had the word sounded so good.

* * * * *

School was over and Angelina walked slowly down the boardwalk. Unbelievable as it seemed, she was missing Kelsey. Reese, too, of course, but mostly Kelsey, who was the closest thing to a loving mother Angelina had ever known. She wondered what would happen to her, now that Reese and Kelsey were married. They probably wouldn't want to have some girl who wasn't even a relative living with them. Maybe she could stay with Papa Joe...

The sound of someone calling her name drew her attention. Looking up, she saw Danny hurrying toward her, a smile on his face. Just seeing him brightened her mood.

"Hi, Angelina." He reached for her books. "Here, let me carry those."

"Thank you. What are you doing in town today?"

"My horse threw a shoe. I was at the blacksmith's when I saw you." He smiled at her again. "I guess horseshoes really are lucky."

"What do you mean?"

"If my horse hadn't thrown a shoe, I wouldn't have seen you today."

"I'm glad to see you, too." With Kelsey gone and the house locked up, there was nothing to look forward to but homework and a long night in her room.

"I had a good time at the dance the other night," Danny said.

"Me, too."

Angelina stopped in front of the hotel. "Well, here we are. Thanks for walking me home."

"Any time."

"Would you…do you want to come up to my room for a while?"

Danny stared at her, his eyes wide, making her wish she could take the words back.

What had she been thinking? No decent woman invited a man to her room, especially when that room was in a hotel.

"Never mind," she said, her cheeks burning with shame. "I shouldn't have said that. It's just that Kelsey's gone and I don't have anything to do and it's so lonely and…"

Danny pressed his fingertips to her lips, cutting her off in mid-sentence. "It's okay. I understand."

"You do?"

"You said it yourself. You're lonely." He looked thoughtful a moment. "Why don't you come home with me and meet my folks?"

"Do you mean it?"

"Sure."

Her joy in being asked was quickly swallowed up by a surge of uncertainty. What would his parents think of her? What would *he* think of her, if he knew who her mother was?

"Angelina?"

"I don't know…" She cast about for a good excuse. "Kelsey will be home today."

"You can leave her a note and tell her where you are. I'll bring you home early."

"All right." She agreed quickly, before she could talk herself out of it. "I'll be right back."

Taking her school books from Danny, she hurried into the hotel and up the stairs to her room. She dumped her books on the bed, brushed her hair, pinched some color into her cheeks. Going back downstairs, she quickly wrote a note for Kelsey and left it with the desk clerk.

Danny was waiting for her on the boardwalk. Hand in hand, they walked down the street to the blacksmith's shop.

"We'll have to ride double," Danny said. "You don't mind, do you?"

"No, I don't mind."

With a wink, he lifted her onto the back of his horse. "Ready?"

She felt her heart skip a beat when he vaulted up behind her, then reached around her to take up the reins.

"Ready," she said breathlessly.

* * * * *

Due to the heavy load in the wagon, the return to Grant's Crossing took a little longer. Kelsey didn't mind. Sitting beside Reese, munching on a licorice whip, she considered the vast changes in her life. Once, she had been certain she would hate living in the Old West. Now that she was actually there, she found that she rather enjoyed the rugged life. It was hard to remember that she had once spent her days in a high-rise office building worrying about invoices and shipping dates or that she had spent hours in front of a computer or on the phone. She didn't miss her job much, although she did miss the comforts of the future. But she knew she would miss Reese even more. And Angelina, too.

She frowned, thinking of the girl. "Reese?"

"Yea?"

"What am I going to do about Angie? Do you think I should tell her that I might be going back to the future? Do you think she'd believe me? And what's going to happen to her when I'm gone?"

"There's an easy answer to all those questions, you know. Just stay here."

It did sound easy, the way he said it. *Just stay here.* Forget about your family and your job and your responsibilities. But how could she do that? She had a loyalty to her boss, assuming she still had a job and a boss. She had bills to pay. And her family, how could she let them spend the rest of their lives wondering what had happened to her? *Just stay here.* Forget about your friends. Give up television and movies and modern medicine and all the wonders of the twenty-first century, like fast food and pizza, her new car, her dishwasher and microwave, her washer and dryer, designer clothes, Godiva chocolates, Christmas with her family.

How could she leave all that behind?

How could she leave Reese?

Of course, when Papa Joe went back, he could tell her parents where she was and that she was all right. He could call her boss, pay off her debts and her lease, sell her car.

She closed her eyes. How could she be expected to make such a decision? If she stayed, would she wish she hadn't? If she didn't, would she wish she had?

She shook off her dreary thoughts. It wasn't a decision she had to make right away. Until the time came, she would cherish every precious moment with Reese. She would memorize the sound of his laughter, the way his eyes crinkled at the corners when he smiled, the rich timbre of his voice. She would bask in his touch, soak up every word, commit the lines and angles of his face to memory so that she could recall them at will.

"Here now, what's wrong?" Reining the team to a halt, he wiped the tears from her cheeks.

"I don't know what to do," she wailed softly, and collapsed in his arms.

He knew her well enough that he didn't have to ask what she meant. Holding her close, he rested his chin on the top of her head, wishing he could help, but this was a decision she had to make on her own. Of course, if it was up to him, she would spend the rest of her life here, but it wasn't up to him. And, from what she had told him about the future, maybe it was selfish of him to want her to give it up for life in the past. He could barely grasp the scope of the things she had told him about, like horseless carriages and wireless telephones and the ability to send words and pictures across the world in mere minutes. A distant part of his mind wondered if it was possible for someone from the past to go forward in time and who would have a harder time adjusting, the one who stayed in the past or the one who went into the future.

She sniffed one last time, then sat back, wiping her eyes. "I'm sorry, I don't know what came over me."

"PMSing, maybe?" he suggested, his tone and expression grim.

He smiled when Kelsey burst out laughing.

"Feeling better now?" he asked.

"Yes." She blew out a sigh. "You always make me feel better."

"I love you, Kelsey. Whatever you decide, wherever you go, I'll always love you."

She couldn't help it. His words, the tender touch of his hand on her cheek, had her crying all over again.

* * * * *

It was near dark when they reached Grant's Crossing. Reese pulled up in front of the house and began unloading the back of the wagon while Kelsey unlocked the front door and went inside to light the lamps.

They had unloaded most of the lighter stuff and were about to lift one of the settees to the ground when Papa Joe showed up.

"What did you do, Kelsey, buy out the town?" he asked.

"Not quite. Where's Angie?"

"She's out at the Hamilton place with that boy."

"What?"

"I got back to the hotel late. When I asked Wexler if he'd seen her, he said she'd left a note for you. I read it and…" He shrugged. "That's all it said."

"You want me to ride out and get her?" Reese asked.

"No, that would just embarrass her. I don't want to do that. And as she's said so often, I'm not her mother. Still, if she's not back by dark…"

Before she finished the sentence, Danny Hamilton rode up with Angelina mounted behind him. Dismounting, he helped her from the back of the horse.

"Hi," Angelina said brightly. "Did you have a good time in Bitter Ridge? It looks like you bought everything they had."

Reese grinned as she echoed Papa Joe's remark.

"Do you need any help?" Danny asked. "I'd be glad to give you a hand."

Kelsey looked at Reese and shrugged and what could have been an awkward moment passed.

Between the five of them, they had everything unloaded and carried inside in no time at all, then Angelina and Kelsey stood in the middle of the room, trying to decide how to arrange the furniture. First, Kelsey had the men put the settees in front of the windows, then facing each other in front of the fireplace, then on opposite sides of the room and finally facing each other in front of the fireplace again. They arranged the smaller dining tables in a half circle around the edge of the room, with the settees the focal point in the middle. She put the one large table in the dining room, in case someone wanted to have a party there, or a meeting of some kind.

The beds came next and after the men set them up, Kelsey let Angie choose which bedroom she wanted and then gave her a set of sheets so she could make the bed.

Reese followed Kelsey into the second bedroom while Papa Joe took the team and wagon back to the livery.

"So," he said, one shoulder resting on the door jamb, "how soon are you gonna open up for business?"

"Probably not for at least a week. I need to buy supplies and try out some recipes first. And I need to make tablecloths and napkins. When do you pay the rent on your room again?"

"Next Friday."

"Then we can move in here on Saturday, if it's all right with you."

"Where's Papa Joe gonna stay?"

"I guess he'll have to stay at the hotel. There's no room for him here."

Pushing away from the door, Reese took her into his arms and kissed her.

"What's that for?" she asked.

"Does a man need a reason to kiss his wife?"

She shook her head, then went up on her tiptoes and kissed him back. They were still kissing when Angelina entered the room. "Oh! Sorry."

Kelsey peeked around Reese's shoulder. "Did you want something, Angie?"

"No, we just wondered if you needed anything else done tonight before Danny goes home."

Seeing Danny standing behind Angie, Kelsey moved away from Reese. "No, I think that's all for tonight. I appreciate your help, Danny."

"Glad to do it," he said affably. "Goodbye Mrs. Reese, Mr. Reese." His voice softened. "Good night, Angelina."

Later that night, after telling Angie good night, Kelsey walked down the hall to Reese's room. It seemed strange, being able to share his room, stranger still to think that her grandfather and Angie were only a few doors away. For a moment, she felt guilty for being in Reese's room and then she shook her head. She was a married woman now and she had every right to be there!

She found Reese sitting on the bed, a hand of solitaire laid out before him. He looked up when she entered the room. "Get all your good nights said?" He placed a red eight on a black nine.

Nodding, Kelsey closed the door. "Black four on the red five."

"We haven't played poker in a while," Reese said, scooping up the cards. "Wanna play a hand or two?"

She frowned. It seemed like an odd way for a newly married couple to spend their time. "Sure, if you want. What'll we play for?"

"Kisses?" he asked.

"We could do that," Kelsey said, "or we could play strip poker."

He lifted one dark brow. "I don't think I've ever played that one."

"It's easy. We'll play five card stud. If you lose, you remove a piece of clothing."

"I'm game if you are," he said, and dealt the cards.

Kelsey won the first hand with three deuces. Reese removed one of his boots.

She won the second hand and he removed the other one.

She lost the next hand and the next and every hand after that until she was left wearing only her bra and panties.

"I like this game," Reese said as he dealt a new hand.

Kelsey looked at him through narrowed eyes. "You're cheating, aren't you?"

He looked shocked. "Who, me?"

"Yes, you. I know you're good, but you can't be that good."

"Honey," he said, sounding deeply offended, "it's how I make my living. Of course I'm good."

Kelsey picked up all the cards and shuffled them twice and then dealt a new hand.

"Don't trust me, huh?" he mused, picking up his cards.

"Not a bit."

Laughing, he tossed his cards on the bed and pulled her into his arms. "All right, I admit it, I was cheating." He ran his hands over her bare back. "Can you blame me?"

"Yes!" She pushed him away. "Pick up your cards."

"Aw, Kelsey, sweetheart, I don't want you to be mad."

"Then you'd better let me win from now on."

"I've got a better idea." Rising, his gaze fixed on her face, he began to undress, first his socks, then his vest, his shirt, his gun belt.

Kelsey felt warm all over as he unbuckled his belt and tossed it aside. She licked her lips expectantly, felt her cheeks grow hot under his knowing smile. And then he was on the bed beside her, unfastening her bra, slipping her panties down her hips.

"My turn." Her hands were shaking as she pulled off his trousers and the long drawers that fit him like a second skin.

Reese drew her close, his arms tight around her. "Not mad anymore?"

"No."

Tucking her beneath him, he nuzzled the sensitive skin behind her ear, nibbled on her lobe and then her lower lip before claiming her mouth with his.

Was there anything more erotic, more pleasurable, than the abrasion of bare skin against bare skin? She had never known that making love could be so heart-stoppingly satisfying or that, with the right man, it could be such a soul-stirring experience. When she made love to Reese, it was more than the mere joining of flesh to flesh. She felt as if she was truly a part of him, as if they were indeed one heart, one soul, one flesh.

She had never felt that way with Nick and she had often wondered what was wrong with her, why a vital spark was missing from their relationship. She knew now that what had been missing was the kind of love she felt for Reese, a love coupled with affection and passion that she had never felt for Nick.

The touch of Reese's hand sliding along her thigh drove all thought of Nick from her mind. There was only here and now, there was only this man, rising over her, his voice whispering that he loved her more than life itself as he buried himself deep inside of her.

And as he carried her over the brink into fulfillment, she prayed that the portal that led back to the past remained closed for all time.

Chapter Nineteen

Kelsey had planned to get up early Tuesday morning and get busy making tablecloths and napkins. Her mistake was in kissing Reese when she woke up, because one kiss led to another and then another and before she knew it, it was almost noon. By the time she dressed and ate a very late breakfast, it was after one, which meant she only had three hours until she had to go to work.

But she couldn't be upset. How could she be, when she had spent the morning in Reese's arms?

She found herself smiling as she walked to the house, already looking forward to the time when she would see Reese at the Square Deal and, later, have dinner with him and Angelina and Papa Joe. But, mostly, she looked forward to bedtime when they could shut the door and shut out the rest of the world.

Kelsey had just finished hemming one of the tablecloths and was getting ready to head over to the saloon when Angelina burst into the room. "Kelsey, Kelsey, help me!"

"What is it?" Kelsey asked, alarmed by the note of panic in the girl's voice. "What's wrong?"

"He's here! He's come to take me back!" Slamming the front door, Angelina turned the key in the lock, then grabbed Kelsey's hands in hers. "Please don't let him take me!"

"Who's here?" Kelsey asked. She glanced around, but there was no one else in the house. "What are you talking about? Who's here?"

"Jed Lynch. I saw him a few minutes ago. He was walking down the street." Angie squeezed Kelsey's hand.

"He's come for me. Mama sent him. I know she did!" She was sobbing now, tears rolling down her cheeks. "Please don't let him take me back!"

"No, no, I won't. Hush, now, Angie, it'll be all right."

"You...you promise?"

"Yes, of course. Come on, let's go find Reese and Papa Joe."

"I'm afraid to go outside. What if he sees me?"

"Do you want to stay here?"

"Alone? No! Don't leave me."

"All right, Angie. Calm down. We'll stay here." She led the girl to the settee. "Sit down and dry your eyes while I think of what we should do."

"I'm sorry."

"There's nothing for you to be sorry about. And nothing to worry about. When I don't show up at the saloon, Reese will come looking for me. We'll just sit tight until then."

Angelina nodded, her eyes wide and scared.

"Who is Jed Lynch, exactly? Does he work for your mother?"

"Yes. He...he keeps the girls in line."

Kelsey had a pretty good idea of how he did that. "Did he ever strike you?"

"No." Her gaze skittered away from Kelsey's.

"Angie, did he ever hurt you?"

"No, but he used to get me alone and...and tell me that he would have me, when I was older."

Just thinking about it made Kelsey sick to her stomach. "Well," she said, "no sense in our just sitting around, waiting." She went into the kitchen, returning with the squares of cloth she had cut out for napkins. "How about helping me finish the hems on these?" It was the last thing she wanted to do but she thought it might help calm Angie if she had something else to think about.

"Now?" Angelina asked.

"Sure." Kelsey threaded a needle and handed it to Angie, then threaded one for herself. Picking up one of the squares, she sat on the settee. "Like this," she said, and showed Angie how to roll and stitch the edge.

Angie bent her head to her task, her hands shaking. Watching her, Kelsey feared she would have to rip out every stitch and do them all over again but she would worry about that later.

Humming softly, Kelsey sent a silent prayer to heaven, praying that Reese would come quickly.

* * * * *

Reese tossed another dollar into the pot, then sat back in his chair, wondering what was keeping Kelsey.

"It's almost four-thirty," Papa Joe said, checking his pocket watch. "Do you think we should go look for her?"

Reese was about to say no when he suddenly found himself on his feet and heading for the door, his cards and winnings forgotten as he walked down the boardwalk toward the house. He was running when he crossed the street. He took the porch stairs two at a time, pounded on the door when he realized it was locked.

"Kelsey? Kelsey, you in there?"

He was about to knock again when the door opened and Kelsey pulled him inside.

"What's going on?" he asked as she shut the door. "Why aren't you at work?" He glanced at Angelina, then back at Kelsey. "What's going on?" he asked again.

"Angie saw a man she recognized. She thinks her mother sent him to take her back home. She doesn't want to go."

Reese dragged a hand across his jaw. "I'm not sure she has any say in the matter until she's a little older."

Angelina bounded to her feet, her whole body quivering with defiance. "I'm not going back!" she cried. "You can't make me!"

"I promised her she wouldn't have to go," Kelsey said, slipping her arm around the girl's shoulders.

"Come on," Reese said, "I'll walk the two of you over to the hotel."

"Maybe we should stay here," Kelsey suggested.

"No, you'll be safer at the hotel." He looked at Kelsey. "What do you want me to tell Pete?"

"Tell him I had to stay home to look after Angie."

He nodded. "Let's go."

Kelsey closed and locked the front door. Angelina kept her head down as they walked down the street to the hotel. Kelsey could feel Angie's body trembling and once again she wondered what terrible things the girl's mother had forced her to endure. Mother's were supposed to protect and comfort their daughters, not sell their favors to the highest bidder.

Kelsey slid a glance at Reese. He was right—legally, they didn't have a leg to stand on. But what about moral rights? What about the promise she'd made to Angie? Right or wrong, she couldn't stand by and let some stranger take Angie back to her mother's house.

Reese walked them up to Angelina's room. At Angie's request, he went in first and looked around. "There's no one here," he said, motioning Angie and Kelsey inside. "I'll see you two later." He started toward the door, then paused. "Angie, what does this fella who's after you look like? What's his name?"

"He's a little taller than I am, with greasy black hair and huge hairy hands. He has a scar here," she said, tracing a long line down her left cheek. His name is Lynch. Jed Lynch."

"What kind of weapons does he carry?"

"He wears a gun in a holster and carries a little hideout gun in the small of his back."

"Does he carry a knife?"

She shrugged. "I don't know. I've never seen him with one."

"What are you going to do?" Kelsey asked.

"Nothing, but I think I might have passed him when I was leaving the Square Deal. I'm going back to the saloon and see if he's inside."

"And if he is?"

"I don't know. I guess the next move's up to him. I'll meet the two of you downstairs for supper at six."

"Do you think that's wise?"

"You can't hide from the guy forever."

"We could leave here," Angie said, her gaze darting between the two of them. "Go to another town."

"It's a thought," Reese said, though it was a decision that would have to be up to Kelsey. If they moved, she'd have to give up looking for a way back to her old life, as well as her new business. He knew what it was like to be on the run. It was a lousy way to live.

"We'll talk about it tonight," Reese said, giving Angelina a reassuring smile. "I'll see you later, downstairs." He gave Angie's shoulder a squeeze, kissed Kelsey on the cheek and left the hotel. Whistling softly, he walked slowly back to the Square Deal.

Stepping into the saloon, he glanced around but he didn't see anyone who fit Lynch's description.

Grunting softly, Reese threaded his way through the crowd to his table in the back corner.

"We were beginning to wonder if you were coming back," Neff remarked. He shuffled the deck and dealt a new hand.

"I was hoping you weren't," Booth said mournfully. "The only time I win is when you're not here."

"What do you want from me, sympathy?" Reese asked, taking his seat.

"That'll be the day," Booth said, picking up his cards.

Reese looked across the table at Papa Joe. "Would you mind going back to the hotel and looking after things?"

"Something wrong?"

"Not yet."

Papa Joe looked at Reese a moment, then scooped up his cash. "I'll catch ya later."

Reese nodded, then glanced at the two men left at the table. "Either of you gents notice anybody new in town?"

Booth shook his head.

"There was a new fella in here a short while ago," Neff said.

Reese picked up his cards. "Black hair, scar on his cheek?"

"Yea. I overheard him ask the sheriff about a girl. Can't remember her name."

Reese felt a tightening in his gut. "Angelina?"

"That was it," Neff said, nodding. "This fella a friend of yours?"

Reese shook his head. "Did you hear what the sheriff said?"

"No. What's this all about?"

"Nothing." Reese glanced at his cards, but his mind wasn't on the game and he folded his hand early.

"Well, I'll be!" Booth crowed when he won the pot. "Hell must have froze over when I wasn't lookin'!"

"Could be," Reese agreed. "Deal me out."

Leaving the saloon, he strolled down the street, thinking about Lynch and turning over the possibilities. He could take the man aside and tell him flat-out that there was no way he was taking Angelina back to her mother's brothel, but he had a feeling that threats wouldn't cut it with a man like Lynch. They could try hiding Angie until the man gave up and left town, but Reese doubted if that would work, either. Too many people had seen Angelina. Maybe the girl was right, maybe they should just pack up and leave town.

Reese stopped in at the Red Queen, but there was no sign of Lynch and no one remembered seeing him there. He had a drink and then headed back to the Square Deal, eager to see Kelsey and to make sure everything was all right.

All they could do was wait until Lynch made his move.

* * * * *

Angelina didn't want to go to school in the morning, nor did she want to leave her room to have breakfast.

Kelsey agreed to let her eat in her room and after seeing how frightened Angie was, she also agreed to let her stay home from school.

"But you can't hide out up here forever," Kelsey said. "It might be better to confront this guy and get it over with."

Angelina shook her head vigorously. "You don't know him! He won't take no for an answer."

"I'm sure Reese and Papa Joe can make him see reason."

"What if they can't?" Tears welled in Angie's eyes. "I can't go back there. I just can't."

With a sigh, Kelsey drew Angie into her arms. "I won't let you go back," she said, and hoped she wasn't making a promise she couldn't keep.

"Wash your face and brush your hair," Kelsey said, patting Angie's back. "I'll go down and order breakfast."

"All right," Angie said, sniffling. "I'm sorry to be such a bother."

"You're not a bother. I'll be right back."

Angie locked the door behind Kelsey, then splashed water on her face. How had Lynch found her? She shuddered at the thought of going back home and facing her mother's wrath. Charlotte Ridgeway had a fierce temper. Angie had felt the back of her mother's hand on more than one occasion. She didn't want to think about what her punishment would be for stealing money and running away, although she couldn't imagine anything worse than bedding Mr. Wellington. He was old and fat and he smelled bad. She couldn't go home, she thought. She just couldn't.

Sitting on the bed, she thought back, remembering how it had been. Charlotte slept most of the day, as did the other girls. Angelina had cleaned the downstairs while they slept, emptying the ash trays, sweeping the floors, dusting the furniture, shaking out the rugs, washing the dirty glasses left from the night before. She had filled the cigar boxes, made sure the liquor cabinet was well-supplied. She had washed her mother's clothes and hung them out to dry, washed the windows, swept the walkway, turned away customers who showed up too early. In the evening, when the girls were downstairs having supper, she had quickly made their beds, changing the sheets, if necessary. And the next day, she did it all again and always, in the back of her mind, the fear that she would end up in one of the rooms upstairs.

Too upset to sit still, she began to pace the floor. If she could only convince Danny to marry her, all her problems would be over. She had failed to seduce Reese, but she wouldn't fail with Danny. All she had to do was find a way to get him alone.

* * * * *

Angelina felt better after breakfast. When Kelsey said she was going to go over to the house until it was time for her to go to work, Angie decided to go along.

"Are you sure?" Kelsey asked. "I thought you didn't want to leave the hotel."

"I don't, but there's nothing to do here."

"Maybe if you wear a kerchief over your hair and keep your head down, no one will recognize you," Kelsey suggested.

Angie agreed and a short time later, they were busily sewing the last of the table linens.

"I think we'll be able to open next week," Kelsey said. "We have everything we need."

"I'll bet you'll be glad to stop working at the saloon," Angie remarked. She folded the napkin she had hemmed and laid it aside.

Kelsey nodded, although, to be honest, she was going to miss seeing Reese. It was nice to look up and see him at the back table, to meet his gaze and feel it move over her like a caress.

Yes, she would definitely miss that.

At three-thirty, Kelsey locked up the house.

"Where's Papa Joe?" Angelina asked as they walked back to town. "I haven't seen him lately."

"I stopped by his room this morning and he was still in bed. Said he didn't feel good. I need to look in on him before I go to work."

"Is he sick?"

"He has gout. It flares up on him from time to time."

"Oh. I hope he'll be all... Kelsey! It's him! Lynch!"

"Where?" Kelsey glanced up and down the street.

"There!"

Angie pointed at a man standing in front of the barbershop. A man who saw them at the same time.

Flicking his cigarette into the dirt, Lynch strode toward them. "Angelina! Wait!"

Angie grabbed Kelsey's arm. "What'll we do?"

But it was too late to do anything.

"Hello, Angelina," Lynch said in an oily voice. "Your mama's been worried about ya."

"I'm fine," Angelina said, her voice quivering.

Lynch's gaze moved over her. "Mighty fine, I'd say. I've come to take you home."

"I'm not going."

"Sure you are."

"You heard her, Mr. Lynch," Kelsey said, taking a step backward and drawing Angie with her. "She doesn't want to go."

Lynch looked at Kelsey for the first time. "Mind your own business," he warned. "Let's go, Angelina."

"You heard the lady. She doesn't want to go."

Relief washed through Kelsey at the sound of Reese's voice.

Lynch's eyes narrowed as he turned around. "I'm gonna tell you the same thing I told the lady," he said curtly. "Mind your own business."

"I'm afraid she is my business," Reese replied. "Now back off."

"She's going with me," Lynch said. "She's underage and her mama wants her back."

He leered at Angie and licked his lips. "When we get home, you're gonna be *my* business."

Angelina shuddered.

A muscle worked in Reese's jaw. "Get the hell out of here, Lynch."

Lynch's hand caressed the butt of his gun. "Who the hell are you?"

"I'm her bodyguard," Reese replied, his voice deceptively mild. "Now get out of here."

Kelsey's arm tightened around Angelina. The tension between the two men was palpable. A dozen or so of the townspeople stood along the boardwalk, pointing and whispering. Surely Reese and Lynch wouldn't resort to gun play!

Hands fisted at his sides, Lynch held Reese's gaze. "This ain't over," he said brusquely and walked away.

Angelina sagged against Kelsey.

Reese watched Lynch until the man disappeared into one of the saloons farther down the street. "Come on," he said, taking Kelsey by the hand, "let's go."

"Do you think we've seen the last of him?" Kelsey asked as the three of them walked to the hotel.

Reese shook his head. He had seen men like Lynch before. When they wanted something, they never gave up.

Chapter Twenty

Papa Joe agreed to stay with Angelina while Kelsey was at work. Knowing how scared Angie was, Kelsey was reluctant to leave her but Papa Joe assured Kelsey that they would be just fine. And after seeing the determined look on her grandfather's face and the rifle he had brought with him, "just in case", she believed him.

"I'll bring you both something to eat when I go to supper," Kelsey said, glancing from one to the other. "Do you want anything in particular?"

"Roast beef and all the fixin's for me," Papa Joe said. "What about you, Angie?"

"Chicken and dumplings."

"All right," Kelsey said, giving them each a hug. "See you soon."

Kelsey found herself glancing over her shoulder time and again as she made her way down the street to the Square Deal. She was relieved to see Reese sitting in his usual place at the back table. Just seeing him was reassuring.

Kelsey was glad to be at work. It gave her something to think about besides Lynch although every time there was a lull, she found herself wondering how Angie and Papa Joe were doing and what Jed Lynch was up to. There was something about that man that made her blood run cold.

At six-thirty, she went to the hotel and ordered dinner for herself, Angie and Papa Joe.

Reese insisted on going with her and she didn't argue. She didn't think she was going to feel safe again until Jed

Lynch was no longer a threat. She said as much to Reese as they made their way upstairs.

"I can handle Lynch," he said.

Remembering how he had "handled" the men who kidnapped her, combined with the tone of his voice, left no doubt in her mind that he could, indeed, handle whatever trouble came along.

Reese knocked on the door; a moment later, Papa Joe asked, "Who's there?"

"It's us, you old fool," Reese retorted, "open up."

"Everything okay here?" Kelsey asked, stepping into the room.

"No worries," Papa Joe said. "Let's eat."

Kelsey sat on the edge of the bed. She looked up several times to see Angie staring at her oddly. "Is something wrong?"

"No, but…" Angelina looked over at Papa Joe, then took a deep breath. "Is it true, what he said?"

"I don't know." Kelsey shivered with a sudden premonition. "What did he tell you?"

"He said you're from the future, both of you. Is it true?"

Kelsey blew out a sigh, unable to believe her grandfather had done such a thing. What had he been thinking? What was Angie thinking?

"Is it true?" Angie asked again.

"I'm not sure what he told you," Kelsey replied. "He's quite a story teller, but it's true that we came here from the future."

Angie's eyes glowed with excitement. "It sounds like a wonderful place! Will you take me there?"

Kelsey scowled at her grandfather. "I don't know if it's possible."

Angie glanced at Reese, then back at Kelsey. It was easy enough to read the girl's mind. She was wondering if Kelsey was going to take Reese when she went back to her own time, or if she was going to leave him behind.

"Well," Kelsey said, "it's time for me to get back to work." She pinned her grandfather with a look. "We'll talk later."

Papa Joe managed to look abashed but not particularly guilty.

Kelsey collected the dishes and stacked them on the tray. "Be careful."

Papa Joe executed a snappy salute. "Sir, yes sir!"

"Very funny," Kelsey muttered.

She was still fuming as she and Reese walked down the street to the saloon. "I can't believe he told her that! What if she tells someone else? People are either going to think I'm crazy or a...a....I don't know, a witch!"

"A witch?" Reese lifted one brow. "I hadn't thought of that."

She punched him on the arm. "You won't think it's funny if they burn me at the stake."

"I think it's been a few years since anybody did that kind of thing and I'm pretty sure it never happened this far west."

"I'm serious! I don't want people looking at me funny, wondering if I'm some kind of nut."

"Who's she gonna tell, sweetheart?" Reese asked gently. "Lynch? Her mother? I doubt either one of them would believe a word she said."

"How about that boy, Danny? Or the kids at school?"

"I'm sure she'll keep quiet about it if you ask her to. And probably for the same reason you haven't told anyone but me. No one would believe her."

"I guess so," Kelsey said with a sigh.

When they reached the saloon, Reese pulled her into his arms and gave her a quick kiss. "Stop worrying, sweetheart. I'm here, remember? I won't let the bad guys get you."

She smiled up at him. "My knight in shining armor," she murmured.

"You got that right." He gave her a playful swat on the fanny, then held the door open for her. "Now, get to work. I've got a poker game waiting."

* * * * *

What with worrying about Lynch, wondering what to do about Angie's new knowledge, stealing time with Reese whenever she had a spare minute and waiting tables, the remainder of Kelsey's shift was over before she knew it. She stopped at the bar to tell Pete good night, then went to Reese's table to see if he was ready to call it a night. She nodded to Neff and Booth. There were two other men at the table that she didn't recognize.

"I hope you've come to take him home," Booth said, tossing his hand face down on the table.

Kelsey grinned. "I don't think he's ready to leave just now," she remarked, gesturing at the pile of greenbacks stacked in front of her husband. "You know he never leaves in the middle of a winning streak."

"Yea," Booth said glumly. "Just my luck."

"Booth, you whine worse than an old lady," Reese said good-naturedly.

"Most old ladies are better poker players than he is," Neff said, grinning.

Reese took Kelsey's hand and gave it a squeeze. "Don't wait up for me."

Booth groaned loudly.

"Buck up," Neff said. "His luck's bound to change sooner or later."

"Well, it better be sooner," Booth said forlornly, "cause I'm about busted for the night."

Shaking her head, Kelsey bent down and kissed Reese on the cheek. "I won't wait up if you promise to wake me when you get home."

"Come on, Kelsey, he deserves better'n that," Neff said with a grin. "Lay one on him."

Blushing, she brushed a kiss across her husband's lips, then hurried out of the saloon.

Reese sat back in his chair, thinking his life had never been better. He had a wife who was as smart as she was beautiful and ever since he'd met her, the cards had been running his way. If this kept up, he'd buy her another house so she wouldn't have to live and work in the same place. Maybe next year he'd take her to Boston or out to California...

Muttering an oath under his breath, he raked in the pot. Here he was, making plans for next year when he didn't even know if his woman would even be here next week.

He was thinking about going back to the hotel and making love to her while he could when Jed Lynch dropped into the chair across from him.

Lynch reached into his pants pocket. "What's the ante?" he asked gruffly.

"Two dollars," Neff said, tossing a couple of greenbacks into the center of the table.

With a grunt, Lynch slid two dollars into the pot.

Booth followed suit and after a moment, Reese did likewise.

Neff dealt the cards. Booth, who usually made wisecracks between plays, remained uncharacteristically quiet.

Little was said for the next half hour. The only sounds at the table were the whisper and slap of cards being shuffled and dealt. Even Booth stopped complaining.

After three hands, two of the players who were strangers to Reese left the table.

Four hands later, Neff and Booth collected their winnings, nodded at Reese and left the saloon.

Lynch tossed his cards on the table and sat back in his chair, one hand on the table, the other out of sight. "I want the girl," he said curtly. "Don't get in my way."

"I'm only gonna say this once," Reese replied. "She's not going with you. Not now, not ever. And if you try to reach for that gun, I'll plug you right here, right now." He drew back the hammer of the Colt in his hand.

The sound, faint as it was, was not lost on Lynch. A muscle flexed in his jaw as he pushed away from the table and stalked out of the saloon.

Reese watched him until he was out of sight. One thing was certain, he hadn't seen the last of Jed Lynch. The man would be back sooner or later and when they met again, only one of them would walk away.

*****

The next few days passed peacefully. There was no sign of Lynch. By Monday, Angelina was sick of staying in the hotel and decided to go to school. There were only a few weeks left until school was out for the summer and she didn't want to get behind in her studies. Reese agreed to walk with her in the morning, Papa Joe said he would walk her to the house when school was over. Kelsey had written a note to Angelina's teacher asking her to keep Angelina at school until either Reese, Papa Joe, or Kelsey came to pick her up.

On Friday, Kelsey told Pete she wouldn't be working for him anymore because she was ready to open her coffee shop.

"I'm sorry to see you go," he said. "If you ever want to come back, your job'll be waitin' for ya."

His words almost made her sorry to be leaving. Almost, but not quite.

On Saturday, she went to the newspaper office and had several flyers made. Later that afternoon, she asked several of the businesses that catered to women if she could place a flyer in their window. All had said yes. She'd also had two dozen menus printed.

It was with a sense of accomplishment and trepidation that Kelsey opened the doors of her new establishment. Now that setting the place up was over and her vision had become a reality, she began to have doubts. What if no one came? What if the women of the town were too busy or just not interested in coming here? What if all the men who had sniggered at the idea of a place for the women to gather had been right? Or, worse, refused to let their womenfolk patronize her shop?

Tying on one of the aprons she had made, Kelsey brushed her doubts aside. She had done all she could. The house looked wonderful; if her business failed, at least she had a nice place to live.

Going into the kitchen, she got down to work. She had cakes and cookies to bake and coffee to make. And if no one showed up, well, then, she and her family would have plenty of dessert to eat after dinner and lots of coffee to wash it down with!

At quarter of eleven, she opened the door for business. And waited.

At eleven thirty, just when she was thinking no one was going to show up, three women came to the door.

"Come in, come in," Kelsey said, beaming. "Please, take a seat."

The women seated themselves at one of the tables near the front window. Kelsey handed each of the women a menu. "I'll be back in a few moments to take your order," she said, smiling.

Women arrived at the coffee shop throughout the day. They came in twos and threes, openly curious. A few stayed only long enough to drink a cup of coffee and satisfy their curiosity, but most came and stayed awhile. Kelsey received numerous compliments on the coffee and the décor and many promises to come back again, often.

She was in the kitchen, brewing a fresh pot of coffee, when Reese came in the back door.

"So, how are you doing?"

"Really well," she said, smiling. "I think we're a hit."

He drew her into his arms. "You are with me," he said, nuzzling her neck. "What time are you closing shop?"

"I'm not sure. I was thinking around five, since most of the women have families to look after. What do you think?"

"I think I'd like to take you to bed."

Kelsey grinned. "Right here, right now?"

"All right by me."

"Men! Do you ever think about anything else?"

"Not often," he admitted. "Don't you ever think about it?"

She did, of course, and now that he was here, being in his arms and in their bed, was all she could think about. But she was a businesswoman. She couldn't just walk off and leave her customers waiting.

As if reading her mind, he pulled her closer. "Are you sure you don't want to sneak into one of the bedrooms for a minute?"

"I'm sure!" She could just imagine the two of them messing up the sheets while half a dozen women sat in the parlor, sipping coffee. "Are you ready to move out of the hotel?" she asked, abruptly changing the subject. "It seems silly to stay at the hotel when we have a two-bedroom house."

He grunted softly. "I can't remember the last time I lived in a house."

"Is that a yes or a no?"

He brushed a kiss across her lips. "If you're gonna be sleeping here, I'll be sleeping here."

Kelsey smiled at him. "I'll pack our stuff tonight after I close up. But right now I have to go wait on table two."

"Not sure I like having a wife that works," he muttered.

"Well, you'd better get used to it."

"Yes, ma'am." He kissed her again, drawing it out until she was limp and breathless in his embrace. "I'll be home early."

She nodded, wondering how she would wait until she was in his arms again.

Chapter Twenty-One

Reese stood on the boardwalk, stretching his back and shoulders. He had spent a profitable four hours at the poker table but he was ready to call it a night, ready to go home and make love to his wife.

Home. Wife. Two things he had never expected to have.

Two things he wouldn't have for long if Kelsey found that damn door and decided to go back to her own time, he thought glumly, so why was he standing out here alone?

Stepping off the boardwalk, he crossed the street. The night was dark and quiet, with only the faint sighing of the evening breeze to break the stillness.

He was turning a corner when a sudden prickling along his spine raised the short hairs along the back of his neck. Years of being on the run, of always looking over his shoulder, stood him in good stead now. Trusting his instincts, Reese dropped to one knee and drew his Colt mere seconds before a gunshot rent the air. Thumbing back the hammer, he fired at the muzzle flash.

With a grunt of pain, a man staggered out from between the newspaper office and the doctor's house. After a few steps, he dropped to his knees, then toppled forward. He twitched once, then lay still. Moonlight glinted on the barrel of the pistol still clasped in his hand.

Gaining his feet, Reese moved cautiously toward the gunman. He kicked the gun from the assailant's hand, then bent down and turned him over.

Jed Lynch stared up at him through lifeless eyes.

Reese muttered an oath. For a moment, he thought about high-tailing it out of town, but only for a moment. He had a wife now, responsibilities. Running would only make him look guilty and he hadn't done anything wrong. Except kill a white man.

He turned at the sound of footsteps to see old Doc Hunter hurrying toward him. "What's going on here?"

"This guy took a shot at me."

Hunter knelt beside Lynch and checked for a pulse, then looked up at Reese. "He's dead."

In moments, a crowd had gathered. Their low murmurs filled the air as they speculated on the cause of the shootout.

"All right, move aside." Sheriff Roger McCain shouldered his way through the crowd, his gun drawn. "What's going on...?" He cast a sharp eye in Reese's direction. "What happened?"

"He took a shot at me from over there," Reese said, gesturing across the way. "I fired back."

"Uh huh. You know him?"

"I know who he is. I don't know him."

The sheriff frowned. "Did he have a quarrel with you?"

"I have something he wanted. I guess he figured if I was dead, he could take it."

"Uh huh. I'll be having that revolver," the burly lawman said, holding out his hand.

Reese hesitated. McCain didn't look formidable but he wasn't the kind of man you wanted to cross. He had a fast draw and was reputed to be bull-dog stubborn. It was said that he had never lost a fight and that he had brought back every outlaw he'd gone after, some of them alive. Those weren't the kind of odds a smart gambler bet against. Blowing out a sigh, Reese handed the sheriff his gun.

McCain took it and shoved it in the waistband of his trousers. "Turn around."

Reese winced as the sheriff slapped a pair of handcuffs on him.

"Stay here," McCain said. He waved the crowd back, then knelt beside Lynch's body. His gaze swept the surrounding area. "He's not armed."

"I kicked his gun away. Over there," Reese said, jerking his chin toward the middle of the street.

Rising, McCain walked up and down the street, then approached Reese. "I didn't find a weapon."

Reese swore softly, wondering if someone in the crowd had picked it up.

"Let's go," McCain said.

Reese glanced over his shoulder. "It was self-defense." He was wasting his breath and he knew it.

"You got any witnesses?"

"No."

"That's what I figured. We'll sort this out in my office. Simms, you and Marv take the body over to Bennett's. The rest of you men go on home. There's nothing more to see."

Swearing under his breath, Reese headed down the street toward the sheriff's office.

* * * * *

For the tenth time in as many minutes, Kelsey went to the window and peered out into the darkness. It was well after midnight. She had expected Reese to be home long before now.

Going into her bedroom, she changed out of her nightgown into a dress and put on her shoes. She wrote a note in case Angelina woke up, and then realized she couldn't leave Angelina alone while she went looking for Reese.

Tossing the note in the wastebasket, she went to the window again. Where could he be?

She was about to wake Angelina when someone knocked at the door. Reese, at last!

She started to open the door, then, afraid it might be Lynch, she called, "Who is it?"

"Sheriff McCain, Mrs. Reese."

A chill ran down Kelsey's spine as she unlocked the door. Lawmen never brought good news, especially in the middle of the night.

The sheriff removed his hat. He was a soft-spoken, middle-aged man with dark brown hair, brown eyes and a grizzled mustache. If it hadn't been for the badge pinned to his vest, she would have pegged him for a cowboy, or maybe a rancher. She never would have taken him for a lawman.

"Sorry to trouble you so late," McCain said. "Do you mind if I come in?"

"No, of course not." She stepped away from the door and gestured at the sofa. "Please, sit down."

"I reckon not."

"What brings you out here at this time of night?" she asked, shutting the door.

"Your husband asked me to come."

Kelsey crossed her arms under her breasts. "Is he all right?"

McCain scratched his jaw. "He ain't hurt, if that's what you mean..."

Relief washed through her, only to be swept away by the lawman's next words.

"But he's in jail for killin' a man."

Kelsey pressed a hand to her heart. In jail! "Who...?"

"Man name of Lynch. You know him?"

"I've met him."

"Would you be knowin' his next of kin?"

"No, I'm sorry."

Kelsey looked past the sheriff when she heard a door open. A moment later Angelina entered the room.

"Kelsey, is something wrong?" Angelina asked, yawning.

"No. Go back to bed, Angie."

Angelina's eyes widened when she saw McCain standing near the front door. "What's he doing here?"

"Angelina." The lawman's eyes narrowed. "That fella, Lynch, was asking about you just the other day," he remarked. "I'd forgotten about that until now. Why was he looking for you?"

Angie moved to stand next to Kelsey, a silent plea in her eyes.

"Mr. Lynch was a friend of Angelina's mother," Kelsey said, putting her arm around Angie's shoulders. "He stopped by one day to see how she was getting along."

"What reason would your husband have for killing him?"

"I don't know. How did it happen?"

"Your husband says Lynch took a shot at him while he was crossing the street, claims he killed him in self-defense."

"Then I'm sure that's how it happened."

"Uh huh. Lynch was unarmed."

"Can I see my husband?"

"In the morning, any time after nine." The sheriff turned his gaze on Angelina. "Don't leave town, either one of you." Settling his hat on his head, he left the house.

Angelina gripped Kelsey's arm. "Do you think it's true, that he's really dead?"

"Of course, why else would they have arrested Reese?"

Angie sagged against Kelsey. "I'm glad Lynch is dead. Now he can't make me go back."

Kelsey nodded but it was Reese she was thinking of. He would hate being locked up.

Remembering that he had told her he was wanted by the law, she bit down on her lower lip. What if the sheriff found an old wanted poster? Was there a statute of limitations on old warrants? If not, and if the sheriff should find out that Reese was wanted for bank robbery, he could be in jail for a very long time.

*****

Reese woke early after a sleepless night. Rising, he paced the floor of his cell, his restlessness growing with each passing minute. Damn Jed Lynch.

He looked at the flyers tacked to the wall across from his cell, wondering if there was an old poster with his name on it among all the others. He gripped the bars. Dammit, he had to get out of here before the sheriff started asking questions he didn't want to answer, before the lawman started going through those old flyers.

He paced for another half an hour, then stretched out on the lumpy cot, his hat pulled low over his eyes.

And that was how Kelsey found him a short time later.

"Reese? Are you awake?"

At the sound of her voice, he thumbed his hat back and swung his legs over the side of the cot.

"Are you all right?" she asked, her brow furrowed.

"Just dandy." Rising, he closed the distance between them, his hand reaching through the bars to stroke her cheek. "You shouldn't have come here."

"How could I not when you're here?" Even as she asked the question, she knew the answer. He didn't want her to see him behind bars.

"How's Angelina?"

"She's fine. Papa Joe is with her. He said he'd come by later."

Reese grunted softly.

"They can't keep you here, can they, not when it was self-defense?"

He shrugged. "I reckon that's up to a jury." His gaze met hers, his eyes dark and intense. "I won't let them send me to prison."

Her insides went suddenly cold. "What do you mean?"

"Just what I said. If they find me guilty, I'll make a break for it."

"No!"

"I'm not gonna let them send me to prison or put a rope around my neck, not for killin' Lynch."

"Please don't talk like that. You're scaring me."

His hand slid down her neck and shoulder, then curled around her waist. Gently, he pulled her closer, closer. And then he kissed her.

Tears welled in Kelsey's eyes as his mouth moved over hers. His kiss was exquisitely tender. They couldn't find him guilty, they just couldn't. She had such a short time left, she wanted to spend every minute of it with Reese.

She felt bereft when he took his lips from hers. "How long until they try you?" she asked.

"The circuit judge will be here at the end of the week."

"They won't convict you," she said fervently. "I know they won't."

"I'm a half-breed, Kelsey. Lynch was a white man."

"What difference does that make?"

"A hell of a lot."

"But that's not fair! It was self-defense!"

"I've got about two thousand dollars in the bank," he said. "If anything happens to me, it's yours, as my next of kin."

"Nothing's going to happen!"

His gaze moved over her. "All right, love, whatever you say."

But he didn't believe it. She saw the despair in his eyes, heard it in his voice. Somehow, some way, she had to get him out of there before it was too late.

*****

"A jail break," Papa Joe said, pacing the floor of his room. "It's the only thing to do."

Kelsey and Angelina exchanged glances.

Kelsey stared at her grandfather. "Are you crazy?" she asked, even though her mind had been flirting with that idea ever since she left the jail. "They can't convict him for defending himself. Lynch tried to kill him!"

"I hope you're right," Papa Joe said, "but this is the Old West and Reese is part Indian…"

His words sent a shiver down her spine. Would a jury really convict Reese because of the color of his skin?

"I'm hoping I'm wrong," Papa Joe said, "but if I'm not, have you got any better ideas?"

She didn't, but she couldn't help thinking that on the inside, her grandfather was jumping up and down at the thought of pulling off a jail break. He really had been born in the wrong time, she thought, but a jail break could be dangerous, not just for Reese, but for Papa Joe and anyone else who got caught up in it.

"It's settled then," Papa Joe said, and there was no mistaking the barely subdued excitement in his voice.

"But…" Kelsey shook her head. "Won't breaking him out of jail just convince everyone that he's guilty?"

Papa Joe made a clucking sound. "It's a chance we'll have to take."

"I don't know." It would mean leaving town in a hurry, abandoning her coffee shop and any hope of finding the door to Nana Mary's. And what about Angelina? "Let's wait and see how it goes," Kelsey said. "I have to believe they'll find him innocent."

Papa Joe snorted. "Right. And maybe pigs will fly."

The next three days passed quickly. Between running the coffee shop, hiring a lawyer and visiting Reese in jail every chance she got, Kelsey didn't have much time to think about Papa Joe's outlandish suggestion. She still didn't think trying to break Reese out of jail was a good idea, but she hadn't been able to come up with a better alternative. The one thing they agreed on was to talk it over with Reese before they did anything.

Jed Lynch was buried in the town cemetery on Wednesday morning. The circuit judge arrived Friday afternoon and Reese's trial was set for the following Monday.

His restlessness grew with the passing of each day. Kelsey couldn't blame him for being worried. Her nerves were stretched taut. Every time someone entered the coffee shop, she was afraid it was the sheriff coming to tell her that Reese would also be tried for bank robbery. She tried to convince herself that the odds of that happening decreased with every passing day. After all, if his past hadn't caught up with him by now, maybe it never would.

Young Danny Hamilton showed up at the coffee shop to see Angelina on Saturday evening. Angie had told Kelsey that she had once contemplated seducing him so he would marry her, but now that Jed Lynch was dead, it was no longer necessary.

Angelina was smiling when she returned to the house that night. Danny had taken her to dinner at the hotel and then they had gone walking in the moonlight.

"He kissed me," Angelina said. "Twice."

"Oh?"

"I think he loves me," Angelina murmured.

"He seems like a nice young man," Kelsey remarked.

"Oh, he is. And he's so polite. I never knew anybody as polite as he is. He opens doors for me and when we were at the restaurant, he held my chair for me." She pursed her lips, her expression thoughtful. "Even though I don't have to seduce him, I think I'd still like to marry him."

"Are you in love with him?"

Angelina shrugged. "I don't know. I've never been in love. But I'd like to have a husband and a home of my own. And no one to tell me what to do."

"That's hardly a good reason to get married. Besides, don't you think you're a little young to be thinking about marriage?"

"Of course not, I'm..."

"I know, you're fifteen years old and you think you know everything."

"I never said that!"

"I know you didn't, but I know that's how I felt when I was your age. I thought I was all grown up. It wasn't until I was in my twenties that I realized just how young fifteen really is. All right," she said, noting the mutinous expression on Angie's face, "I'll stop lecturing. But try to wait until you're at least seventeen, okay? For me?"

Angelina sighed dramatically. "Is this how mothers behave? I mean, mothers who aren't madams?"

"Pretty much," Kelsey said, laughing.

"I'll think about it," Angie replied reluctantly, and Kelsey had to settle for that.

*****

Kelsey spent most of Sunday going to and from the jail. She arrived early in the morning with a pot of fresh coffee and a plate of scrambled eggs, bacon, hash brown potatoes and muffins fresh from the oven.

The sheriff, in her opinion, was being a real jerk. He refused to let her spend the whole day with Reese, insisting she could only stay for twenty minutes every hour.

"He's not in ICU, for heaven's sake!" she said angrily.

The lawman stared at her as if she were speaking a foreign language. "Not in 'eye see you'? What the dickens does that mean?"

"I'm his wife. Why can't I stay?"

"Cause I'm running a jail here," McCain said. "Not a hotel." He jerked his thumb toward the door. "Go on now, get out of here. I've got work to do."

She showed up like clockwork at the top of every hour. She brought Reese a roast beef sandwich and potato salad for lunch.

"Looks mighty good," the lawman said when he checked the tray to make sure she wasn't smuggling any weapons to his prisoner.

"It is good," Kelsey retorted.

"I don't suppose you could..."

"Not a chance," she said.

Nothing she said or did seemed to cheer Reese. Not that she could blame him for being glum. He wasn't the kind of man to take kindly to being locked up.

She persuaded him to play cards with her, hoping it would take his mind off his troubles, at least for a little while.

"Too bad we can't play strip poker," she said as she dealt a new hand.

That, at least, brought a fleeting smile to his face.

* * * * *

Monday morning came all too quickly. Kelsey, Angelina and Papa Joe arrived at the courthouse a few minutes before ten. Kelsey was surprised by the number of people who showed up to watch the trial. Shades of O.J. Simpson, she thought. Apparently it didn't matter what century it was, murder trials seemed to draw a crowd.

She took a place on the side where she would be able to see Reese. Angelina and Papa Joe sat on either side of her. Kelsey had no sooner taken her seat than Reese was brought into the courtroom in handcuffs. Apparently the courts in this day and age weren't concerned about what kind of image that put in the jury's mind. In her day, most defendants weren't handcuffed for fear it would make them look guilty in the jury's eyes.

Reese sat down, his expression impassive.

Kelsey glanced at the jury. Twelve white men, most of them middle-aged. She didn't recognize any of them.

The first witness was Sheriff McCain. He testified that the man identified as Jed Lynch was stone-cold dead when he arrived on the scene. He stated that the deceased had been wearing a gunbelt but that no gun had been found on or near the body. He further stated that to the best of his knowledge, no one had witnessed the shooting.

McCain was dismissed and Doctor Hunter was called to the stand and sworn in.

When questioned, he stated that he was at home on the night of the shooting. He had been in his parlor, reading, when he heard two shots. When he went outside to investigate, he saw the defendant standing over the body of Jed Lynch. Shortly thereafter, the sheriff arrived on the scene.

The doctor was dismissed and the bailiff called Reese to the stand and swore him in.

Reese's lawyer, Robert Kohl, approached the witness stand. "Now then, Mr. Reese," he said in his best Perry Mason voice, "tell us in your own words what happened on the night in question,"

"I was crossing the street when someone took a shot at me from the alley between the newspaper office and Doc Hunter's house. I turned and fired at the muzzle flash and Jed Lynch staggered out and collapsed in the street."

Kohl turned to the jury. "What we have here, gentlemen, is a clear-cut case of self-defense."

The judge looked at the prosecuting attorney. "Questions, Mr. Beard?"

"Thank you, your honor."

Rising, Beard walked to the witness stand. "Do you know of any reason why Mr. Lynch wanted to kill you?"

"We'd had a disagreement earlier."

"About what?"

"About a girl I was looking after."

"You mean Angelina Ridgeway?"

"Yea."

"And why were you looking after Miss Ridgeway?"

"She ran away from home and didn't want to go back. Her mother sent Lynch to fetch her."

"How old is Miss Ridgeway?"

"Fifteen."

"I see. So you refused to send the girl back to her mother? A girl who is underage and for whom you have no legal responsibility?"

"Yes, but..."

"And when Mr. Lynch insisted on taking the girl, you killed him, isn't that right?" Beard turned to face the jury. "There were no witnesses to this crime. All we have is the defendant's word that the killing was in self-defense, which seems unlikely, since the dead man was unarmed." Beard turned and looked down his nose at Reese. "One can only wonder at the defendant's interest in a child of that age."

A muscle twitched in Reese's jaw. "Why, you dirty-minded..."

The judge banged his gavel. "That will be all, Mr. Reese."

With a smile, the attorney sat down.

Reese's lawyer gained his feet. "Your honor, if I may, I'd like to ask the witness a few more questions."

"Granted."

"Mr. Reese, please tell the jury what kind of home Miss Ridgeway ran away from?"

Kelsey slid a glance at Angelina. They hadn't counted on anything like this. Angie's cheeks turned bright red.

"A bawdy house in Colorado," Reese answered.

"Any why had she run away?"

"Her mother was going to put Angelina to work in one of the cribs when Angelina turned sixteen."

"I see." Kohl approached the jury. "T. K. Reese killed a man in self-defense. Not only that, gentleman, but he saved a young woman from a terrible fate. Yes, Angelina Ridgeway's mother is legally responsible for the child but would any of us want to see an innocent young woman..." Here he stopped and pointed dramatically in Angelina's direction. "Used in such a foul manner? I think not! Instead of condemning my client, we should be thanking him. As for Mr. Lynch's missing weapon, anyone passing by could have picked it up. That's all I have to say."

The judge spoke to the jury for several minutes, then the jury was dismissed to reach a verdict. The judge left the room. Moments later, Sheriff McCain ushered Reese out of the building.

Kelsey turned to her grandfather. "What do you think?"

Papa Joe shook his head. "Hard to tell."

Angelina tugged on Kelsey's arm. "Please, let's go."

"All right." Of course the girl was eager to leave the courthouse, Kelsey thought. Everyone in the room was staring at her. Kelsey was outraged that Kohl had identified Angie but she knew she'd forgive him on the spot if it convinced the jury that her husband had done the right thing.

"I'm going to see Reese," Kelsey said when they were outside. "Papa Joe, why don't you take Angelina home?"

"Will do." He patted Kelsey's arm. "Try not to worry."

With a nod, she hurried down the street to the sheriff's office.

Chapter Twenty-Two

Angelina lay curled up on her bed, her cheeks damp with tears. Soon, everyone in town would know about her, about how she ran away from her mother's brothel. Danny Hamilton and his parents would know. The thought brought a fresh wave of tears. Danny would never want to see her again when he found out. No decent boy would look at her now. Even though she wasn't sure she loved Danny, she still wanted to be his friend. She wished she could just crawl into a hole and disappear! She couldn't stay here any longer, couldn't face the condemnation or the pity she was sure to see on everyone's face. She just couldn't.

She jerked upright as a new thought occurred to her. Her mother knew where she was. She had sent Lynch to find her. When Lynch didn't return, Charlotte would send someone else.

Angelina wrapped her arms around her middle. She had to leave Grant's Crossing as soon as possible. Where to go? She had no money. If she wanted to leave town, she would have to walk.

She shook her head. She would never make it to the next town on foot. Maybe she could convince someone to take her, someone like Papa Joe. She could trust him. She bit down on her lower lip. The sheriff had told her not to leave town. Would he come after her if she did? Would he lock her up? Notify her mother?

Caught up in her fears, she began to cry. Sobs racked her body. She was afraid and she didn't know what to do. Reese was in jail and it was all her fault. They might hang him.

Kelsey was her only friend in the world, but Kelsey would hate her if they hanged Reese.

"Angelina?"

She stilled at the sound of Papa Joe's voice.

"Angie, honey, open the door."

Sniffling, she let him into her room.

He took one look at her and drew her into his arms. "Honey, what is it?"

Her fears poured out of her in a torrent of words. Though most of them were incoherent, he seemed to understand.

"There now," he said, patting her back, "don't you worry your pretty head about going home. Kelsey and I won't let anyone take you back there. Your mother ought to be horsewhipped for even thinking of selling your favors. By damn, if I had a horsewhip, I'd do it myself!"

The idea of Papa Joe taking a whip to her mother brought a smile to Angelina's face.

"There now, that's better." Papa Joe pulled a handkerchief from his back pocket and dried her tears. "And don't you be worrying about what the people in town will think about you, either. It's not your fault that your mother is a…" He cleared his throat. "Well, what she is, any more than it's your fault that your hair is blonde and your eyes are blue."

Angelina rested her cheek on the old man's chest. She had never known her father or her grandparents, never had anyone take her side, especially against her mother. Papa Joe was right. She hadn't done anything wrong.

"Feeling better now?" Papa Joe asked.

She nodded. "Thank you."

"Come on, let's go over to the sweet shop. I've got a hankerin' for some peppermint."

* * * * *

For once, Sheriff McCain didn't send Kelsey away after twenty minutes. He even let her visit with Reese inside his cell.

She sat beside him now, his hand clasped in hers. She could feel the tension radiating off him like heat from a furnace as they waited for the jury to reach a verdict. She had run out of small talk long ago. Her own nerves were strung tight as she tried to decide if the fact that it was taking the jury so long to decide his fate was a good sign or a bad one.

A muscle throbbed in Reese's jaw. What would he do if they found him guilty? He had told her he wouldn't go to prison and he wouldn't let them hang him. Thinking about the tone of his voice and the look in his eyes when he'd said it sent a chill down her spine. Was he planning his own escape attempt? Should she tell him that Papa Joe was way ahead of him?

Muttering, "I hate this," Reese stood and began to pace the floor. His long legs carried him quickly from one end of the cell to the other. Back and forth, back and forth, restless and angry, his hands clenching and unclenching at his sides.

Kelsey watched him, wishing she could think of something to say that would ease his mind, wishing she could think of something to allay her own growing fears.

It was a little after four when the sheriff announced that the jury had reached a verdict.

He ordered Reese to approach the cell door and had him turn around so he could cuff his hands behind his back. When that was done, he unlocked the door. Gun drawn, he escorted Reese out of the office.

"Reese, I'm going to go get Papa Joe and Angelina," Kelsey said.

He nodded curtly but didn't reply.

Kelsey hurried toward the house, her heart pounding heavily in her breast. Reese's future would be determined in the next few minutes.

* * * * *

Kelsey decided that the news about the verdict must have spread quickly through the town because the courthouse was even more crowded now than it had been earlier in the day.

All the seats were taken and people were standing shoulder to shoulder along the walls. She saw Nate Osgood and Pete Muldoon in the crowd, along with the men Reese played poker with at the Square Deal. Heedless of others, she made her way along the wall until she found a place where she could see Reese. He was looking straight ahead, his gaze fixed on some point behind the judge's bench. He sat so still, he might have been carved from granite.

The jury filed into the room and the judge followed a few minutes later. The bailiff called the court to order. The judge asked the jury if they had reached a verdict and the foreman replied that they had. He handed a slip of paper to the bailiff, who handed it to the judge.

Kelsey's heart was in her throat as she waited for the judge to read the verdict aloud.

"We, the jury find the defendant, T. R. Reese..."

Her heart was pounding so loudly she could scarcely hear the words. Reese remained as still as stone save for a muscle that throbbed in his jaw. She knew, before the final words were spoken, what the verdict would be.

"Guilty of manslaughter."

Guilty. The word seemed to echo in Kelsey's mind...*guilty, guilty, guilty.* She looked at Reese. His expression hadn't changed.

The silence in the courthouse was deafening as the spectators waited for the judge to pronounce sentence.

"The defendant will please rise."

Reese pushed his chair back and stood tall and straight. The only sign of the tension pulsing through him was the clenching of his fists.

"You have been found guilty of manslaughter," the judge said. "I hereby sentence you to ten years in the territorial prison. Court dismissed."

Kelsey braced herself against the wall as her legs threatened to collapse. She couldn't believe it. Ten years. Oh, but it wasn't fair. She didn't have ten years to wait for him. It was only a few months until the portal to her own time would be open again.

Needing to touch him, she pushed her way through the crowd.

"Reese..." She looked up at him as words failed her. What could she possibly say to make it better?

"Excuse me, Mrs. Reese," Sheriff McCain said, his voice uncharacteristically kind, "I need to get him back to jail."

"Yes, of course," Kelsey murmured. Rising on her tiptoes, she gave her husband a quick kiss on the cheek. "I'll see you soon."

Reese nodded once, curtly, then turned and headed toward the door.

Papa Joe and Angelina hurried toward Kelsey.

"Well, they gave him the benefit of the doubt," Papa Joe said as they left the courthouse.

"What do you mean?" Kelsey asked.

"They could have found him guilty of murder and sentenced him to hang." He shook his head. "I've always been a good judge of men and I'd be willing to bet my pension that it was self-defense." He shook his head again. "That verdict was a load of..." He looked at Angelina and clamped his mouth shut.

"A load of manure?" Angelina supplied.

"That's not what I was going to say, but it'll do," Papa Joe allowed.

"It's not right," Kelsey said. "He shot Lynch in self-defense."

Papa Joe grunted. "Well, as I understand it, manslaughter is the unlawful killing of a person without malice or premeditation, whereas murder is done with malicious intent."

"But it was self-defense!" Kelsey exclaimed. "They should have acquitted him."

Though her grandfather didn't say the words, she could hear his silent "I told you so." He'd been right, after all, she thought. And so had Reese. The jury had convicted Reese on the color of his skin and nothing more.

Papa Joe's gaze moved from Kelsey to Angelina and back again. "So, where do we go from here?"

"I can't let him go to prison," Kelsey said.

"So, we're gonna break him out of jail?"

"Break him out of jail?" Angelina exclaimed. "Are you two kidding?"

Kelsey blew out a sigh. "I wish we were."

Angelina stared at the two of them and then she smiled. "What can I do?"

* * * * *

The wagon that would carry Reese to the territorial prison wouldn't arrive for three days.

Kelsey used that time to pack what she could take with her. She closed the coffee shop. They ate what they could of the food in the kitchen and she disposed of the rest.

Papa Joe went to the livery and made sure Reese's horse was ready to travel. He bought horses for Kelsey, Angie and himself, then took care of picking up enough supplies to last the four of them for at least a week. He bought derringers for Kelsey and Angie, a new rifle for himself and ammunition for all three weapons, as well as for Reese's Colt. Enough ammunition, Kelsey thought, to fight off a small army.

Kelsey took Angie shopping and they each bought a pair of dark-colored trousers, dark shirts, boots and hats.

Tomorrow they would tie up whatever loose ends remained. Tomorrow night Joe St. James and his gang would hit the jail.

*****

Reese shook his head. "Forget it, Kelsey. I don't like it."

She leaned closer to the bars and lowered her voice. "Have you got a better idea?"

"Just bring me a gun. I'll take care of the rest."

"How do you suggest I do that? McCain searches me every time I walk through the door."

Reese swore. "It's too risky, sweetheart." He stroked her cheek. "Besides, if you get caught, you'll all be here in jail with me."

"I don't care. The best chance we have of freeing you is while you're in here. Once the prison wagon comes for you, you'll be handcuffed and surrounded by guards. This way, we only have to worry about McCain and getting out of town."

Reese shook his head. "No. I don't want you putting your life in danger."

"You might as well save your breath. You can't talk me out of it."

"Dammit, Kelsey, what chance do you think a young girl, an old man and a city girl have of getting me out of here?"

"I guess we'll find out tonight, won't we?"

* * * * *

Reese stood looking out at the sky through the tiny, barred window of his cell. It was after midnight. With every passing minute, he expected St. James and the girls to come charging to his rescue. He didn't know what they were thinking. None of them had any experience on the wrong side of the law and the last thing he wanted was to find Kelsey in the cell next to his.

Reese grunted softly. What was the old man thinking to let Kelsey side him in such a mad scheme? On the other hand, knowing Kelsey, he didn't know how the old man could stop her. He had to admire his bride's grit and determination. She was a woman to ride the river with.

The passing of another hour was marked by the chiming of the courthouse clock. When another hour passed, Reese decided that his would-be rescuers had come to their senses and changed their minds.

He should have known better.

He was stretched out on his cot, staring blankly at the white-washed ceiling, when there was a commotion at the door. Stilling the urge to rush to the cell door, Reese remained where he was, feigning sleep.

Through slitted eyes, he watched McCain's deputy, Matt Stover, draw his pistol and peer through the office door's narrow window. Apparently satisfied with what he saw, Stover lowered his weapon and unlocked the door.

Angie stood in the doorway, her face wet with tears. "Come quick," she said, "Mrs. Reese heard someone prowling around the house. She's afraid one of Lynch's friends might be snooping around, looking to get even, you know?"

After a glance over his shoulder, as if to make sure his prisoner was still locked up, the deputy followed Angie outside and closed the door.

Overtaken with a fit of nervous energy, Reese began to pace the floor. He didn't have to wait long. Moments later, the door opened and Papa Joe slipped into the office. Wordlessly, he rummaged through the sheriff's desk until he found the keys to the cell.

"Hurry!" Reese urged.

In minutes, he was out of the cell and buckling on his gunbelt. He opened the loading gate to make sure the gun was loaded, then moved toward the door. Opening it a crack, he glanced up and down the street. "Now what?"

"Horses waiting around back. Kelsey and Angie will meet us at the abandoned line shack beyond the ridge. The rest is up to you."

With a nod, Reese slipped out the door. Keeping to the shadows, he rounded the building. Two horses waited in the shadows.

Reese swung into the saddle and rode out of town. The old man rode out behind him.

* * * * *

Stover circled the house, then went inside and checked each room before returning to the parlor where Kelsey and Angie waited. "I searched the premises inside and out," the deputy said. "I didn't find anything."

"Thank you, deputy," Kelsey said, clinging to Angie. "You know how frightening it can be for two women alone."

"Yes, ma'am," Stover said, smiling indulgently. "My own ma gets the night frights sometimes."

"She's lucky to have such an understanding son," Kelsey said. "Thank you so much for coming. I feel ever so much better now."

"I'm sure it was just the wind rustling the tree outside your window," Stover said.

"I'm sure you're right," Kelsey said. "Can I fix you a cup of coffee?"

"That's right kind of you, ma'am, but I'd best get back to the office and look after my prisoner..." His voice trailed off and a dark flush spread up his neck, no doubt caused by the recollection that it was Kelsey's husband he had locked up back at the jailhouse.

"Well, thank you again for coming out at this late hour," Kelsey said, walking him to the door.

"My pleasure, ma'am." He tipped his hat to Kelsey, nodded at Angie and left the house.

Kelsey waited until he was out of sight, then shut the door. "Are you ready?" She was peeling off her robe as she spoke. Sitting on the sofa, she reached underneath and pulled out a pair of boots.

"Yes." Angie removed her own robe and shrugged into a warm jacket. "My boots," she said, panic in her voice. "What did I do with my boots?"

"They're under the other sofa. Hurry!"

Moments later, they were running through the night toward the back of the livery where Papa Joe had left their horses.

If they hurried, they could meet up with Reese and Papa Joe before McCain and Stover knew what had happened.

Reese and Papa Joe were waiting for them at the line shack. Dismounting, Kelsey threw herself into Reese's arms.

"We don't have time for that now," Papa Joe warned.

"Then we'll make time," Reese said, and lowering his head, he claimed his bride's lips in a searing kiss.

Kelsey blew out a sigh when Reese took his mouth from hers. "Papa Joe's right," she said regretfully. "We need to go. We're cutting this mighty close as it is."

"Reckon so," Reese agreed. He lifted Kelsey into the saddle, then swung onto the back of his own horse. "Let's move out."

They were on the run. It was frightening and exhilarating, racing through the dark night with only the moon and the stars to light the way. Kelsey's imagination kicked into overdrive. In her mind, every tree and shadow, every rock and hill, held menace. Fear pounded through her, the frantic beat of her heart keeping time to the rhythm of her horse's hooves as the animal flew across the prairie. A gopher hole, a misstep on her horse's part, could send horse and rider crashing to the ground with a broken leg or worse.

She risked a glance over her shoulder. She couldn't see Angelina's expression in the dark. Was the girl as scared as she was? And what about Papa Joe? She knew, somehow, that he was enjoying all this.

They rode all through the night and into the dawn, stopping only when the horses needed rest.

When, at last, they stopped to get some sleep, Kelsey took Reese aside. "Where are we going?" she asked, and knew the answer even before he replied.

They were on the run and they needed a place to hide out while they waited for the portal to the future to open again. Where else would they go but to the one place no one could follow?

Chapter Twenty-Three

It was after dark when they arrived at the Lakota village. As Kelsey had already deduced, Reese had decided that holing up with the Lakota would be the wisest move. No one would look for them there, not McCain and certainly not Angelina's mother.

Reese spoke to the sentry that materialized out of the shadows. Moments later, they rode into the heart of the village. A dozen barking dogs announced their arrival. Kelsey saw several men peering at them from out of their tipis.

Kelsey wasn't surprised to see Hantaywee standing outside her tipi waiting for them, a smile on her weathered face.

"She always knows when I'm coming," Reese murmured as he reined his horse to a halt in front of the old woman's lodge.

Dismounting, he embraced Hantaywee, then turned and lifted first Kelsey and then Angelina to the ground.

"Hantaywee," he said, "this is Angelina and this is Kelsey's grandfather, Joseph."

"Welcome," Hantaywee said, smiling at Angie and Papa Joe. "Come inside and eat. Your lodges have been prepared."

Angie looked at Kelsey, then glanced around. "Lodges?"

"Tipis," Kelsey said, gesturing at Hantaywee's home.

"How did she know we were coming?" Papa Joe asked, frowning.

"Hantaywee is a medicine woman," Kelsey explained. "She can see into the future."

"That's impossible," Angelina said.

Kelsey grinned at the girl as she took her hand and gave it a reassuring squeeze. "I'm beginning to think nothing is impossible. Come on, let's eat."

"What do Indians eat?" Angie asked, hanging back.

"Mostly venison and vegetables," Kelsey said. "But whatever it is, just eat it."

"Hold on a minute," Reese said. "There's a few things you need to know." He looked at Kelsey. "Things I should have told you when we were here before but what with one thing and another..." He shrugged. "Anyway, when you go into a Lakota lodge, it's considered polite for the men to go to the right and the women to go to the left. Also, it's impolite to pass between the fire and a guest. Men and women rarely look directly at each other, although that's a custom Hantaywee doesn't practice much. It's also custom for men to be served first."

"Anything else?" Papa Joe asked. "I don't want to offend anybody while we're here."

"If I think of anything else, I'll let you know," Reese said, and ducked into Hantaywee's lodge.

One by one, the others followed him. Inside, Kelsey and Angelina turned to the left and sat down, Papa Joe followed Reese to the right.

Again following Reese's lead, they sat down and accepted the bowls that Hantaywee offered them.

"*Pilamaya,*" Reese murmured. Thank you.

Noting that Angelina wasn't eating, Kelsey leaned toward her and whispered, "Don't worry, it's just venison stew."

When they finished eating, Hantaywee showed the four of them to the lodges she had erected for them.

Papa Joe thanked Hantaywee for her hospitality, hugged Kelsey and Angelina and ducked into his lodge, obviously ready to turn in for the night.

The lodge beside Papa Joe's was for Kelsey and Reese.

"Where's mine?" Angelina asked.

"You will stay with me," Hantaywee said.

"Why can't I stay with Kelsey?"

Hantaywee smiled indulgently. "Kelsey and Tashunka Kangi need to be alone."

Angelina looked imploringly at Kelsey. "But..."

"You'll be fine," Kelsey said, patting the girl's shoulder.

Reese put his arm around Angie. "You'll love her once you get to know her."

Looking doubtful, Angie followed Hantaywee back to her lodge.

"Maybe we should have let Angie stay with us," Kelsey said.

"Maybe tomorrow night," Reese said, "tonight I want you all to myself."

His words sent a shiver of anticipation down her spine.

She stood in the center of the lodge, her heart pounding with excitement because she would soon be in his arms. Reese closed the flap on the tipi, assuring that they wouldn't be disturbed.

Padding toward the center of the lodge, he stirred the banked fire in the pit. Tiny flames licked at the dry wood. Shadows danced over the lodgeskins.

"Come here," Reese said, his voice low and husky.

She moved toward him, her gaze on his face, every nerve and cell quivering in anticipation of his kiss, his touch.

His hands slid up and down her arms, making her shiver with delight, and then he drew her into his arms. His mouth swooped down on hers, teasing, tasting. She reached for him, her hands hungry for the touch of his skin. The muscles in his arms bunched and relaxed as she explored the width of his biceps.

He groaned low in his throat as she thrust her hips against his in open, blatant invitation.

Unable to wait longer, he lowered her to the blankets spread beside the fire. He was all too aware of how fragile life was, of how quickly their time together was coming to an end. His hands trembled as he undressed her, his lips caressed each inch of newly bared flesh.

Her own hands were none too steady as she made short work of his clothing and then they were lying side by side, skin to skin, on the blankets.

"You're beautiful," he murmured, "so damn beautiful sometimes it hurts my eyes to look at you."

"You are," she replied breathlessly. She moaned softly as his hands, his large clever hands, stroked her from shoulder to thigh.

"Now, Reese," she gasped. "Now, now, now."

"Easy, sweetheart, we've got all night."

She writhed beneath him. "I can't wait. Please, Reese."

"I like a woman who says please," he murmured, rising over her.

She wrapped her arms around his neck, her legs around his waist, cried out with pleasure as his body meshed with hers. She cried his name as he pleasured her, his loving so complete, so exquisite, it was almost painful in its intensity.

Completion found him moments later. She cradled him to her, feeling tender and protective as shudders racked his body.

Resting on his elbows, his breath hot against her neck, he whispered that he loved her, would always love her.

And she wondered once again how she would ever leave him.

* * * * *

The next few days passed without incident. Kelsey set up housekeeping in their lodge. She and Reese had little other than their clothing. Reese had his weapons, of course. Kelsey had packed her tunic and moccasins and she laughed out loud at the surprised expressions on the faces of Angie and her grandfather the first time they saw her in her Indian clothing.

"I wish I had my camera," Papa Joe said. "Mary would have loved to see you in that getup."

Within days, Papa Joe and Angelina were both wearing Lakota garb.

Papa Joe took to Lakota life like a fish to water. Among the Lakota, elders were revered and although Papa Joe didn't speak the language, the Indians accorded him the respect due his age.

Angelina was slower to accept her new lifestyle, though she quickly grew fond of Hantaywee and began calling her *Unci*, which was pronounced *uhn-chee* and meant Grandmother.

Now that they were going to be there for who knew how long, Kelsey spent more time observing the Lakota people. She noticed that the boys were taught to use a bow and arrows when they were very young and that both girls and boys were taught to ride almost before they could walk. The boys played war games that, at times, seemed quite fierce. The little girls, like little girls the world over, played with dolls. As the girls grew older, they put their dolls away and began helping their mothers with household chores, like cooking and cleaning. Older girls were also expected to look after their little brothers and sisters. They were also taught how to tan hides, as well as quilling and beadwork. All the children Kelsey met were soft-spoken and polite. They treated their elders with respect and never entered a tipi without knocking on the side of the lodge first.

By being observant, Kelsey learned that colors were often more than just decoration. According to Hantaywee, colors were used to represent the different Lakota gods and to express emotions and character traits, as well. *Wi*, the god of the sun, was represented by the color red, as were all of the things that the People held sacred. *Maka* was the Lakota god of the earth, his color was green. Kelsey thought that made perfect sense, since grass and leaves and many edible plants and vegetables were green. Yellow was the color assigned to *Inyan*, the Rock. *Skan*, the most potent of the Lakota gods, was the god of the sky. Not surprisingly, *Skan's* color was blue. The nature of mankind was represented by black and white—black for anger and white for happiness.

The colors chosen for clothing often depicted the wearer's personality. Garments that were colored red proclaimed that the wearer was *wakan*; green told of generosity; yellow stood for bravery. Few things were painted blue, for blue was the symbolic color of *Wakan Tanka*, the Great Spirit and was used for spiritual things only.

Not only did the Lakota paint their lodges, their clothing and themselves, but their horses, as well. A red hand print, known as a blood mark, painted on a horse's flank, meant that the rider had killed an enemy in hand-to-hand combat. A rectangle meant the warrior had led a war party. Painting a red circle around a horse's nose was believed to give the animal a heightened sense of smell; red or white lines drawn around the animal's eyes were believed to add strength to its sight. To increase a horse's speed, warriors painted streaks of lightning running from a horse's rump down its hind legs and from its head down its front legs. To boast of coup counted in battle, a warrior painted short horizontal lines on his mount's nose. Warriors also painted red circles around scars that their mounts sustained in battle.

In these, the last days of summer, the Lakota were busily preparing for the fall hunt and the winter to follow. Autumn was a busy time of year. The women spent hours gathering vegetables and nuts and drying meat for the coming winter. The men went hunting at every opportunity, sometimes burning the prairie so that the buffalo would come nearer the hunting camps.

"The tribe will be moving to the Black Hills soon," Reese told her late one afternoon.

"Are we going with them?"

"That's up to you. We can either hole up there until it's time for the portal to open, or we can hunker down in Deadwood until October."

Neither option was particularly appealing. An early winter could leave them snowbound in the Hills. Deadwood was a wild town, filled with con men, gamblers and women of ill repute, hardly a fit place for Angelina.

It was Angie who made the decision. To everyone's surprise, in the short time they had been in the village, she had not only picked up a little of the Lakota language, but a beau, as well.

Chapter Twenty-Four

Angelina walked along the riverbank beside Hehaka Luta. Though he spoke very little English and she spoke only a smattering of Lakota, they managed to communicate quite well, most likely because what they felt for each other was beyond words. She had been fond of Danny Hamilton but what she had felt for Danny was nothing compared to what she felt for Hehaka Luta. He understood her in ways no one ever had before. He knew when she was feeling sad or lonely or lost and best of all, he knew when she needed to be held and when she needed to be left alone.

What he didn't know was how to kiss, but that was something that she quickly remedied.

In the days that followed, Angelina and Hehaka Luta invented many ways to meet by accident so they could spend time together. And with every passing day, she grew to love him more.

She was sitting in Hantaywee's lodge one evening, learning to make moccasins, when Hantaywee informed her that Hehaka Luta had come courting. Angelina hadn't realized Indians courted one another, although, thinking about it now, she supposed it shouldn't come as a surprise. They married and had children, after all.

Pleased that Hehaka Luta had come to call and curious to find out what courting involved among the Lakota, Angelina followed the old woman outside to where Hehaka Luta was waiting.

Angie smiled a greeting, then widened her eyes in surprise when Hehaka Luta shook out the red blanket draped over his arm and held it over their heads and around their shoulders, hiding them from sight in a cocoon made of wool.

It was quite cozy, she thought, overcoming her surprise. Shut away from passersby, she could touch him and kiss him to her heart's content and she did. He moaned softly as her hands caressed his chest and his back. She ran her fingertips over the muscles in his arms, felt them quiver at her touch. Cupping his face in her palms, she kissed him, a long lingering kiss that he returned with great enthusiasm.

It grew warm very quickly inside their cloth cocoon. Considering the heat of their kisses, Angelina was surprised the blanket didn't go up in flames. One more kiss, and then one more, and Hehaka Luta lowered the blanket so they could breathe.

Angelina was startled to see Hantaywee standing a short distance away talking to several other women. For a moment, she had forgotten anyone else existed. Hidden in the folds of the blanket, there had been no one in all the world but the two of them.

She smiled, her cheeks hot, as Hehaka Luta bid her goodnight and walked away. She slid a glance at Hantaywee, wondering if the old woman and everyone else in the camp knew what had transpired beneath the blanket.

Later that night, as she lay in bed staring up at the sky through the smoke hole of the lodge, she heard the sweet, lilting notes of a flute. The music seemed to wrap around her, as if a ghostly lover were caressing her in the darkness.

"It is Hehaka Luta," Hantaywee said.

Angie sat up. "It is? How do you know?"

"I know. He is hidden somewhere in the dark, hoping you will hear the music he makes and know that he cares for you."

"Did he make the flute himself?" Angie asked, growing more curious by the minute.

"No. A Big Twisted Flute can only be made by a man who has dreamed of the buffalo. It is a powerful instrument, made to express love. Such a flute might cost a young man a fine horse, but it is a small price to pay."

Angie smiled as she settled under her blankets again, thinking she had never heard anything more hauntingly beautiful, or more romantic, than the music Hehaka Luta played on the big twisted flute.

Hehaka Luta came courting the next night and the next. It was exciting, being courted in such a way, but it didn't really give them a chance to be alone the way Angie wanted and so, being young and resourceful and eager, she and Hehaka Luta conspired to meet by accident when Angie went to gather wood or water. There was no shame in meeting this way, as it was expected that young lovers would seek to be alone.

On this day, they met by the river early in the morning. And it was there, sometime later, that Reese found them.

"Hantaywee's waiting for that water."

Angie looked up, startled at the sound of his voice. "Oh, it's you."

Reese glanced from Angie to Hehaka Luta and back again. "How serious are you two?"

"Very," Angie said. "Hehaka Luta wants to marry me, but he doesn't know who to ask."

"I reckon that would be me," Reese said.

Taking Angie by the hand, Hehaka Luta rose to his full height. "It is my wish to take Angelina as my wife," he said, speaking in Lakota.

Reese nodded. "I'll think about it," he replied, also in Lakota.

"I will bring horses to your lodge before the sun sets," Hehaka Luta said. He looked meaningfully at Angie, then walked away.

"Are you sure about this?" Reese asked. "You haven't known each other very long."

"I'm sure. You won't tell him no, will you?"

"Not if you're sure this is what you want. You'd best give it a lot of thought. It won't be easy, living with the Lakota. They don't have much in the way of fripperies and stuff. Along about December it's gonna start to snow and the tribe will move to the Black Hills to spend the winter. It's a hard life at the best of times. You ready to give up pretty dresses and the comforts of livin' in a town?"

"I've thought about it a lot," she said. "I know I'll miss some things, but I'd miss Hehaka Luta more. You can argue all you want, but my mind's made up. If you won't let us get married, then we'll just run away."

A muscle worked in Reese's jaw. "Is that right?"

She nodded. "We already talked about it."

"I won't say no."

"What happens next?"

"Hehaka Luta will bring horses to my lodge. Kelsey and Hantaywee will help you build a lodge for the two of you."

"When will we get married?"

"When the lodge is done, Hehaka Luta will take you to it and you'll be married."

"Just like that? No one marries us?"

"No, not in the white man's way. Lakota marriages aren't sanctified by a church. Marriage among the Lakota takes place here," he said, placing his hand over her heart. "Once you're married, you'll become part of Hehaka Luta's family. You'll have to learn to get along with his sisters and female relatives and banter with his brothers. And if it doesn't work out, all you have to do is walk away."

"What if his family doesn't like me, because I'm not Lakota?"

"I don't think that'll be a problem, but if it is, then it's something else you'll have to adjust to, just like he'd have to adjust to the prejudices of your people if you took him home."

Angie thought about that for a few moments, then nodded. She was used to being looked down upon. In her whole life, she'd never had any friends. The decent women in the town didn't want their sons or daughters associating with the daughter of a harlot.

"All right, then," Reese said. "As long as you're sure this is what you want, let's go tell Kelsey and the old man."

* * * * *

"Are you sure about this?" Kelsey asked. "You hardly know him." She felt a little hypocritical as she said the words. Who was she to talk? She hadn't known Reese much longer when she married him. And she had to admit that Hehaka Luta was a fine young man and obviously very much in love with Angie.

"I don't suppose hearts have calendars," Papa Joe remarked.

Kelsey nodded. Marrying Hehaka Luta would certainly solve most of Angie's problems, although it might add just as many more. How would Angie feel about staying here when the rest of them went back to Grant's Crossing? Still, it was Angie's decision. Even though Kelsey felt responsible for the girl, she had no legal right to tell her what she could or couldn't do.

"I hope you'll be happy," Kelsey said, giving Angelina a hug.

"Me, too, honey," Papa Joe said. "So, when's the big day?"

"Just as soon as I have a lodge of my own," Angie replied, smiling. "Hehaka Luta said he would bring horses to Reese this evening. How many do you think he'll offer?"

"I don't know," Reese answered. "Depends on how wealthy he is."

"Is he going to buy them?" Angie asked, frowning.

"No. Lakota measure their wealth in horses."

"Well, come on," Kelsey said, taking Angie by the hand. "Let's go talk to Hantaywee."

Later that day, just before the sun went down, Hehaka Luta left eight horses in front of Reese's lodge.

"Eight horses seems like a lot," Angelina said, stroking the neck of a lovely paint mare.

"It's a respectable number," Reese said. "It means he holds you in high esteem. They're all fine-looking animals, too. I reckon he's a wealthy young man."

She considered that a moment, then asked, "Who do they belong to?"

"According to Lakota custom, they would belong to your closest male relative, but since you don't have any family here, I reckon they're yours."

"Mine?"

"That's right," he said, grinning. "I reckon that makes you a wealthy young woman."

"I want you to take one of them," Angie said with a shy smile, "for being so nice to me."

Reese's gaze moved over the horses. "I'll take the black mare, if it's all right with you."

Angie nodded. "Maybe you should take one for Kelsey, too," Angie suggested.

"That's right nice of you."

"Do you think she'd like that pretty chestnut?"

"Reckon so." Angie was going to fit right in, he thought. The Lakota were a warm and unselfish people. Generosity was a trait highly valued. A man who acquired wealth and didn't share it was looked down upon, while a man who couldn't accumulate wealth was to be pitied. Young people shared what they had with their elders, women offered gifts to orphans and widows, hunters distributed their catch with those who were too old or too sick to hunt.

Feasts were often given by families to celebrate a successful hunt or a marriage or a successful raid. Everyone in the village was invited to such occasions and gifts were exchanged.

In fact, it was hard to think of any special occasion that didn't involve the exchange of gifts.

"Won't be long now until you're a married woman," Reese remarked.

The mere idea made Angelina smile. Tomorrow, she and Kelsey and Hantaywee would begin to build her new lodge. Hantaywee had told her that a wife was expected to have food ready whenever her husband was hungry. She would be in charge of fire-keeping and bed-making, of keeping their lodge clean and rearing whatever children they might be blessed with. She would be expected to entertain her husband's friends and treat her in-laws with respect.

She could do it. She could anything she had to, as long as she could be with Hehaka Luta.

*****

"Do you think she'll be all right?" Kelsey asked.

Reese shrugged. "I reckon that's up to her." He drew Kelsey closer, aware, as always, of time passing. Each day brought them closer to parting. They would have to talk about it soon, but not now. If she had decided to go back to her own time, he was in no itching hurry to find out about it.

"She's so young," Kelsey said.

He grunted softly. "That's a good thing, to my way of thinking. Young'uns adjust to new situations quicker and she'll have a lot to get used to. Tipi livin' won't be easy for her, but she's young and strong and she's tough inside."

"Maybe, but she's innocent, too, in spite of the way she was raised. It just seems like such a lot to take on, all at once, a new husband, a new culture, a new way of life."

Reese grinned into the darkness. "By this time next year, she'll be as Indian as Hehaka Luta."

Kelsey laughed softly. "I hope you're right."

"Sweetheart, I'm always right."

Kelsey shook her head. She had never yet met a man who didn't believe the same thing. Right or wrong, they were always right! She frowned, trying to remember something she'd read or heard that seemed to echo those sentiments. How did it go? Something like, *I'm never wrong, but I might not be as right as I usually am.*

"Do you think..." Before she could finish her thought, Reese began to caress her.

"I don't want to talk about Angelina," he said, his voice husky with mounting desire.

"No?" she asked, her pulse quickly speeding up. "What do you want to talk about?"

"You," he said, nuzzling her cheek.

"What about me?"

"Everything, like the way your voice trembles when I touch you here...and the way your breath catches in your throat when I do this...the way your skin tastes when I run my tongue across your belly..."

She moaned, all thoughts of Angie and Hehaka Luta stricken from her mind by the sensual touch of her husband's hands exploring her body, the heat of his tongue laving her skin, the press of his erection against her thigh.

With a low groan, she turned in his arms and began a slow seduction of her own.

* * * * *

Angelina soon discovered that building a tipi wasn't easy. There were poles to be cut and hides to be measured, cut and sewn together. A small tipi required seven hides, larger ones used twelve or more. Hantaywee's gift to the bride was nine hides that had already been tanned, along with food and drink for the women she had invited to help her and Angelina build the lodge.

While they worked, Hantaywee explained to Angie and Kelsey that, with practice, a tipi could be struck and packed and its furnishings and contents loaded on a travois in a very short time. In making camp, two women could raise a tipi and set up housekeeping in less than an hour.

Hantaywee also informed them that once the lodge was completed, she would make a dew cloth, which was also made from hides. This would be fastened to the poles on the inside of the lodge and would be roughly shoulder-height. Dew cloths were used to keep dew out of the tipi and also acted as insulation, keeping the lodge warmer in winter and cooler in summer. Warriors often painted their war records on the lining and sometimes invited their friends to come in and do the same.

So much to do, so much to learn, Angie thought as she struggled to sew two of the hides together. Not that she minded the work. Every stitch brought her home closer to completion, closer to the day when she would be Hehaka Luta's wife. Excitement mingled with trepidation when she thought about living among the Lakota. She didn't really belong here. Would she always feel that way? She wondered if the young women would make her welcome or if they would shun her because she was an outsider?

With a shake of her head, Angie she put such thoughts from her mind. Though she hadn't made any real friends among the Indians yet, the young women smiled at her when they passed by, the young men nodded respectfully. The women who were helping her build her lodge seemed friendly enough. She didn't speak the language well enough to follow their rapid conversation but she didn't feel excluded. They spoke slowly when they spoke to her, sometimes laughing behind their hands when she stumbled over a word, but there was nothing cruel or mocking in their tone. They were laughing with her, not at her.

That evening, on the pretext of going to the river for water, Angelina ran into Hehaka Luta. Taking her by the hand, he quickly drew her off the path and into the cover of the trees.

"*Mitawin*," he murmured. My woman.

"Yes," she whispered, dropping the waterskin to the ground. "Oh, yes."

Because he was still shy about being intimate, she wrapped her arms around his waist and pulled him to her. He smelled of smoke and sage, of horse and leather and she loved it. Lifting one hand, she ran it through his hair. It was longer than her own, thick and black.

His eyes grew hot as she rained butterfly kisses on his bare chest.

"You are bold, for a woman," he said.

"Oh! I'm sorry." Chastened, she backed away from him.

Hehaka Luta frowned. "Have I offended you?"

"No, but I, that is..." She looked away, her cheeks burning. They had caressed each other under the courting blanket, perhaps that was the only time it was permissible.

With a gentle smile, he drew her into his arms and kissed the top of her head. "I did not mean for you to stop."

She looked up at him, confused. "I thought you didn't like it."

"Foolish woman," he replied, his dark eyes sparkling.

She smiled up at him; then, rising on her tiptoes, she wrapped her arms around his neck and kissed him. Kissed him until her toes curled. Kissed him until his body trembled against hers. Kissed him until he suddenly put her away from him and disappeared into the underbrush.

Only then did she hear the voices of two other women coming down the path.

Smoothing her hair and her skirt, Angie picked up her waterskin and stepped out onto the trail.

She smiled at the two women, both of whom she recognized. They were about her age, both tall and slender, with beautiful black hair and dark eyes.

They both smiled back at her, a knowing expression on their faces as they continued down the path toward the river.

* * * * *

And suddenly the day of her marriage was upon her. Angelina stood in Hantaywee's lodge, wishing she had a mirror so she could see how she looked in the doeskin tunic the old medicine woman had made for her. She ran her hands over the material. It was cream-colored and buttery soft. Yellow beads adorned the yoke. Long fringe dangled from the sleeves and the hem. Tiny silver bells had been sewn to the fringe, the bells chimed softly each time she moved. Hantaywee had made her a new pair of moccasins decorated with yellow beads, as well.

Angie looked over at Kelsey, who was also wearing a new dress courtesy of Hantaywee.

"You look lovely, Angie," Kelsey said, smiling.

"Do I?"

"Look into Hehaka Luta's eyes when he sees you and you'll know just how pretty you are."

"You look nice, too," Angie said. Kelsey's tunic was similar to Angie's, although the yoke was plain and the fringe wasn't as long or adorned with silver bells.

Hantaywee placed her hand on Angie's arm. "Are you ready, *cunksi*?" she asked.

Hearing Hantaywee call her "my daughter" brought a quick sheen of tears to Angie's eyes. Impulsively, she hugged the old woman. "Thank you," she said. "Thank you for everything."

Hantaywee nodded. "You are one of us now. You have no family here, so I will be your family, if you wish."

"Oh, I do!"

Hantaywee smiled. "Your young man is waiting."

Suddenly nervous, Angie lifted the door flap and stepped outside.

Reese and Papa Joe were waiting outside, but Angie had eyes only for Hehaka Luta. He wore a buckskin clout, a vest painted with suns and moons and moccasins. His long black hair fell down his back, a wide copper band circled his left biceps, a single eagle feather adorned his hair. He was beautiful.

There was no official wedding ceremony, but Hantaywee had prepared a feast to celebrate their marriage. Everyone in the village had been invited. There were gifts for the bride and groom—backrests and blankets, cook pots and fly whisks, a string of bells to tie to one of the lodgepoles, a tool for scraping hides.

Angie was touched by the generosity of the Lakota people. As the feast went on, she grew more and more anxious for the time when she and Hehaka Luta would be alone.

At dusk, Hehaka Luta rose. Taking her by the hand, he led her to their lodge, which was located a short distance from Hantaywee's. He lifted the flap for her, then followed her inside.

Angelina stood in the center of her new home, her heart pounding. According to Lakota custom, they were married, but she didn't feel married.

"There should be words," she said, looking up at her new husband.

He raised one brow in question.

"We should promise to love one another," she said haltingly, "you know, in sickness and health, for as long as we live."

"Ah." Hehaka Luta took her hands in his. "I will love you and protect you for as long as I live," he said, his voice quiet and all the more powerful because of it.

"I'll love you as long as I live," Angie said. "I promise to be a good wife and to take care of you if you get sick and to stand beside you no matter what."

He squeezed her hands. "I will care for you and provide for you and for our children, always."

Children. Angie's cheeks grew hot at the thought of how children were conceived.

"Do you want children?" Hehaka Luta asked.

She nodded, suddenly unable to speak. She could get pregnant tonight. Was she ready to be a mother?

"*Mitawin?*"

With a sigh, she went into his arms. At the touch of his mouth on hers, all doubts and fears for the future melted away. She was his now, as he was hers. Tomorrow would take care of itself. Today, she wanted to learn more about her husband, what he liked, what he didn't like. She wanted to taste and touch and explore every inch of him.

She sighed with pleasure when he led her to their blankets in the rear of the lodge and stretched out beside her, as eager as she to begin their journey of discovery, a discovery that, hopefully, would never end.

Chapter Twenty-Five

When Kelsey saw Angie the following morning, her first thought was that the expression on the bride's face was exactly like the one Scarlett had worn the morning after Rhett Butler had swept her into his arms and carried her up that long flight of stairs. Kelsey had a feeling she had worn a similar expression after Reese made love to her the first time. She smiled at the memory.

"Good morning," Angie said, sitting down beside her.

"Good morning."

"Isn't it a beautiful day?"

"Indeed it is," Kelsey said with a grin. "How are you feeling this morning?"

Angie's cheeks turned bright red.

"There's nothing to be ashamed of," Kelsey said, hoping to ease Angie's mind.

Angie glanced around, her cheeks turning even redder, if possible.

"What's wrong?" Kelsey asked, puzzled by the girl's embarrassment.

"Nothing, but..." She fidgeted with the hem of her tunic. "Everyone knows what we did, don't they?"

"Is that what's bothering you?"

Angie nodded.

"Believe me, no one is giving it a second thought."

"I guess..." She blew out a sigh. "I don't know how to explain it. I spent my whole life thinking what went on between a man and a woman was shameful, you know, something dirty."

"There's nothing shameful about it when a man and a woman are in love," Kelsey said. "It's the most beautiful way two people can express their feelings for each other."

"He was so gentle," Angie said softly. "I never knew anything could be so wonderful."

Kelsey put her arm around Angelina's shoulders and gave her a squeeze, grateful that she would have one less thing to worry about when she went back home.

In the days that followed, Kelsey and Angie learned a good deal about Lakota housekeeping. Reese and Hehaka Luta spent their days hunting while Hantaywee taught Kelsey and Angie how to tan the hides their men brought home. It was, Kelsey thought, a rather disgusting process. After staking the hide out on the ground, Kelsey scraped away the meat and gristle with a chisel-like instrument Hantaywee had given her. It was an arduous task, hard on the knees and the back.

Once the hide was scraped clean, it was left to dry in the sun for several days and then it was scraped again with a short tool that reminded Kelsey of a hoe. The purpose of this scraping was to even out the thickness of the hide. When that was done, the hide was turned over so the hair could be removed.

When she finished scraping away the hair, the hide was hard and stiff, making Kelsey wonder if she had done something wrong, because there was no way in the world that that hide could be used for anything other than a door mat, or maybe a bulletproof shield! But, not to fear, she wasn't done yet. Following Hantaywee's directions, Kelsey soaked the hide in water for two days and *voila!* It was soft and pliable.

Now came the most disgusting part of all. Hantaywee showed Kelsey and Angie how to make a mixture out of brains, liver, fat and red grass, which was to be rubbed thoroughly into the skin.

Kelsey glanced at the mess in the pot, then glanced at Angie, who looked as horrified as Kelsey felt at the idea of rubbing the mixture into the hide. Grimacing, Kelsey got to work, figuring that the sooner she got started, the sooner she would be finished. When she was done, the hide was again left to dry.

The next time they got together, Hantaywee showed them how to stretch the hide.

When the hide was finally ready to be cut and used, Kelsey realized she had spent ten days preparing the thing. Ten days! Shopping for clothes at Nordstrom's was definitely easier!

Hantaywee taught them how to cook over an open fire and how to butcher a deer carcass, which was even grosser than tanning the hide.

To Kelsey's surprise, Angie quickly mastered everything she was taught. She soon overcame her aversion to tanning and butchering. Her ability to speak Lakota grew by leaps and bounds and by early fall, Reese's prediction had come true. Angelina Ridgeway was just as Indian as Hehaka Luta. But for her long blonde hair, she could have easily passed for a Lakota woman.

Reese, however, remained a man apart. Kelsey often thought it must be difficult for him to be there when the place and the people held so many unhappy memories, but he never complained. He spent most of his days away from the village, hunting with Hehaka Luta, but he spent his nights with Kelsey. Though they hadn't spoken of parting, it was always there between them. Their lovemaking grew more frequent. Sometimes quick and intense, sometimes slow and exquisitely tender, they made love as if each time might be the last time.

Kelsey ran her hands over every inch of his body, imprinting the touch of it, the warmth of it, the musky scent of it in her memory. Mentally, she recorded his laughter and his smile, the husky sound of her name on his lips, the warmth of his breath against her cheek, the touch of his calloused hands on her skin, the sweet sensation of his fingers in her hair, the heat in his eyes when he rose over her in the dark of the night, the tinkling of the bells outside their lodge. She wished she had a camera with her so she could photograph him from every angle, waking and sleeping.

Now, sitting on the riverbank in the moonlight, Kelsey gazed at the slow moving water, her thoughts turned inward. The days since Angie's marriage had quickly turned to weeks, the weeks to months. All too soon it would be time for her and Papa Joe to return to Grant's Crossing to await the opening of the portal that would take them back home.

Home. She wondered if her condo would ever feel like home again. How would she explain her long absence to her parents, her boss, her friends?

How could she leave Reese?

How could she stay away from her family and everything she was familiar with?

Feeling the onset of tears, she blinked rapidly, afraid if she started crying she would never be able to stop. Maybe she didn't have to leave him, at least not permanently. Maybe she could spend six months here, with Reese, and he could spend six months in the future, with her. But that wouldn't work. She couldn't leave her job for six months every year and even if she could, there was no guarantee that she would step through the portal into this exact time and place. As for Reese going with her to the future, they had never even talked it. Was it even possible? For all she knew, people from the past couldn't travel to the future, although it seemed that if you could go from the future to the past, you should be able to go from the past to the future.

She tried to imagine Reese in her time, tried to imagine what a nineteenth-century man would think of the world she knew. Would he take to cars and technology, or would he forever feel out of place, always longing to go back to the world he had known? It would be harder, she thought, for him to adjust to the future than it had been for her to adjust to the past. After all, she had known a little of what the Old West was like, so it hadn't been a complete shock. Even if movies and TV romanticized the wild west, she'd still had a vague idea of what to expect. But Reese had no inkling of what life was like in the future. Sure, she had told him about it as best she could, but there was no way to prepare him for crowded freeways or airplanes or shopping malls.

She massaged her temples with her fingertips in an effort to avert the headache she felt coming on.

"Here, let me do that."

His voice sent warmth spreading through her.

"What are you doing out here alone?" he asked, sitting down behind her.

"Just thinking."

Cradling her body between his thighs, he began to massage her temples. "What were you thinking about?"

"Nothing. Everything."

"Like going back to Grant's Crossing," he guessed.

Closing her eyes, she made a soft sound of assent.

"You're going, then?"

"It's where I belong."

"Is it?"

"I don't know." She turned imploring eyes on him. "Oh, Reese, what am I going to do?"

Drawing her into his arms, he said, "I can't make that decision for you, sweetheart."

"I know." If only he would beg her to stay, tell her he couldn't live without her, but that wouldn't be fair. This was something she had to decide for herself. She knew how he felt about her, he knew how she felt about him.

The decision would have to be hers. But he wasn't above pressing his case, she thought, as he lifted her into his arms and carried her to their lodge where his every kiss and every caress was a silent plea for her to forget the world she had left behind and stay in his world, with him.

*****

The days flew by on winged feet and, all too soon, it was time for Kelsey, Reese and Papa Joe to begin the journey back to Grant's Crossing.

It was a tearful farewell.

Angelina clung to Kelsey. "I'll never see you again, will I?"

Fighting back tears of her own, Kelsey said, "Probably not. Be happy, Angie. Take good care of Hehaka Luta. He loves you very much."

"Promise me you'll come and see us if you ever..." Angie sniffed back her tears. "If you ever come here again."

"I will, you know I will."

Angie hugged Reese and Papa Joe, then retreated to her husband's arms while Hantaywee said her goodbyes.

"It was so nice to see you again," Kelsey said, giving the old woman a hug. "Thank you for everything."

Hantaywee patted Kelsey's arm. "Thank you for bringing Tashunka Kangi home. Because of you, old hurts have faded, though new ones may come to take their place."

Kelsey nodded. Reese's heartache at Chumani's loss seemed to have healed. She didn't have to ask who would be the cause of any new grief in his life. Though he hadn't said so in words, she knew he would grieve for her when she returned home.

Hantaywee drew Reese into her arms and held him tenderly. "She is meant to be yours," she murmured, for his ears alone. "In this time or another, you are meant to be together."

Stepping back, the old woman smiled at each of them. "I will pray that *Wakan Tanka* will bless you with a safe journey."

There was nothing more to say. Reese lifted Kelsey onto the back of her horse, then swung into the saddle of his own mount and rode out of the village.

It surprised him that he was sorry to leave. Even though he was still considered an outcast, the Lakota were his people, the land itself was a part of him. The scent and smells and sounds of the village were in his blood.

He would take Kelsey back to Grant's Crossing and then he would come back here. When Chumani died, he had turned his back on who and what he was and sought solace among strangers. He would not make that mistake again. If Kelsey returned to her own time, he would return to the land of the Black Hills and the red-tailed hawk.

Back where he belonged.

Chapter Twenty-Six

Kelsey couldn't shake off her sadness as they left the Lakota village behind. She had grown to love Angelina and she knew she would miss the girl in the days to come and that she would think of Angie often when she was back home where she belonged. She was anxious to see her parents and her brothers and sisters and all their kids, anxious to see Nana Mary's face when Nana was reunited with Papa Joe.

Kelsey smiled inwardly, thinking of the fun it would be to recount her adventures in the Old West, to tease Nana Mary for keeping Papa Joe's trips to the past a secret. He wouldn't have to keep it a secret now. No one in the family would think he was losing his mind, not when he had Kelsey to back up his story. Maybe one day they could all take a trip back in time, just for the day. She realized now that the reason she had never found the portal was that she had stepped through it only moments before it closed for the duration.

She was going home. Back to her job, if she still had one, and the excitement and satisfaction of closing a multimillion dollar deal. Back to hurried lunches and quick shopping trips. Back to her cell phone and her microwave. Back to movies and television and spending a quiet evening curled up in her favorite chair, listening to country music on her iPod. Back to shopping malls and all-night grocery stores. Back to her new car and her Jacuzzi. Back to high gas prices and crowded freeways, air pollution and wars in the Middle East, property tax and income tax.

She shook her head. You had to take the bad with the good. And as much as she had enjoyed being here, in the past, she missed the life she knew.

"You all right?" Reese asked, riding up beside her.

"What? Oh, yes, I'm fine," she said, fighting the urge to cry.

"I guess you're anxious to go back home."

She nodded, unable to speak past the lump in her throat.

"We had some good times."

"Yes."

He blew out a sigh, thinking he had best change the subject. It would take them a few days to get back to Grant's Crossing. Plenty of time for goodbyes when the time came.

"Should you be going back to Grant's Crossing with us?" Kelsey asked. "I mean, you're a wanted man there."

"Don't worry, once I see you safely to town, I'll be moving on." The thought of her going back to her own time was like a knife in his gut, a knife that twisted a little deeper every time he thought about it.

"Oh. Where will you go?"

"Back to my people. Hantaywee is growing old, she needs someone to look after her."

Kelsey nodded. The thought that he would be with his own people, with someone who loved him, made her feel a little better.

Several times on the long ride back to Grant's Crossing, Reese thought about asking Kelsey to stay, but she didn't belong here, would never be happy here, trapped in the past. Her life was in the future. She had family there, friends, a home.

What if he went with her to the future? He had considered it before but always dismissed it as a foolish notion. What would he do in the future? Her world was as alien to him as his was to her.

He grunted softly. She had managed to get along in his world. Surely he could get used to living in hers. He had no ties to keep him here, no family, no friends to speak of, no one, save Hantaywee, who would miss him when he was gone.

He thought about it all that day and the more he thought about it, the more convinced he was that it was the right thing, the only thing, to do.

Later that night, with Papa Joe snoring softly a short distance away, Reese drew Kelsey into his arms. She snuggled against him, her face buried in the hollow of his shoulder.

She had grown quieter and more withdrawn with each passing day. Now, he felt the warmth of her tears on his shirt, felt her body tremble with the force of her sobs.

"Hey," he said, stroking her back, "don't cry."

"I can't help it. I don't want to leave you."

"What would you think about me going to the future with you?"

She looked up at him, her eyes filled with hope. "Would you? Oh, Reese, that would be wonderful!" Laughing and crying, she hugged him tight. "I can't wait to show you my world. You'll love it, I know you will. We could move out to the suburbs, get a big house, have some horses. Oh, I love you!"

He crushed her close, thinking that giving up his life here was a small price to pay for the happiness shining in her eyes. He laughed softly. One thing about going to the future, he wouldn't have to keep looking over his shoulder, worrying about the last Crenshaw boy creeping up on him to exact vengeance for the deaths of his brothers.

Overcome with happiness and the relief that they would stay together, Kelsey rained kisses over Reese's cheeks, his nose, his chin, his lips. One kiss led to another. One caress led to another and soon they were entwined in each other's arms, trying to undress one another under the blankets, trying to keep their lovemaking quiet so they wouldn't disturb Papa Joe. At any other time, Kelsey would have been reluctant to make love when her grandfather was so close by but not now.

On this night, she needed to be in Reese's arms, needed to show him how much she loved him, how grateful she was that he had decided to go with her into the future.

She surrendered to him with a soft sigh, relieved that she wouldn't be leaving her heart behind when she returned to the world she knew.

* * * * *

It was late on a cold and windy night when they reached Grant's Crossing. Skirting the town, they went to the house to spend the night. As near as Papa Joe could figure, the portal would be open the following day.

"Assuming I haven't made a mistake in keeping track of the days," Papa Joe said.

"I'll bet Mary's worried sick. I've never been gone this long before and she's probably worried to death about you, too."

"She'll forgive you," Kelsey said, yawning.

Papa Joe chuckled. "Yeah, but she'll be madder than a wet hen for a week or two. I missed her birthday and our anniversary, you know. She won't like that."

"No, she won't," Kelsey agreed. Nana Mary was a tiny thing, barely five feet tall, but she had a temper big enough for a lumberjack. Kelsey yawned again. "I don't know about you two, but I'm going to bed."

"See you in the morning," Papa Joe said.

Nodding, Kelsey kissed her grandfather on the cheek, then left the room.

Reese's gaze followed Kelsey. "I reckon I'll turn in, too."

Papa Joe grinned a knowing grin as Reese left the room.

* * * * *

Kelsey rose early after a restless night. She had slept little and when she did, her dreams were dark and troubled, though she couldn't remember them now.

Turning on her side, she saw that Reese was awake and watching her. They had made love last night. Reese had been tender, gentle, almost as if he was afraid she might shatter beneath him. She had felt a peculiar tenderness herself, almost as if they were making love for the last time. But that was silly. He was going back with her.

He brushed a lock of hair from her brow, then wiped his thumb across her cheek. "You were talking in your sleep," he said.

"What did I say?"

"I'm not sure. You were crying."

"Crying?" She lifted a hand to her face. Her cheek was still damp. "I don't remember what I was dreaming about," she murmured, "only that you were in it."

He drew her into his arms, one hand stroking her back. "Am I the one who made you cry?"

"I don't know." She usually remembered her dreams, it was odd that she couldn't remember this one.

There was a knock at the door. "Hey, you two awake in there?"

Kelsey lifted her brows in a gesture of resignation at the sound of her grandfather's voice. Rising, she wrapped a blanket around her nudity and padded to the door. "We're up."

"There's nothing to eat in here," Papa Joe said. "I'm going over to the hotel to get some breakfast. Want me to bring you something?"

"I'll have whatever you're having," Kelsey said. She glanced over her shoulder at Reese. "Do you want anything?"

"Steak and eggs and black coffee."

Kelsey repeated Reese's order, then returned to the bed. "I hope we've got the date right," she remarked. "It's dangerous for you to be here."

He kissed her bare shoulder. "Stop worrying."

"I can't help it, it's what I do best."

After breakfast, Kelsey made the beds while Papa Joe returned the dishes to the hotel.

"What are you gonna do with this place?" Reese asked while they waited for Papa Joe to return.

"I told Angelina it was hers to do with as she pleased, unless you wanted it, but now you're going with me, so…"

Reese nodded. "She might have need of it one day."

"Maybe, or she can just sell it. I'm sorry our coffee shop never really got going. I think it would have been a success."

"I think anything you turn your hand to will be a success."

"Flatterer."

"Who, me?"

"Yes, you."

Papa Joe arrived a few minutes later. "Town's real quiet," he said.

Kelsey stared at the food Papa Joe had brought her. It looked wonderful, but she was too nervous to eat. After a few bites, she pushed her plate away, waited impatiently for Reese and Papa Joe to finish theirs.

Kelsey shivered when they left the house. Standing in the backyard while Reese and Papa Joe saddled the horses, she felt a strange ripple in the air. She glanced at Reese and her grandfather, but neither man seemed to notice it. She was sure the horses did, though. They shook their heads and stamped their feet and seemed reluctant to leave the yard. She wondered if it had something to do with the portal opening.

They rode out of the yard in single-file, with Papa Joe in the lead.

Kelsey's emotions were in turmoil. She was thrilled at the prospect of going home, yet oddly reluctant to leave the Old West behind. She would miss Angie and Hantaywee and even Pete, the bartender.

The air felt oppressive as Papa Joe led them into the alleyway between the bank and the newspaper office.

"Well, here we are," Papa Joe said, dismounting. "What'll we do with the horses?"

"Unsaddle 'em and turn 'em loose," Reese said. "Somebody will pick 'em up. Kelsey…"

"T. K. Reese, throw down your iron and get those hands up where I can see 'em! a voice hollered. "This is the law."

Reese swore a vile oath. His first instinct was to run, but there was nowhere to go.

Papa Joe stood in front of him, Kelsey's horse blocked the only way out.

Sheriff McCain and his deputy, Matt Stover, stepped out of a recessed doorway in the building across the way, their guns drawn.

Moving slowly, his hands over his head, Reese swung his right leg over the saddlehorn and slid to the ground.

"Your gun," McCain said curtly. "Ease it out of your holster nice and slow and kick it over here, toward me."

Still mounted on her horse, Kelsey held her breath as Reese slid his gun from the holster, placed it on the ground and kicked it toward the sheriff.

"I had a hunch you were somewhere close by when I saw old man St. James leaving the hotel this morning," McCain said. "Turns out I was right."

Kelsey looked past Reese to her grandfather, who was ever so slowly circling around behind the two lawmen. With their attention focused on Reese, neither McCain or Stover seemed to notice.

McCain pulled a pair of handcuffs out of his back pocket and tossed them to his deputy.

"Cuff him."

"What about the girl and the old man?"

"We've got nothing on them."

"You know they helped him escape last time!" Matt Stover exclaimed.

"We don't have any proof of that."

"But..."

"I can't arrest them for something they might have done." McCain gestured at Reese with his gun barrel. "Cuff him and let's go."

Reese looked up at Kelsey. She knew, in that moment, that he was going to make a break for it. She shook her head, silently beseeching him not to try it. But it was too late.

After holstering his gun, Stover moved purposefully toward Reese.

Reese dove under the belly of Kelsey's horse, rolled to his feet and darted toward the head of the alley.

McCain fired two quick shots. The first one went wide. The second one caught Reese in the back. He staggered forward a few steps, then slumped against the side of the building, one hand pressed against the wound.

Papa Joe grabbed a rock and brought it crashing down on McCain's head before the sheriff could fire another shot.

Fumbling to get his gun clear, the deputy hollered, "Stop or I'll shoot!"

Kelsey slammed her heels into her mount's flanks. Startled, the horse leaped forward, slamming into the deputy and knocking him off balance before he could fire at Reese.

Papa Joe ran forward, rock in hand, and rendered Stover unconscious while Kelsey scrambled out of the saddle and ran toward Reese.

She slipped her arm around his waist, her nostrils filling with the scent of blood. "How bad are you hurt?"

"I'll be all right. Bullet went through. I think it cracked a rib."

She offered a quick, silent prayer of thanks that it wasn't worse. "Hurry," she said, "we can get through the portal before they regain consciousness."

With Kelsey supporting Reese, they followed Papa Joe to the portal. The door, which she hadn't noticed in all the excitement, shimmered with a ghostly silver light.

"Hurry!" Papa Joe said. He put his hand on the door and it swung inward. Beyond the threshold, Kelsey could see the inside of the house. It looked exactly as she had left it.

Smiling, she walked toward the doorway, her arm around Reese's waist.

Almost there, she thought exultantly. Another few steps and she would be home again.

Papa Joe hurried inside, holding the door open for her and Reese. Kelsey had to release her hold on Reese in order to step across the threshold. She frowned when Reese didn't follow.

"What's wrong?" she asked, turning around.

"I can't get in."

"What do you mean?"

He took a step forward, his hand reaching for hers, but some invisible force kept him from entering the house.

It was just as she had feared, she thought dully. You couldn't cross from the past to the future, only from the future to the past.

"Come on, Kelsey," Papa Joe said. "The door won't stay open much longer."

She glanced at her grandfather and the room beyond. The house represented her whole life, her family and everything that was familiar. How could she leave it all behind?

Reese didn't have to see her face to know what she was thinking, feeling. Ever since he had seen her that first night, all she had wanted to do was go back home and now she was where she belonged, where she wanted to be.

"Go on, sweetheart," he said quietly. "I'll be all right. I'm not hurt that bad."

She stared at him, at the blood on his hand, the love in his eyes and knew she couldn't leave him. He might be all right without her, she thought, blinking back her tears, but she would never be all right without him.

Turning, she kissed her grandfather on the cheek. "Tell mom and dad that I love them. Kiss Megan and Amy and Rose for me. And hug Keith and Ryan. Tell them I'll think of them often. And tell Ryan he can have my Mustang." Her youngest brother, Ryan, had been drooling over her car since the day she drove it home.

Papa Joe shook his head. "Kelsey, are you sure?"

"I can't leave Reese," she said, tears welling in her eyes. "I can't live without him."

She kissed her grandfather again and then she darted back through the portal and into Reese's waiting arms. Home at last.

Epilogue

Kelsey sat in front of her lodge, her month-old daughter Kimi cradled in her arms. When she left the Lakota village thirteen months ago, Kelsey had never expected to see it again. Now, she couldn't imagine living anywhere else.

Angie had been thrilled when she learned that Kelsey and Reese had decided to make their home with the Lakota. Kelsey and Angie pitched their lodges close together and often did their chores together. Gathering wood and water or hunting for berries was more enjoyable when there was someone along for company.

As usual, Hantaywee had been waiting for Kelsey and Reese when they arrived. It had been Hantaywee who delivered Kelsey's baby. Hantaywee who had made the two traditional "sand lizards", one of which would be used to hold the baby's umbilical cord. The amulets were fashioned in the shape of a lizard, although they were sometimes made in the shape of a tortoise. Both animals were revered by the Lakota because they were hard to kill, thus their protective powers were enlisted to guard the baby's cord. When Kelsey asked why Hantaywee had made two amulets, Hantaywee explained that one would be used to hold the cord while the second would be used as a decoy to guard the baby against malevolent spirits.

Hantaywee also made a cradle for the baby. Such things were usually crafted by the father's sister, but Reese had no kin among the Lakota.

Four days after the baby's birth, everyone had been invited to a feast for the naming of the baby. Reese and Kelsey had given gifts to Angie and Hehaka Luta and Hantaywee, as well as to several of the widows in the village.

The gift giving had been followed by feasting and then Reese had informed the guests that their daughter would be called Kimimela in honor of his mother. When that was done, Reese gave a horse away.

Kelsey stroked her daughter's downy cheek. In the time that they had been in the village, Kelsey had grown to love the people and their customs. She spoke the language like a native. And she was happy, happier than she had ever been in her life but, more importantly, her husband was happy.

Of course, there were days when she missed her family and the conveniences of the world she had left behind, but those days grew fewer as the months went by.

In spite of Reese's protests that he hadn't been badly hurt, their flight from Grant's Crossing had nearly cost him his life. They had spent the first night out in the open. They'd had no food, no water and no shelter. She had spent the night at Reese's side, afraid to close her eyes, afraid that he would die in the night. The next day, they reached a small town where Reese received some rudimentary medical attention rendered by a doctor who was half-drunk. Kelsey would go to her grave convinced that it had been her urgent prayers that had saved her husband's life. Due to his cracked rib, it had taken weeks before he could move without pain. But he had survived and they had come here, back to those they cared for, back to those who cared for them.

Kelsey smiled when she looked up and saw Reese striding toward her. As always, her heart beat a little faster when he was near. He was every inch a warrior now. Sunlight glinted in his long black hair and caressed the warm copper color of his skin, skin her fingers itched to touch.

Her hungry gaze moved over him. It had been too long since they made love, she thought. Much too long.

One look into her husband's eyes and she knew he was thinking the same thing, and suddenly she couldn't wait for nightfall.

Rising, she took her husband's hand and led him into the shelter of their lodge, and in the warmth of his arms, she found home once again.

Also by Madeline Baker

༄

Apache Flame

Hawk's Woman

Lakota Love Song

Wolf Shadow

About the Author

༄

Madeline Baker started writing simply for the fun of it. Now she is the award-winning author of more than thirty historical romance books and one of the most popular writers of Native American romance. She lives in California, where she was born and raised.

Madeline welcomes comments from readers. You can find her website and email address on her author bio page at www.cerridwenpress.com.

Tell Us What You Think

We appreciate hearing reader opinions about our books. You can email us at Comments@EllorasCave.com.

Why an electronic book?

We live in the Information Age—an exciting time in the history of human civilization, in which technology rules supreme and continues to progress in leaps and bounds every minute of every day. For a multitude of reasons, more and more avid literary fans are opting to purchase e-books instead of paper books. The question from those not yet initiated into the world of electronic reading is simply: *Why?*

1. *Price.* An electronic title at Ellora's Cave Publishing and Cerridwen Press runs anywhere from 40% to 75% less than the cover price of the exact same title in paperback format. Why? Basic mathematics and cost. It is less expensive to publish an e-book (no paper and printing, no warehousing and shipping) than it is to publish a paperback, so the savings are passed along to the consumer.
2. *Space.* Running out of room in your house for your books? That is one worry you will never have with electronic books. For a low one-time cost, you can purchase a handheld device specifically designed for e-reading. Many e-readers have large, convenient screens for viewing. Better yet, hundreds of titles can be stored within your new library—on a single microchip. There are a variety of e-readers from different manufacturers. You can also read e-books on your PC or laptop computer. (Please note that

Ellora's Cave does not endorse any specific brands. You can check our websites at www.ellorascave.com or www.cerridwenpress.com for information we make available to new consumers.)

3. *Mobility.* Because your new e-library consists of only a microchip within a small, easily transportable e-reader, your entire cache of books can be taken with you wherever you go.

4. *Personal Viewing Preferences.* Are the words you are currently reading too small? Too large? Too... ANNOYING? Paperback books cannot be modified according to personal preferences, but e-books can.

5. *Instant Gratification.* Is it the middle of the night and all the bookstores near you are closed? Are you tired of waiting days, sometimes weeks, for bookstores to ship the novels you bought? Ellora's Cave Publishing sells instantaneous downloads twenty-four hours a day, seven days a week, every day of the year. Our webstore is never closed. Our e-book delivery system is 100% automated, meaning your order is filled as soon as you pay for it.

Those are a few of the top reasons why electronic books are replacing paperbacks for many avid readers.

As always, Ellora's Cave and Cerridwen Press welcome your questions and comments. We invite you to email us at Comments@ellorascave.com or write to us directly at Ellora's Cave Publishing Inc., 1056 Home Avenue, Akron, OH 44310-3502.

Cerridwen Press

Cerridwen, the Celtic goddess of wisdom, was the muse who brought inspiration to storytellers and those in the creative arts.

Cerridwen Press encompasses the best and most innovative stories in all genres of today's fiction.

Visit our website and discover the newest titles by talented authors who still get inspired—much like the ancient storytellers did...

once upon a time.

www.cerridwenpress.com

CPSIA information can be obtained at www.ICGtesting.com
Printed in the USA
LVOW081006290412

279585LV00001B/146/P